*Anne Barbour,* one of the Regency genre's most popular writers, won Best Regency Novel Award from *Romantic Times* for *Lord Glenhaven's Return.* Her newest title is *Buried Secrets.*

*Elisabeth Fairchild* won the 1995 *Romantic Times* Best Regency Novel Award for *Miss Dorton's Hero.* A newcomer to the Signet list, she has become an instant hit with readers and receives a great deal of fan mail. Her latest title is *Breach of Promise.*

*Carla Kelly* is a highly regarded Regency author who has won two RITA Awards, and has received a Career Achievement Award from *Romantic Times.*

*Allison Lane,* a highly talented newcomer, won the 1996 *Romantic Times* Reviewer's Choice Award for Best First Regency for *The Rake's Rainbow.* Her newest title is *The Beleaguered Earl.*

*Barbara Metzger,* one of the stars of the genre, has written over twenty Regencies and won numerous awards, including a *Romantic Times* Reviewer's Choice Award for Best Regency, and National Reader's Choice Award in 1995. Her newest title is *Saved by Scandal.*

# The Grand Hotel

Anne Barbour

Elisabeth Fairchild

Carla Kelly

Allison Lane

Barbara Metzger

A SIGNET BOOK

SIGNET
Published by New American Library, a division of
Penguin Putnam Inc., 375 Hudson Street,
New York, New York 10014, U.S.A.
Penguin Books Ltd, 27 Wrights Lane,
London W8 5TZ, England
Penguin Books Australia Ltd, Ringwood,
Victoria, Australia
Penguin Books Canada Ltd, 10 Alcorn Avenue,
Toronto, Ontario, Canada M4V 3B2
Penguin Books (N.Z.) Ltd, 182–190 Wairau Road,
Auckland 10, New Zealand

Penguin Books Ltd, Registered Offices:
Harmondsworth, Middlesex, England

First published by Signet, an imprint of New American Library,
a division of Penguin Putnam Inc.

First Printing, June 2000
10  9  8  7  6  5  4  3  2

REGISTERED TRADEMARK—MARCA REGISTRADA

Printed in the United States of America

# Contents

# The Background Man
## by Carla Kelly

It was on days like this—when the rain poured from sodden skies onto slate roofs, to roar down overtaxed drainpipes—that Charles Mortimer missed the heat of India. Naturally, through some cosmic conspiracy, such days seemed to collaborate with Mondays. Chin in hand, he stared out the front window across the lobby, watching London's workers hurry along the sidewalk, staying well back to avoid spray from the coaches and carts.

His honesty required an amendment; Mondays made little difference to him. As manager, he lived at the Grand Hotel, and while he was granted days off, he generally had nowhere to go, and nothing to spend his money on. Mrs. Wheelwright, the housekeeper, had quizzed him once about his solitary life. "A day off to you only means coming to the front desk two hours later than usual, is that it?" she asked, and he had agreed.

*And here we are, open on July 1, right on schedule,* he thought, *even though I cannot get into my rooms behind the lobby because they are still full of boxes that I suspect belong in that other hotel my employer is opening in Kent.* He sat up straight and frowned. *And the carpenters are still banging away in the upstairs linen closet. I suppose that Sir Michael Moseley will poke his head in the door now to declare that Mr.*

1

*Simmons has recovered from the gout, and I can return to deputy manager instead of manager.*

*I should be a prophet,* he thought, startled, as the footman opened the entrance door upon the owner himself. Charles held his breath while Sir Michael Moseley let the footman remove his many-caped cloak. *Now if only my employer will be hard of hearing,* he thought.

Sir Michael was not. "What do I hear, Mortimer?" he asked, his voice thundering across the great and elegant space between door and desk.

Charles sat up, his Monday morning reverie at an end. "That, sir, is the sound of hammering," he stated. "The carpenters forgot to line the linen closet shelves with cedar."

Sir Michael sniffed, and then sniffed again. "Paint? Paint? Do I smell paint?" His face was long and lined, and when he turned it upon Charles, it seemed to the hotel manager that he bore a remarkable resemblance to a basset hound. "I was led to believe by Mr. Simmons—from his bed of pain, mind you, where all men tell the truth—that the Grand Hotel was finished."

"I believe it will be by six of the clock, Sir Michael," Charles said, "or so the workers have promised me." He managed a slight smile. "Sir, there are always kinks to work through." He coughed, wondering at his own presumption. "But you know that far better than I do, Sir Michael. Is this your sixth hotel?"

"It is, Mortimer." The owner made his stately way across the lobby, pausing to stare at the muted blue and yellow tones of the wallpaper as though for the first time, even though Charles had it from Mrs. Wheelwright that the man had been making a nuisance of himself with the workers for the past month. "You would think he had never built a hotel before, Mr. Mortimer," she had confided over tea belowstairs last night.

*I will allow my employer his idiosyncrasies,* Charles considered. *He has employed me in his other hotels since my return from India, and I have observed—and endured—his bluster.*

Sir Michael stood before him now, on the other side of the marble-topped front desk. "I worry when things are not done and guests are already arriving. Is my trust well placed in you, Mortimer, to run one of my establishments?"

*Should I be humble or honest?* "Yes, it is, Sir Michael," he replied.

"Then the workers will be gone tomorrow?"

"If the Grand Hotel is done, and not one moment before. I have standards, too." He waited for the blast to come.

Sir Michael glared at him. "So you will not bow and scrape and tell me lies, eh?" he asked.

"I shouldn't think so," Charles murmured. "It's not my usual pattern."

The owner rested his elbow on the desk. "It is just that you seem somewhat meek, Mr. Mortimer, and that will never do. Your position requires a certain dignity, combined with an element of humility and deference." He waved his arm. "Let them know who is in charge, but at the same time . . ." He paused.

*Lick their boots?* Charles thought in wry amusement. *I've done that a-plenty in twenty-five years of the working world. Bow and defer and speak softly and arrive at solutions to problems they have not even voiced? I am an expert. Make suggestions that guests far grander than I can adopt without any nagging sense of plagiarism? I am your man, Sir Michael.*

"Sir Michael, you may be certain that the Grand Hotel is in good hands," he said. It was prosaic, but entirely what he should say.

"I'll judge that, won't I?" his employer stated. His words only avoided being menacing by the fact that most men who look like basset hounds cannot be thought sinister, or so Charles reasoned.

"To be sure, Sir Michael."

Sir Michael continued to regard him. "We shall see.

I hope I have not misplaced my trust by making you a manager at last," he said, then looked behind him. "And now you have a customer. Good morning, madam." Sir Michael bowed to someone behind him that Charles could not see, then turned again. "Mortimer, I will be checking on you." He turned from the desk in an elaborate motion worthy of the regent himself and headed for the grand staircase, obviously intent on exploration upstairs. *Go in peace,* Charles thought with fervor, and turned his attention to the lady who stood before him now.

He wasn't surprised that he had not noticed her behind Sir Michael's impressive bulk, because she was short. And Charles couldn't be surprised that he had not noticed her entrance when he was occupied with his employer, because there was nothing about her calculated to attract attention. She was one of hundred, no thousands and millions of women who inhabited the world in quiet, possessing no air to make a man look twice, or maybe even once.

That is, unless the right man took time out for a second perusal, Charles Mortimer decided as he looked again at the lady before him. No question in his mind: She was a lady. She had a pleasant face with a sprinkling of freckles across her nose and a cleft in her chin. Her brows were thick, and her eyes lively. Her face was wet, which surprised him, because she carried an umbrella. *I wonder if she dislikes those as much as I do,* he thought as he cleared his throat and then smiled at her.

When she smiled back, he took a third look, and for the first time in forty years of ordinary living, surrendered himself to someone he did not know. He could not credit the strange way he felt as he continued to smile at the lady. *My word, she is beautiful,* he thought. *How is this?*

She cleared her throat this time, and he knew he should say something. He continued instead to smile at her, even as his brain protested somewhere inside his skull that he was looking stupider by the half second.

"Excuse me, sir, but I believe I have a reservation," she said. "Millicent Carrington, from Edgeley, Kent."

"Oh, yes, of course," he told her and dragged his attention to the card box where all reservations nestled in precise alphabetical order. *Oh, please don't let her be encumbered with something as distasteful as a husband,* he thought. *I will have to remember how to shoot and then call him out.* "Millicent Carrington," he declared, holding up the card as though she were the first visitor of his life, and not one of thousands. "Mrs. Carrington?" he asked, remembering his manners and hoping for information that would prevent the purchase of dueling pistols.

She shook her head. "Miss Carrington, if you please."

He could have fallen in a heap behind the desk, such was his relief. *I am being stupid,* he told himself as he smiled back, and was rewarded with a smile of her own that made her blue eyes fairly glow at him. *I wonder if she smiles at every man like that,* he thought with a jab of sudden jealousy. *A man can only fight so many duels in one lifetime.*

She cleared her throat again. "Sir, is there a register I sign?"

Register. Register. "Yes, of course, Miss Carrington," he replied. "Things are so new here that I seem to have misplaced it."

"Um, I believe it is right here in front of us," she said, after a moment's pause.

"Heavens! There it was, all the time!" he said, looking down at the book that rested on a prominent stand between them. "And open to Monday, July 1," he said, wincing at his inanity, he who was the most unflappable of men. "Fancy that."

She leaned forward to sign the register, while he admired the top of her bonnet, and the faint fragrance of lemon that rose from her skin. He could hear her breathe. Miss Carrington looked up at him then. "Sir, is there a key?"

A key. A key. Now why would . . . of course there was. He glanced at her card. He had planned to put her in 301, at the opposite end of the hall from his own temporary quarters, but he took the key to 318 from the pigeonhole next to his own. *Why am I doing this?* he asked himself. He handed her the key, then motioned to the other footman positioned by the grand staircase. "Devost will take your bags and show you to your room, Miss Carrington." Was that *his* voice cracking? Good Lord, he was nearly thirty years from his voice change.

"Thank you, Mr., Mr. . . ."

"Mortimer, Charles Mortimer," he replied. "If I can do anything for you, you need only ask." *Oh, please do,* he thought. *Tell me that you think Devost is a scoundrel and you'd rather that I carried your bags upstairs. Anything.*

To his dismay, she seemed to have no qualms about his footman, and surrendered her luggage with good grace, pointing to the portmanteau by the front entrance that the hackney driver had deposited there. "This is your first hotel, Mr. Mortimer?" she asked while she waited.

*I must seem greener than a Spanish lime,* he thought with a wince. "The first hotel where I am manager, Miss Carrington," he said. He hesitated a moment, wanting to tell her more, wondering if she expected it. "Actually, I have worked for Sir Michael Moseley for over ten years . . . ever since my return from India." There. That seemed enough, without being too much.

She looked at him with what he hoped was real interest. "India? My brother was with the duke's own Thirty-third. We shall have to talk about India, Mr. Mortimer."

She nodded to him then and followed Devost and her luggage up the stairs. He watched until she was out of sight at the stairs' turning, and wondered if she was seriously interested in more conversation with him. Reason told him no, that she had only been filling time until the footman should return with her baggage. And yet. After another moment, he braced himself and returned to his duty.

By the time his day ended hours and hours later, Charles had convinced himself that no, he was not relapsing into malarial fever, and yes, he was a foolish fellow. It was an easy conclusion to arrive at, considering that in his forty years on the planet, he had never been overly concerned with women. It wasn't that he didn't like them; he did. The problem was a matter of simple ciphering: As the ninth of ten children of an earnest vicar unencumbered with either a good living or money of his own, the necessity of earning his bread had somehow always superseded any attempts at wooing.

*I suppose I could have chosen a different venue to begin my career,* he thought, not for the first time. Clerking for the East India Company had plunked him down in a corner of the world that while exotic offered little opportunity for matrimony with a proper British lady. And come to think of it, the Hindu women hadn't been eager to give him any of their time, either. The Mogul ladies? They were only a rumor, shadows on the street in their head-to-toe wraps, and otherwise kept behind high walls like mad uncles in England. India wasn't the place to find a wife; he might as well have lived on the moon.

He thought about the matter while he ate dinner in the kitchen belowstairs and reread, "On the Proper Administering of Hotels," Sir Michael Moseley's primer on hotel management, with its plethoras of do's and don'ts. He had returned to England with Wellington's Thirty-third, brought out of the country by the direst necessity, afflicted as he was with malaria. He wanted to die at Port Said, but the vessel's surgeon wouldn't hear of it; he had no alternative but to live.

The attacks of malaria were less frequent now, but he could never deny that they held him back from advancement in Sir Michael's hotel empire.

Or had until now, when Mr. Simmons's gout had reached such a degree of agony that the poor man yelped when anyone even walked close to his foot and stirred up a breeze. He glanced up from the rule book to see Henri DuPré eyeing him across the cutting board. "Excellent chicken soup, DuPré," he said, never quite sure what to say to a French chef with more than his share of arrogance.

"*Mon dieu,* monsieur! It is soup à la reine! Can't you taste the almonds and veal stock?" the chef snapped, banging down his French knife and decapitating an entire rank of unsuspecting carrots. "Chicken soup! Chicken soup! You might as well call Napoleon a private on half pay!"

"Yes, I might," Charles said under his breath. "Excellent soup, DuPré," he repeated. "Almonds and veal stock, you say?" *I suppose that is my problem,* he thought as he returned his attention to the rule book. *I don't have any imagination in the kitchen.* He smiled into the bowl, so DuPré would not see. *Still tastes like chicken soup to me.*

He did take a turn around the dining room after he finished his dinner, pausing to bow to the few guests already assembled, and listen to their complaints about the banging and clanking and strong smell of paint that lingered still. He made a mental note to send them each a box of Copley's Crunchy Toffee. Nowhere did Sir Michael mention it in his pamphlet, among the admonitions and caveats, but Charles knew from long experience that giving people something to eat that they didn't pay for invariably reaped dividends. *I should write my own booklet,* he thought. *Actually, I should run my own hotel.*

Miss Carrington came into the dining room just as he was completing his circuit and mentally girding himself for a diplomatic discussion with the carpenters.

How nice, if only for a moment, to tuck away the up-coming unpleasantness and look upon a pretty woman.

In the soft light of midsummer that streamed in the tall French windows, Miss Carrington did not disappoint. He moved closer, as the maître d'hôtel seated her, then cleared his throat, not wishing a repeat of his adolescent falsetto earlier that afternoon. "Miss Carrington, would you wish to be seated with another lady? Some of our single guests request it."

She smiled her thanks, but shook her head. "No, Mr. Mortimer. I prefer to sit alone." She smiled again. "Would you think me terribly ill-mannered if I read while I am waiting? Father never allows such liberties at home."

She could have done a fandango on the table, and he wouldn't have objected. "Not at all, Miss Carrington," he assured her. "I always read when I eat."

"Then we are two dull dogs, indeed," she told him, and he laughed out loud. The maître d' looked at him, his eyes wide. *Yes, Washburn, I do laugh,* he wanted to say. *I've even been known to want a woman, although it's been a while.*

She took a small book from her reticule, so he could think of nothing else that would keep him by her table. He bowed and left the dining room.

The carpenters occupied him to the utmost levels of diplomacy for another hour. Patiently he listened to their catalog of troubles and delays, accepting blame when nothing else would work, and offering gentle admonitions of an avuncular nature when that seemed apropos.

The carpenters left at ten o'clock, cheerful again, armed with his quietly voiced suggestions, and ready to finish in the morning. He relieved the night clerk at the desk so the man could eat and indulge in a restorative nap, and then spent the next two hours catching up on correspondence, filing reservations, and forwarding invoices to Sir Michael at his office on Oxford Street. When he looked up again it was midnight.

Another day gone. When Chaseley returned, re-
freshed from his nap, Charles Mortimer went to his
room.

He opened the door and sighed out loud. Everything was jumbled where he had left it that morning,
when he vacated his rooms off the lobby. He moved
a few boxes to one side, located a towel for his morning bath, and then carefully arranged his clothes across
a chair. *This inconvenience will last for two weeks,* he
thought, *or three at the most, until Wellington's big
party ends.* He sat on the bed, smiling to himself, and
thinking suddenly of his father, that worthy man, and
his sermons.

"The sermon," he said out loud, that homily on
inconveniences and problems, the sermon that had
shaped him more than he knew, until he had applied
it at the worst moment of his life. He lay back on the
bed, his hands behind his head. "Yes, Father, how I
wish I could have told you," he murmured, and closed
his eyes, thinking in odd, telescoping fashion backward
to India, and then the Deccan, and Assaye, and Kaitna
Ford, and then smaller still to the cannon where he
passed ammunition all the hot afternoon, until the moment when he was the only one left to fire the gun.
And then he was touching the punk to the hole, his
entire energy focused on that effort, and kept from
fear by the certainty that this was a problem, and not
merely an inconvenience, and how refreshing it would
be to tell his father that he knew for himself now.

*I promised myself then, Father, if that if I avoided
being cut into bite-sized chunks by those Mahratta
swords that I would always know the difference between an inconvenience and a problem,* he thought.
*Father, malaria is an inconvenience; a problem is hav-
ing only one canister remaining to fire at a foe grudgingly sharing the same spit of land between two rivers.*

It hadn't been a problem for long. Wellesley himself
(this was long before he was Wellington) brought him
canister shot from the rear that was only the rear be-

cause it was twenty yards farther back. They had stared at each other for the briefest moment, Wellesley muttered something about East India clerks expanding their repertoire, and then mounted his horse again.

After the battle, when Charles amused himself by the realization that he was still alive, he sat down on an ammunition box, only to find himself joined on another by Wellesley again, the man as black from powder as he was and as exhausted. Wellesley sat there with his elbows on his knees, his head far forward, his eyes closed. After a long pause, he turned his head slowly, as though every part of him ached. "Mortimer, are you ready to return to pushing a quill across a page at Fort William?"

"Can you doubt it, sir?" he replied.

Wellington grinned suddenly, his teeth amazingly white in his black face, and then gave that horse's laugh of his. "You're welcome anytime to serve my guns, Mortimer," he said. "Thank you with all my heart."

"You're welcome," Charles said as he lay there on his bed in the Grand Hotel. "Why didn't I tell him that? Why did I just blush and mumble?"

He opened his eyes and glanced at the night table next to the bed, then sat up, looking around. The table was there, of course; there was always a night table at a Moseley hotel. The manuscript was missing. In a moment he was on his feet, searching for it. He retrieved it from the neat folder of hotel business that he kept in his room, and placed it on the table. *Wellington in India.* He knew it was a simple title, but he had never managed a better one. He ruffled the pages, his evening's work for many years, secure in the knowledge that the manuscript would be complete soon enough to present it to the great man during the summer's fetes.

"And so I shall," he murmured, tired now and ready for the release of sweet sleep.

He slept peacefully and well—the times of night-mare were long over—and woke to the sun coming in the window, and then a scratching at his door. "Come, please," he said, alert now and ready for the day's first emergency, early as it was.

Betty the 'tween stairs maid opened the door, peek-ing in to make sure that he was dressed, he thought, then pausing outside when she saw that he was still in bed.

"Oh, come in, Betty," he said, sitting up and tucking the blanket around his waist. "I'm probably twenty times more harmless than Mr. Simmons, if I can be-lieve rumors. Is there a problem?"

She smiled at him then and came into his room, although no farther than the wall by the door. "Mr. Mortimer, there's trouble with the drain in the public bath down the hall. The lady in there thought you should know."

He frowned. "It's not draining?"

"That's what she said." Betty grinned. "She was awfully nice about it. Oh, haven't we seen some guests flutter up into the boughs over little?"

*Oh, we have,* he thought, then waved her away so he could dress. *Everyone expects perfection in a Mose-ley hotel.* While buttoning his trousers he looked at his manuscript, knowing that there wouldn't be any time to write this morning. India would wait.

There were two public baths on the third floor, un-like the second floor, which had private baths in each chamber. Even though he was certain that the lady would not have remained there, he knocked.

" 'Make thee an ark of gopher wood,' " he heard a woman say in a deep voice. He laughed, and knew without knowing that Miss Carrington was on the other side of the door.

"I'm coming in, Mrs. Noah," he said, and opened the door to gaze upon Miss Carrington clad in a perfectly respectable but entirely fetching robe, her hair wrapped in a towel, her feet bare, her ankles so fine.

"You know your Genesis," she began, not rising from her perch on the side of the tub, or her contemplation of its recalcitrant drain. The steamy room smelled radiantly of that exultant lemon essence she wore.

"I am the child of a vicar," he said, coming closer to join her in staring at the drain.

"Are you?" she asked, the interest evident in her voice. "Then you must be well acquainted with the entrancing delights of waiting your turn for the tub."

He laughed again. "I am the ninth of ten, Miss Carrington. Not only did I queue up for the tub, I usually got hand-me-down water."

It was her turn to smile, and twinkle her eyes at him. "That was not my intention in summoning you from sleep, sir," she replied, then blushed, probably from the suggestion of her reply. "I followed the time-honored ritual of lifting the stopper, but as you can tell, the result was less than satisfying."

"Shall I send a dove for the plumber?" he asked.

"By all means, sir," she said, and rose gracefully. "As if you did not have one hundred other pesky duties incumbent upon opening a hotel. I can wait here for the plumber, if you wish."

He did not overlook for one moment that he could summon Betty back, or call for the underfootman, but he nodded. "I will bring you tea," he said.

" 'An ever-present help in trouble,' " she quoted.

He thought a moment. He felt the years drop away in that peculiar fashion that happened among friends, but never with a woman before, or someone he scarcely knew. " '. . . Though the waters thereof roar and be troubled.' "

She clapped her hands. "Mr. Mortimer, you are amazing! That is even the same psalm!"

With a nod to her, and a feeling of real satisfaction at his own wit, he hurried belowstairs to summon the plumber. He ordered a pot of tea and biscuits for the third floor west bathing room, which brought such an elevation to Mrs. Wheelwright's eyebrows that he feared for her hairline.

He was not destined for an immediate return to the third floor. The carpenters had arrived, and needed his soothing ministrations. He supervised the changing of the guard at the front desk from a bleary-eyed Mr. Chaseley to the much more alert Mr. Kipling. One foot on the stairs, he was recalled to solve a complaint of an Italian guest who had misplaced either her husband or her dining table—he couldn't be sure which, because his Italian was untested ground. She did seem happy to see a peculiar-looking dog when it strolled into the lobby, and even happier when it was followed by a little boy. He smiled, bowed, and resolved to consult his Italian grammar that evening.

He did so hope that Miss Carrington wouldn't have exchanged her robe for a dress and shoes by the time he returned to the third floor, but time had passed; she was dressed, and seated by the tub, this time with a sketch pad in her lap. She looked up and smiled when he came in, gesturing toward the plumber.

"Do you know, Mr. Mortimer, that water swirls counterclockwise above the equator and clockwise beneath it?"

He wondered if she had any idea how entrancing she was, sitting here in a rectangle of sun from the skylight, her hair still damp and spread like a fan across her back. "I don't know that I ever considered the matter, Miss Carrington," he told her.

"Mr. Wilson here tells me that it is so," she replied. "Do you know that he was an able seaman on one of Captain Cook's voyages of discovery to the South Seas? I am astounded at what a person can learn, watching a drain. And here my father told me that I would find London a bore."

He shook his head in amazement. *I have never met*

*anyone like you,* he wanted to say. "Wilson, wasn't it two voyages with Cook?" he asked.

The plumber looked up from the drain, where he was snaking down a pliable copper rod. "It was, sir."

Miss Carrington gazed upon him with what he hoped was admiration. "You know your employees, sir."

He felt faint surprise at her comment. Of course he knew those who worked for him, right down to their birthdays. "Miss Carrington, I worked with Wilson in Harrogate. When Sir Michael was building this hotel, he moved the manager and me down to run it, and some staff chose to follow."

"That speaks well of you, sir," she said.

He knew he was blushing when Wilson laughed. "Ah, miss, don't make 'im get all flustery!"

She smiled, and inclined her head toward him. "My apologies, Mr. Mortimer, but Sir Michael must certainly repose some confidence in you."

The plumber snorted, and returned his attention to the drain. "I say it's high time!"

"Oh, Wilson, leave off," Charles protested, more amused than irritated.

The plumber forced the snake farther down the drain. "Miss, it's only Mr. Mortimer's little souvenir from India what holds'm back."

"Malaria," Charles said when Miss Carrington gave him an inquiring look. "It comes back like unwanted relatives." He tried to make light of it, because it embarrassed him to be talking about himself. "It's hard to run a hotel with the fever and shakes."

"So you're always second-in-command?"

"It works better that way, Miss Carrington. Except what does Mr. Simmons do but contract the gout? I am now manager by default."

"There are some of us what didn't mind that, either," Wilson muttered under his breath.

Charles was spared any further discourse by the plumber, who grunted in satisfaction as the snake stopped. He tugged gently, turned the snake, and then pulled out a glob of plaster. "There y'are, Mr. Mortimer. Happens all the time with new construction."

"Excellent, Wilson. Do have a biscuit."

"I believe I will, sir," the plumber replied. "Any of that tea left, Miss Carrington?"

"Just enough for you," she said, pouring him a cup. "Since you didn't come back, Mr. Mortimer, I knew you wouldn't mind if Mr. Wilson used the other cup."

"Of course not." Charles sat down on the stool at the dressing table. He looked at the sketch pad in her lap, thought about all the rules in Sir Michael's book that he and Wilson were probably fracturing, and set them aside. "Are you an artist, Miss Carrington?"

"I pretend to be," she said, passing the teacup to the plumber, who sat on the lip of the tub and took it from her as nicely a though the three of them inhabited a drawing room. "It's hard to draw water swirling, and here was my perfect opportunity to practice a sketch." She smiled at the plumber, who smiled back. "And what does Mr. Wilson do but regale me with stories of watching the transit of Venus, and cannibals in Fiji. I had no idea that Moseley hotels could be so . . . so entertaining. I have been totally diverted."

"Best not breathe a word of this to Sir Michael," Charles said after a moment's pause. "He would probably wonder what any of us are doing taking tea in a bathing room at nine in the morning."

"Absurd, isn't it?" she agreed. She stood up and closed her sketch pad. "I don't know why this is, but I always seem to stumble into the most agreeable situations and meet the most interesting people. Good day to you both. I had better be about my business."

He watched her go, then turned to regard the plumber. "Wilson, did you ever?"

"Not me, sir," Wilson said, then chuckled. "But you know, I think she meets interesting people because she asks questions, and glory be, she *listens!*"

"How rare in a guest," he said.

He went about the duties of the day then, knowing how busy he would be soon, with the grand fete for Wellington approaching. However shy of visitors the new hotel was, he knew that the Moseley reputation for order and efficiency would soon fill it. It was his duty to make things run smoothly. "Each employee must be polite, thoughtful, and capable," or so the rule book stated. *I am all those things,* he reminded himself as he was tempted to contemplate Miss Carrington.

*Maybe even a little bloodless, too.* Mr. Simmons had accused him of that once; or maybe it wasn't so much an accusation as a comment on his subdued personality. He had thought about his supervisor's comment, mulling it about during a solitary walk (the only kind he ever took), and then deciding that he was not so much bloodless as he was resigned. He had decided years ago that certain things in life—a wife, children, a home—would never be his. His breeding was good enough, except that it was unmatched by even the smallest inheritance to grease his way. He had never regretted, until now, his personal honesty that had never allowed him to cheat his way to a fortune in India, as many other clerks in the East India Company had done.

He knew he was a quiet man, one not inclined to trumpet himself to the notice of others. He liked his solitude, relished it even, after a long day of dealing with the petty inconveniences of spoiled hotel guests. In time, he had come to prefer it. If that resigned him to a bloodless existence, then so it was. He had found his niche—even if it was a step or two down from what his breeding should have allowed—and tailored it to suit himself, the perfect existence.

Except that suddenly it wasn't so perfect. Somehow between yesterday and today, a page had turned in his book of life. He had been mindful of a page turning at Kaitna Ford, when he went from youth to man in one horrific afternoon. Time had passed and more pages had turned, but now they seemed to be turning back to a chapter he had skipped, overlooked, or simply ignored, because the possibility of fulfillment was so remote. The rain thundered down again that afternoon, and he knew, with despair in his heart—that place where he usually felt nothing—that he wanted not only a wife and little ones, but that he wanted Millicent Carrington.

The thought jolted him. He knew from long practice that he could get rid of it; enough work and worry over this opening and Wellington's fete would push Miss Carrington so far back in his mind that he would soon forget her. He had the ability, except that this time he hesitated to dismiss her from his brain, and most certainly from his heart. *I am being absurd,* he told himself as he greeted guests, spoke with them in the lobby, let Mr. Kipling check them in, and summon the footmen for their luggage. He knew Mr. Kipling was wondering at him, wanting to ask why he was not squirreled away in his office as usual, doing the hotel's paperwork, like the super-efficient clerk he was. He could never tell his day clerk that he, Charles Mortimer, was waiting like a mooncalf for Millicent Carrington to appear in the lobby. He wished he had the nerve to ask her day's business.

To take his mind off Miss Carrington, he looked through the reservations for the month and was gratified to note members of Parliament, clergymen, and military officers. He sighed. And royalty. "Oh, Lord, we must bow, we must scrape," he murmured as he fingered the card with the name of Princess Henrika Hafkesprinke.

And Americans, apparently. He held up a card, marking the place in the file box with his finger. "Malachi Beach, Boston, Massachusetts, the American Society for Abolition," he murmured, then replaced the card and picked up the next one. "Mountrail, Lady Augusta. God help us." He replaced it quickly, remembering her from previous visits to the Grand

Vista in Harrogate, a lady tottering on the brink of death—or so she told everyone—who lived only to torment his staff. *"The guest is invariably correct,"* he murmured to himself, quoting Sir Michael's first rule.

He hoped, as he always did when he saw her name, that she would forget to arrive, or die, whichever seemed more convenient to her. As the morning wore on and his stomach began to gnaw itself at the prospect of her arrival, he thought he would circulate a warning throughout the hotel, rather like that fellow in the colonies who warned the Minutemen. As it turned out, there wasn't time.

She came as she always came, preceded by her dresser, a thoroughly cowed woman who, if she could have, would have flattened herself against the wall and slithered in, so as to escape all possible notice. Charles Mortimer, who had faced sword-wielding Mahrattas, stared down malaria, and survived ten years in Sir Michael Moseley's employ, felt his courage sink to cellar level.

"You have Lady Mountrail's reservation, I trust," the dresser asked, her voice scarcely above a whisper.

He could easily have turned the matter over to Mr. Kipling, but one glance at his day clerk's pale face told him that it would be useless. Lady Mountrail could smell fear like a bulldog. "Certainly, Smith. We have placed her in the Grand Garden Suite on the second floor. Here is the key."

He looked up then while the dresser registered for her mistress, knowing that Lady Mountrail would make her entrance now.

The riders from her post chaise came first, bearing her luggage, to be followed by the lady herself, bundled in fur and turbaned to guard against a chance bit of chill air on a July morning. Under her arm she carried a lapdog with a pushed-in face registering the same utter disdain as her mistress. Lady Mountrail was thin and wizened like an apple forgotten in the bottom of the bin. Mr. Simmons claimed that she knew everyone and forgot nothing. As Charles gazed on her, he felt icy fingers down his back: the guest from hell.

She moved with surprising grace for one of such antiquity. For all he knew she may even have been a gazetted beauty at one time, perhaps during the earlier days of the Roman Republic. He smiled at the thought, then wiped the grin from his face when she skewered him with a stony stare.

"Mortimer, is it? I thought we had seen the last of you at Harrogate."

"I was transferred here, my lady," he managed. Out of the corner of his eye he saw Millicent Carrington descend the staircase and then pause.

"Let us hope that you have not brought along your typical mismanagement," she snapped, slamming her walking stick down on the desk, coming within inches of his nose. "I have not forgotten that time you checked me into a room where the sun struck my face at ten in the morning! Or the time you—you, Mortimer—allowed them to serve me Darjeeling tea instead of Lapsang souchong!"

"How could I do that?" he murmured, wishing that Miss Carrington would hurry on, and not stand there to witness his humiliation.

"I trust you have learned something in the six months since our last conversation."

"I trust I have, my lady," he agreed, and bowed. "Smith has your key, and you know that we are at your disposal."

She slammed down the stick again, and Mr. Kipling, cowering by the reservations, began to tremble visibly. "Simmons always shows me to my room, Mortimer," she said in an awful voice that made his hair rise on the back of his neck. "Have you *already* forgotten?"

Without a word, he came around the desk and extended his arm for Lady Mountrail. The lapdog snarled at him, but Lady Mountrail gave a vicious jerk on its diamond collar. "That's enough, Teddy," she growled back. "Save it for the footman!" They started across the lobby, followed by underfootmen with luggage and the dresser. Progress was slow, with the witch on his arm keeping up a steady diatribe about the weather, the general nastiness of London drivers, the odor of new paint in the lobby, the height of the carpet in the corridor, and the way the sun glanced off the windowpane and reflected in her eyes. Charles didn't think she paused for a breath.

He knew the suite wouldn't be to her liking: the windows too tall, too short, too wide, too narrow; the bed too soft, too hard, or both; the bell pull too far from the chair he sat her in. He fled the room as soon as he could, after promising to send up a footman to walk her nasty dog.

Miss Carrington still stood in the lobby, frowning. "Heavens, Mr. Mortimer, do you ever contemplate a different career after her visits?" she asked as he came near.

"Every time."

She touched his arm, which brought some measure of peace to his heart. "Do you know, if there are any Sicilians in town for the duke's fete, perhaps you could arrange an accident?"

He laughed out loud, and amazed himself by clapping his arm around her shoulder and giving her a squeeze. She looked at him in delight, but he remembered Sir Michael's rule book and released her just as promptly. He wanted to ask her to luncheon in the dining room, something also forbidden he knew, but she nodded to him and bid him good day.

He didn't know it was possible for a day to extend itself as this one did. His darted glances at the clock in the lobby only frustrated him because the damned timepiece seemed to be on some cosmic pause, once Miss Carrington left the building. He knew his job better than anyone; he greeted guests, solved problems, coaxed the carpenters to unimagined heights of efficiency, while all the time some corner of his brain waited to astound Millicent Carrington with his wit upon her return.

Lady Mountrail did not reappear in his lobby, but a footman came and went with the dog. On his return, the man muttered that next time he would push the little beast into oncoming traffic. His best upstairs maid came down to him in tears because the cucumber sandwiches she had served with tea weren't all the same length, and Betty the 'tween stairs maid had fled in terror when Lady Mountrail accused her of staring at her. "Honest, Mr. Mortimer, all I did was sweep a little coal dust from the hearth!" she declared as she sobbed and he patted her shoulder.

As the dinner hour came and then went, he wondered if he had missed Millicent Carrington somehow. He thought about asking the footmen, but they would want him to describe her, and what could he say about someone who looked as ordinary as she did, except that she was wonderfully, magnificently original, qualities that didn't show?

The dining room had been empty for an hour and shadows were lengthening across the lobby when the footman opened the door for Miss Carrington, looking a little blue-deviled. He was sitting down at the desk behind the counter where he knew she could not see him. He leaned back in his chair and watched as she crossed the lobby in silence, with only a nod to the footman, until she stood before the great vase of flowers that Sir Michael Moseley mandated for all his lobbies. As Charles watched, fascinated, she slowly untied her bonnet, lifted it off, and set it on the bust of Sir Michael that was also de rigueur in each Moseley hotel. Mr. Chaseley at the desk started forward.

"No, Chaseley," he said, his voice low, "leave her alone."

"But, Mr. Mortimer," he began. He took another look at the bust with its bonnet and deep green tie. "Does look festive, doesn't it?"

"Most certainly," he agreed. "It's a wonderful hat. I'm certain she'll remove it eventually."

After another long look, Chaseley busied himself putting letters in pigeonholes. Charles got up quietly and stood at the front desk, his eyes on Miss Carrington. She had returned her attention to the vase, which she surveyed for a moment, then began to rearrange the flowers. She worked with a sure hand—a rose here, a gladiolus there, more baby's breath bunched in one corner—until she was satisfied. She stepped back again, and he noticed that the high lift to her shoulders was less pronounced.

Without looking at her face, he could tell that she had reached a certain equanimity. *Writing does that to me, Miss Carrington,* he thought. *After a dreadful day, I can return to India with ink and paper. You do it with flowers.*

She stood admiring the much-improved arrangement, and with a sigh that he could hear all across the lobby, she removed the bonnet from Sir Michael. On impulse, Charles left the desk and crossed the lobby. "Miss Carrington, would you like some tea?"

One foot on the step, she turned around; he watched her smile center itself somehow in her eyes. He couldn't help but smile back and wonder, just for a second, about the many ways a woman was beautiful. *My God, I can't be the first man to have noticed this about Miss Carrington,* he thought. And then, *I wonder if other men feel this way about their dear one? And then, I am presumption personified.*

"I think I would like tea more than anything, Mr. Mortimer," she replied, to his heart's delight, he who was self-contained, regulated, and sufficient unto himself. "It might just keep me from throwing myself under a dustman's cart, or prevent me from taking the king's shilling."

The idea of Miss Carrington enlisting was so amusing that he laughed out loud. "Surely your day has not been so terrible," he said as he walked her into the dining room and seated her.

She relaxed visibly. "Mr. Mortimer, I came into your hotel positively long-jawed this evening, and you kindly let me arrange the flowers! I shall have to tell Sir Michael that he was wise to transfer you here . . . that is, if I knew him."

He ordered tea and biscuits. "Would you like anything else?"

She shook her head. "No. The activities of this day have quite caused my appetite to vanish."

That was an opening if ever he had heard one. *She is a guest, Mortimer,* he reminded himself. *She surely cannot want you to delve into her life. She can't mean you to pry.* "That bad?" he asked, mentally tearing up the rule book and scattering the pieces around in his brain.

But she was regarding the ceiling now with that same degree of interest she had reserved for the bathtub drain only that morning. "Do you know, Mr. Mortimer, I rather think that I would duplicate that ceiling design around the top of the wall there," she said, not shifting her gaze. "It would make such a declaration, if you bring down the blue and yellow from the ceiling medallions."

He followed her gaze. "I believe you are correct," he said, after considering the matter. He took a deep breath. "You've changed the subject, Miss Carrington. Why was your day so horrible?"

The tea came; she took a sip, and then another before answering him. He had the strangest feeling that she was measuring him. "Such a restorative! Mr. Mortimer, I am a clergyman's daughter. I will be thirty at Michaelmas." She paused, and moved her chair closer to his, which gratified him no end. "Papa would gladly support me forever, and my brothers are already clamoring for me to visit them." She returned to the tea, took another sip, and then stared into the cup as though she planned to read her fortune there.

"Then you are probably more fortunate than most of England's females." Charles felt himself on firm ground. He worked with women every day who were compelled by necessity to labor outside of their own hearths.

"I don't want to burden my family," she said simply. "I told Papa I was coming to London to find myself a position as governess. I speak Italian, play the pianoforte, know the rudiments of grammar and history, and I can sketch. Do I not sound like a governess already?"

"You sound like an accomplished lady to me," he replied. "If you don't need to seek employment, why do it?" He took a deep breath, and retreated further from Sir Michael's book of rules. "I do not understand why you have chosen not to marry, Miss Carrington."

"No one ever asked me, Mr. Mortimer," she said simply. "My marriage portion is respectable, but I've never been fond of losing at chess, just because it's the ladylike thing to do, or agreeing with a man even if what he says is stupid." She looked at him then, and there was some color to her cheeks. "I'm sorry, Mr. Mortimer, but do you know, you have an air about you that rather invites me to speak my mind."

"Do I?" he asked, startled. "This is certainly a mutual discovery."

She returned her attention to her tea, and there was a look of sudden confusion about her that he found entirely endearing. She blushed then, and he turned his attention to the ceiling again. *Bless her,* he thought. *She might like me to think she is more confident than is really the case. It must be a daunting thing for a lady to go to an employment agency.*

"No luck at the agency, Miss Carrington?"

She took another sip, then sighed and settled back in the chair. "On the contrary, sir, too much luck! Every lady between here and Galway Bay seems to want a governess to educate the young. I have only to pick and choose."

He frowned. "Where is the difficulty? If there is a dearth of intelligent men willing to propose, and you don't want to become the aunt-in-residence, have you changed your mind about . . . about governing?"

She laughed. "I have not! It is merely this, Mr. Mortimer, plainly put: I had wanted to spend at least a week in London, just enjoying the place, before I chose a position." She leaned forward. "But I find that I do not have enough money to remain at the Grand Hotel." She put her hand on his arm for a moment. "Oh, I will never escape in the middle of the night, sir! I have enough for last night and this night."

He found the notion of Miss Carrington shinnying down a rope hugely appealing; he had not a doubt that she could do it. He shook his head. "No, my dear, you would have to knot the bedsheets together, and I am not certain that the height of the building from your window and the length of the sheets are entirely compatible. You might be a floor short of success." He frowned again, wondering why someone as well dressed as she should be short of funds after so brief a stay in London.

"And now you are wondering why I am at such a low tide," she said, and he was struck again how they seemed to read each other's thoughts. "When I was returning here, I happened by a family that had been evicted. There they were, sir, with their belongings all around them on the street." The reminder seemed to galvanize her, and she shook her finger at him. "Mind you, such a thing would be unheard of in my father's parish!"

She didn't need to say any more. "So you emptied your reticule on them?" Charles asked.

"It's what any Christian lady would do."

*Oh, you're a green one,* he thought. *Totally dear, but a green one all the same.*

He studied the matter a moment, thinking to leave it alone, but knowing that if she was plainspoken, he should be, too. "Was it off Bayswater Road?"

"Why, yes. Are all landlords there so unfeeling?"

"Miss Carrington, there is a family in that vicinity whose career in life is to gull passersby from out of town."

She said nothing for a long while. While he did not look at her directly, he could watch her expression from the corner of his eye, and how it went from shocked disbelief, to argumentation, to real embarrassment, and then—ah, relief—to humor.

"And no one but visitors stop, is that it?" she asked.

"Precisely. Everyone else who knows the scam just walks by. Eventually someone will tattle on them and the Runners will show up."

"But by then they've packed their bundles and are off in search of another street corner," she finished, her expression thoughtful. "And they are probably well acquainted with the Runners and their habits."

"Can you doubt? Rumor has it that they have put one son through medical school in Edinburgh on the strength of that dodge."

She groaned, made a face at him, and drank the rest of her tea. "I depend upon you not to tell anyone!"

"The thought never crossed my mind," he replied, the helpful hotel manager again. He touched her hand this time, intensely aware of what he was doing, but unable to resist because of the doleful look on her face. "If it's any comfort, I fell for the same dodge when I arrived here two months ago."

"You?" she asked in amazement.

He smiled at her then, his fingers still light on her arm. "Miss Carrington, I am a clergyman's child, too." He was relieved to see the frown leave her face.

"Better to be cheated than to have passed up an opportunity to relieve suffering?" she asked in a low voice.

"Of course."

She shifted slightly in her chair, and he withdrew his hand quickly, only to discover that she was moving closer, and not farther away. *Let it go, Mortimer,* he told himself.

"So I will march back to the Steinman Agency tomorrow morning and engage an employer, then return virtuously, pay my bill, and leave," she told him.

"I could loan you some money," he offered. *Sir Michael, have I now broken* every *rule?* he asked himself.

"I wouldn't accept it."

"You could write your father."

"And tell him what I have done? He would know that I am a babe and unfit to be loosed on an unsuspecting world."

"Then I suppose we are at *point non plus,* Miss Carrington."

"Well, I am, at any rate," she replied. "It's not your problem." She rose then, and he rose, too. He wished there were some way to detain her longer in his empty dining room, but thought of nothing. "Good night then, sir," she told him. "I suppose I was unfair to unburden myself like that."

"Just one of the many services we provide at Moseley hotels," he teased, even as he understood in his heart how seriously he had just flouted his own rule of disinterest, not to mention all of Sir Michael's.

"Oh, I doubt that Sir Michael is concerned about much beyond the last entry in the ledger, Mr. Mortimer," she said. "Good night."

She left him then but looked back at the ceiling as she stood in the arched doorway. "Yes, if I ran this Moseley hotel, I would bring down that color. Good night, sir."

When he returned to the lobby, glum-faced he was sure, Chaseley looked up from a London *Times* some guest must have left behind. "Miss Carrington, sir?" he asked.

"Yes. She had some slight problem and needed a little advice."

"Could you help her?"

"No."

"That's not like you, Mr. Mortimer." Mr. Chaseley leaned his elbows on the counter, which Charles should have frowned on, but overlooked instead. "I know we have not known each other long, Mr. Mortimer, but do you know what a reputation you have throughout the Moseley enterprises?"

This was turning into a day of surprises, Charles decided. He came closer to his assistant, even though the lobby was as empty as the dining room, and lowered his voice. "I don't know what you mean."

The younger man gave him what he thought was a charitable look, the kind he, as a young man, would have reserved for elder statesmen. "Everyone knows how good you are at solving problems. Haven't you ever wondered why Sir Michael moves you around from place to place?"

He had never considered the matter before. "I've always assumed it was because he couldn't find me a niche, but that I was too useful to sack."

"Lord, no, Mr. Mortimer!" Chaseley exclaimed. "You are the perfect background man. You do everything right and by the book." He leaned closer. "Sir Michael told me so himself, when he moved me up here after he replaced Mr. Simmons with you. 'Study him,' he told me. 'He's the kind of employee every entrepreneur wants—the perfect background man.' Honest, Mr. Mortimer, that was what he told me."

Charles wondered if this was a compliment, then decided that it must be, or he would have been sacked years ago, after that first reoccurrence of malaria had rendered him immobile and sweating for days in decidedly untropical Glasgow. " 'Pon my word, Mr. Chaseley."

His assistant must have decided that he had overstepped his bounds, because he mumbled something about needing to file some reservations, and returned to his duties. He looked up long enough to say good night, and add something about "too bad you couldn't help Miss Carrington."

It was too bad, he decided as he sat down later in his room, his manuscript open before him. Sir Michael Moseley had always made it perfectly clear that any guest who could no longer pay his bill at a Moseley hotel must be invited, nay, urged, to leave. He had certainly done his share of ejecting through the years, but Miss Carrington needed no encouragement to vacate. Tomorrow she was going to cheerfully pay her bill and vanish from his life into some estate schoolroom, where she would likely be underappreciated. If he thought it would have made a difference, he would have dropped a wad of his own money—after all, what did he ever spend it on?—in front of her door, except that he knew she would merely return it to the front desk and encourage the clerk to find the rightful owner.

Moody now, he rested his chin on his palm and stared down at the manuscript, which only awaited that final chapter chronicling the last string of victories that put the seal on Wellington's years in India. After returning to Fort William after Assaye, he had admired the great man from a distance, hearing from others of the victories at Argaum, that steaming plain, and then the fortress of Gawilghur, sieged and then taken at so little cost. Ordinarily the mildest of men, Charles had not even flinched at the stories of Mahrattas thrown alive from the battlements of Gawilghur to break apart on jagged rocks far below. He had fought them at Assaye, and had earned his cynicism.

How far away it all seemed now as he sat in his quiet room. He wrote too late, or at least until his eyes began to feel sandy. Leaving the last page open to dry, he stood up, stretched, and went into the corridor. He stood a moment, hands in his pockets, shirt open at the collar, then did what he always did every night. Weary with writing—why was it that something so sedentary could wear him out so fast?—he took off

his shoes and walked quietly through his sleeping
hotel. In a few hours, the maids would be rubbing
slumber from their eyes as they came down from the
attic. Chef DuPré would coax the kitchen fires into
life again, and shoo his assistant outside with orders
to return with only the freshest produce from London's great open-air market.

He went into the dining room and stood for a moment by the table where he and Miss Carrington had
taken late-night tea. *I would like to sit here with her
again,* he thought, then shook his head at the impossibility of it all. He pushed open the French doors and
strolled onto the terrace that overlooked a most pleasing vista of Kensington Park's new-planted shrubbery.
The view was handsomer in Harrogate and he wished
himself back there, even as assistant manager again.
London was too large, and when Miss Carrington left
it, he knew it was going to be too much trouble.

After a moment breathing in London fumes, he
shook his head and closed the French doors again. He
was halfway up the back stairs and headed to his bed
when he suddenly decided that some of Sir Michael
Moseley's rules deserved to be broken. *I wonder if
Miss Carrington will agree,* he thought as he walked
quietly down the carpeted hall, his eyes on that angle
where wall met ceiling. Who better to bring down the
color than the guest who suggested it? Why should
this London hotel look like all the others? The paint
could certainly come out of his own pocket; the painters, too, for that matter. And if Sir Michael sacked
him, well, he could find another job. He returned to
his room, wrote a quick note, then tiptoed next door
to 318 and quietly secured the note to the door with
a tack, something never done at a Moseley hotel.

He was up early as usual, despite his late night. A
glance outside his door showed him that the note was
gone. He listened then, a smile on his face; someone
was humming in the bathroom, and he didn't think
it was the plumber. He dressed quickly and hurried

downstairs. He stayed long enough at the front desk
for the changing of the guard from Mr. Chaseley to
Mr. Kipling, then went into the dining room to wait
for Miss Carrington.

She did not fail him. She made herself comfortable
and looked at him expectantly. "Your note said you
had a brilliant idea."

The imp of self-doubt bounded into the room like
a Gibraltar ape and hoisted itself onto his shoulder.
*This is insane,* he thought in sudden panic. *What was
I thinking?*

He knew he was just sitting there staring at her, and
he wouldn't have been surprised if she left the room
without a backward glance. To his amazement, she
only smiled and nodded. "I've had brilliant ideas that
turned a little soggy by morning, too," she said. "Oh,
and here is some tea. May I pour you a cup?"

He nodded, touched by her charity. He took a sip,
and reminded himself that he was forty-one years old,
and by most reckoning an adult. He had faced down
hundreds of Mahrattas, each intent upon killing him;
surely he could make a harmless suggestion to a
pretty woman?

He thought he could, but the issue hung in some
doubt. The only thing that made it possible for him
to speak finally was the utter conviction, coming from
where he knew not, that Miss Carrington took him
seriously. "Miss Carrington, would you consider accepting a temporary position at the Grand Hotel?"

He could tell that he had surprised her by the way
her eyes widened. "Doing what?" she asked finally.

"Painting and arranging flowers," he replied, after
listening with super-sensitive ears for some wariness
in her voice, and finding none. He looked over her
shoulder to the wall. "I like your idea of adding color
to the walls there. You're not afraid of heights, are
you?"

"With three brothers and an apple orchard? I
wouldn't dare be," she said. She paused a moment,

and he crossed his fingers that calm good sense would not overtake his lovely companion. "You are serious, aren't you?" she asked.

"Never more so, Miss Carrington." He cleared his throat. "And both Mr. Kipling and I observed yesterday that you have a superior talent with roses and . . . and whatever those things are."

"Gladioli," she said, her eyes lively again.

"Of course, I wouldn't recommend another bonnet on Sir Michael's bust," he said.

"No, he's more a turban man, I should think," she said promptly, then held out her hand while he laughed. "I do so want another week in London. Let us shake on this, Mr. Mortimer, before either of us changes our mind!"

Shaking her hand, he almost asked her why she wanted another week in London. He knew his own reasons, however skewed they were: He wanted another week to enjoy her presence before she left his life forever. Of course, he reasoned, there was always the chance that she could register at his hotel again someday. He also knew how awful it would be if she came as a guest someday with a husband in tow, and two or three children. Which would be worse, he wondered as he watched her drink her tea and look thoughtfully at the opposite wall, to see her married or see her still single?

It was food for thought far less nourishing than breakfast, he decided after he finished taking ham and eggs with Miss Carrington. He left her there in the dining room because she wanted to think about the wall. Her only request was a tape measure, which he procured from the laundry room. By the time he returned with it, she had already cajoled someone on his staff into locating a ladder.

He felt a knot growing in his stomach as he sent the footman on an errand to summon the painters again. His anxiety was not without cause. When the painting crew arrived, all gloomy with sullen looks and

filed with pointed disfavor, he knew it was time for a
brave front. "Ah, and here you thought you were
done," he began, wincing at the trio of sour expressions.

"We were, Mr. Mortimer," the chief painter said.
"Do you have any idea how busy every painter in
London is right now? We might decide that we don't
want to help you."

"You might," he agreed, totally in sympathy. "I
would understand. Would you just follow me into the
dining room? I'll let you judge for yourselves." He
started for the dining room, hoping the men would
follow. To his relief, they did.

He opened the door, heard the crew chief sigh, and
knew that the painters were his. Tape measure draped
about her neck, and chin in hand, Miss Carrington
perched on top of the ladder, staring at the wall. She
gave him a cheery smile—at least he thought it was
directed to him—that made the chief painter sigh
again. "Reinforcements?" she asked.

"Pardon me, ma'am, but you shouldn't be there,"
the crew chief said, hurrying forward to grasp the ladder. "Tell me what you want, and I'll do it."

Charles could only stand there with his arms folded,
and hope that his own countenance was sober, should
the crew chief decide to look at him (and which
seemed unlikely in the extreme, especially since Miss
Carrington's fine ankles were just so discreetly evident).

What a lady, he thought as she gave the painter a
look of vast understanding. "You are kindness itself,"
she told the man, who had been joined by the other
two painters, each of whom now had a grip on the
ladder. "What I want to do is stencil this edge to
approximate the furbelows in the ceiling." She looked
down, the picture of good humor. "And then it would
be our task to paint the design." She who was anything but helpless gave Charles a helpless look. "Of
course, I can imagine that you are so busy right now,

and probably weary of the thought of one more day here at the Grand Hotel."

A chorus of no's, followed by vigorous headshakes and general murmured disagreement, came next, and Charles could only look away and consider the lilies of the terraced lawn, and how they grew. *Men are clay and putty,* he thought. *There are probably even some of us who think we rule the world. Idiots.* Standing behind the painters, he grinned up at Miss Carrington and winked.

With only the barest glance in his direction, she gazed down at the painters. "Of course, you may have already decided not to take on this picayune project."

"We have oceans of time for this little thing," the crew chief declared, perjuring himself, Charles knew, beyond all hope of redemption. "We will tell you what we need, and Mr. Mortimer can arrange delivery."

Unwilling to ruin Miss Carrington's diplomacy by any words of his, Charles bowed and left them to work, feeling more satisfied than in many a week. All afternoon he wanted to return to the dining room, but every glance he made in that direction seemed to be intercepted by his day clerk. "Mr. Kipling, what is your problem?" he finally asked in exasperation as the day dragged on. He must have startled Kipling; he knew he startled himself. *I'm rarely that rude with my staff,* he thought.

Kipling was all fumbles and stammerings then, and Charles felt instant remorse. "I was only thinking that it . . . it is a good thing that . . . that Sir Michael doesn't know what Miss Carrington is do . . . doing."

*Oh, Lord, let us pray he never finds out,* Charles thought. *He'd have my guts in a bucket if he knew I had bartered work for a room fee. There is nothing in the Moseley hotel handbook that even comes close to this subject.* "You're so right, Kipling," he said. It was lame, but at least Kipling stopped his fluttering.

The painters, all smiles still, left in midafternoon. "She's finishing the stenciling now," the crew chief told him, handing over a list of supplies. He leaned closer. "I didn't want to disappoint her, but we do have a project to complete tomorrow. She seemed quite agreeable when I told her we would be back tomorrow evening to work."

*Am I in some sort of handyman heaven?* Charles asked himself as he took the list in nerveless fingers. *Did someone in the construction business actually* tell *me his plans for the next day?* He thought of all those strange disappearances of painters and carpenters through the years—here one day, gone tomorrow— and could only marvel at the effect of a pretty lady with nice enough ankles. In a daze, he gave his regards to the painters, handed the list to the footman, and went into the dining room before anyone else could waylay him with demands that ordinarily would never ruffle him, but which right now would cause him some irritation.

Miss Carrington had traded the ladder for the floor and, using a rule that the painters must have left, was busy outlining a stencil. He watched her from the doorway of the empty dining room, inching her way along the floor as she drew the design that would be stenciled onto the wall. His viewpoint was all a man could ask for, he decided as he felt the duties of the day slip from his shoulders. *Miss Carrington, you have a lovely backside indeed.*

He must have made some noise (he hoped he wasn't breathing hard) because she looked around, then scooted sideways quickly. "Mr. Mortimer, what do you think?"

In an amazingly short time he thought of many things, most of them involving no one but him and Millicent Carrington. He walked closer to look at the floor. "This is the center section," she said, sitting back now. "We've already stenciled the corners."

He looked where she pointed. With obvious skill, they had replicated the curlicues and furbelows from the ceiling onto the top of the wall. "The painters—

oh, Mr. Mortimer, they are such *nice* men!—said they would be back tomorrow after the dining room closes and we will paint."

He was going to sit down, but she held up her hand to him, so he pulled her to her feet. Standing so close to her, he wished there was some reason to continue holding her hand. He could think of none, so he released her, cursing his lack of imagination, or maybe his want of backbone. He could only look at her and smile.

She smiled back, then stooped to pick up her chalk and stencil. "I think I will prefer working at night, because that will give me time in the day to view London's attractions. What would you recommend I see?"

"The Elgin Marbles," he said promptly, thinking of an editorial he had read in the morning paper about the disgraceful way the Greek treasures were housed. "I believe they are stored in some kind of shed, somewhat open to the elements. You could draw them," he suggested, warming to the topic. He took a deep breath. "I could escort you there tomorrow morning, if you wish."

*There now, I have fractured another rule in Sir Michael's handbook on hotel management,* he thought. *Make no attempt, beyond polite, unvarying service, to encroach upon the personal lives of the patrons.* He could see the words emblazoned on the page in his mind's eye.

"I think that is a perfectly wonderful idea," she told him. "Do you have the time?"

"I believe tomorrow is my day off," he replied.

"How fortunate." She smiled at him. "Mrs. Wheelwright will be so pleased."

"Mrs. Wheelwright?"

"Your housekeeper," she reminded him gently. "She took us belowstairs at noon for a sandwich and confided that you never take a day off."

He laughed, pleased that Mrs. Wheelwright was also

breaking Sir Michael's rules. A guest belowstairs? Unheard of. "I suppose I don't take many days off," he
said. "There's so much to do, to get ready to open
a hotel."

"That may be," she said, "but Mrs. Wheelwright
claims that you are legendary at Sir Michael's hotels
for *never* taking a day off. What is so fun about never-
ending toil? I live to be lazy."

He doubted that, but he did find her reply amusing.
"Miss Carrington, I have no one on whom to lavish
time." There. It sounded bald to him, but he hoped
not pathetic.

"You don't even have a diversion?" she asked.

"One." He had never told anyone about his manuscript, but something told him that she would be interested. "I am writing a history of Wellington in India.
It is nearly done."

She leaned toward him in that confiding way of hers
that he was already finding indispensable. "I think that
is marvelous, Mr. Mortimer. Perhaps you would let
me read it?"

"You're serious?" he asked, surprised.

"Never more so." She leaned closer. "In turn, I
could show you my sketches of India. I told you my
brother was with Wellington's Thirty-third, didn't I?"

He nodded. "Did he describe India to you?"

"He did in his letters, and then I looked at books.
He gave me some constructive criticism during his last
furlough." She sighed. "Perhaps you could tell me
how accurate they are."

"Just ask him," he said.

"I would if I could, but he died of the fever a year
later in Madras." She touched his hand before he
could mumble any platitudes. "Stay right here. I'll go
get my sketches."

She hurried from the room. The Grand Inquisitor
himself with a staff of thousands could not have
budged him from the dining room. He sat down and

willed himself to relax, letting the day slide from his shoulders.

When he opened his eyes Miss Carrington was sitting beside him. "You'll think I am lazy," he said in apology as she removed her drawings from a large folder.

"I think you are a man who needs to take a day off now and then," she replied. "Tomorrow I will require nothing more strenuous than that you carry my sketch pad. Here they are."

She spread her sketches before him, and he was enchanted—graceful women in saris, an ox pulling a big-wheeled cart, sun shining through a pipal tree, entrepreneurs in turbans squatting in an open-air market. "Rob thought I had captured the look of India," she told him, "but I credit his descriptive letters. What do you think?"

"They make me want to return to India," he said simply. He picked up a sketch of a boy with a monkey on his shoulder, the long tail curling around the child's neck. "I liked it there."

"So did Rob," she said, her voice soft, as though she did not wish to interfere with his memories. "Are they accurate?"

"For the most part." He ran his hand over a water buffalo on a road lined with tall grass. "I should rather tone down the size of that beast through the shoulders here, and elongate the horns a little. Yes, right there. And Indian women are a little narrower through the waist and wear more bangles on their arms. They are beautiful people, Miss Carrington." *But not as lovely as you,* he wanted to add.

"Now you must share your manuscript with me," she said, after another long moment as the dining room sank into deeper shadow.

"Very well, Miss Carrington." He stood up. "It is a work in progress." *And so am I,* he reasoned with himself, discarding forever the notion that he was mature, ordered, and prepared for any of life's eventualities. "Wait in the lobby if you wish. I will bring it down."

When he returned, she was seated on one of the overstuffed sofas in the empty lobby, her legs tucked under her. He stopped on the stairs to watch her a moment, struck by the serenity of her appearance. "I think it will put you to sleep," he told her quietly.

She held out her hands for the pasteboard box that contained his labor of four years. "It might," she agreed, "but I doubt it." She looked at the first page. "Your handwriting is so legible," she told him. "Of course, you were a clerk. It should be readable."

If another lady had said that, he reasoned, it would have sounded like a setdown. From Miss Carrington, it was only an affirmation of his life's work, almost conspiratorial, as though she said, "See here, you were a clerk and I am a painter of walls and soon a governess."

He gave her the manuscript with a bow, ushered the startled Mr. Chaseley off to a late dinner below-stairs, and sat at the desk basking in their camaraderie, even though she was halfway across the lobby from him. In a few moments he was engrossed in reservations. She minded her own business, looking up at him occasionally—he was aware of her every glance, even as he concentrated on his work—as if taking his measure in this history. "You were at Kaitna Ford," she commented once. When he nodded, she said, "So was Rob. Desperate work."

She did doze once or twice, resting her head along her arm. The lobby was so quiet he could hear the clock ticking. The few guests returning from late-night ventures took their keys from him in silence, almost as though they did not wish to disturb Miss Carrington, either. When Mr. Chaseley returned to duty, Charles sat down next to her on the sofa. She opened sleepy eyes. "It is not boring," she assured him, "but I think I am ready to retire for the night." She held up the few chapters remaining on her lap. "Trust me with it?"

"Of course. Good night, Miss Carrington. When do you wish to begin our expedition tomorrow?"

"By nine o'clock at least," she said promptly. "That will give you time to manage any number of crises, and still feel virtuous about leaving for a few hours." She laughed. "Do I understand you, sir?"

"Quite well, Miss Carrington. Good night."

It was an easy matter to walk upstairs with her, but harder to just let her go into her room next to his and shut the door on him, after a good night smile. He was awake a long time that night.

In spite of little sleep, Charles Mortimer was up early enough to console himself with a quick bath, and a quicker bowl of porridge belowstairs with Mrs. Wheelwright, who informed him that Sir Michael Moseley had already made his stately way through the kitchen that morning. Charles sighed and took a firmer grip on his coffee cup. "I suppose he is upstairs waiting to pounce?"

Mrs. Wheelwright observed him over the top of her spectacles. "As sweet as you please, I told him it was your day off, and what does he do but laugh? Mr. Mortimer, you're going to have to take a day off one of these days."

"Today, as a matter of fact," he told her. "I am escorting Miss Carrington to the Elgin Marbles." He held up his hand. "I know, I know! Sir Michael's rule book says this is a great malfeasance."

"But you're also employing her, or so she told me," the housekeeper said, leaning closer. "Good for you, I say, Mr. Charles Mortimer."

He blushed, which only made his housekeeper laugh. "You might mention that I'd like her to arrange two vases of flowers in the cooling room before you drag her to look at some dusty marbles."

By now he was at the door, coffee cup still in hand.
"She is a pretty thing, isn't she, Mrs. Wheelwright?"

"A real bloomer, sir, a real bloomer." She winked
at him, and he felt the color rush to his face again, he
who had given up blushing years ago for Lent. "I
think you ought to find her all kinds of walls to paint."

Sir Michael paced back and forth in the lobby,
which apparently had flustered Mr. Kipling into dropping a file of reservation cards. They littered the floor
in front of the check-in desk, and there was his deputy
manager, on his hands and knees gathering them.
"Steady, Mr. Kipling," Charles murmured as Sir Michael broke off his distempered pacing and bore down
on the desk. "Mustn't show fear."

"There you are!" Elaborately Sir Michael dragged
out his watch and glared at it. "I can't imagine why
you would trust the front desk to this . . . this butter-
fingered lackey who calls himself a deputy manager!"

"It's my day off, sir, and I have complete confidence
in Mr. Kipling," he said calmly. "Hurry up there,
Mr. Kipling."

*Now or never,* Charles thought. He strolled over to
his employer with what he hoped was an air of su-
preme confidence. "Sir Michael, I want to show you
what we are doing in the dining room, at the suggestion of one of our guests." He led the way into the
dining room, which was inhabited by a few patrons
who relished breakfast, that unfashionable meal. He
pointed to the stenciled outline high on the wall. "She
suggested that we could duplicate the colors from the
ceiling and achieve a thoroughly pleasing look. I agree
with her."

Sir Michael stared at him in amazement. "This has
never been done in a Moseley hotel!"

Charles Mortimer had no idea where his huge vat
of confidence was coming from. "Well, you might
want to consider it for your other hotels. I think the
effect is going to be quite charming. I would urge you
to return in a day or two and see."

It seemed to Charles that Sir Michael stared at the stenciled outline long enough for Napoleon to have made his retreat from Moscow half a dozen times, with room in between for the entire Tilsit negotiation. After another long moment, Sir Michael clasped his hands behind his back and began to rock on his heels slightly. "You could be right, Mortimer," he said finally. "A guest suggested this, you say?"

He nodded, scarcely daring to breathe. "A lady from Kent, daughter of a vicar, I believe. Bit of a painter herself."

Another pause. Sir Michael chuckled. " 'Pon my word, Mortimer. I don't know that any other hotel manager has ever gone to so much trouble to please a guest."

"I am not any other hotel manager, Sir Michael," Charles assured him, in voice quiet, then nearly fell over backward at his own temerity. "And this is no ordinary hotel."

Sir Michael was smiling now. He unclasped his hands and allowed Charles to walk him from the dining room. "I might refer you to my rule book for hotel management, Mortimer," he admonished, but there was no sting in his words. "A vicar's daughter from Kent, you say?"

"Yes, indeed."

"Well, carry on then! I'm flat amazed that you could cajole a crew of painters to help. I think every journeyman in town is touching up something or other for the duke's festivities."

"They're coming at night, sir."

"And not charging you dear?"

"No."

"You must have amazing powers of persuasion that I have been unaware of all these years, Mortimer," Sir Michael said when he recovered himself.

"I rather think it was a good look at the vicar's daughter," he offered in all honesty, and his employer burst into laughter.

"Lord help us, Mortimer!" he said when he could talk. "You are amazingly diverting!"

"Not as much . . .

". . . as the vicar's daughter!" the two finished together, completely in charity with each other.

*Pinch me and wake me up,* Charles thought. "Do trust me, sir," he said.

"I suppose I must, considering that someone has stenciled the dining-room walls." Sir Michael looked at the footman, who started forward with his hat and cane. "Oh. One thing more: Here's a little tidbit for your chef. The duke himself will be early at Carlton House at the end of this week to judge a pastry contest, of all things. It is some harebrained scheme of our regent. The hotel that makes his grace's favorite confection will have his patronage during all future visits to London. Do you think that scoundrel DuPré can manage to not embarrass us?"

"Certainly, sir," Charles replied. He accepted a broadside from Sir Michael. "These are the rules of the contest?"

"Yes indeed. See that you give them a little more consideration than you have given my rules of hotel management, Mortimer."

"Certainly. Good day, Sir Michael."

He was content to finish more hotel paperwork while Miss Carrington, blooming as a posy herself, went belowstairs to arrange flowers. She wore the prettiest blue muslin, almost a Wedgwood color that set off the rose and cream of her English complexion. *So you are rising thirty,* he thought as he watched her go. *Thirty never looked so good to me. Are blondes still in fashion? How should I know? I love brown hair. And freckles? Miss Carrington, I love those, too.*

When she came upstairs with a rose tucked in the roll of her hair where she had gathered it low on her neck ("Mrs. Wheelwright insisted," she told him, not without a blush of her own), he showed her the broadside Sir Michael had left. "I suppose you know his grace better than some," she teased. "What does he like for dessert?" She put down the paper and her expression changed. "Oh, Mr. Mortimer, what a time you had in India."

"Do you like the manuscript?"

She nodded, looking him in the eyes long enough to start a curious feeling in his stomach. "It's a wonderful work. I want you to finish that last chapter as soon as you can. I will insert my sketches, and you can give the whole thing to the duke."

The peppery fragrance of the rose in her hair mingled with the lemon cologne on her skin and he felt himself going quite light-headed. He hoped it wasn't a malarial relapse. "What a lovely idea, Miss Carrington," he told her. He had the strongest notion to kiss her right there across the front desk, but it was midmorning, and there was Mr. Kipling. "But now I think we had better locate the Elgin Marbles before some dustman carts them away, Miss Carrington."

"Or you find yourself trapped into working through another day off."

After some days of rain, the sun shone so brightly that he squinted, then almost regretted the necessity of securing a hackney. He helped her in, again captured by the sweet smell of her. They rode in silence, not so much because he was tongue-tied this time, but because she seemed as content as he to enjoy without words the pleasure of an extraordinary July day.

"Do you know," he said finally, "I am convinced I know precisely what will win that pastry contest."

"I thought you would."

"Plum duff."

She looked at him in delight. "There is no more plebeian dessert that I know of," she said at last, leaning forward in that way of hers that gave him her complete attention.

"He always asked for it in India." He sat back and laughed. "Henri DuPré will suffer a major convulsion if I suggest it."

"But you will, I hope. I believe I could even make plum duff, if he chooses not to." She shook her head. "No one else in London will even think of it. Mr. Mortimer, you are the most clever of hotel managers."

He only smiled, and looked out the window again, content to bask in the warmth of her approbation.

The Elgin Marbles were no anticlimax, despite his sole interest in the woman who shared the hackney with him. After paying a small fee, they picked their way among the rubble and weeds to gaze in silence at a caryatid from the Erechtheum. Miss Carrington sighed and leaned against his arm, completely caught in the magic of the fluid robes and grace unexpected, even in marble. He held his breath, hoping that she would not notice what she was doing. Casting all caution away, he put his arm around her shoulder. She only leaned closer, to his unimaginable delight. She was a short woman, but not tiny. Her shoulder felt strong.

Bound together, they strolled toward a collection of three figures, one headless woman reclining in the lap of another, which must have formed the most acute angle of the pediment. "Look at the lines, Charles," Miss Carrington murmured, his name sounding like music to him. She touched his hand that rested so lightly on her shoulder, so he knew she was aware of him. "Oh, they are glorious. Please, can we stop here?"

He did as she said, removing his arm from about her and handing her the sketch pad he carried in his other hand. Eyes on the figures, she seated herself on a column fragment. He sat down to watch her sketch.

She sat for a long time with her hands folded in her lap, looking first at the caryatid, and then the group of three. As he watched in pleasure, and then growing disquiet, her expression changed. She frowned. She shifted on her marble perch. In another moment, he saw her dab at the corner of her eyes.

"Miss Carrington?" he asked, uncertain of himself. "Millicent?"

She looked at him then, and her eyes, to his horror, filled with tears. "These should have never been taken from the Parthenon," she said in a low voice. "Oh, Charles, think how beautiful they must have been on the Acropolis! What was the matter with Lord Elgin?"

He didn't know what to say, so he handed her his handkerchief. The moment was so personal, and she had said his name again. In another moment he perched himself beside her on the marble slab, his arm about her again as she sniffled into his handkerchief and blew her nose.

He knew he shouldn't have, but Charles kissed her hair and sat in silence, thinking about India and Wellington, and Napoleon on Elba now, and change, and death. "Better we should stay on our own little island and never bother anyone else, eh?" he asked softly. "Better the Turks should use these figures for target practice and blast them to rubble? The world's a complicated place, Miss Carrington, isn't it? The older I get, the fewer answers I have, anymore. And here I had hoped to be wise someday."

In the circle of his arm, she rested her head against his chest. "You must think I am silly," she confessed.

He chuckled and drew her closer. "No, none of it. I think you're sensitive to waste." He sighed. "Maybe I am, too. I work in a hotel that is utter perfection, with everything planned out for the total accommodation of pampered people. I move around quietly in the background, seeing that things are always done right." He sighed. "For dreadful creatures like Lady Mountrail."

She pulled away a little to look at him. "And have you constructed a life out of always doing things quietly for others? Is it enough?"

"Not anymore."

She touched his face. He knew it was an amazingly intimate, forward gesture on her part, one he never expected, but he was overwhelmed with a feeling of protection. *I am safe with this person,* he thought as he kissed her.

He couldn't recollect that he had ever kissed a woman before, and he enjoyed the moment as none other in his life, even more than moments of greater intimacy with lesser women. Her hand pressed against his neck at his hairline and her fingers were as warm as her lips. She murmured something low in her throat and the sound made his lips tingle in a pleasant way. He kissed her again when she pulled away slightly, and she made no objection. He heard the sketch pad slide from her lap and onto the ground, as the sun shone on his face, and mingled with the fragrance of lemon on her skin. Every feeling and sound seemed to magnify itself into a moment of total completeness. He kissed her and understood awe, and it had nothing to do with statues or vistas, or battles won and celebrated. It had only to do with him and her.

And then the moment ended; he thought they both pulled away at the same time. He was relieved to see no wariness in her face, no revulsion. She only watched him with that same expression of amazement she had first reserved for the now-ignored triumphs of Greek civilization that stood or reclined in the weeds of a forgotten yard.

"I . . ." He shook his head and waited another moment. "I should apologize, Miss Carrington, except that I do not wish to."

She smiled, and his heart began to circulate his blood again. "It's Millie." As he sat beside her, still so close, she picked up the sketch pad, and with fingers that shook a little, drew his own face. Surrounded by wonders of the ancient world, she drew his face.

On the ride back to the Grand Hotel, he wanted to tell her he loved her, but he was as silent as she. Quiet, they sat close together hand in hand. He realized with a jolt that throughout his life he had never put himself forward except once at Kaitna Ford in India, and all his doubts returned.

They went into the lobby together, standing farther apart now, calling no attention to themselves. He stopped her at the entrance. "Miss Carrington, I must have been out of my mind," he said quietly.

If he had disappointed her, she did not show it. "I doubt you ever take leave of your senses, Charles," she told him.

*How serene you are about all this,* he marveled as she continued her graceful way through the lobby, a slight smile on her face.

They hadn't taken more than three more paces when Mr. Kipling left the desk and hurried to him. He bowed to Miss Carrington, and all but plucked at Charles's sleeve. "I thought you would never get here," he whispered.

Charles felt himself on sure ground, except that he could almost feel himself blending into the background again. "What could possibly be the matter, Mr. Kipling?" he asked.

With only the slightest gesture toward the desk, the deputy manager inclined his head. "Do you see that man there, that man of color?" he whispered. "He is trying to check in!"

"He's not a servant?"

"No! He claims he is a free man from Boston in Massachusetts and actually wants to stay in a second-floor suite!" He noticed Miss Carrington. "Begging your pardon, ma'am," he said.

"This has never happened before," Charles said. He could see Sir Michael's book of rules in his mind. Page three, column one, he thought wearily. Oh, Lord.

"I've tried to direct him back to the docks—those hotels take anyone—but he says his money is good." Mr. Kipling was wringing his hands now. He looked at Miss Carrington. "Ma'am, you wouldn't think a black man would have so much gall, would you?"

Charles was almost afraid to look at Millie. "Really,

Mr. Kipling," he murmured. "Let us leave our guest out of this. Excuse us, Miss Carrington."

*I know what to do,* he thought as he walked to the desk and went behind it. *I know what Sir Michael expects.* "May I help you?" he asked. "I am Mr. Mortimer, the manager."

"I have a reservation, sir," the man said. "Malachi Beach of Boston. From the American Society for Abolition." He leaned forward, and there was no mistaking the exhaustion on his face. "Actually, I made a reservation at every good hotel in London, and you are my last stop."

Mr. Kipling must have taken out the card from the file box because it lay between them on the desk. Charles picked it up, then looked at the man in front of him, someone about his own age, tired, with travel-worn clothes. *I could send him on to a lesser hotel, where he will get the same rude treatment,* he thought. He has obviously spent the better part of a day looking for a room. *Or I could step out from the background.*

He glanced at Millie Carrington, who had quietly come closer, and could not overlook the concern in her face. The thought came to him—it was an odd, stray thought—that he wasn't sure if she was concerned about Malachi Beach, or Charles Mortimer. He smiled at Malachi Beach, then turned to the key rack as Mr. Kipling sucked in his breath.

"Here you are, sir," he said, and handed the man a key. "I am sorry you had to wait." He nodded to the footman, who stood as still as Parthenon marble. "Devost here will take your bags. Dinner is served from six to nine, if you do not have another place to dine." He laughed quietly, and was relieved to see his guest smile. "Even though we've barely opened, we're already going through some renovation in the dining room. What can I say? I hope you enjoy your stay."

"I believe I shall, Mr. Mortimer."

He watched Devost take the man's bags and lead

the way upstairs. Charles ignored his deputy manager's tug on his sleeve. He rested his elbow on the check-in desk, contemplating nothing more than the marble on the counter. *I wonder why I did that?* he thought first, and then, *How soon before the news travels to Sir Michael Moseley?* He waited for dread to set in, but nothing happened. *This has been a strange day, indeed,* he thought. *I wonder what else will happen?*

"Mr. Mortimer, you know what the rule book says!"

Charles turned to gaze for a long moment at his deputy manager. "Do you know, I think it's a foolish rule, Mr. Kipling. Don't you? We're running a business, Kipling."

From the way he blinked his eyes, Charles could see that Kipling had never considered the stupidity of some of Sir Michael's rules. And did Kipling seem to regard him with a degree of deference he hadn't noticed before? Strange indeed.

"Well done, sir," Millie said as Kipling turned away to distract himself with interminable filing.

"Thank you," he said, pleased to note that his plainspeaking had somehow driven away any shyness regarding Miss Carrington.

It was her turn to lean toward him across the counter that separated them. "Aren't you a little fearful of losing your job if Sir Michael finds out?" she asked.

He considered her question and shook his head. "Likely I could find another, Miss Carrington." *I love you, Miss Carrington,* he wanted to add, but he knew he hadn't the courage.

The painters arrived in the evening after the dining room was empty of patrons. He stood in the doorway, charmed with the effect of the blue and yellow design now making its way around the top of the wall. Millie smiled at him from her perch on the scaffolding that the painters erected.

He would have invented some reason to stay and watch, but he strolled into the lobby in time to nod good evening to Mr. Kipling and welcome aboard Mr. Chaseley for the night shift. Restless, he paid a visit belowstairs. He asked himself how Henri DuPré would feel if he broached the subject of plum duff for Wellington as the Grand Hotel's entry in the dessert contest.

His suggestion was met with the disdain he expected, as well as a sprinkling of "bahs!" and "sacré bleus" until he found himself—he, the mildest of men—gritting his teeth. *Frogs,* he thought as DuPré raved on, flinging his arms about. *I do not know that I would miss the French, if some rare disease suddenly swept them from the earth. I doubt anyone would, come to think of it.*

"It was only a suggestion, sir," he said when the chef paused to take another breath. "You're certainly welcome to make your entry. It's just that I know the duke, and he . . ."

*Oh, dear, that was unwise of me,* Charles thought in dismay as DuPré burst into derisive laughter.

When DuPré collected himself, leaning against the counter to hold himself up, and wiping the tears from his eyes, he elaborately offered Charles a chair. "I think you have been touched by the sun, Mr. Mortimer," he said, and Charles almost winced from the disdain in his voice. "If you know His Grace, the Duke of Wellington, then I am Caroline of Brunswick!" He started to giggle again.

Charles regarded the chef for a long moment. "No, I don't see any resemblance. Her mustache is lighter than yours," he said softly, more to himself than to the chef. "Well, monsieur, you won't mind if I make a little plum duff anyway, will you?"

The chef gave him a dark look. "Only if you place it far, far away from my meringue *glacés*"—he held up a bony finger and struck a pose—"soaked in raspberry sauce. I will call it Triomph de Toulouse, in honor of his final victory over Napoleon, that most misunderstood of men."

"No one will ever know our recipes came from the same kitchen," Charles assured him. "I'll never tell the duke." He left the kitchen, disgruntled and dogged by DuPré's laughter. *DuPré is an ass, but I wonder if Wellesley will remember me?* he asked himself as he went upstairs again. *He's never really seen me with my face devoid of black powder. If my plum duff wins, I will take the opportunity to present him with the manuscript. And Miss Carrington has promised her sketches.*

The painters were leaving when he came upstairs, and the lobby was quiet. Mr. Chaseley looked at him and smiled, raising a handful of letters. "Sir, I do believe that the Grand Hotel will be full to the rafters in two weeks for the celebrations."

"Excellent, Mr. Chaseley. And by the way, let me compliment you on the way you handled that rather intoxicated patron last night."

The night clerk beamed at him. "Oh, I've just watched the way you handle'um, sir."

*Well, what do you know,* he thought. He looked in the dining room, hoping to see Miss Carrington, and there she was, standing on the terrace, breathing deep of the night air. She turned around when he approached, and without a word, embraced him and raised her face for a kiss, which he willingly shared with her. They stood in the circle of each other's arms. "This is beyond belief," he said finally.

"I know," she agreed, but made no move to leave.

But she did move finally, standing away from him until he lowered his arms. Before he could feel too disappointed, she took his hand and led him to a table. "Let's sit here a moment," she said. "There's something . . . something I have to tell you." She looked down at the table. "I don't think you'll like it very much."

*Here it comes*, he thought, willing himself numb before she began to speak. *True, we are both the children of gentlemen, but as in India, there are many layers to our British castes. Say on, lady, I knew this was coming.*

She couldn't look at him for the longest moment, and as she opened her mouth to speak, Mr. Chaseley flung open the dining-room door he had so carefully shut, and stood there, obviously searching for them in the dark.

Alarmed, Charles leaped to his feet. "Chaseley, I am here," he said. "What is it?"

There was no disguising the urgency of the night clerk's voice. "Mr. Mortimer, you have to hurry. Lady Mountrail. Second floor."

He took the stairs two at a time, Miss Carrington right behind him, after admonishing Chaseley to stay at the desk. He pounded up the stairs and looked down the long corridor to see Lady Mountrail's dresser, that meek woman, kicking Betty, the 'tween stairs maid. "Oh, I say, please stop!" he insisted as he ran down the hall.

He wrenched the sobbing child from the dresser's grasp just as the door swung open and Lady Mountrail stood there. "She was snooping around this door!" she shrieked.

Heads popped out of other doors. "Please don't concern yourselves, ladies and gentlemen," he said as he held Betty close to him. "Please, Lady Mountrail, may I come into your room to settle this in quiet?" he asked, his voice low.

"Absolutely not!" she declared. "I'm a lady!"

*I have my doubts,* he thought, in a rage. "Hush, Betty," he said, and gave her a little push toward Miss Carrington, who folded Betty in her arms. "Very well, Lady Mountrail, we'll talk right here in the hall like commoners."

She gasped, and yanked him into her room with a grip he hadn't expected. Miss Carrington followed with Betty, giving the dresser such a look that Charles wanted to cheer.

"What happened here?"

Before he could stop her, Lady Mountrail reached forward and gave Betty's hair a sharp tug. Miss Carrington turned to shield the child. "Don't you touch her again, you dreadful woman," she warned.

"Please, Miss Carrington. Watch your tongue," he said, his voice sharp. He flinched inwardly at the look she gave him.

"Lady Mountrail, what has happened?" he asked again.

"That gutterscamp was lurking around my door," she screamed, all but jumping up and down in her fury. "I am certain I am missing half my jewelry!"

"I sincerely doubt it," he said quietly. "Betty, what were you doing?"

He took Betty by the arm and Miss Carrington reluctantly released her grip. "Come, now. How can I help you if you won't talk?"

"Help her? Help her? *I* am the injured party!" Lady Mountrail insisted. She sank into a chair and the dresser began to fan her.

Betty burst into tears and sobbed into Charles's shoulder. He held her in a firm grip, patting her back. "Come now and tell me, my dear," he murmured.

"Mrs. Wheelwright said I was to close the draperies and turn down the bedclothes," she said finally, speaking through the handkerchief he had given her, and dabbing at her nose. "She said the other maids were busy, but they don't like coming in here any more than I do!" She looked at him, and he was appalled to see the hopelessness in her eyes. "I was afraid to go in, so I . . . I walked up and down trying to get my courage. Mr. Mortimer, I would never steal anything."

"I know you wouldn't."

She stood on tiptoe and spoke into his ear. "I'm afraid of her, too, Mr. Mortimer."

He would have smiled, if the situation had been different. "I am, as well, Betty." He took a deep breath and turned to Lady Mountrail. "Perhaps you should examine your jewel case now."

"She just said she didn't steal anything!"

He looked around, surprised at Millie's outburst, then filled with shame that she should see any of this. "I have to ask, Miss Carrington. It's my job."

"Part of the rules?" she snapped.

"Yes, as a matter of fact. Lady Mountrail?"

The woman made a gesture to her dresser, who brought the jewel case and set it on her lap. Heads together, the two women brought out each bauble while Betty shook and sniffled in his arms and Miss Carrington stared stonily ahead.

After they had sorted through the little pile twice, he asked, "Well, Lady Mountrail?"

"I think there is a pearl necklace missing."

He noted the confusion in her eyes now, and felt the tiniest twinge of sympathy for the old harridan. "But you're not sure if you may have left it behind on your estate?" he suggested gently.

Lady Mountrail said nothing for a long moment. "I am not certain, Mortimer, not certain! You'll turn her off though, won't you?"

"Yes, I will," he replied, dreading the explosion from Millicent Carrington, even as he tightened his grip on Betty, who sobbed in earnest now.

"How can you?" she said, her voice low with scorn, which he decided was worse than all of Lady Mountrail's ravings.

"It is one of Sir Michael Moseley's rules, Miss Carrington," he said. "Any suspicions are dealt with this way."

The next sound was the door slamming. *Oh, well,* he thought. *Oh, well.*

He left the room fast enough himself, after assuring Lady Mountrail again that Betty would be let go. His arm around the young girl, he led the weeping child down the backstairs to the kitchen, where he sat her down at the table to a good cry, tea, and Mrs. Wheelwright's combination of admonition and sympathy, which helped the tears stop.

"I didn't pinch anything, Mr. Mortimer," Betty said again, when her eyes were dry.

"I know you didn't," he said quietly. "It's not in you to steal. I still have to let you go, but let me tell you how I'll do it."

She listened in fear, and then, to his relief, relaxed when his quiet explanation began to make sense. "You're an orphan, I know," he said, "and maybe you'd just like a change of scenery . . . at least until this ill wind blows somewhere else."

"The manager at Harrogate will take me in?"

"Positive. I know him well, and what's even more to the point, he's suffered through a visit or two from Lady Mountrail himself." He rose and stretched, wondering what time it was. "I'd never just turn you off, and I don't care what Sir Michael Moseley says."

'Tween stairs maids don't have many possessions, and Betty was packed by the time he had finished his letter to the new Harrogate manager, a dependable man he had shared the front desk with when they both worked in Glasgow. He took the child in a hackney to the closest mail coach stop, paid her wages (and a little more from his own), bought a ticket, and gave her the letter.

He walked back to the Grand Hotel contemplating his evening's work and his own hypocrisy in keeping some rules and flouting others, and the obvious loss of Miss Carrington. He beat himself with a few more stripes, then reminded himself that she had been about to let him down anyway when Chaseley intervened with Betty's crisis. "Some things just aren't going to happen," he said out loud as he stood in front of his hotel, looked at its magnificent facade, and found himself sadly wanting. And his head was starting to ache.

It was too late to go to bed and too early to rise, so he sat down in his room to finish *Wellington in India*. The narrative warmed him as it always did, and gave him comfort as he wrote steadily, consulting his voluminous notes. He was sweating so he opened his window and leaned out to get a breath. *I don't know that I like London so well, myself,* he thought as he rested his arms on the windowsill and tried to breathe deep. *Simmons's gout can't last forever, and I will gladly recommend Chaseley for a promotion to my position. Maybe Harrogate needs a night clerk; it's all the same to me now.*

He finished the last chapter just as he heard the maids coming downstairs to begin their morning's work. He went to add it to the other pages in the pasteboard box, but remembered that Miss Carrington still had possession of his manuscript, unless she had dumped the whole box outside his door, or in the nearest dustbin. In a few days he would begin a fair copy of the whole thing and present it to Wellington somehow before the conclusion of the upcoming festivities. *Then what will I do?* he asked himself as he lay down on the bed, his hand to his head. *I have no other diversions.*

It took him a long time, but he finally summoned the energy to put the final chapter in front of Miss Carrington's door, then crawled into bed. He managed to sleep for an hour, until Mr. Kipling, all aflutter that he was not at the desk, pounded on his door and woke him. In a haze—his head was pounding now in good earnest—he washed and dressed and took his usual place at the front desk.

He was seated at his desk behind the check-in counter when Miss Carrington left the hotel. When he noticed her in the lobby, he thought she might slam her key on the desk, but she didn't. In fact, she had no luggage, so he knew she wasn't leaving. He reasoned that she would never leave the dining room half-painted, and had to thank her for that, at least.

She returned less than an hour later carrying a package. He wanted to say something to her, but she refused to look at him. *And what would I say?* he thought. *Please excuse me for being a hypocrite? I'm sorry I fell in love above my station? I could at least tell her that Betty wasn't out wandering the streets and hungry.*

He didn't' see her for the rest of the day, but there was plenty of work for him. He was aware of the painters arriving that evening, and despite the buzz in his ears, heard her laughing with them in the dining room. He could only stand up now when there was something to lean upon, and he knew his temperature was shooting through the roof. Any moment the chills would begin, and his semi-annual malarial relapse would be firmly under way. *Drat the luck,* he thought. *My Indian friend, my cursed companion, couldn't you have waited another month until the festivities for Wellington were over?*

He watched the painters leave, and then Millie followed after a time. He wondered if she had lingered in the dining room for him, but dismissed the idea. When she crossed the lobby, he thought she hesitated. He couldn't be sure; his entire goal was already focused on climbing those same stairs and hoping he could make it to his room.

But first he had to see the dining room. He knew that Chaseley had been watching him all evening since he came on duty, staying close as though ready to offer assistance, and he was grateful for the man's perspicacity. *I certainly shall recommend that he fill my position here,* he thought.

It wasn't so hard to cross the lobby because there were enough sofas and chairs to lean upon. The expanse from the last chair to the dining-room door was daunting, but he had faced worse inconveniences. *Just inconveniences, Father,* he told himself. *The only problem I have now is that I will spend a lifetime without Miss Carrington, and I cannot bear that.*

Someone, probably Millie, had left a lamp burning in the dining room. With a force that made him stagger, he started to shiver. He pulled up a corner of a tablecloth to wipe the sweat that poured off his face, and then stared at the wall trim. Despite his discomfort that was growing by the second, he smiled. *Miss Carrington, you were so right,* he thought. *It is beautiful. You have a flair.*

That was his last conscious thought before the convulsive shivers reached his legs. He clutched the tablecloth as though it could hold him up, then sank to his knees when it didn't, and sagged against the table. From miles away he heard it crash and then remembered nothing more.

The relapse followed its usual, dreamy course. One moment he was staring intently at Mr. Chaseley's mouth as the man slowly, slowly formed words. Another moment, and he was wishing the people in his room would not rush about too fast for his eyes to keep up with them. He was colder than a naked man on an ice floe; he was hot, sweating, and in the humid Deccan again. Someone raised his head enough for him to swallow bitter medicine, and then his ears began to ring, even as his shivering slowed.

Was it days? Was it minutes? He finally opened his eyes on a nearly normal world, except that Miss Carrington sat beside his bed. He knew that was a hallucination, especially when she rose, put a cool hand to his forehead, and then darted from the room. He closed his eyes again and let the tears slide into his ears.

He kept them closed, even when the door opened and someone held his wrist. He heard a watch case snap, and after a year or two, someone spoke so loud that he flinched.

"Well, Mr. Mortimer, you've given us scare, you have. Are they always this severe?"

He nodded, and went back to sleep. The doctor released his hand, but someone else with lemon-scented skin pulled the blanket to his chin when he started to shiver again. In another moment there was

a cloth-covered hot-water bottle at his freezing feet,
and gentle hands rubbing his legs.

He felt better when he woke again. He had a sense
of time now, and he knew without opening his eyes
that it was afternoon sun that rested on his hands
folded across his stomach. He panicked first. *They're
laying me out,* he thought, then raised a cautious hand
to his cheek. *No, even a London undertaker wouldn't
bury me with this much stubble on my face.*

"You're a little hairy, but you were shaking too
much to shave."

He knew the voice, and opened his eyes anyway.
"Millie. Why?" he asked, frustrated because the words
in his head weren't coming out of his mouth. "The
painting. Done. What day?"

"Four nights ago Mr. Chaseley came to your rescue
in the dining room," she said, leaving her chair to sit
on the edge of his bed.

"Four. Lord. Who in charge?"

"A sentence! Hooray!" she said in all good humor.
"Mr. Chaseley. Mr. Kipling wasn't up to it, so Mr.
Chaseley staged a coup d'état. I thought it was a good
idea. I kept Uncle Moseley out of it but he will be
here tonight and . . ."

He couldn't have heard her right. "Uncle?"

She must have leaned closer, because the next thing
he knew, she was rubbing her smooth cheek against
his stubbly face. "Heavens, Charles, you reek. I told
you I had something to tell you that you wouldn't like
very much."

He invoked deity again and slept.

When he woke it was darker, and his room was lit
with a soft light. He managed to raise his head off the
pillow. He wanted to lean on his elbow, but it was
still made of melting wax so he didn't try. He lay back
and Millie propped a pillow behind his head.

Sir Michael Moseley paced back and forth at the
foot of his bed. Millie's chair was pulled up as close
to the bed as she could contrive it, and Mr. Chaseley

grinned at him from his perch on the window ledge. Mrs. Wheelwright, daring him to object, ran a warm cloth over his face, and then down the front of his nightshirt and under his arms. He wasn't about to object; it felt wonderful. "When we think you won't drown, the footman will help you bathe," she told him.

"Sir Michael, I am sorry," he said finally.

This was all the opening his employer seemed to require. He stopped his pacing and leaned on the foot rail of the bed, pointing his finger. "You have been deceiving me," he began.

Charles opened his mouth to agree, but Sir Michael was pointing his finger at Millie. Charles looked at her with a question in his eyes. She took his hand. "That's what you won't like, Charles. I'm Sir Michael's niece. He's married to my father's older sister. I almost hate to say this, but he planted me in the hotel to see what kind of a manager you were."

"Millie!" he said, unable to hide his disappointment.

"Charles? Millie? Oh, worse and worse!" Sir Michael thundered. "For more than a week now, Niece, you have told me that everything was going fine here at the Grand Hotel! You're a positive viper in an uncle's bosom!"

Charles started to shiver again. Millie leaped to her feet and right into her uncle's face, a wren squaring off against a great blue heron. "Don't shout!" she shouted. "He's still in a weakened state!" She put her hand to her mouth. "Oh, I'm sorry, Charles."

He only smiled. "Sit down, Millie." She sat. "First things first," he said, looking at his night clerk. "Betty?"

"I got a letter two days ago from Williston at the Grand Vista," Chaseley said, coming off his window perch. "She's fine and working as an under housemaid. It seems Williston was short-staffed."

"Thank God. Lady Mountrail?"

With a glance at Sir Michael, and after a deep breath, Mr. Chaseley spoke. "Would you believe that she discovered that her dratted necklace had never been packed in the first place?" Mr. Chaseley ran his finger around his collar. "I . . . I told her what I thought." He glanced at Charles. "I suppose I rather thought that's what you would do."

Charles smiled.

Millie glared at her uncle as though daring him to speak. "Uncle Moseley, the guests are *not* always right. Sometimes you have to trust your manager not to be a slave to rules."

*This is daffy,* he thought. "Sir Michael, you *planted* Millie?"

"I always do that with new managers," he said, speaking softer now. "Well, not Millie." He glared at her. "Never again Millie! She was here in town to secure a position as governess—if that wasn't hare-brained enough—and I thought I could use her." He threw up his hands and started to pace again. "And what does she do but encourage you to break all kinds of rules!"

"They were stupid rules, Uncle," Millie insisted.

"Your father's not a vicar?" he asked.

"Oh, yes!" she declared. "I wouldn't lie to you . . . well, about that."

He couldn't help grinning. "No wonder no one's ever dared to marry you, Millicent Carrington."

"Sir!" she exclaimed, but she was smiling, too. "Oh, Charles, it just so happens that we are a wealthy family. It's the damnedest thing."

"Millie!" her uncle said, shocked.

"I said I would stay at the hotel, and find out if you were a good manager." She gave her uncle a long, measuring look. "Oh, Uncle Moseley, Charles Mortimer is imaginative, kind to his staff, listens to them, knows a good idea when he hears one, and . . . and isn't afraid to let people stay here who you might not consider . . . consider . . ."

"Kipling tattled to me about the man of color from Boston," Moseley said. He cleared his throat. "Were either of you aware that Mr. Beach was invited to London to address Parliament about enforcing that 1807 law against the slave trade in our empire?"

"No!" Millie said. "He never said that."

"I had a visit from Lord Dickinson only this morning, thanking me for extending him the hospitality of the Grand Hotel. It seems that Mr. Beach was quite eloquent."

"Good," Charles said.

"Everyone's been giving me an earful," Sir Michael growled, except that this time he sat on the end of the bed. "Who should come to me in tears but that wretched chef Dumbass . . . no, no . . ."

"DuPré," they all said together.

"It seems he entered a pastry with some froggy name in that contest last night, and it met with foul play." He sighed. "Millie, are you responsible for this, too?"

"I'm not sure," she said uncertainly. "Charles, don't you dare laugh! What . . . what kind of foul play?"

"Oops," said Chaseley from the window. "I'll tell what I did if you'll tell what you did, Miss Carrington."

"I don't want to hear it!" Sir Michael said, throwing up his hands.

"Mrs. Wheelwright distracted him, and I slipped cream of tartar in the raspberry sauce," she confessed. "It probably tasted awful."

"I'm to blame then, because no one ever tasted it," Chaseley admitted. "It seems that at Carlton House, DuPré tripped over my foot and landed face first in the Triomph de Toulouse. *Sacré bleu*," he concluded solemnly, and Millie burst into laughter, which she quickly smothered with a corner of Charles's bedsheet.

"What entry won?"

"Why, Mr. Mortimer, can you doubt? Millie's plum duff, of course," Chaseley said. "His Grace said it was always his favorite dessert." He looked at Mrs. Wheelwright. "Don't you just love military men and their total lack of culinary curiosity?"

"That is uncalled for, you young chub!"

Surprised, everyone in the room turned to look toward the door, except Charles, who knew that voice. *Oh, I am weak,* he thought. "Your Grace," he said, raising his head up from the pillow again. "Do come in and join the rest of London in my room."

His Grace, the Duke of Wellington, resplendent in his uniform and fairly bristling with medals, entered the room. Millie quickly stood up and offered the great man her chair, which he accepted with a nod. He looked around. "I do beg your pardon. I hate to squelch a perfectly rousing donnybrook—it must be the Irish in me—but I only have a few minutes before the next silly event begins and I wanted a word with Charles."

Sir Michael's eyes fairly popped from his head. "My God!" he exclaimed in a strangled tone.

"Oh, no," said the duke calmly. "That title belongs to our first minister, if rumor suffices." He turned his attention to Charles. "You look fit for a midden. Could you use some more quinine, or have they dosed you with too much? Ears ring?"

"I think I'll survive, Your Grace."

"Thank goodness for that." He glanced at the door. "Crauford, give over that manuscript, if you would. Thank you." He placed the pasteboard box on the bed. "This came with the plum duff. I read it last night—stayed up far too late, drat you—and came here to ask your permission to send it 'round to Epping and Stanley."

"The publishers?" Millie asked in a whisper, her eyes wide.

"The very same. By the way, is this your handwriting? You have quite an elegant fist."

"Thank you," she said. "It's only partly copied, Your Grace," she said to Wellington. "I can finish it in a week." She looked at Charles. "I started copying it that morning after I was so rude to you."

"Which morning was that?" he teased.

Her eyes filled with tears. "Oh, I am so glad you can quiz me about it now. I thought you were going to die." She came closer again to dab at her eyes with the bedsheet. "And that would never do, because I love you."

Sir Michael groaned in despair. "Millicent, this is extremely unsuitable!"

"Far from it, Uncle," she replied calmly. "I love this man. As I am your favorite niece—don't deny it!—we will except the gift of a hotel on our wedding. Don't you think Charles and I could run a fine hotel? I recommend the Grand Whatchamacallit in Kent. Isn't it opening soon?"

Sir Michael Moseley winced, then thought a moment. "It is. You may be right."

"Sir Michael, if I may," Chaseley began, after clearing his throat. "I think I can vouch that any staff member where Mr. Mortimer has served will be happy to follow him to the ends of the earth." He looked at Charles and shrugged his shoulders. "You may deny it, but you have a certain something."

"There you are, Uncle," Millie said.

"Charles, you are a lucky dog," Wellington said. "Let me put my oar in. Everyone's been after me to write my memoirs, and dash it, I haven't the time. *Wellington in India* will do for starters. Perhaps you and I will collaborate on the Peninsular Wars. The illustrations are excellent, by the way. Miss Carrington, when you have copied it entirely, send it round to Epping and Stanley. They are expecting it." He looked up at Sir Michael. "Charles Mortimer is talented. What can one expect from a man who served the guns so well at Kaitna Ford? He probably has many hidden talents. How lucky you are to employ him, Sir Michael."

"Yes, Your Grace."

The duke looked at Millie. "These are your drawings, are they not?"

She nodded. "I did them for my brother, Major Robert Carrington."

"I remember him well, my dear." He paused, remembering. "You're a pretty thing. Has Charles Mortimer proposed yet?"

"Not yet," he said from the bed. "I thought the matter was hanging in some apprehension."

"I doubt that," the duke replied, after a long look at Millie's blushing face. "My dear, Charles Mortimer is just a late-bloomer. I was one, myself. Perhaps you are, too?"

She nodded.

"Give him a week, and he'll be on his feet again." The duke looked toward the door and sighed. "Crauford is dancing around and nervous that I will be late to the next event. Miss Carrington, take the manuscript so you can continue." He took Charles by the hand. "Thank you again for Kaitna Ford."

"You are welcome, Your Grace. I . . . I have wanted to tell you that."

Without another word, the duke kissed his forehead, stood looking at him for another moment, released his hand, then left the room. He must have sucked all the air out with him; exhausted, Charles closed his eyes and slept.

He left the Grand Hotel on a stretcher the following morning, bolstered by another dose of quinine, and Millie standing close. He had tried to protest when she stayed by his bed all night, but he couldn't really form any words until morning. He didn't think she would have listened, anyway.

He hadn't the energy to voice any objection to Millie's plan to take him to Kent and the vicarage for a full recuperation, but no objection had occurred to him. *Perhaps the vicar will marry us,* Charles thought. *I shall ask him, when I am able. While I am not precisely a father's dream of a husband for his wealthy daughter, Millie likes me.*

*Millie loves me,* he amended as dawn approached and his strength returned. His words still came out halting and disjointed, especially after that next blast of quinine. She seemed to consider "Love you," and "Marry me?" as complete sentences of amazing eloquence, and responded to both in the affirmative.

He would have preferred to exit the Grand Hotel as a normal biped, but he couldn't manage to get the mattress off his back. Mr. Chaseley, totally in charge now, directed the footman to put him—"Gently now!"—onto a stretcher.

Their slow progress across the lobby halted when a familiar voice hailed him and he opened his eyes.

"Mr. Mortimer, call it Providence; my gout is better."

Simmons swam before his eyes, then came into focus. True, the man was leaning on a cane, but there he was, none the worse for three weeks off his pins. "Glad to hear," Charles said, wishing that his voice was not so faint.

"The first thing to do is remove those boxes from my rooms behind the lobby, Mr. Mortimer," the manager said, shaking his cane at his former assistant manager. "Really, Charles, if you were only more forceful, so much would be accomplished." He sighed. "If only you were a man of action."

Charles smiled, and closed his eyes. *Charles Mortimer, man of action, that I am,* he thought in amusement as he managed to wave good-bye to his staff (and remind Chaseley to plan for a move to Kent soon as his new assistant manager), then take Millie by the hand as she walked alongside his stretcher. *I am a detail man, a background man, and soon a husband and lover.* He put his hand on Millie's arm as the footman prepared to lift the stretcher into the carriage. "Feel lucky?" he asked.

Right there in front of the Grand Hotel, with his whole staff looking on and Mr. Chaseley cheering, she kissed him thoroughly and well.

# Love Will Find the Way
## by Elisabeth Fairchild

*Meet me at the Grand Hotel,* her last letter had ended. So, here he was, Lieutenant James Forrester, lately of His Majesty's Eighteenth Brigade Hussar, in London, striding up Bayswater Road, dodging scaffolding, piles of brick, and bricklayers with their buckets and trowels. The box in his arms grew heavier with every step. The saddlebag banged his knee. He was looking for Leinster Terrace, on his way to meet Miss Annabelle Grant.

He was in love with her, and they had never met, never spoken, not face-to-face. He had no idea how her voice sounded—only the cadence of her sentence structure, the careful loops and curves of her lettering, the turn of a phrase. These were as familiar to him as his own. James had read her letters time and again, night after night, a box full of them.

*Annabelle,* a name like music. She had been prolific in her correspondence, each folded sheet of crossed and recrossed paper a gift to him, through Archie, who could not see. He deciphered each one first for his friend, later for himself, because they were so full of life in the midst of death and the dying, so gently funny in a rough and unamusing world, so affectionate amid the anger and hatred of war.

Of course Archie talked of his Belle. Hours of ramblings, about their childhoods together, the trees they had climbed, the ponies they had ridden. James knew her hair was flaxen fair, her eyes the color of blue spruce, not quite blue, or green, or gray, but a dark blend of all of these. She had a beauty mark beside her mouth, another high on her left shoulder. Archie wanted to discuss little else in the end.

James had no choice but to fall in love with her—the illusion of her anyway. She had been beauty in the midst of everything grim. She had been England, an icon of all that the lads yearned to live for, to return to.

And now he returned to a city unfamiliar, quiet, and clean. It smelled of cabbage, coal dust, sausage, fresh horse dung, and, of course, the humid sewer of the Thames, fine perfume compared to the stench of gunpowder, and rotting horseflesh and septic wounds that had too long soured his nostrils.

He was, himself, unfamiliar, out of uniform, his clothes too crisp, smelling of dye, soap, and starch, not sweat, horses, and fear. No clink of Marmaluke sword at his hip. No spur at his heel. He still wore his Hessians, silver tassels swinging, and chalk white breeches, but no weight of silver lacing weighed upon his chest, and his hat was that of a gentleman, not a heavy fur shako with aigrette feather cockade. His stride made no music, other than a steady tapping. No jingle of silver spurs to remind him who he was. He was, in fact, a stranger to himself when he caught sight of his reflection in the windows he passed. The space he occupied, the very placement of his feet felt off balance, all wrong, foreign.

Who was he, if not a lieutenant for the Eighteenth Brigade? What goal had he now that his fighting days were done? He possessed only one thought at present, that of finally meeting Annabelle Grant, his reason for staying alive.

He had imagined many times their meeting. He had dreamed of it, of a shadowy, fair-haired figure with a beauty mark beside her mouth, who fell upon his chest and wept upon his shoulder. He had held countless imagined conversations with Annabelle Grant.

*Meet me at the Grand Hotel,* her last letter had ended. How those words had made his heart leap! But now that he was here, standing in the shadow of the bow-fronted house across the street from the hotel, it struck him that he was in love with illusion, an illusion he had clung to too desperately, an illusion about to be shattered.

He took a deep breath, ready for the plunge, and hitching the saddlebag a little tighter stepped across the street.

The doors of the hotel opened, as if to welcome him, but no, a calvacade of people were leaving: a gentleman on a stretcher, a woman at his side, grasping his hand as they went, murmuring something comforting.

At the bottom of the steps, right there on the walkway, the gentleman proved himself not completely disabled in kissing the woman, much to the amusement of his stretcher bearers, who made noises of mock disapproval and ribald remarks.

"Nah, nah, now, Mr. Mortimer. Plenty of time for that once you are married," someone said.

James smiled. *Lucky fellow.* Was this how it would have been for Archie?

Annabelle stood at the window of her room examining the raw, new, ever-expanding London before her, the bundle of letters from Archie, in Mr. Forrester's handwriting, clasped to her breast.

Below her in the street, a cluster of people poured from the hotel. A gentleman on a stretcher, four men carrying him, another hailing a passing hack. A woman clung to the man's hand. She would have liked to cling to Archie's hand in just such a way, one last time.

The woman kissed the man, right there in the street, turning heads, giving pause to a passing horseman.

Archie would have tsk-tsked. He had not believed in
public displays of affection.

"Too maudlin," he would have said. "Best left to a
private moment."

She had never agreed. Still did not. The woman
looked happy. Her face glowed with it.

She thought about the day they had parted. He had
kissed her that morning in bed, but not on taking his
leave. His hand on her cheek, a murmured, "I love
you."

No more than that. No more kisses, ever. More than
two years ago, now. Could it really be so long?

She wondered briefly if Archie had found her daily
letters too public a display of her affections. He had
responded only once a week until he was injured. The
letters had been more frequent then. Changed.

The crackle of paper beneath her fingers was not
changed, the imprint of her husband's signet in the
stiff, slightly greasy blob of wax beneath her thumb
all too familiar to her touch. She knew every word.
Like the ache of an old wound, the faint whiff of
gunpowder ghosting up from the pages brought tears
to her eyes. The horizon swam, a blur of grays and
greens, an unfinished watercolor that threatened to
run.

She sniffed, blinked, wiped a tear from her cheek,
and stiffened her back. She must not cry in front of
the man. She must not go to the door teary-eyed. She
had cried enough surely, in the past year and a half,
cried again the night before, letters spread upon the
bed before her, each of them memorized, every last
word.

No, she would not cry. Even the toughest of soldiers
became helpless in the face of a woman's tears. She
would not waste Lieutenant Forrester's time with an
excess of emotion. She would not have him regret in
any way his inclination to come to her today.

His task was not an easy one. She would not make
it more difficult. She owed him that much. He had

been kind, throughout the roughest patch of life she had ever traversed. Too kind.

And in meeting him she bridged past and present. She must begin anew, as new as the Grand Hotel smelled: of paint, plaster, varnish, and fabric dyes. It looked out over an area just as raw and new as it was, the painted faces of the houses and businesses fresh, the trees planted down the center of the boulevard before her no more than saplings. Beyond the edge of the bow-windowed house across the street Kensington Park's recently planted trees waved tender green in the breeze.

She turned from the window as Hettie, her quiet little maid, the only one of her servants she could now afford to keep, drifted through the room, asking if she required anything from downstairs.

"A bite to eat, miss? I hear the French chef here is quite remarkable."

She was not hungry, never really hungry anymore. Not for food at any rate. "Not right now, Hettie," she murmured. "I will wait and take a little tea with our guest."

"Yes, marm."

She turned to the window again, though it was ridiculous of her to watch the street. Even if she saw the lieutenant she would not recognize him. She had no idea even as to how old he might be.

She had envisioned him. One could not help but speculate given the intimate nature of the correspondence that had passed between them. A bewhiskered, fatherly figure she imagined, like her Uncle Grover, a gentleman of wisdom, years, and sensitivity. A face lined with a lifetime's worth of experiences. Far more mature than Captain Archibald Grant had proven himself, this Lieutenant Forrester, despite the discrepancy of their ranks. He had known just what to say in his final letter, dreadful as it was. She must not think of it, or she would end up weeping again.

She concentrated on the room, instead. Very modern, the hotel, with the latest lighting fixtures, and a new sort of fireplace surround, all finished off in the faux Greco-Roman motif that was popular of late. Archie would have hated it, his tastes too staunchly English to appreciate foreign influences no matter how Classical. She smiled, the smile crumpling. It had been almost a year now—and still the stupidest things set her off.

Youth and promise and new beginnings surrounded her as she made a new beginning herself. She must grow, and flourish—be green again. And yet, she felt terribly old—weary.

She did not care to be in London, certainly not for the reason that brought her, certainly not in the midst of a celebration that fired everyone she met with bright-eyed glee. The war had ended, Napoleon abdicated. All of London celebrated, but she.

The knock came upon the door in the middle of her musings, the sound of it freezing her, a rush of expectancy firing her veins. Eyes fixed nervously upon the door, she put the letters down on the secretary, glanced briefly in the mirror, fingered a stray lock of hair into place, pinched wan cheeks, and smoothed the white lace at her throat.

Taking a deep breath, she opened the door.

It was not the rush of air that accompanied the opening of the cupid-topped door that stole his breath away, it was sight of her—at last—his imagination given flesh. Annabelle Grant stood regarding him, just as Archie had described her, her complexion paler than he had imagined, perhaps it was the gray dress. Funny, he had never pictured her in mourning, even knowing what he knew. A form of denial, he supposed.

"Mrs. Grant?" he said.

"Yes?" Her voice was breathier than he had imagined, her tone one of surprise. "Are you Lieutenant Forrester?"

The beauty mark beside her mouth moved in an intriguing manner when she spoke.

"I am James Forrester," he said, trying to hold forth his hand without dropping the box or the saddlebags that grew heavier by the minute. "I bring you . . ."

A whey-faced, mob-capped maid stepped from the room across the hallway, and though she kept her head bowed subserviently and appeared to pay them no mind, something in her posture, and the tight-lipped set of her mouth, gave him the feeling he said the words too loud. He lowered his voice and leaned forward to say quietly, "Your husband's effects."

Annabelle Grant eyed the box as if it contained a serpent, held the door wider, gestured him inside, and said, "How kind of you to come, Lieutenant. Will you be so good as to put those there, on the table?"

He strode into an elegant sitting room, saddlebag thumping his thigh. This was a far cry from the hospital tents and commandeered quarters he had known as home for so long—far nicer, too, than the room he had taken at the George Inn. But, of course Archie, first in line to inherit his father's fortune, had had money. His widow would be accustomed to fine things.

The fire surround alone must have cost a fortune. White marble, it boasted carved stone inset intaglio medallions of Greek gods and goddesses, charioteers and archers. An annoyingly civilized and symbolic representation of conflict, of combat, heroic and bloodless. Fiction.

A breath of her perfume met his nose as he passed her, distracting him. He closed his eyes, the better to savor the familiar scent. Her letters had smelled the same. Lavender.

The odor triggered memories of Archie, and the smell of sulphur and camphor, gunpowder and rotting canvas. For an instant he heard the shriek of cannonball, the shout and thunder of the charge, the pounding hail of gunfire, the scream of horses and men.

He took a deep breath, shook away the past, con-

centrating on the present, and the table top: white,
smooth, cool, solid, untroubled by bad memories, the
table legs black lacquered. Gold-leafed caryatids sto-
ically bore the weight of the marble.

His hands shook a little as he released his burden.
His arms ached in letting go. Too long had he clutched
the awkward shape.

Archie's Annabelle stood watching, hands clenched at
her sides, gaze fixed on the box, as she caressed the
leather saddlebag.

"Will you cut the cord?" she asked.

He would, and did, with the silver-handled dirk he
kept tucked in his boot, thinking as the twine was
severed how wonderful it would be if he might so
easily cut the cord to his past.

In no way did he match the picture she had formed
in her mind. He was all wrong. No uniform, no fatherly wisdom staring back at her as he bent gracefully
to slide the wicked little dirk from his boot. No whisk-
ers to be seen. This brown-haired lad with satin fine
locks that slid down into his eyes had not the look or
manner of a man who had experienced tragedy, who
had killed—and led others to kill.

He looked younger than Archie, not much older
than herself, surely.

Archie, fond of pranks and laughter, never without
companions. She should have known it was a chum
he would find rather than a father figure among the
ranks. And yet, could it be true that this boyish imp
had sat beside him throughout his illness, even as he
died? It seemed highly improbable.

The cotton cord put up no resistance to the keen-
edged assault of the dirk. As the cord slid to the floor,
the lieutenant bent to retrieve it, with long-legged,
coltish grace, and tucked away the blade again in one
fluid motion, rising to look at her, hazel eyes warm,
expectant. Deep in that golden darkness sorrow

lurked, and concern, hiding behind the friendly twinkle, at odds with the hesitant smile.

Deep waters, she thought. There was more to Lieutenant Forrester than first met the eyes.

"Shall I leave you to go through his things in private?" he asked. "Or would you prefer company?"

"Company," she said, her voice as uneasy echo to his. And then, as if her request required further explanation. "You may know something of significance in connection with his things."

Her hands were pale, small, in undoing the saddlebag's clasps. They trembled as she delved into the last earthly possessions of Captain Archibald Grant. He knew exactly what she would find there, having carefully packed the things himself.

The box held Archie's cape, carefully wrapped around his sword, pistol, boots, and spurs. The saddlebags held a bit of horse tackle, shoes, stockings, leggings, trousers, breeches, and an article bag containing Archie's watch, his coin case, and rings. She lingered over these, chewing her lip a bit, setting them carefully down upon the marble-topped table as if they were bird's eggs, an equal amount of white space around each treasured item. Archie, come home.

He stood, unmoving, uncomfortable with his own presence in the room, unsure where to look, unwilling to draw attention to himself in clearing his throat, or shifting his weight. There was little he could say in connection with these ordinary things, other than that they had seen extraordinary violence. Archie would have begged him to hold tongue on that. He knew that for a certainty, and as he had thus far honored the dead man's every wish he saw no reason to open his mouth.

She came very close to tears in sliding the wedding band onto her thumb and off again. With a sigh, she placed it carefully on the table beside the engraved gold watch that had timed many an advance into battle. It made a faint pinging sound when she lifted it and flipped open the cover.

"Love will find the way," she said.

"B-beg pardon?"

She looked up from the watch, her eyes as gray as the dress she wore, and sad, so very sad. "Is it broken? It should play a tune when the casing is opened."

"Perhaps it is," he said.

He swallowed hard, and studied the garlanded plaster border that decorated the room, more plaster gods and goddesses to match the fireplace in round and rectangular bas relief between the decorative arches that led from the sitting room to the bedchamber. *Love will find the way?* Such promise in the words, in bedchambers. A room he should not indulge himself with thoughts of in connection with his best friend's widow, and yet the more he told himself inwardly not to think in that direction, the more his mind strayed.

She brought him back to his senses with a gasp.

He reacted instinctively, dove for the little pot of pipe clay that slipped her fingers, almost caught it. It bounced from the tips of his fingers. The marble flooring was unforgiving.

The pot smashed with a tinkling of broken pottery, pipe clay scattered everywhere. With bruising force he fell beside it, hand outstretched, empty.

"Oh, dear," she said, hands flying to her mouth. Tears welled instantly to her beautiful blue-green eyes, but she blinked them back, mouth set in a tight line. "Are you all right?" She held out a hand to help him to his feet.

"It is nothing," he said. "Just a bit of pipe clay."

"It came so far, unscathed," she said, head down, lashes fluttering, composing herself, and he knew she mourned not the thing that was lost, but that it had been Archie's.

She took up the captain's spyglass then, and distracted herself in going to the window, where she elongated it to examine more closely the neighborhood, her figure cutting a very pretty silhouette against the light, the sun creating a glowing halo of her hair. For an instant he saw not her, but Archie, freckled hands clasping the spyglass, his locks burnished a glossy roan.

"Set your sights upon the far horizon, my dear, and that is where I am," Annabelle said, lowering the glass.

James licked his lips, nonplussed.

"Archie said that." Her voice was faint. "When he left me."

The remark did not require a reply, and yet he felt compelled to say something, that silence did not dangle between them awkwardly.

"Did it help?" he managed to spit out. Stupid question.

She turned, the light upon one pale satin cheek, the line of her jaw smooth.

"A little." She folded up the glass with the familiar slide of metal on metal and came back to him—back to the box. "Did you leave behind any words of wisdom for the women awaiting your return?" she asked.

He thought of his mother, shook his head. "No women waiting," he said with forced lightness.

Her hands stilled. She looked up at him with her incredible blue-gray eyes, quizzically, as if he said something quite ridiculous.

"Oh, but you are wrong," the breathy voice contradicted. "*I* have been waiting. Eighteen months I have waited."

Since the day he had first written to her of Archie's injuries.

The lieutenant's lips parted, the brown of his eyes deepening as he looked back at her, dark lashes, thick as a girl's, fanning down to cover the gleam she had lit there. His jaw moved, as if he meant to reply.

The door opened behind him, breaking the growing

tension. Annabelle jumped back a step, as if they had been interrupted in something illicit.

In stepped Hettie, behind her a tea cart rattling, pushed by one of the hotel's maids. "Here we are, miss," she cried cheerfully. "But, what's this mess on the floor? Hold on now, Molly, my dear. This will have to be tidied before we roll in on top of it."

"At once, miss." The girl bobbed a curtsy, and backed out of the door.

"Clumsy me, Hettie," Annabelle said. "I should have seen it was picked up."

"No trouble, miss. The captain's things have arrived, have they? Then this must be the famous Lieutenant Forrester, whom we have been looking forward to meeting for so very long. Do you mean to stay to tea?"

"Yes, please," Annabelle pleaded, but he was shaking his head, the silky brown mane of hair drifting boyishly into his eyes.

He swept it back with an impatient rake of his fingers, and plucked up his hat from the table.

"As much as I would like to, I've another appointment."

She tried not to allow her disappointment to show. "Perhaps another day? I have so many questions."

He nodded, hair sliding, the hat gripped tightly, and stepped to her side of the table as the cart rattled past. "Mrs. Grant, I hope you will not find me too forward . . ."

His voice was very low, meant for her ears alone, and yet the maid, pale-faced, her mouth a forbidding line, turned her head as she returned with whisk broom and pan.

"What is it?" Annabelle asked, fascinated by the play of boy and man across features that had faced death unflinching and yet quailed a bit in the presence of a forbidding servant.

He licked his lips. Well shaped they were, and firm

with youth and good health. The rich, brown depths of his eyes slid away from her regard uneasily.

"Would you care to accompany me to the prince's fete honoring the Duke of Wellington tomorrow evening?"

A fete? The last thing she felt like doing was celebrating. Surely he understood. "I do . . . I do not . . ."

"I know you are probably not in a mood for the noisy crush it will be." His gaze met hers again, with an earnestness and pained understanding that took her breath away. "Many of the officers who knew Archie will be there," he said carefully. "I know they would like to meet you, perhaps regale you with a tale or two of his bravery. Archie spoke highly of you. It was a much envied common knowledge that you wrote to him almost every day."

His features held no mischief now, only expectant concern. His dark brows furrowed a little, the boy again hovering in his features, as if he feared he asked too much.

He did. It sounded like an emotionally wringing evening, a crowded, unpleasant affair among strangers, pity in their eyes, and a lurking curiosity as they wondered how much she suffered, and considered how glad they were death had not similarly touched them. She did not know if she could bear it.

"I know it is not easy," he said, as if he read her mind. They shared the loss. She had not stood by Archie as he walked through the valley of death. The lieutenant had.

"I will swiftly extricate you from the melee, should you care to leave." There was a steady quality to his voice, an earnest certainty. She began to see what he might have been like helping Archie meet his Maker.

"It is very kind of you to offer, but I am not very good company," she said uncertainly. *Coward!* she thought.

"I hate to go alone," he said, his hands awkward. "You would do me great honor."

There was an air of tension in him, as if he found it most difficult asking her to go.

Almost as difficult as she found it to accept.

"When should I expect you?"

He crossed the lobby of the Grand Hotel the following evening in full dress uniform, his last occasion to wear the high-collared, silver-braided, frogged, and embroidered blue coat. The lacing at his veed cuffs was a trifle worn. The gold tassel that dangled from his cummerbund had seen better days, but he saw no point in replacing it. Let the next fellow do it. What was his name? Chris—Christopher Fagan? The young fool who meant to buy his colors, as soon as he could put together the capital.

"A pity Napoleon has abdicated," Fagan had said as they reached an agreement.

"How so?" he asked, suspecting he knew what Fagan meant to reply. The stupid lad did not disappoint.

"Fun's over," he complained. "Dull days ahead with no one to fight, and little chance for advancement."

Small chance the fool would get his head blown off either, James refrained from pointing out. Small chance he would leave behind a sweetheart, or a wife like Annabelle Grant, to mourn his passing.

He wondered a moment if Archie had bought his colors with the same foolish enthusiasm for a fight. What other reason had he for joining, a wealthy young lord with the world on a silver platter: horses, home, an inheritance, a wonderful wife who loved him to distraction?

James shook his head at the cupid that topped the door to Annabelle Grant's lavish rooms. *Thrown away! Happiness wasted.*

She was ready when he tapped, not the sort of woman to keep a fellow waiting. He liked that in her. He liked, too, that she chose to wear gray, a silvery shade of silk that molded admirably her form, not black as she might have, not playing the part of widow to the hilt. She mourned, he knew, and deeply, but it was a private, between-the-lines sort of grief. She made no spectacle of her loss.

She looked him up and down in the mirror by the door as her maid helped her don evening cloak and gray-feathered hat, eyes brightening when their gazes met, but he could not tell if she was glad to see him, or if her eyes glistened with a wash of unshed tears. The truth was quickly hidden behind a downward sweep of pale lashes.

"You are looking very handsome tonight in uniform, Lieutenant," she said.

The uniform! Of course it brought her memories of Archie.

He waited a moment to reply, so that her gaze rose again to the mirror, her eyes shining that beautiful spruce blue Archie had so eloquently described. Definitely a hint of tears there. The beauty mark beside her mouth trembled.

"Is he with us, do you think?" she surprised him in asking.

"Tsk, tsk," Hettie murmured, guiding her mistress's hands into a pair of pearl-gray gloves.

He had no similar urge to brush aside her question. He had often wondered as much, himself. In the days following Archie's death he had felt his presence keenly—as if he hovered about the tent, as if he whispered something too soft to hear. But, the man's widow did not want to hear that, surely.

He held out an arm to her, saying, "He enjoyed such events, didn't he?"

"Far more than I," she admitted.

"If he is with us, Archie is beaming with pride."

Her fair brows rose.

"You are a vision in that dress, Mrs. Grant."

She smiled, a faint flush coloring her cheeks, the upward tilt of her lips moving the beauty mark beside her mouth in the most intriguing manner. "You are too kind."

She took his arm. Her touch, long anticipated, seemed a startling thing, an unimaginably powerful connection between them. It raised the hair on his arms. He felt like blurting, *No, not at all—not kind. Not me. It is another emotion entirely that brings me here.*

He said nothing, of course.

Her hand had always been meant to rest in the crook of his arm. It offered him the greatest comfort as they walked downstairs, through the elegant lobby, past the briskly nodding desk clerk and into the night.

She turned solemn face to the sky, to pinprick stars and a moon as waxen and pockmarked as a wheel of cheese.

The night always spoke to him of man's insignificance in the grand scheme of creation, of his mortality.

He turned the question back on her. "Have you some sense of his being with us, here, tonight?"

Her eyes had gone gray in the darkness, far darker than the color of her gown, which glowed like starlight as he opened the door of the vehicle he had hired, her palm to his, even gloved, a wondrous thing, a contact long dreamed of.

She waited until he had settled opposite, and then she spoke quietly as the horses set the carriage in motion, her voice barely audible above the noise of the wheels, her face thrown into shadow as they pulled away from the lampposts outside the hotel.

"He haunts me," she said.

An uneven spot in the pavement threw him forward in the seat, swaying him as much as her words.

"Nothing frightening, of course." Her voice seemed to come from a well of darkness. "That was not Archie's way. But I feel him near me at the oddest moments, or hear his voice in the wind. The day he died I thought I saw him in the apple orchard."

Too close to his own experience, this. James remem-

bered Archie's thin-voiced description of the trees, of
the crisp, firm-skinned fruit. "You met him there,"
he said.

"He told you everything?" she asked.

*Everything about you,* he wanted to tell her. "I
asked him."

"Did you?" She cocked her head, just as Archie
had described, her hair silvered in the moonlight, so
that it was for the moment she who seemed ghostlike.

"I asked him when it was he fell in love," he
clarified.

She laughed, her laughter bordering on tears. "And
he told you from the moment we met? The liar. He
teased me mercilessly, and called me all manner of
unpleasant names."

"Ding dong bell," he said. "And Anna-ring-a-ling."

"Dear me," she sighed. "He did tell you everything."

"It is a lad's way to be cruel to the one he loves."

"Were you cruel, then, James Forrester, when you
were a lad? I cannot picture it."

He might have left her with that impression, that
he was above such meanness of spirit, but he had no
desire to lie to her any more than he already had. "I
dipped a girl's pigtails in an ink standish," he said
quietly, not at all proud of the memory. "I believed I
would marry her one day."

"And where is she now, your sweetheart?"

"Married to a friend of mine. A curate."

"Oh!"

"They are a very good match, far better than we
ever would have been. They named their firstborn
after me."

They jolted along in silence, his gaze locked on her
face, what he could see of it. Light and shadow played
across its contours. She studied her gloved hands,
clasped in her lap.

"I shall miss him," she said at last.

"I know," he said. He would, too. *We shall name
our firstborn after him,* he thought.

\* \* \*

The prince had spared no expense in preparing Carlton House for the celebration. Annabelle had read about it in the *Times*, never dreaming she would have opportunity to see the huge, octagonal brick building that had been constructed in the garden. It boasted an umbrella-shaped, leaded roof. Huge banks of silk and paper flowers had been arranged in the center of the building to resemble a temple to house two bands to provide constant music. Above them, the ceiling of the new building was painted to resemble draped muslin, complete with real gilded cords. On every wall there was more muslin, and mirrors, and in them she saw herself time and again, clutching tight the arm of Lieutenant James Forrester, a forced smile on her lips, a milling crowd, all color and movement, on all sides.

She liked the manner in which the lieutenant gently guided her through a forest of uniforms, a wash of glittering satins and silks. He was a handsome fellow, not striking, not eye-catching as Archie had never failed to be, with his fiery hair and boisterous manner. No, the lieutenant was quiet and steady, his features as even as his manner, the sleek forelock of his hair sliding down to mask his eyes, just as his mildly humorous asides to her masked the seriousness with which he took his task as escort.

The prince arrived, looking well pleased with himself and his gathering, resplendent in his field marshal's full dress uniform, English, Prussian, French, and Russian orders completing his ensemble. The queen made an exceptionally long appearance. The duke was met with respect and affection by all.

The lieutenant was well known and respected as well. Many a superior officer made a point of acknowledging him. James met them with gracious aplomb and impeccable manners. He made a point of introducing her to everyone they encountered. He even prepared her as many of them approached with telling, succinct little biographies of their connection to her husband.

She was met with sympathetic smiles and many a "Good man, Grant. Pity he cannot be here to celebrate with us today."

When her cheeks tired of studied smiles, and her heart ached to think so many had returned, well and whole, while Archie had perished, James Forrester seemed to know she could take no more. He led her away from the throng along a draped promenade to a Corinthian temple in the garden. He did not stop, nor speak until they reached the bust of Wellington that had been strategically placed atop a column in front of an engraved mirror.

She found herself strangely comfortable walking in unbroken silence with him, as if they had known each other forever, as if the silence spoke as eloquently as their moments of conversation. Archie had never been comfortable with silence.

"There," he said, pointing at one of the many tents that littered the lawn. "There we shall find those who knew Archie best."

He indicated a supper tent, hung in white and rose curtains, regimental colors decorating the entrance flap. The same colors James Forrester wore.

She stopped, regarding it with trepidation. "Do you mind if we walk a little longer?" She hoped against hope he would not find her too craven a coward in delaying the inevitable.

"Not at all," he said. "There is another promenade just through there."

The crook of his arm beneath her hand was a comfort, the little pat he gave her knuckles familiar in a brotherly way. They traversed a dark patch of garden. He caught at her elbow, steadying her when she tripped over uneven ground. The strength and support of his grasp took her breath away.

He leaned close. "Are you all right?"

His breath, warm against her nose, smelled faintly

of the mushroom tarts they had sampled from a passing tray. Inexplicably, she longed to lean closer, to rest her head against the familiar blue wool covering his shoulder.

She did no such thing, of course, but she missed in that moment Archie's strong arms, the warm comfort of his embrace. She had missed it every night as she lay her head upon the pillow she kept wrapped in one of his linen shirts—that she might catch some whiff of him.

In that darkness, face-to-face with this stranger who had loved Archie almost as much as she, she felt compelled to blurt, "I begin to forget his face. A horrible thing to admit. I've a painting of him, and a miniature to remind me, and yet they are only poor likenesses. I do not forget all of him. It is silly, really. What I remember best are his hands. All freckles, with the biggest thumbs."

He inhaled abruptly—closed his eyes—she lost their gleam in the darkness. The sheen of his hair caught what light there was as he flung back his head, rubbed at his nose, and sniffed.

She might have wept then. Her eyes welled with tears to think that the lieutenant was probably even more loath than she to remember the loss of those beautiful hands. One sooner than the other.

*Blown clean away.* Archie had made him write her. *The right, blast it! Makes writing you myself an impossibility. My dear friend, Lieutenant Forrester, is kind enough to do the honors. You will notice he has a better hand than I in every way.* Always a jester, dear Archie. Even when it was not at all appropriate. He had never mentioned his loss again. Never mentioned the pain of losing it, said only in the end, *Wounds gone septic, my dear. Might lose the arm. A pity. I did so enjoy wrapping both of them about you.*

Would that she had only lost half of his embrace.

The lieutenant stepped out of the shadows. When he spoke his breath warmed her cheek. "If anything haunts me, it is Archie's feet. Cannot purge them from my brain," he complained.

She laughed. The remark was so unexpected.

He chuckled. "Did not like to keep them tucked under covers, our Archie, and he so tall they dangled off the end of the cot like two great, pale, finless fish."

"Flounder," she agreed with a chuckle.

His smile flashed, teeth catching the light. "They were the first thing I saw of him every morning, and the last thing at night."

"All bones and angles," she said. "He had very slender feet, and long. The cobbler who made his Hessians remarked on them."

He nodded, smile fading in the darkness. "The oddest things trigger my recollections of him."

She dabbed at her eyes, sniffed once, and said, "Yes. Thank you for reminding me of his feet."

He led her from the darkness into the second promenade.

Draped in green calico, it had been hung with large transparencies of battle scenes. They bore titles he found vaguely offensive given the current turn of his mind. "Military Glory," one was called, and another, "The Overthrow of Tyranny."

Had the artist ever been to war, he wondered.

"It is not like this, is it?" She paused before one of the transparencies.

He marveled at how tandem their thoughts ran. "No," he agreed. "It is not so orderly a business."

"Curiously bloodless these depictions," she suggested.

*God, the blood.* He did not want to remember. "Mmmm."

"And, of course, a painting captures only a visual. They lack sounds, smells."

"Thank God," he blurted.

She looked at him a long searching moment. "You will introduce me, now, to the others?"

"My pleasure," he said.

\*    \*    \*

They met her with kindness, with sympathy, with curious gazes, some of them deep into their cups, some completely sober. It was not so difficult as she had imagined, and far more so in ways she had never dreamed.

"Brave lad."

"A pleasure to serve under him."

"A pity he is not here today to drink your health."

They welcomed her into their midst like a visiting dignitary, on their best behavior, fetching a chair, filling a plate. She nibbled at what they brought her, unwilling to appear ungracious, though she had no hunger.

"But of course we should have known James would bring you tonight," a Captain Waters said when Lieutenant Forrester briefly abandoned her to fetch glasses of negus.

"Obsessed with repaying his debt to Captain Grant," a gentleman she knew only as the paymaster agreed with a nod.

"Debt?" she echoed, baffled.

A dark-haired young man with the drawn visage of a much older fellow, who had been introduced as Boffard, the company surgeon, asked, "He never told you?"

"The shots Archie took were meant for Lieutenants Forrester and Golding," Captain Waters said.

"Meant for them?" The idea made no sense. They spoke all at once, incomprehensibly, from all sides, some of them murmuring hushing noises. Others suggesting it was Archie's place to tell her.

"That he was a hero?" A young lieutenant who attempted rather unsuccessfully to hide his inebriation spoke from behind her. She had to twist her head to look at him, and he breathed brandy fumes when he nodded in an exaggerated fashion and said, "Without a doubt, a hero."

She searched their faces. "Tell me."

They did not want to look her in the eyes. Their gazes slid sideways among themselves, settling at last on the young man as he blurted, "James and I were done for. Horses down. Shots flying on all sides. Archie rode right into the thick of it—rescued us."

A bright-eyed young man agreed. "Lost his horse in doing so. It took shot after shot, but he managed to keep the poor beast upright. Used it as a shield as they made their way to cover."

"Then the shell hit." The paymaster smoothed his mustache, remembering. "One minute the horse was there, the next, nothing but a red mist."

"Kellinger!" the others objected as one.

"You go too far, sir."

"Hold your bloody tongue, man! A lady does not want to hear such detail."

The drunken lad attempted to console her, saying, "Put the beasht schwiftly out of its miz'ry."

"And Archie?" she dared ask, hand to throat.

"We were sure the captain was lost, Mrs. Grant," the paymaster said.

Annabelle swallowed hard. Her mouth tasted foul. Archie had mentioned none of this in his letters. Or was it Lieutenant Grant who had refrained from writing it?

"The lieutenant went back after him," someone said.

"Put 'imself in 'arm's way. Said the captain 'ad risked 'is life for him. 'E could do no less."

"Lieutenant Forrester?" she verified.

"Aye."

They fell silent, exchanging uneasy glances.

"Blames himself for the captain losin' 'is 'and, Mrs. Grant. 'E were carrying the captain over his shoulders, you see, 'im bein' knocked out as it were."

"They took some fire."

"The cap'n took a hit to the hand. The lieutenant one to the leg."

This news stunned her. "Lieutenant Forrester was hit? He never mentioned . . ."

"Flesh wound," Boffard dismissed the injury. "Ball was spent. Your husband was not so fortunate. Shrapnel made a mess of his hand and face, poor man. So covered was he in his horse's blood and guts I was stunned to discover he still breathed."

Someone suggested, "Less color, Boff."

"Yes, quite." Boffard fell silent a moment, carefully arranging his words. "Admirable fellow, your Archie. The will to live was strong. 'Can't see, Boffard, old man,' he said to me when I reached him, when of course it was perfectly clear to me he would never see again. 'Must patch me up,' he said, as if he required no more than a bit of sticking plaster. 'Patch me up and send me home to Belle.' "

Annabelle's breath caught in her throat. Tears stung the backs of her eyes.

"I'm very sorry I could not better oblige him, Mrs. Grant," Boffard's voice dropped.

"Mr. Boffard. You are the one who wrote to me, dissuading me from crossing the Channel to be with him as he died?"

"I am, I did. I . . . I pray you may find it within you to forgive me." He licked his lips nervously, his face a picture of regret. "A mistake, that. But he swore me to it. 'Keep her out of harm's way,' he said, and I, convinced each breath must be his last, was certain you would arrive too late."

A horrible quiet fell. Annabelle sat staring at the tips of her best shoes, a beribboned satin pair she had bought to welcome Archie home in, since dyed black. While she had been worrying over how pretty her feet might look to him, Archie had suffered, horribly, alone but for these men.

"No remaking the past."

James Forrester said it, his voice mild, his agitation to be witnessed in the sway of the liquid in the glasses he had brought. "No use beating oneself up over what might have been." He handed the surgeon a drink, seemed to address his remark to the man, and yet Annabelle took it to heart.

*No remaking the past.*

Boffard tossed back his spirits in a single gulp, his guilty gaze straying again to Annabelle.

The lieutenant held out a glass to her as well, but rather than take it, she rose, ready to be gone, and yet realizing they watched her, waiting to hear what she might say.

The surgeon blinked when she turned her attention to him. He flinched when she leaned forward to press her hand to his shoulder. "Thank you," she said. And turning to the others, she managed to say, "A pleasure to meet Archie's friends."

She walked blindly out of the tent then, with tear-blurred gaze sought the friendship of darkness, some spot where none could hear the sobs that collected at the back of her throat.

The lieutenant followed, but she did not know it until she stopped at last in a far corner of the garden, in the shadow of a tall shrub, and tried her best to collect herself.

Stifled sobs wracked her, shook her shoulders as if in a gale. Rising emotion threatened to tear her in half, but she would not allow herself to cry, not here, in so public a place, not in front of these men. She must restrain her sorrow, maintain an outward show of calm.

Then he touched her, his hand upon her shoulder, a little thing really, and yet it was too much. It broke the damn of grief, flooding her.

Knowing that Archie had saved this man, and lost his own life doing so, knowing this man blamed himself for her loss, she turned into the welcome strength of his open arms. She lay her head upon his shoulder. Her fingers grasped the silver frogging that made his chest the same uncomfortably bumpy pillow she had encountered when Archie had left her. Her tears could no longer be contained.

"Annabelle," he said gently, one hand smoothing the hair at the crown of her head, the other beating a gentle tattoo on the flat of her back. "Forgive me. I should not have brought you here."

He cradled her in his arms, the warm width of her shoulders a precious gift, the humid weight of her head a benediction. He offered up his handkerchief for a soaking, and wondered if he could ever part with the uniform now that her tears had drenched the shoulder. Archie's Annabelle, in his arms, as he had dreamed, the softness of her breasts pressed to his, the smell of lavender perfume intoxicating. He wanted to crush her closer, to kiss the damp curve of tear-stained cheek, to seek out the humid need of her mouth. His body stirred with involuntary ardor.

And yet he felt such crushing guilt in holding her, his hands alive to the warm, wet splash of her tears, to the silken softness of her hair. *His* hands. Why his? Why had Archie been the one to die? Why did he survive? Why, oh, why had he allowed himself to become fixated on his savior's wife?

The moment was wrong and right all at the same time. A confusing paradise in a purgatory. He clung to her until she pushed herself free, one hand against his chest, her face averted. "I am so angry with him," she said, her voice tight with emotion. "He need not have gone, need not have played hero. He certainly need not have kept me away in the end. We had a good life, a quiet life. Why did he choose to give it away? Why?"

He had no answers for her.

"I would go now," she said, dabbing at her eyes.

He walked her out of Carlton House Garden by a side gate with the assistance of one of the numerous footmen, hailed the hired coach by some miracle, and sat opposite her when they climbed within, his shoulder cold now, empty. He yearned to reach out and grasp the hands that twisted his handkerchief into a ball.

Withdrawn and introspective, she could not look at him, staring instead at the floor, light playing across tear-swollen features.

He did not know what to say, what to do. He sat mute and helpless, unmanned by the intensity of her grief, by the untimely strength of his desire for her. How vain of him to think he could ease her pain. All he had done was exacerbate it.

He would treasure this evening, nonetheless, treasure her gracious kindness to the men who had so wantonly revealed what Archie had meant to keep secret. He wondered if she would ever want to set eyes on him again once he had returned her to Hettie and the safe elegance of the hotel.

All too soon they were there, and he was opening the door of the carriage, and offering her his arm as she navigated the step. They stopped before the huge Wedgwood blue door, the color an attractive frame for her fairness. He asked her if she would like him to walk her to her room.

"No, thank you," she said, unwilling to look at him. Distance yawned awkwardly between them in the guttering lamplight. She wished to be rid of him.

"Thank you for the use of your handkerchief." She returned it to him swiftly, careful not to touch his hand. Was she afraid he might cling to her? Did she regret now the intimacy of their tearful embrace? He hated to think so.

"Thank you for accompanying me," he said.

She turned her face to the moon, her tear-swollen profile silhouetted like that on a coin against the stark white Doric columns framing the door. Moths fluttered darkly above the pale flax of her smoothly coiled hair.

"And so you saved him," she said.

She had a way of disconcerting him—going straight to the heart when he least expected it.

"I did but offer short reprieve," he objected bitterly.

"I am greatly in your debt."

"No."

She turned her face to him, her mouth fragile, and very serious.

"He did the same for me," he tried to explain.

"And so all debts are quit?" she asked, and made a noise like laughter that had nothing to do with amusement. "Exactly what Archie would have said, and yet it is not true. We are bound forever by your act, by his."

"I suppose we are," he admitted.

She turned before the door, hand upon the latch. "I wonder if you will do me a favor while you are here in London?" she asked.

"Anything," he promised wildly, in earnest.

"Call upon me again. Talk to me on occasion of Archie's final days. I know all too well now that here are things he left out of his letters." She sounded weary. Her shoulders seemed to carry a great weight.

He meant to do all he could to lighten that burden. He had with every letter he had ever penned.

"Tomorrow?" he asked. "Is two a good time?"

"Perfect," she said with a sigh that made him question whether anything in her life would ever be perfect again.

He nodded and stepped back as she wished him "Good evening," and disappeared inside.

He stood at the bottom of the steps, watching the window in the stairwell until her pale hair caught the light in passing. Then he boarded the hired carriage humming a tune. Was it what the band had played that evening as he held her in his arms? He could not remember, but it sounded right to him. It sounded right.

Four o'clock in the morning, and Annabelle sat inelegantly cross-legged, hair down about her shoulders, on the beautifully accoutred bed that brought her no sleep. Archie's stained, worn, and battle-torn things were scattered on the pristine counterpane like treasures washed ashore from a shipwreck, and indeed it was the shipwreck of her life she combed through. An exercise both painful and cathartic.

A shoe-polishing ball left a black mark upon the sheet. A rust-blighted razor and scissors dusted everything they touched with fine sienna. His pistol weighed down the coverlet. His sword glittered ominously from the floor. His boots she had placed beside the bed, as if he might rise to step into them at any minute.

She wore one of his shirts. The fine linen grazed her nipples, reminding her of his touch. His cloak warmed her lap, gave scratchy caress to her thighs. A lover's touch. The faint whiff of cordite and gunpowder that rose from the fabric whenever she moved was enough to pluck at her heart like a violin string, high and achingly sad.

Hettie had long since gone to bed, her faint snores a comfort from the far side of the door.

Archie hovered, watching, his voice not quite loud enough to hear, and yet she knew he talked to her, knew exactly what he would have said to her as she clutched his down-at-heels shoes to her chest, and tried not to imagine how the spattering of stains on the left toe had been gained.

*"Belle,"* she could hear him say. *"Why cling to those dirty old things. Throw them out, my dear. Time for a step forward. One foot at a time. You cannot cling to the past forever."*

The floor creaked, muffled footsteps sounded in the corridor. She was not the only soul awake in the dead of night. She and her memory of Archie had sat quietly in the midst of Archie's things for several hours, time passing like a river, and she completely unaware of the flow, conscious only of the faintly yellowed state of his linens, the carefully darned toes and heels of his stockings. Whose careful stitches, these? Archie's? Lieutenant Forrester's? One of the lads she had met tonight, assigned such menial duty for her husband's sake?

She fingered a hole in a pair of flannel drawers, considered darning them, and again he spoke in the depths of her mind. *"Don't be a goose, Annabelle. Give them away, my dear. The poorhouse has better use of them than you, or I."*

She imagined him laughing in her mind, a man to jest on all subjects, even his own demise.

She wondered if Lieutenant Forrester thought her a goose as well. She must give him something of Archie's, something to remember him by—but what? She combed through Archie's article bag. A gold stickpin? His emerald ring? No, his watch. Of course! It must be his watch.

The watch was not in the bag. It was not among the things strewn on the bed. She knew she had seen it on the day Forrester first arrived. She remembered the weight of it in her hand as Hettie and the maid had arrived with the tea trolley. Perhaps she had left it on the marble-topped table. Perhaps it had fallen onto the rug beneath.

She would check first thing in the morning. Her head felt too heavy to lift at the moment, her limbs too weighted with exhaustion.

Hettie let her sleep in.

"Hadn't the heart to wake you, marm. Tuckered, you looked, curled up among 'is lordship's things."

"Have you seen Archie's watch?" Annabelle asked over a steaming cup of cocoa that Hettie claimed was the best she had ever tasted, and yet nothing tasted good to Annabelle. The cocoa was no exception.

She had already peeked under the marble-topped table. No gold watch.

"Oooh, miss, has it gone missing?" Hettie asked, eyes round with the wonder of it. "There is some talk, you know, that one of the maids is suspected of stealing from the rooms."

Annabelle laughed. "Stolen. Nonsense. I have only misplaced the thing."

And yet, several hours later, Lieutenant Forrester

tapping at the door, and still the watch had not been found, and she was not so certain.

She said as much to James as they walked past the shops along Leinster Terrace to Kensington Gardens for a stroll before their tea.

"I find it hard to believe a stranger would take from me this precious remnant of Archie. That no sooner is it returned to me than it is lost again forever. How could anyone be so cruel?"

"Human frailty I understand," he said, quietly. "But I struggle mightily to understand why God would have me save Archie only to lose him."

"Silly me. To fret over a watch."

"I understand," he said. "It was his."

"I had meant it for you."

"Had you?" His gaze rose from studying of the traffic that bottlenecked in Bayswater Road due to a cavalcade of carts carrying what looked like perfect, miniature replicas of British and French frigates, sails furled.

She smiled at him. "You gave Archie time. It seemed only fitting." Then to ease the sudden awkwardness between them, she waved a hand at the carts. "What in the world are they doing?"

"On their way to Hyde Park," he said. "A mock battle is scheduled for the Serpentine on the first. Part of the celebrations."

"Do you mean to go?"

"Shall I take you?"

"How kind of you to offer."

"Kind of you to think I might want the captain's watch," he said. "He told me you gave it to him as a going-away gift."

Of course, she thought. Archie had told him everything.

He could not tell her she was his perfect remembrance of the captain, that he could not look at her without hearing the man's voice, husky with pain, momentarily transported from his sufferings by mere mention of his darling Annabelle.

He could not explain how bittersweet was the pleasure of strolling along a light-dappled walk in the company of a beautiful woman who need not fear for her life or virginity on a daily basis, as had the young women in war-torn France. That she happened to be the wife of the man who had died to save him added a special poignancy.

He did not blurt out how beautiful, how fragile, how luxurious he considered the weight of her hand in the crook of his arm. He did not wax poetic on the quality of the light, the flutter of green leaves, the peaceful serenity of the park. She would not understand, could not. He would not have her understand. Such an understanding changed one forever. Life was precious, to be cherished.

"And so you mean to stay housed at your husband's estate, in the company of his brother's family?" He wanted to know how Archie's death affected her life, wanted to know every nuance. He was responsible for what became of Annabelle Grant.

She nodded.

"Do you not find such an arrangement a trifle awkward?" he asked.

"Not at all. My brother-in-law and his wife require far more space than I do, and they mean to have a large family. It is only right they should have the estate, while I inhabit quite cozily the dowager house. My sister-in-law, who is currently with child, has indicated she would greatly appreciate any assistance I might give her in rearing my impending niece or nephew."

"I see," he said. She had gone in an instant from lady of the manor to the penniless, widowed female of the family, a pawn who must make herself useful— an extra set of trustworthy hands to care for the ill, infantile, and elderly.

"My parents would welcome my return, of course,"

she said, "but they can make little provision for me with five of my sisters yet to leave the nest. I mean to serve as an escort to them as much as I can—introduce them somewhat to society."

A society he had little connection with, a society that would most likely reject her if she were to have him as he hoped, as he prayed. Was it fair? Was it enough, what he meant to offer her?

"Ah," he said with a nod. "It sounds as if you mean to keep happy—busy."

They came to the Serpentine, the water almost the color of her eyes. A crowd had gathered to watch the launching of the frigates from the carts. They were craft large enough to hold a half dozen or so men, each fully outfitted with rigging and flags, portholes and cannon. No mean feat to transfer them to water, where they were ferried about by smaller craft manned by sturdy oarsmen.

"Do you not imagine yourself remarrying?" he asked, picturing a better future for her, a changed future, in fresh waters, society be damned. "Children of your own?" He had to ask, had to know if someone already vied for her affections.

She sighed. "Perhaps. Someday."

It did not sound as if she held anyone in mind for the role. It pleased him that she did not hasten to another man's arms, another man's bed. Sunlight dancing on water cast her face in a new light. He could not take his eyes from the glimmer of light across her lips, her brow.

"What of you? I heard from your mates that you have sold your colors, that you do not mean to remain with the military."

"No," he said, turning his back to the frigates. "I plan to marry," he admitted. "Have a houseful of children, herd sheep." He watched her reaction with keen interest.

"Sheep? Are you well versed in sheep?"

"I am. My father raised sheep, and his father before

him. I once thought it a rather boring way to spend one's life. My recent experiences have given me fresh appreciation of an orderly country life." *In battle,* he thought, *we were sheep, led to a slaughter.* "I would be shepherd now," he said.

"And have you a young lady in mind to share this new life of yours?"

A strand of hair threatened to fall into eyes that went blue backed by sky. He reached out to brush it away, provoking a sudden flush in her cheeks, her gaze, downcast, rising to regard him, eyes changed to green as they passed into the meager shadow of the trees.

"I do," he said.

"Ah. Does she know sheep?"

His brow furrowed. "I don't know. Do *you* know sheep, Mrs. Grant?"

She looked at him a long moment, her lashes sunlit, a thick fringe of gold to frame heaven. Her mouth distracted him when she parted her lips to say, "Annabelle. You really cannot continue to stand on form with me, Mr. Forrester. Surely you consider us as intimately connected as I do, given what brings us together."

"You will call me James, then?"

"Yes, James, and yes, I do know sheep—a little."

Shocking how much his name from her lips moved him! How pleased he was she did not hold sheep in contempt.

"Come," he said, turning into a new pathway. "They have built a castle in Green Park. A sight to behold."

She followed him, readily enough, bemused by their conversation, a trifle disappointed, though she had no right to it, that he spoke to her of his future with another. And yet, had he? There was something in his eyes whenever he looked at her, something in the way he had asked if she knew sheep . . . to make her wonder.

"And where will you keep your flocks?" she asked. "Have you a castle tucked away in the hills?"

"Nothing so grand. I've a bit of land in Yorkshire, and a house, abandoned for some time, that requires extensive renovation."

"And you left such prosperity to fight Napoleon?"

He laughed. "To the contrary, it was in fighting him I obtained the means to buy them by way of a solicitor, who invested all of the earnings I posted home to him."

"Ah. When do you mean to set out upon this shepherding venture?"

"I . . ." He did not really have an answer. "I've business that keeps me in London," he said.

"You will want to stay for the celebrations," she suggested, reluctant to lose him to his future. Too soon she must step into her own.

"Yes. And you?" He seemed anxious for her answer.

She frowned, and as swiftly erased the frown with a smile. "I must stay at least until I've seen a mock battle on the Serpentine."

He smiled swiftly.

"Will it not bother you a little?" she asked.

He did not pretend to misunderstand. His expression changed in an instant from boyish delight to an all-too-mature seriousness.

"There is something disconcerting in honoring battle," he said. "Something in a way perverse to honor the killing along with those killed."

"Did Archie die in vain?"

"No." He stopped in the path before her and took her hands, and she let him, enjoying the strength of his grasp, the very maleness of him. His voice rang with authority, with the certainty she craved.

"Strife brings out the very best and the very worst

in man. It brought out the noblest part of your husband. I shall never forget his valor, his fearlessness."

She pulled away from his grasp at the mention of Archie, feeling disloyal to the dead, unable to look him in the eyes. Was this the worst in her, that she was so strongly drawn to this young man? That she longed to rest her head once more upon his shoulder?

"Did it bring out the best or worst in you?" she asked.

He exhaled heavily. "I could not say, I know only that I am a changed man."

She nodded quietly.

He had read of her loneliness, of her fears, between the lines of her letters to Archie, their tone too cheerful, as she kept up a brave front, tending the home fires, waiting, wondering.

"I know," he said.

She considered him a long moment with spruce blue eyes, questions there. She did not voice them. A bird distracted her gaze. She began to walk again, and when he fell into step at her side, she was the one to tuck her hand in the crook of his arm, as if it belonged there.

A thoughtful quiet fell between them as their stroll took them deeper into the park, away from the rows of newly planted trees, into the open grassy area and bright flower beds of Green Park. They had no trouble finding the castle. It was huge, positioned in front of Buckingham House, at least a hundred feet tall, its walls embattled.

"The Castle of Discord," Annabelle said. "I have read about this. The *Times* decries daily the expense of the coming celebrations, and this was one of the items they made the greatest noise about."

"And what do you think of the thing?" he asked, wondering what went on inside her fair head. She remained in some ways a complete mystery to him, a mystery he wanted to explore. He found something wonderful in his every moment in her company, in the careful consideration of her gaze whether it turned upon him, or fanciful follies like the castle before them. Her tongue was not given to idle chatter. Her posture and movements had quiet dignity.

She cocked her head. "Well, I do not think it puts us to shame in front of visiting dignitaries as they would have it. I understand there is to be quite a production surrounding it, the night of the fireworks. A magical transformation." Her smile faded. "You say war transformed you?"

This unexpected return to their earlier topic by such a path intrigued him. "Yes."

Her eyes were downcast, her mouth gone soft, serious, kissable. He longed to tilt her chin and taste her lips.

"Did you find Archie changed as well?"

Again the shadow of the dead came between them, shaming him for his thoughts, his desire. He considered his answer carefully. "I would not presume to know," he said, "having not known him before."

"I found him changed," she said softly, turning to regard him with an unnerving focus. "By way of his letters."

"Did you?" he asked stiffly, wondering if she knew of his deception, fearing she might mistake his reason for it. "Might I ask, how so?"

She considered her answer carefully before responding, "There seemed an added sensitivity to his communications, to the way he regarded the world. At the end, especially, he wrote with unusual eloquence, with a spiritual awareness I would never have credited him with."

"Impending death inspires depth of thought in the simplest of fellows," he said, noncommittally, unwilling to look at her, afraid his eyes would give him away.

"It did occur to me"—she paused—"that his correspondent might be responsible." Her gaze drifted across the vastness of the park before coming to rest on him with disconcerting keenness. "That in transposing words to paper—in transferring thought to ink—he might have allowed his own opinions, or beliefs, to voice themselves."

He licked dry lips before allowing a hint of a smile to lighten his expression. "That's entirely possible," he agreed.

She was a shrewd one. Archie had told him as much.

She continued to study him a moment as if she might divine from his features how close to the truth she came.

"They are very precious to me," she said. "I will never part with those letters."

He could not meet her eyes, could not allow her to see too deeply. Let her hold on to the illusion that Archie had been lucid enough through the last of his days to offer her deep thoughts and words of comfort. What good did it do to reveal that he had perpetuated a lie? To tell her the poor man lay for days in a delusional fog unable to string two words together seemed an unnecessary cruelty.

And what excuse had he, for instigating such falsehoods? Was it her feelings he had wished to spare? Indeed, that had played some part in his decision to continue the correspondence, but the selfish truth of the matter, if he were completely honest with himself, had been that he could not relinquish the pleasure of *her* letters. He feared losing her, his best friend's wife. What a twisted web he had woven.

His mother was not a writer. His father dead. He had no other source of regular correspondence, and he had been, sight unseen, completely infatuated with the sweet, steady, unfailing Annabelle Grant.

Could he tell her how much her letters had meant to him? So much that he had fostered a hoax of sorts, a harmless fabrication, one that would have pleased Archie, may even have brought him some level of peace as he died. One that kept Archie's wife from the painful truth. One that kept the letters coming, letters he had read to Archie, even in the end, when he fell into a rouseless slumber. Did it really matter that in his heart of hearts he began to think of the letters as his?

It did. Of course it did. He liked to consider himself an honest man, a true friend. He would not go on deceiving her.

"There is something I must tell you," he began.

"Yes?" She turned to him with trust in her gaze—respect.

A beautiful sight, such a look in the eyes of the woman one loved. He could not destroy that. He simply couldn't. And yet she waited for what he would tell her.

He told her what she wanted to hear.

"The captain spoke of you often, with great fondness. He loved you dearly. He wanted to return to you more than anything. Because of that desire he clung to life longer than anyone anticipated."

He would not tell her how painful was the fight, nor that poor old Archie had called out her name in his last moment with an anguish that would live in his memory forever. He would not tell her this was part of the reason he had determined to meet her, to continue writing her, the female whose memory was enough to keep a doomed man fighting to free himself from death's irresistible clutches.

"Did he suffer much?" she asked. "In the end?"

Clever girl. She suspected the truth. Perhaps she knew without his saying a word. He had known she would ask eventually. That she asked him in that instant caught him a little off guard, but he had his answer ready. One last favor for Archie, who had allowed no word of his agonies to make their way into that correspondence he *had* dictated.

"He knew he was dying," he said. "And in it, he found peace."

Her footsteps slowed. She stared intently at the

ground, as if to find her own peace. At last, with a
catch in her voice that wrung his heart, she said, "I
see," and lifted her head, and set off again, no tears,
no more questions, no turning into his arms again
for comfort.

They walked the row of kiosks in Hyde Park twice.
Once that day, as they were in the process of being
assembled, and again late in the morning of August
the first when they were finished and manned, and the
park crowded with an absolute mob of revelers.

The day had begun with showers and some fear that
the celebrations would either be canceled, delayed, or
miserably sodden, but then the sun chased away the
clouds, brightening everyone's outlook considerably,
and a crowd began to pour into the parks.

The kiosks were a hurly-burly avenue of sausage,
fish, fruit, and gingerbread vendors, outdoor ale-
houses, tobacconists, and trinket kiosks. The ground
in and around this tent city was soon churned into a
sea of hard-packed mud as hundreds of feet wore
away the grass.

Nibbling happily at sausages on sticks, and slices
of hothouse melon, the grass brilliant with emerald
raindrops beneath their feet, James and Annabelle
strolled Green Park, the Castle of Discord a fanciful
backdrop to a Mr. Windham Sadler's balloon ascension, an intriguing contraption that drew grasps and
cheers as, freed from its moorings, it rose gracefully
into the sky. Sadler leaned out over the side as he
went, releasing a paper rain across the park of printed
broadsides detailing upcoming events in the celebration.

"Oh, my," Annabelle turned to James with sparkling eyes. "That was certainly worth seeing! Ar . . ."
She stopped herself, started again. "What next?"

She avoided mention of Archie. She had not spoken
of him for several days, several awkward days when

his name came quite naturally to her tongue, and yet she stifled it.

"Archie would have wanted to climb into the basket with Sadler, wouldn't he?" James said, wearying of her nipped-off sentences, and the stricken look that followed.

"You read my mind," she said sheepishly.

"You need not avoid mentioning him."

She made a face. "I begin to feel like a parrot with a limited vocabulary. Everything Archie this, and Archie that."

"He leaves a great gaping hole in our lives. It is only natural we should still try to fill it."

She sighed. "I hear his voice, in my head, saying, 'Get on with it, Annabelle. Stop liv—'"

"Living in the past." His voice joined chorus with hers."

She laughed. "I forget sometimes how well you knew him."

*I can never forget,* he thought.

With Mr. Sadler's balloon growing rapidly smaller in the sky above, as small as his hope that they might ever get past the past, they retraced their steps to Hyde Park.

The desk clerk at the Grand Hotel had kindly provided them with a picnic basket, into which they put their purchases: a jug of cider, two paper tricorns full of fried cod, roasted potatoes liberally sprinkled with salt and vinegar, a jar of pickled chestnuts—a favorite of Annabelle's—a pair of rosy-cheeked pippins, and two gingerbread men specially decorated to look like Royal Hussar.

Thus fortified, they made their way out of the melee, and across the park again, to the Serpentine, where the sharp crack of mock gunfire and small brass cannons booming sent birds winging.

They settled companionably in the grass, and made a feast of their provisions, avoiding the crowd at wa-

ter's edge as the miniature frigates floated grandly
down from the top of the Serpentine, and proceeded
to make war on one another.

The spectacle held their attention for some time,
but then Annabelle became fascinated with the faces
of the onlookers, marked by a variety of expressions
from avid interest to solemn melancholy.

Most of all she watched Lieutenant Forrester—
James, she must remember to think of him as James
now. He was no longer a lieutenant in silver-fronted
regimentals. He was a country gentleman, on brief sojourn in the city, before he closeted himself away in
the wilds of Yorkshire to tend his sheep.

And yet, there was a level of grim awareness as he
watched the ships on the Serpentine try to outmaneuver
one another, the English frigates far outnumbering the
French flying American colors. His experiences were betrayed in furrowed brow, and tight-set lips. He would
never be just a country gentleman. War had touched
him, marked his soul, made him wise beyond his years.
She wondered how it would have been had Archie
lived. Would he have returned a stranger? No longer
content with his old life? With her?

James turned to look at her, as if he felt the weight
of her thoughts. "What do you think?" he asked, all
grimness gone.

For her he put on a good face.

She smiled. She could keep up a brave front as well.
"I watch the crowd," she said. "So much of human
nature is revealed when they do not think they are
themselves watched."

"And what do you see in me?"

"That would be admitting I watch you."

"Do you not?" he asked in a teasing manner, brows
arching. He was a handsome young man, his face, his
presence dearer to her by the day. And they had spent
some part of almost every day together since his arrival. He had squired her to entertainments for the
brigade, to private parties celebrating the end of the

war. There was much talk of the coming peace talks in Versailles, of the anniversary of the Battle of the Nile, and the accession to the English throne of the House of Hanover. Fireworks and music were scheduled, plays and balls. Visiting dignitaries and the local street sweepers—all of London rejoiced.

"I was thinking," she said. "How much I dreaded this week. Our encounter."

His brows arched higher. His features came alive, boyish with curiosity. "Oh?"

"Yes. I expected the very worst. An emotional turmoil. A deep melancholy in the midst of everyone else's glee. And yet, you have made it bearable. My spirits are not downcast as I expected. You have, in fact, for quite some time, made this horrible turning point in my life less of a trial. Thank you."

"I am pleased to think I am in some way repaying a favor," he said.

She nodded, looked away, saddened. "To Archie," she said, wistfully.

He frowned, opened his mouth to say something, and closed it again as he rose to his feet. "Come! They have started the fireworks along the Kensington side. Let's leave this Serpentine massacre of innocents. They mean to end the thing with fireships taking the French, and I've little stomach to watch any more ships go up in flames, even pretend ones."

She took his hand when he offered to help her up, his hold firm, this brief contact a comfort. It brought with it a sense of security, a feeling that in the midst of chaos there was stability.

Gathering their belongings they set off arm in arm toward St. James's. "There is a pretty Oriental pagoda and bridge across the canal there," he said.

She fell into step beside him willingly, his legs, his stride, of a length that suited her own, different from Archie's. He had always seemed to be a step ahead, as though even in walking there was a competition to be won.

No competition here. She and James walked in companionable silence to the bridge, sharing occasional glances, laughing simultaneously at a duck that waddled across their path. She felt as if they had known each other forever.

The bridge was a fantasy of yellow and black paint and pretty Japanese lanterns like windblown flowers leading to the pagoda in the middle, tall and narrow with six sections, each growing smaller like a layer cake, each section iced by an upwardly curled blue lacquer roof.

It was on the bridge, as they stood staring down at the colorful reflection of the towering pagoda, that he said, "It is not Archie's favor I wish to repay with our outing today so much as it is yours."

His remark seemed as unreal as the rippled reflection of reality. "You confuse me," she said, turning to look at him, the light on the water below them casting his face in an unusual light that shimmered and changed as he spoke, as if he, too, were a chimera.

"What great favor have I done, to merit days of your undivided attention?" she asked.

His eyes locked on hers. Dark pools, shimmering with the reflection of the water below. "Your letters . . . They were far more important than you may imagine."

"To Archie?" she said.

His brow furrowed. "They kept Archie fighting, yes, but—" The furrow between his brows smoothed. His dark eyes sparkled as he said with surprising intensity, "You've no idea how welcome your words were, arriving as they did, almost every day—the voice of England—a breath of home."

"Such a sadness he is not with us here, today," she said.

Words died on his lips. The pucker returned to his brow. The light faded in his eyes. "But he is," he said, staring down into the water, the silk of his hair, like a curtain, hiding his expression. "In our thoughts, our memories. I feel as if would the water beneath us but hold still, we might see him clearly reflected there, standing between us." He pointed.

She studied their uneven reflection, half expecting to see Archie's familiar silhouette. But there was only a space and the reflection of a bit of blue sky, and what looked like disappointment in the reflected features of her companion.

Their gazes met by way of his dancing mirrored image.

"He would have liked the boats far more than I," he said, raking his hair away from his face with a gesture grown familiar. "The sound of gunfire and cannon always fired him with enthusiasm."

"Did it? Did he like battle?" She found the notion a matter of curiosity—and a trifle unsettling.

He nodded, as if it were not at all unusual. "He enjoyed a challenge, enjoyed leading others. He was a good captain to follow."

She had been drawn to Archie's robust enthusiasm from the start. He had been a neck-or-nothing rider, a first-over-the-fences hunter. He had always bagged more than his fair share of game, and yet, that he might relish the killing of men had never occurred to her. A disquieting thought.

"Any other man in the regiment would have left us to die," he said, dissipating her doubts. "I can never repay the debt I owe him."

She knew in that instant exactly why he spent so much time with her. If he could no longer repay Archie, she offered poor substitute.

And in that same instant she admitted to herself that she had hoped, had begun to believe their relationship grew out of something else, something separate from Archie.

It pained her to find herself mistaken.

The rest of the day passed pleasantly enough, and yet he could tell something had changed between them. She smiled as pleasantly and spoke to him as before, and yet there was a distance to the look in her eyes, a lack of depth to the subject matter she broached.

They ate dinner at the hotel, a wonderful meal prepared by the Grand Hotel's well-known French chef, Henri DuPré, before venturing into the park again to watch the staged production at the Castle of Discord.

It involved players and fire and fireworks and set scenes of destruction and battle that reached a smoky crescendo in which it seemed all was lost, the castle fallen.

The park was crowded, the tiered stadium seats erected for the performance filled to overflowing. More gathered on the green, jockeying for position that they might see better. A hush fell over the crowd as smoke billowed from the castle, and it appeared to be consumed in flame.

It was supposed the source of smoke and fire for the production had gone awry, producing far more of a cloud than was necessary, all of the actors, the castle itself, engulfed—obliterated.

Then the smoke cleared.

The castle had disappeared! In its place another structure stood, almost as large. A fanciful folly with column-framed arches, flowing fountains, mural-painted walls, a pinnacled tower, and a balconied gallery from which great clusters of flags waved.

There rose from the crowd a united sound of awe and delight and thunderous applause, and everyone moved forward, the better to view the transformation.

"The Temple of Concord," Annabelle said with a laugh, eyes sparkling with pleasure. "I read somewhere it took the work of fifty men behind the scenes to create that little bit of sleight of hand."

"Sleight of castle," James said, amazed and amused by the spectacle. "How did they do it?"

They passed beneath the shadow of one of the few great, old oaks in the park.

A sudden piercing whistle arced above their heads, and without thinking, the smell of smoke triggering instinct, he grabbed Annabelle's arm, roughly threw her to the ground, and himself atop her, his body shielding hers. A loud bang followed, as he had expected, but no earth-shaking explosion. Not rockets and mortar fire. The series of crackling pops was not gunfire but fireworks.

He could see the shower of gold, like falling stars in his eyes, as she lay looking up at him, as her chest rose and fell against his, her breath, warm against his cheek, smelling of apples and ginger. He thought of kissing her.

"Mr. Forrester," she said gently.

Her legs stirred beneath his, stirring him.

"Oh, God!" he whispered, humiliated. Clusters of people passed quite near them, some careful not to look, others openly staring.

"What have I done?" he gasped. He did not want to move, did not want to end this mistaken heaven of warm, solid contact with her, but neither did he wish to make a spectacle. "I thought . . ." He rolled away from her. "I do beg your pardon. I thought . . ."

She sat up, one gloved hand clasping his wrist, the other pressing finger to his lips, stilling the cascade of apology. "Shhh. I know. I know," she said.

Another pop. It seemed a white star exploded in each of her eyes, the brilliance from within. She gazed at him, not with revulsion, or offended honor, but with what looked like admiration.

"F-f-fireworks," he stammered.

A boom, another explosion of color against the sky, this one a tree, with twinkling green leaves.

"And you thought it the real thing," she said, "and tried to save me." She smiled, her teeth flashing in the darkness, her face illuminated faintly by a starburst of pink.

A flurry of crackling explosions, and color like a confetti of luminous roses, sprinkled the sky as she took the hand he offered and stood. "How wonderful!" she said, and he must agree, for it was not the sky she gazed at in saying so, but him, and in gaining her feet, she quickly planted a soft, apple-scented kiss upon his cheek.

The pagoda was burning. Not a staged fire, like the Castle of Discord, a real one. They could not walk the Oriental bridge and enjoy the fireworks display as she had suggested.

The fireworks were the problem. A stray Roman candle had taken a downward route. Now flames licked the highest curly lipped rooftop, scorching blue paint. Smoke smudged the sparkling sky.

A crowd gathered to watch from the ground beside the bridge, along the banks of the canal. Several boats in the water drifted close, the oarsmen's heads upturned, mouths agape. The pretty yellow pagoda became the next in a series of spectacles. It went up like a huge sparkler, cinders starring the sky, competing with the fireworks that continued to boom and glitter—a pretty backdrop for smoking destruction.

"Can nothing be done?" Annabelle asked.

"No," James said.

"A pity." She turned away, heart empty, a void within, her emotions wiped blank. She had cried herself out over more important matters. She had no more tears for the destruction of the prince's folly.

Only one regret. She would never again walk the bridge with James. A shame. She had, she realized, begun to think of it as their special place, fool that she was, believing he was interested in her, for her sake, not Archie's. She had kissed him! And enjoyed it.

But, with the smell of burning wood, with the ugly collapse of the burning folly, steam rising from the canal as bits of it fell into the water, dousing the flames, too late, reality took over. She realized she must steel her heart against foolishness, against her own loneliness and gratitude. This fine, dear young man who had quickly become so vital to her daily happiness hoped to wed another, a country girl who would learn to love sheep. She must remember that.

She must not put either herself, or him, in a position to suffer more heartbreak. Surely they had had their fair share.

He had become a fixture at her hotel. The staff knew him by name, from the lowliest scullery maid to the manager. The waiters in the dining room knew his tastes well enough to recommend certain dishes. The temperamental chef no longer complained when he asked for his sole broiled without the sauces DuPré took such pride in.

As they came to know him better, he felt her withdraw. Day by day, she pulled a little further away. He could not pinpoint exactly when, or why, but a door closed to him in her eyes. She no longer opened up the depths of heart and feeling to him, and no matter how hard he tried, he could not regain the ground that was lost.

He took her to the theater, to Astley's, to an opera. They walked in the parks, watched the kiosks disassembled, the burned mess of the Oriental bridge torn down, the frigates on the Serpentine carted away. It was as if the celebrations had been their tie, and daily the bonds unraveled.

She remained polite, cordial, pleasant—grateful. No more crying on his shoulder. No ore revelations about Archie. The distance between them yawned, a heartache.

His love for her did not falter, and yet he felt no urge to share his feelings, not when he had no indication they were in any way returned. He might have given up, gone to Yorkshire, to purchase the flock she asked him about more than once. But every so often, he caught her watching him, and in the instant that their eyes met he thought he caught a glimpse of such desire there, such sad longing, that he could not abandon all hope. Would not.

There was, too, a moment in the stairwell one evening, as he saw her to the door of her room.

The Grand Hotel possessed a grand stairway, as richly appointed as the rest of the hotel. Statues of scant-clad goddesses and decorative medallions manned by centaurs and Greek archers looked down on them. Doric columns, framing every doorway, had been painted so cleverly one was prepared to swear they were marble until one examined them closely. A gallery of windows at the top gave a glimpse of stars.

She outshone all of these beauties. And he had her, for the moment, all to himself. His voice echoed when she turned to him, her hand light as thistledown on his arm, and said, "Tell me more of her."

He thought for a moment she must mean the singer they had heard perform that evening.

"Your sweetheart," she said, catching him off guard, as she was wont to do, with the directness of the question, unprefaced by any warning she meant to broach such topic.

"What would you know?" he asked, surprised, and yet hopeful that this might be the doorway to possibility opening again.

"What made you fall in love with her? Is she pretty?" She paused in the window that looked out over the front door of the hotel, her face in profile, the night a frame. Lord, what a lucky man Archie had been, to win such beauty, such grace. What a fool to leave it.

"I fell in love with her sense of humor," he said. "Her way with words. The levelheaded turn of her thoughts. The positive way she went about her life. Her unfailing faithfulness."

"Stop," she said, hand raised, a wistful smile touching the tilt of her lips. "Sounds a paragon." She looked at him, indirectly, by way of his reflection in the windowpane.

*You are,* he almost blurted, but she gave him no opportunity.

"I mean to send you off in pursuit of her. Relieve you of all obligations to me." Turning to mount the remaining flight of stairs, she said, "I leave London the day after tomorrow."

The words echoed, the stairwell suddenly a cold, unfriendly place. He had dreaded this death knell to his hopes of convincing his love to love again. "So soon?"

She paused to look down at him, her left hand clutching the banister, the gold of her wedding ring glinting in the lamplight. So dear, her face, and yet so distant, as if she imagined already what she would do when she returned to the home she had shared with Archie. "I was sure you would be glad to be rid of me," she said.

*Two more days! Only two.* He had been foolish to let time slip through his fingers.

"I am sorry to hear it," he said. "What would you do in those two days? How might I entertain you?"

"Oh, but you need not feel obliged."

He hastened up the risers. "I can think of nothing I would rather do. Please, do not say this evening is good-bye."

She hesitated on the landing. "Oh, but surely we will meet again. You must invite me to your wedding."

"My wedding?" He chuckled bitterly. "But of course. Such was ever my intention."

Emotion flickered in her eyes. What emotion he could not divine.

"A walk in the park tomorrow? After noon?" he asked. "There is much I have yet to tell you."

Her head tilted, hair painted gold by the light from the arch that led to her floor. "Yes," she said with a decisive nod. "One last walk."

He came prepared to declare himself, given the slightest opportunity, and yet none came, though they spent the entire afternoon walking and talking uninterrupted, in the calm green of the park. She wore the same dress she had met him in, that first day—dark gray—trimmed in white lace. A gray straw bonnet covered the brightness of her hair. Her eyes seemed to lose much of their color in its shadow, going deep gray, and completely serious in their outlook.

Her manner matched her appearance. She seemed subdued, devoid of color, her voice not much given to enthusiasm, her lips unsmiling.

*I love you. Marry me!* He had rehearsed the words, but to utter them seemed hasty and inappropriate given that all she wanted to talk about, after more than a week of silence on the subject, was Archie.

He ached with the need to tell her, to explain his feelings and desires for their future together, but she seemed, more than ever, trapped in the past.

"I need to ask you some questions you may not wish to answer with regard to my husband's death," she said as the day wound down, the dinner hour fast approaching. "I beg you will answer them anyway."

The breeze caught at the brim of her bonnet. The sun glittered briefly on wisps of trapped gold. God help him, he could not stop staring at her, afraid this would be his last chance to look his fill.

She, on the other hand, seemed unwilling to look in his direction, gaze fixing, more often than not, on her feet, her hands, or the ground. Odd, he thought. She had always been unusually fascinated by their surroundings in the past, and the day was bright, the sky cloudless. There was much to observe in their ramblings.

"Ask away," he suggested.

She glanced up briefly, the shock of her gaze like a jolt of nearby cannon fire, deafening his senses to all else, rocking his equilibrium.

"Would you be so good as to describe what a typical day was like before he was injured," she began.

It was easy enough to oblige. He spoke of their

passage by boat, of the daily care and exercise of the horses, of the manner in which camps were set up and torn down and moved.

She asked him about their encounters with the locals, and how they obtained supplies. She asked for specifics about the food, and laundry, and even who had darned Archie's socks, a service he owned up to reluctantly.

"How did you meet my husband?"

He told her of the day he had been assigned to the captain, told her whatever she wanted to know without hesitation until she asked him, "What exactly were the nature of my husband's injuries?"

When he did not immediately open his mouth to respond, she said, "Please, Lieutenant Forrester, I need to know."

"Why?" he asked.

"Why not?"

"Archie preferred that you didn't."

She studied her feet for a moment, before she lifted her face to him, dear, beloved face, troubled now by a sorrow he could not begin to reach. "I've a ready imagination, sir, and it will not be still. I imagine the worst. I know it was bad. I must know how bad. The truth will trouble me far less than my suspicions."

"And if the truth is worse than you imagined?"

Her eyes widened, dark gray pools of bottomless anguish. "Was it?"

How could he begin to explain?

"You do not understand Archie's gift," he said.

"What?"

"Your not knowing. Your remembering him as he was, not what he became. That was important to him—vital. It kept his spirits intact, his pride alive."

"But he is dead now. Don't you see? His wishes were met. Now I would have questions answered."

"I do not see, at all. He would not have you suffer any more than his death, then or now. Is it not enough? Must you pick at the wound? It will only revive the pain, the suffering, slow the healing. Do you wish to go on hurting?"

"Lieutenant!" she gasped. "How dare you?"

"I dare, because *I* would not have you suffer. *I* wish your wounds to heal. I—" *I have good reason,* he almost said. *I love you. I want to build a future with you.*

But, she turned her back on him. "You will return me to the hotel now."

She was angry. The taut line of her jaw, the rigid stiffness of her spine, evidenced her pique.

"If you wish to go back," he murmured.

"I do," she said, voice brittle.

*More's the pity,* he thought, *when all I wish is to go forward.*

They smelled smoke on the wind before they were halfway across the park, and in the distance the bells of a water wagon clanged insistently. An ominous dark smudge stained the evening sky in the direction of the hotel.

"Fire!" she said, and broke into a run. "Hettie! Oh, God, Hettie!"

"Wait," he cried, running after her. "It is probably not the hotel."

He was wrong. It was.

Flames cast odd shadows off the shopfronts along Leinster Terrace. They lit the cluster of water wagons that jammed the road in the half-light of dusk in Queen's Garden Road with an unearthly orange glow.

"No!" Annabelle gasped. With a fresh burst of speed she ran toward the blaze, into a fearsome heat, crying, "Hettie! Hettie!"

James wound between the water wagons after her, dodging leather-booted firemen—at least three different brigades judging from the varied uniforms, red, green, and brown. They manned their pumps with a will, indeed, they seemed to be gaining on the fire. It had, in the very least, been contained, limited to the end of the hotel nearest the dining room, and the rooms above.

Her rooms! The windowsill was charred, the exterior columns scorched black. A frightful sight. He felt a knee-weakening surge of uneasiness to think Annabelle might have been in those rooms preparing for her journey!

He found Hettie before she did, spotted her among a group of stunned onlookers, mouths agape, watching the firemen.

He caught up to her easily enough, standing, face upturned to what had been her room, next to a bedraggled-looking couple, faces smudged with smoke, the woman clutching a dog, the man clutching the woman.

She was too shocked to notice them.

"Annabelle." He caught hold of her arm.

She whirled, cheeks tear-streaked, mouth shaking with grief. "My room! Do you see my room? Oh, God. Hettie!"

And with that, she burst into tears and flung herself against his chest.

"Hettie is fine, my love," he said, stroking the crown of her head, her hair like satin beneath his hand, the smell of burning all too familiar, rousing a bitter taste in his mouth, bitter memories. "Hettie is there, see?"

Her head rose to look. She stilled her crying, and yet he ached to see the sparkle of tears on her cheeks.

"The letters!" she moaned.

"Things," he said. "Just things."

"They can never be replaced," she said sadly, fresh tears flowing.

"Not his, no. But yours are safe."

"Mine?" She dug in her pocket for a handkerchief. As she pulled it forth something fell to the wet street with a clatter, and a tinkling of glass.

He bent to pick it up for her. A familiar gold watch. The glass face had shattered with the fall.

"Archie's watch!" she gasped. "Was it in my pocket all along?" She clutched at it like a lifeline.

"All is not lost," he said, glad for her. "The glass is easily replaced, and perhaps the chime can be fixed. You said it used to sing?"

" 'Love Will Find the Way.' " She dabbed her cheeks, smiling. "What a happy accident," she said. "What a happy, happy accident."

Hettie joined them then, crying, "Oh, marm. A dreadful thing, this. Is it not? How glad I am to see you safe with Mr. Forrester."

"Safe, yes." She nodded, her smile transforming into a puzzled awareness as she turned the cool blue-green of her eyes in his direction.

Hettie said, "I shall just go and check with Mr. Simmons, the manager, shall I, to see what is to be done in the way of accommodation for us tonight."

She left the two of them alone again, her mistress's attention never wavering. "You said my letters were safe?" she asked.

"Yes." He regretted telling her now. "I have them."

Still she appeared confused.

"Your correspondence to Archie."

"You kept them?" Her baffled look grew, her eyes searching his in a most penetrating manner.

He nodded. Was she angry? He could not tell in the dimming light. "Archie gave them to me." He wanted her to know. "He knew how much they meant to me."

"Gave them—to you? I—I do not understand."

"They are yours if you want them."

"I want . . ." The reflected glow of the ebbing fire was alive and heated in her eyes. He thought for a moment she might say—you. Instead, she said, "I want to know how much they meant to you. Why you kept them." He thought she held her breath, awaiting his answer.

She had him on the spot—offered the opportunity

he had waited for for so long. The heat in his cheeks was not merely that of the fire.

Courage, now, he thought with a laugh. He shook his head, and turned away an instant. The fire was dying, night closing in on them in the smell of damp ashes. Steam rose with a hissing noise from the areas where the bucket brigades still flung water. He cleared his throat and turned back to her.

"Your letters kept alive within me the embers of hope, of happiness, of all that is good and true within me. I feared war, and death, and the killing would douse my better self, and yet almost daily came your letters and fired me with hope for better things, a better place."

She blinked, and looked away with a confused expression.

He crooked a finger beneath her chin, lifting it, forcing her to look at him again. "I came to London with but one purpose," he admitted, voice low, as the last glowing embers smoldered and faded, plumes of smoke, and starlike ashes rising like little flumes of fireworks as the firemen took axes to fallen wood. "I came to meet you face-to-face, to return to you Archie's things, and to work up courage enough to tell you I love you."

He could say no more, dared no more.

Torches bobbed, scarring the growing darkness, bright as the hope within him.

"By way of the letters," she said quietly, starlight in her eyes.

"Yes." He leaned closer, determined to see what shone in her eyes for him. "Is there hope for me, Annabelle? Tell me there is."

She closed her eyes on more welling tears, pressing her lips together tightly before she said, so softly he must lean close to hear above the shouting of the firemen, the blows of their axes as they sought out the last remnant of heat.

Somewhere in the melee a dog barked.

It seemed an eternity of the two of them drowning in each other's eyes, before she leaned forward to whisper, "You gave me hope, when I had none. It is only fair I should give it back to you."

"Yes?" he asked, joy rising, and yet he was reluctant to give in completely.

"Your letters." Emotion changed her voice. "In the end, it was not Archie at all, was it?"

He frowned and shook his head. "I—"

"Walked with me through the valley—"

*Of the shadow of death,* he thought when she could not say the words.

"You lifted my spirits," she managed, "on the worst days, when I knew, deep in my heart, that Archie would not . . . was not—that I would never see him again." She sniffed, and this time her smile was genuine. "You must have this." She pressed the watch into his palm.

He laced his fingers through hers, the watch clasped between them. "I would have you," he leaned close to whisper. "Does Archie stand too much between us?"

"Archie?" She made a little noise deep in her throat. "I believe he planned this."

He laughed. He could not help himself. Too highly charged their conversation. His mood teetered between elation and despair. "He planned that I should fall in love with you?" he asked in disbelief.

She started to laugh, an expression not so much of amusement, as of her relief. "No. Yes. I don't know. All I know is that he spoke, briefly, before he left, of the potential of his death, when I gave him this watch."

She raised their hands, together, turning hers in such a way that the watch was revealed.

"No!"

"Yes. I . . . I did not want to hear it, but he insisted we must discuss it. He made me agree that I must marry again. That I seek, if not love, at the very least close companionship. He made me promise. He said I would know when the time was right."

He stared at their hands, at the watch in disbelief. "He made me promise to come to you."

"Did he?"

"Yes. Made me swear on a Bible."

"Dear Archie," she said.

"Dear Annabelle," he echoed.

She leaned forward to kiss him then, soft and quick, upon the cheek.

"Is it time, Annabelle?" he asked very quietly, his voice thick with emotion.

She smiled, her features soft, her eyes very dark, and she kissed him again for answer, this time her mouth against his.

He wrapped his arms about her as she did so, and would not let her go when she was done. Not that she really wanted to be let go.

"And will you marry me, Mrs. Grant?" he murmured as their lips parted. "And go with me to Yorkshire? I do not want to let you go."

And in his hand, without provocation, the watch began to chime "Love Will Find the Way."

He knew the words. They ran through his head as the high, sweetly tinny voice of the watch gave plinking sound to the notes. "Over the mountain, and over the waves, under the fountains, and under the graves . . ."

The chime stilled. Not another note forthcoming.

"Love will find out the way," he murmured.

With a glance heavenward she smiled, and said, "It would seem it is time, Mr. Forrester."

Time to shower her with kisses, he thought, and silently blessing his dear friend Archie, he swept the watch safely into his pocket, and Annabelle Grant once again into his arms.

# The Castaway
## by Anne Barbour

### 1

The carriage was very fine. The young woman perched stiffly on the edge of one of the plush seats glanced about her in appreciation. She removed one glove, neatly darned in several places, to draw her hand over a velvet curtain swagged across the window.

Idly, she ran her fingers over the modest carpetbag placed on the seat opposite her, pausing at the initials MF stitched near the top. Martha Finch. For how long, she wondered with a shiver of anticipation, would that be her name? If only she could convince Lord Branford of her credentials.

It wouldn't be an easy task, she reflected with a sigh. From what Seth Pinfold had told her, the earl was formidable—and suspicious. At least, she mused, trying to force herself into a more optimistic frame of mind, Lord Branford had sent this elegant vehicle for her, and provided for a comfortable, leisurely journey from York. She wondered what sort of hotel he had chosen for her lodging in London. Odd he would choose one so out of the way. She could well imagine his purpose in doing so, however.

Absently, she touched her hair, balled into a tight knot atop her head. Perhaps she should have lightened it. On the other hand, if she managed to keep her enterprise going, it might be difficult to apply lemon juice at frequent intervals, to say nothing of the evil-smelling chemicals suggested by the apothecary. At any rate, it might be supposed that the golden curls of a small girl would later darken to an indeterminate brown.

The carriage slowed and Martha looked out the window once more. They had turned off the Bayswater Road and were pulling up before a large edifice, obviously new and intimidatingly stylish. Bas-relief columns, interspersed with Grecian medallions, embellished the front of the building. Emblazoned just beneath the pediment over the door were the words GRAND HOTEL. Minions in livery bustled about the entrance; one of them scurried to let down the carriage steps and fling open the door almost before the carriage had drawn to a halt.

The footman, poised to assist Martha, halted suddenly to gape at her in surprise. He drew himself up to ask in a supercilious tone, "Are you a guest of the hotel, then—ma'am?"

Putting out her hand, Martha replied calmly, "Yes. I believe I am registered—as the guest of the Marquess of Canby. I understand that Lord Branford made the arrangements."

At this, the footman's eyes fairly bulged. Recovering himself, he assisted Martha from the carriage with a flourish and issued instructions to another underling as to the disposition of madam's luggage.

Straightening her skirts, Martha reflected ruefully that she could not blame the footman for his misperception. The sort of young woman who might patronize the Grand Hotel would certainly not arrive sans abigail and dressed in a plain gown of cheapest muslin. In addition, the sort of young woman who might be presumed to be under the protection of Lord Branford would not, in all probability, be tall and plain and thin as a bedpost.

She sighed. None of that could be helped. At least, Lord Branford was familiar with her station in life and

would expect nothing more than her very undistin-
guished person.

Drawing herself up, she swept into the lobby of the
hotel. She refrained from gaping at the grandeur about
her, but walked swiftly to the desk. There, a middle-
aged gentleman of sober mien, his thinning hair
brushed back severely, greeted her. When she gave
him her name, he bowed courteously.

"Of course, Mrs. Finch, we have been expecting
you. I am Mr. Simmons, the hotel manager. Your suite
is ready. If you will follow me?"

Martha said nothing, merely nodding regally. Mr.
Simmons led her across an expanse of thick blue carpet to a broad staircase that led upward in a lavish
sweep.

Martha was by now thoroughly awed by her surroundings, but she stiffened her back. She must assert
her right to take her place in these exalted surroundings.

Martha followed Mr. Simmons up the stairs. At the
top, he led her through a corridor embellished with
Greek statuary. He paused at a door, painted a rich
cream, and knocked discreetly.

Martha held her breath at the sound of soft footfalls
on the other side of the door, but the figure who
swung the door wide was obviously not the Earl of
Branford.

"You must be Martha Finch!" exclaimed the plump,
middle-aged woman who confronted her. Mr. Simmons stepped aside to allow Martha to enter the
room, and bowed himself away.

Martha scarcely noticed his departure, her attention
wholly on the woman who ushered her unceremoni-
ously into the room.

"I am Carolyn Coppersmith," she announced, smiling a welcome. "I am to be your companion during
your stay here." She hesitated a moment. "I believe
it is *Mrs.* Finch, is it not?"

Martha nodded, smiling. "Yes, Mrs. Matthew Finch. My husband passed away two years ago."

Mrs. Coppersmith's returning smile was warm and sympathetic. "I'm so sorry. I, too, am a widow. It's been twenty-five years since I lost my Roger." She did not wait for a response from Martha, but turned to a young maidservant who had entered the room. "Peters, take Mrs. Finch's things. I'm sure her luggage will be up in a few moments. And I think we'd like a nice cup of tea." To Martha she said, "Do come and sit down. You must be exhausted."

Martha, mentally reviewing her pampered journey from York, smiled. "Thank you," she murmured, accepting Mrs. Coppersmith's gesture toward a cherry-striped satin settee. "You're very kind."

She glanced about. "Is Lord Branford—?" she began.

"Branford will be so sorry you arrived ahead of him," interposed her new companion. "He should be here momentarily. In the meantime—"

She was interrupted by a peremptory knock on the door. The young maid, Peters, who had returned to the room a moment earlier scurried to open it and was almost flung aside by the gentleman who strode into the room.

Watching him as he mouthed a brusque apology to the maid, Martha reflected that it was as though she observed the advent of a force of nature. The Earl of Branford was not overly tall, nor was he extraordinarily large, and he certainly could not have been described as handsome. His features were harsh and his nose was large and shaped rather like a scimitar. It had apparently been broken at one time, for it seemed to change course midway down its impressive length, curving to a blade-edged hook at the end. Despite these flaws, however, he was—well, magnificent. There was an energy about him and an air of command that was both compelling and a little frightening. His eyes were dark and brilliant and penetrating, and above

them, black brows lifted in a straight, heavy slash
toward his temples. His hair, also black, and thick as
coal dust, was neatly trimmed and shorter than the
current fashion.

The carelessness of his clothing almost proclaimed
him a Corinthian. However, his fawn pantaloons and
his coat of Bath superfine were expertly tailored, and
he wore them with an offhanded elegance.

His gaze swept past the maid and Mrs. Coppersmith
and, like a falcon sizing up its prey, focused on
Martha.

"Mrs. Finch, I presume?" he asked in crisp, well-
modulated tones.

Drawing a deep breath, Martha rose, extending
her hand.

Gabriel Storm, the fourth Earl of Branford, stood
at the door for a moment, surveying the woman who
approached him so calmly. Good God, Wister had described her as a tall, thin nonentity! Was the man
blind? To be sure, she was somewhat on the spare
side. Her light brown hair strayed in untidy wisps from
the unfashionable knot that sprouted from the top of
her head like a belligerent mushroom. However, she
stood tall and proud as a goddess. Her eyes, large and
luminous, were extraordinarily expressive. He thought
he saw a hint of apprehension there, as well as humor
and an unexpected intelligence. Her gaze was calm
and assessing. For a single, uncomfortable moment, he
felt it was he on trial here, rather than the woman
before him, who, all his instincts told him, must be
an adventuress.

"Branford!" exclaimed Mrs. Coppersmith, hurrying
to him with outstretched arms. "It is so lovely to see
you again. I want to thank you for suggesting me to
Canby for this position." She refrained from actually
embracing the earl, perhaps because he had stiffened
so alarmingly at her approach, but she grasped one of
his hands in both of hers. "And what splendid accommodations you have procured for us." She gestured

toward Martha. "Mrs. Finch arrived a few moments ago, and we were just introducing ourselves."

Another knock at the door heralded the arrival of a servant with a tea cart, complete with an impressive silver service and plates of sandwiches and cakes. While Mrs. Coppersmith dealt with this largesse, Branford moved to Mrs. Finch and, nodding for her to be seated, settled himself beside her.

"I trust you had a pleasant journey," he murmured in a noncommittal tone.

"Yes," replied Mrs. Finch, smiling slightly. "I must thank Lord Canby when I meet him for making sure my journey was such a comfortable one, and, of course," she added hastily, "for Mrs. Coppersmith."

Her voice was pleasant, noted Bran. She spoke in low, well-modulated tones. Hmm. Hadn't she claimed to have been raised in a fishing village? Contemplating her words, he grinned. Was Mrs. Finch throwing down the gauntlet with this subtle assumption that she would, of course, be meeting the marquess in the near future? Or was it merely an expression of her disappointment at not being invited to Canby House in the first place? Lord, if it had been up to the old man, the female would have been ushered into his best guest chamber upon receipt of Wister's report. It had taken all Bran's powers of persuasion to induce the marquess to follow a more circumspect path.

At Mrs. Coppersmith's direction, the tea apparatus was set out on a marble-topped table near the settee, and the next few minutes were occupied in pouring, stirring, and passing the exquisitely thin sandwich and cake plates.

Conversation was general during this ritual, dealing with the extraordinary expansion of London in the last few years, the marvels of the peace celebration, and the notables who had come to participate in the festivities. Bran noted, again with some surprise, that Mrs. Finch seemed to know her way around a tea table. She ate with delicacy and spoke quietly and with sense. When the cups had been drained, however, and the last sandwich lay curling on its plate, he turned purposefully toward her.

She obviously knew what he was going to say. He watched in amusement as her hand hovered for a moment over the sandwich. Under his gaze, she phased the movement into a genteel brushing of her lips with the tip of one finger. She stared straight into his eyes and straightened her shoulders as though readying herself for battle.

"Now, tell me, Mrs. Finch," he began, as one opening the first salvo in a skirmish, "why I should present you to the Marquess of Canby as his long-lost granddaughter."

2

Martha stared at Lord Branford as he continued meditatively.

"There have been many claims over the years by enterprising young women claiming to be Lady Felicity Marshall, granddaughter of the Marquess of Canby, miraculously rescued from the sea some twenty years ago—under unvaryingly dramatic circumstances, I might add. These claims have, not unexpectedly, also proved unvaryingly false. It is almost certain that Felicity perished in the same boating accident that claimed the lives of her father, the marquess's heir, and her mother. Stewart, the Benningtons' son, escaped the tragedy since he was visiting friends when the rest of his family embarked on their yachting vacation. The bodies of the other shipwreck victims were recovered, but Felicity was never found. Hope dies hard, and the old gentleman has never ceased his search.

"Lord Canby is a very old and valued friend. Eventually, the steady stream of claimants to his fortune and his affection—primarily the former, I must say—

became too much for him, and he asked me to represent him in filtering out those whose claims were patently false. Thus, Mrs. Finch," he concluded colorlessly, "while I am willing to listen to your no doubt touching story, I make no promise that you will ever come to Lord Canby's personal attention."

Lord Branford gazed at Mrs. Finch, assuming an expression of bored expectancy.

For a long moment, Martha remained perfectly still, her rigidly controlled features revealing nothing of her inner chaos. Lord Branford had made every effort to put her at a disadvantage. Despite this, oddly, she stood in no fear of him. On the contrary. From her first sight of his forbidding countenance, she had felt— she could find no other words to describe the sensation—a peculiar bond. It was as though something in her recognized and cherished something compelling in his makeup.

She shook herself. This was no time for such nonsense. Her moment had come. The moment for which she had so carefully prepared. She opened her mouth, knowing that the next few minutes would decide her fate for the rest of her life.

"My lord," she began slowly. "I do not claim to be the marquess's granddaughter. I say only that I might be. I have come because I am searching for myself— for my history, that is. When I heard recently that the Marquess of Canby has been searching for his relative for a number of years, and when I discovered the circumstances in which she was lost to him, the possibility occurred to me that the son and daughter of the Marquess of Canby were my parents."

"I am pleased, Mrs. Finch, that your motives are pure." The earl crossed his booted legs. "Pray continue."

Martha flushed, and lifted her chin.

"I have no recollection of my infancy. My earliest memory is of waking one morning on the beach after a storm at sea. I was about six years old, and I lay in the remains of a small boat, having been secured there with a rope. I was wrapped in a fine shawl embroidered with the initials 'FEM.' Around my neck I wore a silver locket, containing portraits of a dark-haired man, and a woman with fair hair. Both were elegantly dressed.''

" 'FEM,' " murmured Lord Branford, brushing a bit of lint from his sleeve. "Felicity Elizabeth Marshall. Most affecting. It does seem odd, though, that a small child would have been placed, unattended, in a lifeboat.''

Martha felt beads of perspiration break out on her forehead. She had known this would be difficult, but she had underestimated the earl's antipathy. She drew a deep breath.

"Yes. It was thought that perhaps one or both of my parents had embarked in the boat with me, but were washed overboard. At any rate," she continued hastily, "I was found by Josiah Sounder. Josiah was a fisherman who lived with his wife, Margaret, some distance from the village of Tenaby, which lies on the North Sea some forty miles north of Scarborough. They had both yearned for children for some years, so they made little effort to discover my identity. I became their daughter.

"Fishing was the village livelihood, and in the years following my rescue, I helped Josiah in that pursuit, or busied myself with chores about the cottage. Josiah and Margaret were elderly and lived some distance from the village. They kept to themselves. Margaret died when I was twelve, and Josiah did not live long after her death. I left the village then. I decided to make my way to London and I earned money for my journey in stages. I worked in a variety of employment along the way.'' She smiled tentatively. "Extremely menial employment—mostly as a scullery maid in various inns. I would work at one place until I had enough money to move on.''

"Why did you wish to go to London?"

"I don't know. I suppose, like so many others, I thought of London as a font of riches for someone who possessed a modicum of intelligence and a willingness to work hard. I had visions in my head of finding employment in a noble house where I might work my way up from scullery maid to housekeeper."

"Or perhaps to catch the eye of a wealthy protector?"

Martha stared in affront. "Had that been my goal," she snapped, "I did not lack the opportunity. However, though I was open to almost any sort of employment, I drew the line at renting out my body."

For a moment, a startled flash leaped into the earl's dark eyes. "My apologies," he said, his lips twitching.

"As it happened," she continued stiffly, "I never did reach London. In fact, it took me about a year just to get as far as York. I was fourteen, and work was hard to find there."

She closed her eyes for a moment against the memory of endless hours trudging the streets of the city, accepting rejection with the little dignity remaining to her. How many nights had she returned, cold and shivering, to a ragged nest created in a doorway or a stairwell? She had lived by her wits, stealing food and evading the attentions of the many predators who prowled the malodorous streets of this major metropolis.

She drew a deep breath and continued. "I was fortunate at last to find a position as kitchen maid in the house of a rising merchant. I did my best, and my work pleased the Murchisons' cook. She was a kind woman, and when a position of upstairs maid became vacant, she recommended me. I became friends with another maid—a young woman who acted as abigail for the daughter of the house. I learned from her the duties of a lady's maid, and filled in for her several times when she became ill and could not work."

Martha lifted a hand to her eyes. "The poor girl died of the white sickness when I was seventeen, and I was chosen to become Miss Emily's abigail."

"You seem to have been greatly favored by circumstances, Mrs. Finch." There was nothing but a sort of remote curiosity in his voice, and Martha felt herself bristle.

"I have found, my lord, that circumstances are what you make of them, and any favor I found came through my own endeavor."

"Now, that I have no difficulty in believing."

The implication of this statement was not lost on Martha, and a tide of heat rose to her cheeks once more.

"At any rate, when I was nineteen I met Matthew Finch, who owned a bookshop in St. Martin's Lane, not far from the river. He was a fine man, and not long afterward, he asked me to be his wife. I was widowed when I was two and twenty."

She twisted her hands in her lap and felt compelled to speak once more to forestall the comment she saw forming on his lordship's lips.

"Perhaps I should mention here that Mr. Finch was in his sixties when we married. No, it was not what would one could call a love match—although I did love him—very much. He was a good husband, and—" Her voice caught. "I grieved at his passing."

Lord Branford yawned. "I suppose you did."

Bran closed his mouth immediately, rather shamefaced. That was not well done of him. Though he might think her story a tissue of lies from start to finish, he had been able to ascertain before he met her that she was, indeed, a widow. As such she might well grieve for a husband, elderly or no, and he had no right to belittle her loss. He found he was having a difficult time maintaining his skepticism with this woman. She was vastly appealing and a peculiar recognition of spirit tugged at him. He almost felt as though she were a dear friend, unrecognized but returned to him after a long absence.

What nonsense. He straightened in his seat.

"And now you find yourself without a provider," he said.

He observed with some amusement the growing anger that Mrs. Finch was unable to hide beneath her supplicant exterior.

"I have no need for a provider," she replied austerely. "Mr. Finch left the bookshop to me and I have been running it since his death."

"I see." Bran shifted in his chair. "It has been a pleasure making your acquaintance, Mrs. Finch. However, I must say you have shown me no evidence other than a story that could have been made up of whole cloth to indicate that you are Felicity Marshall. Therefore, I think it is time to bring our interview to a close."

If he expected his statement to discommode Mrs. Finch, he was doomed to disappointment.

"But what if I did not make it up?" she asked reasonably. "What if it is all true? Do you not think it is up to the Marquess of Canby to accept or dismiss what I have to say? It seems to me, my lord, that it behooves you to let him make that decision."

"Of course you would think that," Bran retorted somewhat waspishly. This female had an extraordinary gift for bringing out the worst in him, he reflected. "You mentioned a locket," he said after a moment. "I suppose that was conveniently lost during your travails."

Mrs. Finch said nothing, but smiled sweetly as she reached for her reticule.

3

Martha struggled to conceal her exultation as she picked up her reticule. From it she produced a tiny bit of silver, which she handed to the earl.

"Yes, my lord," she murmured. "The locket is still in my possession, though I had some difficulty in keeping it all these years." Tears stung her eyes as she recalled the tenacity with which she had clung to the keepsake. She'd made up stories in her head about the people in the portraits, creating elaborate fantasies in which she became a beloved daughter, the center of their doting attention.

Martha observed the surprise in Lord Branford's dark eyes, and watched, scarcely daring to breathe, as he turned the little silver scrap over in his fingers before opening it.

For a moment, Bran said nothing, merely gazing at the two miniatures, his expression shuttered. He did not recognize the small piece of jewelry, but he knew the two faces as well as he knew those of his own parents. Much better, in fact. He had tried for so long not to think of his parents at all that now his memories of them were faded and fragmented. He turned hastily to his perusal of the portraits. They were copies of two larger works that hung in the family gallery at Canby Park, in Bedfordshire. The subjects were the Earl and Countess of Bennington, the son and daughter-in-law of the Marquess of Canby. Bran concealed his surprise, telling himself it was more than likely that the Widow Finch had purchased the locket in a bits and pieces shop, perhaps some years ago. On discovering the identities of the pair pictured inside, she had seized the opportunity to make her claim.

Staring at the two smiling faces, Bran was struck with his own memories. Memories of Canby Park, and in the background, a small, vivacious girl, busy about her own pursuits. Felicity. A golden-haired cherub— an imperious, brown-eyed imp—a mischievous whirlwind—a demure tyrant. A plaguey nuisance, he and Stewart called her, through privately Bran adored her. Felicity returned his affection, following him about like an engaging puppy. When she was five she announced to Bran that he must not seek a bride when

he grew up, for she intended to marry him herself.
Ten-year-old Bran, scoffing loudly, secretly tucked
away her promise, building dreams of a family that
would be his alone.

Bran glanced up to observe Mrs. Finch gazing at
him, a flicker of hope shimmering in her expressive,
brandy-colored eyes. Felicity Marshall's eyes? He
shook himself. Lord, he was becoming as maudlin on
the subject as the old gentleman. He became aware
of a sense of danger emanating from the slender figure
opposite him. This was perfectly absurd, of course, yet
he felt somehow threatened by that wispy sense of
recognition and by the fleeting vulnerability he saw in
a woman who seemed to wear her self-possession like
a steel cage.

"And the fine woolen shawl?" Branford asked
casually.

"N-no," Martha stammered. "It was stolen from me
in the very first inn where I worked."

Bran noted the tears that glistened briefly in her
eyes. A nice touch that, he noted sourly. Stolen, indeed. Lord, there was certainly very little to indicate
that she was anything but an enterprising bookshop
owner from York. Bah! If it were up to him, he would
send her packing, along with her false pretensions and
her pretty, wistful manner. Unfortunately, it was not
his decision. He stood.

"Very well, Mrs. Finch. Lord Canby wishes very
much to see you, and you have told me nothing so far
to prevent me bringing you to him. He will meet with
you this evening."

Martha almost cried out in her relief. Instead, she
nodded serenely. She came to her feet, as well, holding
her hand out to the earl. For a moment, he stared
blankly at the extended hand.

"You are left-handed," he said colorlessly.

Martha knew a moment of panic. Oh, Lord, she had
not thought of that. Had she ruined everything?

"Felicity was left-handed," the earl continued, still in that toneless voice.

Martha sagged in relief. She cast her thoughts briefly to Mary. Dear Lord, her acquaintance with the child had been too brief to notice such a detail.

"I shall leave now," Lord Branford said coldly, "and return at six o'clock this evening. We will take an early supper here at the hotel before setting off for Canby House. Will that be acceptable?"

Martha nodded. "Of course. But—" she added quickly, "my locket!"

The earl frowned as though she were a street beggar who had just importuned him for a coin. "It will be returned to you after the marquess has had an opportunity to examine it. In addition," he continued in a slightly softer tone, "on my way here this afternoon I heard two maids gossiping in the corridor about jewel thefts that have apparently occurred here in the hotel. Your locket will be safer in my keeping."

He bowed slightly to her and to Mrs. Coppersmith, he snatched up his hat, gloves, and walking stick and left the room.

To Martha, it seemed as though the room expanded at his departure, and grew somehow dimmer, though the sun still streamed through the tall windows of the sitting room. She sank back into her chair, exhausted.

"There now!" exclaimed Mrs. Coppersmith. "Was that not a comfortable coze? Such a charming young man, do you not agree?"

Martha could have laughed. Charming? To her, the man seemed part ogre, part jungle predator, and part immovable object. The unexpected attraction she felt for him was threatening, for he was dangerous and hostile, and posed a threat to her immediate future. She could only pray she would have better luck with the old marquess.

Mrs. Coppersmith rose. "I am so anxious for us to talk together, as well, for I very much wish us to be friends, but I shall let you rest now."

Rising, she led Martha into an elegant little dressing room, from which could be seen an airy bedchamber.

"When you wake, ring for Peters and she will help you with your preparations. You have plenty of time for a nice long nap."

She hesitated for a moment, then pressed a soft kiss on Martha's cheek before hurrying from the room. Martha, unfastening the muslin gown, moved into the bedchamber.

Never had she been surrounded by such luxury. She pulled off her serviceable shoes and lisle stockings and padded barefoot toward the bed. Her toes curled in the thick softness of the carpet and her gaze traveled over furnishings of heretofore unimagined elegance. Besides the bed, the chamber contained a dressing table, a Grecian reclining couch, and several scroll-backed chairs.

Sighing, she lay down and stared up at the richly designed bed canopy. If all went well, this sort of luxury would form her milieu for the rest of her life. She would be done with pinching pennies, days with only a scrap of bread for dinner. She closed her eyes. The first thing she would do after being installed at Canby House as Lady Felicity Marshall would be to order roast beef for dinner every night. With good wine to go with it. No watered beer for her ladyship! Then, she'd have some of those little cakes she'd seen in pastry shops, all covered with colored icings. In the summer, she'd cool her tongue with sherbets and in winter she'd warm herself with hot, spiced punch. She would— She stopped abruptly. Good Lord, she'd better stop thinking about her belly and concentrate on her strategy. She had a long way to go before she'd have the ordering of dinner at Canby House.

She contemplated the forthcoming meeting with the Marquess of Canby. Seth Pinfold had told her that over the years the old man had become almost obsessed with discovering his granddaughter's whereabouts. Without his young friend, the Earl of Branford, to protect him, he would have embraced the first claimant to come down the pike, an enterprising actress, according to Pinfold, whose story had proved to be as full of holes as Martha's oldest pair of drawers.

Her own background, she thought with some complacency, should hold up under any but the most intense scrutiny. She had told the truth—in the most part—to Lord Branford. She'd merely left out one critical fact. She had, she told herself, a perfectly legitimate right to declare herself the granddaughter of the old marquess. One could almost say she was doing the man a favor. He wanted a granddaughter. Martha Finch stood ready to assume that position.

Her eyelids grew heavy and her breathing deepened. After four days spent in relative idleness of travel in a well-sprung coach, she should not be tired, but she felt drained, as though her carefully contrived design was a leech, fastening to her flesh and gathering nourishment from her life's blood. Just before she sank into sleep, however, an image floated from the back of her mind. A small face and fine curls, bright as fairy gold falling over a pale forehead. Dear God—Mary.

"Mary. Please forgive me, little one," she whispered. "I do you no wrong—and you know I would have . . ." Her voice trailed off and she slipped into the blessed darkness of sleep.

4

"My boy, it is she! It must be she!" cried the Marquess of Canby.

Bran stood in the center of Lord Canby's study, an elegant but comfortable chamber that featured roomy leather armchairs glowing with the patina of age, and several massive tables littered with pictures, mementos, and items of everyday life. Canby House itself was a sedate mansion set in Grosvenor Square, and had been in the family's possession since the first development of Mayfair some two hundred years ago.

Though approaching his seventieth year, the Marquess of Canby stood straight and tall, his silver hair still waving luxuriantly. At the moment, he was nearly dancing about the room in his delight, and watching him, Branford thought his heart might break. He loved this old man more than anyone else on earth. Certainly more than his own parents. He shrugged. Perhaps he could not fault his father and mother for busying themselves so thoroughly in their own pursuits. Even the servants had virtually ignored him. It was Lord Canby and his family who had taken note of his unprepossessing self and seen the boy beneath, lonely and unloved. Bran had grown up more on the adjoining Canby estate than his own. The sun seemed to shine with more warmth there, and the sound of laughter filled his heart.

His throat tightened now as he strove to answer the old gentleman. How many times had the marquess reacted in just this manner to the news that another female had turned up, declaring herself to be Felicity Marshall? It was always like this. The marquess's hopes would flare almost to combustion point, only to be dashed on the rocks of reality when the claimant invariably proved to be an unscrupulous confidence artist.

Branford sighed. "It is, of course, possible that Mrs. Finch is the genuine article, sir, but we must proceed cautiously."

"Bah! How could she *not* be Felicity. Look at the locket!" He waved the bit of silver in the air. "I recognized it immediately. I gave it to the little darling on her fifth birthday. Do you not—? No, I don't suppose you would remember, but—"

"Sir, the woman could have picked up the locket almost anywhere."

"Good God, boy!" the marquess exclaimed impatiently. "Why are you always so pessimistic?" He halted abruptly, his shoulders sagging. "All right, Bran. I know I have leaped to unwarranted conclusions in the past. If it were not for you, we would have some scheming adventuress installed here as my granddaughter. But," he continued pleadingly, "this does not mean that the Finch woman is not Felicity. It seems to me, despite your arguments to the contrary, the locket is quite conclusive. And what about the shawl?"

"I think, sir, that we may safely conclude that the shawl is a convenient fabrication—no pun intended."

"Possibly," responded the marquess with a sigh. "But, still—Jennifer frequently embroidered monograms on the children's clothing. And Mrs. Finch is left-handed! In addition," continued the old man hastily as Bran opened his mouth, "Wister told us she is the right age. Tell me more about her. What does she look like? Is she pretty? Does she have brown eyes the color of a pansy's heart? Felicity's hair was the most beautiful gold—like that of an angel, I always told her. Does—?"

"No. Mrs. Finch has light brown hair. And no—" Branford frowned. "She is not pretty. I would call her attractive, rather—or at least she would be if she were not so—scrawny—and did not pull that brown hair back in a ridiculously tight bun. Her eyes are a sort of coffee brown—though sometimes they seem more amber—like brandy." Branford halted abruptly, reddening. "She is tall and thin," he concluded colorlessly.

"Well, of course she would be tall, would she not? Ben was well above average height—and Jennifer was willow-slim. And Stewart was tall as well." The old man's eyes glistened suddenly. "When he went off to war, he topped—oh, God, Branford, if only he had listened to me. I begged him not to go a-soldiering. 'Leave it to others.' I said. 'There are plenty of young men who have no responsibilities at home.' But he was army mad, and he didn't listen. He never listened, did he? And he never returned." He extended a shaking hand to Branford, who grasped it convulsively.

"I, too, tried to dissuade him, sir," he whispered. "But Stew never followed aught but his own drumbeat."

The marquess straightened and cleared his throat. "So, she has brown hair. I think that's a good sign, don't you?"

"I beg your pardon?"

"Well, Felicity's hair color as an infant is well known. If Mrs. Finch were a fraud with brown hair, surely she would have dyed it."

"With all respect, sir," Branford responded austerely. "It is difficult to dye one's hair convincingly, and it requires constant attention once one has done so. I'm sure Mrs. Finch has considered that Felicity's golden curls might well have faded to a sort of light, wheaten brown."

The marquess nodded reluctantly. "You are right, of course, I should have learned my lesson by now, after all the disappointments. I don't understand," he mused softly, "how anyone can be so cruel as to engage in such a pretense. To embark deliberately on such a fraud, knowing the heartache that will result when the hoax is penetrated."

Branford sighed once more.

"I can only say, my dear sir, that I wish you had not bruited it about so publicly that once having Felicity restored to you, you would make her your heiress. You are an extraordinarily wealthy man, after all, and only a small portion of that wealth is entailed. In fact, your heir will be left with little besides the title and Canby Park—and this house, of course. A not insignificant portion, but—"

The marquess waved an impatient hand. "My nephew will do well enough. In any case, I am not

concerned with him. It is of Felicity I wish to talk. I
am anxious to see her."

"I plan to give her an early dinner at the hotel, and
then I shall bring her here."

"Excellent. How do you find the hotel, by the by?
Is it acceptable? I would much rather you had put her
up at Grillon's or the Pulteney, but—" He interrupted
himself hastily. "Yes, very well. I can see the wisdom
of keeping her in a more out of the way spot until we
verify her bona fides."

"The hotel is all one could wish, sir. It positively
reeks of *tonnish* excess, and the clientele seem entirely
unexceptionable."

"Good-bye, then," said Lord Canby, walking with
Branford to the door of the study. "I shall see you
later this evening."

As Bran made his way back to his lodgings in Duke
Street, his thoughts were full of the enigmatic Mrs.
Finch. He wished she were not so compelling, with
her earnest air of candor and her extraordinarily expressive eyes. Yes, their color did resemble the velvety
heart of a pansy, he reflected, and it had seemed to
him he had observed in them flashes of pain when she
talked of her past. He wished that irritating sense of
connection with her would go away. She was not what
he would call diffident, for her demeanor was composed. Yet she did not push herself forward. Was this
merely a masterpiece of strategy, or was she truly only
interested in discovering her true background?

The vision of the vibrant, golden-haired child
flashed before him once more.

*"When you are grown, you will* not *marry anyone
but me! Now you must kiss me good night, for Nurse
will be coming for me soon."*

Her lips had been warm, her arms around him were
soft, and she smelled of warm milk and daisies.

Bran sighed. He might find Mrs. Finch's motives
highly suspect, but he was somewhat unnerved at the
desire she had created in him to believe her.

5

Martha sat stiffly on the edge of her chair in the dining room of the Grand Hotel, feeling very much like a frowsy brown sparrow in a room full of peacocks. As thickly carpeted and as elegantly furnished as the rest of the hotel, the chamber provided an appropriate setting for birds of luxurious plumage. She told herself that no one was taking any notice of her, but she expected at any moment that some person in authority would sweep down to order her immediate removal from the sanctified precincts of this haunt of the *ton*.

Not that such an outrage would likely be visited upon a guest of the Marquess of Canby. Or his surrogate, the Earl of Branford. She would be allowed to remain unmolested, but made to feel the veriest interloper under stares of contemptuous indifference from the other patrons. Chief among these, of course, was the earl himself.

For the first several minutes after she was served a portion of tasty, tender cutlets, smothered in an indescribably delicious sauce, she addressed herself solely to its consumption. When she looked up, she found the earl gazing on her in startled bemusement. She flushed, realizing the picture she must present of a starving street urchin. It had been a long time since she had eaten to her fill.

"It's very good," she remarked brightly, gesturing with her fork.

"Yes, though the hotel is quite new, the chef here has already made a reputation for himself as a premier artist with spatula and spoon. French, of course, and, I hear, wildly temperamental. And now," he continued, "do tell me about your life in the fisherman's cottage."

Martha provided him with details of that brief, idyllic time in her life. "My days were busy," she concluded. "In addition, Margaret, who could read and write, taught me my letters."

Bran watched her narrowly. She certainly appeared to be telling the truth. In any case, her story could be easily verified by the agent he had sent to the village of Tenaby. He pictured her as a child. Despite her description of sunny days on the seashore, life would have been hard and lonely for the child of fisherfolk scrabbling for a living on the isolated shores of the North Sea. Had her hair been golden then? He started, aware that she was speaking to him.

". . . but how is it that you became such close friends with the marquess?"

Clever minx. He did not thwart her transparent attempt to turn the subject, but answered easily. "I believe I mentioned that his grandson, Stewart—Felicity's brother—and I grew up as best friends. We were constant companions as striplings, and went to both Eton and Oxford together. Later, we spent the requisite period idling about London at great expense to my parents and his grandfather respectively. Stewart was a hey-go-mad youth, always ripe for any spree. After the loss of his father at sea, he was, of course, Canby's heir—and the light of the old gentleman's life. After Stewart left for the Peninsula, the marquess lived most of the time in London, in Canby House. I visited him there often. We would talk of Stew for hours, comparing notes from the letters he sent.

"When Stewart was killed, I thought for a while the old man would succumb as well, for he lost all desire to live. He returned to Canby Park and became a virtual recluse. I had returned to my own home, Winstead Priory, after I acceded to the title. I spent as much time as I could with the marquess. He was always available for advice on the management of my estate, which I appreciated greatly. My father—" Bran paused. "My father had taken little care that I be made familiar with the running of the Priory, and later, as young men will, I had found life in Town much more worthy of study."

Bran had been gazing down at his plate as he talked, his mind many miles and many years away, but now he looked up suddenly. He could not remember ever having spoken at such length about his relationship to the Canbys, or about any other aspect of his private life, for that matter. What had got into him to gabble on as though his tongue were on wheels? Was it that intangible bond he felt between them? Perhaps it was Mrs. Finch's air of silent but empathetic—and no doubt feigned—interest. Whatever the case, he realized somewhat irritably, he had opened up like a thirsty petunia in a rain shower.

He grimaced inwardly. He was not ordinarily so susceptible to feminine wiles, and he would take care not to be so lulled again.

"Tell me about your bookshop," he said, somewhat testily. He thought he observed a slight stiffening of Mrs. Finch's spare form. "You have been running it for, um, two years?"

As though her food had suddenly gone tasteless, Mrs. Finch pushed a forkful of peas around her plate. "Yes."

"A successful enterprise, I trust?"

The widow lifted her head abruptly. It was odd, mused Bran, how the color of her eyes varied. Ordinarily a deep chocolate, they appeared to lighten when she was startled or overset. Right now, they were a sort of cinnamon.

"Things were very difficult, at first, particularly since we were not doing well when my husband was in good health. He—he was not a businessman, although he loved books. I have little skill myself, though I, too, love to read. Through necessity, I forced myself to learn the mechanics of running a shop, and though I am not yet showing much profit, things are beginning to turn around. While I shall never become wealthy as a seller of books and papers, I am surviving."

"Yes, I can see you are a survivor, Mrs. Finch. However, I would not, if I were you, take the fact that you will soon be meeting his lordship as an indication of his subsequent acceptance of your claim."

Martha felt a tide of desperation rise within her. Dear God, what was she going to do if the marquess turned her away? "Beginning to turn around," indeed. She could not return to the bookshop and certain ruin. She had vowed she would never work as a scullery maid again, but her options were painfully few.

A waiter appeared to remove their plates and a few moments later, dessert appeared—a towering *croquembouche*. The earl spoke again, and Martha reluctantly turned away from the spectacular delicacy.

"What was the name of the family for whom you served as ladies' maid, Mrs. Finch?"

"Murchison, my lord. They were very kind to me, and I was sorry to leave them. But," she continued, making a sudden decision, "if I may ask, why are you interested in my former employers? Do you think I am lying about my association with them? What reason would I have for doing so? After all, I am not relying on how I lived the last twenty years to convince you of my identity as Felicity Marshall. It is not what I did that should concern you, my lord, it is who I am."

Martha held her breath for a moment. She hoped she had not made a critical error in taking such a bold stance. She had known only that were she to continue quailing defensively under his questions, the earl would soon simply roll her up and throw her away. She watched intently as what seemed to her a spark of amusement flared in his dark gaze.

"Yes," he responded softly, "but since there is so little actual evidence of who you are, it is necessary for me to delve as far as possible into what you are. You might be Felicity Marshall. Or you might not. I think you must agree I would be a fool were I to take everything you tell me at face value."

*And you are certainly no fool, my lord,* thought Martha rancorously.

"Thus, in determining the veracity of your claim, I must ascertain your general truthfulness. If I find you are lying about your employment with the Murchisons, for example, it will be difficult to accept your touching story of being found on the beach wearing the silver locket."

Martha forced a smile to her lips, grateful once again that she had not been forced to lie—about the Murchisons, at any rate. "Of course, my lord. In fact, I take leave to tell you I very much appreciate your candor. I prefer to keep matters strictly aboveboard and open. That way, each of us will know without a doubt where the other stands. I can understand your skepticism, and will do everything I can to assist you in your search for the truth. For that is my goal, as well."

"Very well put, Mrs. Finch. In view of your admirable sentiments, I'm sure we shall deal well together."

*When hell freezes over,* added Branford to himself.

*When pigs sprout wings,* thought Martha privately.

"By the by, Mrs. Finch, I cannot help but notice that although you say you were raised in Yorkshire, you speak with no trace of the dialect of that region. How—?"

"Why, thank you, my lord. I have worked very hard to speak in more genteel accents. I must give Mrs. Murchison credit for my transformation. She was gently bred, and when I became maid to her daughter, she was kind enough to teach me to speak like a lady. She gave me lessons on the pianoforte, as well, and Mr. Murchison opened his library to me."

"Mmp. How extraordinarily condescending of the Murchisons."

"Yes," Martha said simply. "They were very nice people."

She could not keep the weariness from her voice as she continued. "My lord, I know you look on me as a thieving adventuress, but I have told you nothing that is not the truth. The locket I showed you has been in my possession since I was cast up on the beach at Tenaby eighteen years ago."

"A rather slim testimonial, I think you will agree." He threw up his hands. "However, I suppose it will accomplish your purpose."

Martha gaped at him. Had she heard aright? Was Lord Branford admitting defeat? She struggled to regain her poise. Did this mean she would now achieve her goal? She felt no joy—only a curious emptiness. At least, for the moment. She supposed that once the shock wore off . . . She had not realized how important it was to her that she find the love and acceptance of a real family. How she had yearned for the warmth and security she would find there—of people who would love and cherish her. She glanced once more at the earl. Dear God, he looked as though he were waiting for someone to hand him a fiery sword with which to banish her from London—or at least from the environment of the Marquess of Canby. Seated opposite her, she was intensely aware of the aura of controlled power that emanated from him like lightning shooting through a bank of storm clouds. And yet, she realized with some surprise, she was not intimidated. Instead, she felt oddly comfortable, as though she'd sparred with him in the past to their mutual enjoyment.

"You have estimated to a nicety the effect the locket will have on Canby. I am impressed by the excellence of your mind."

Martha laughed shortly. The fleeting sense of rapport vanished. The arrogance of the man! Did he think her a sniveling hinney who would wither under his contempt? "I suppose I must thank you for the compliment, my lord."

"No, you must not, for I did not intend it as such. To my mind, your intelligence makes your actions all the more heinous. You must realize the effect of your inevitable exposure on an old man who has lived for many years on the hope that the last remaining member of his immediate family would be returned to him from the dead. What you are doing will destroy him, Mrs. Finch, and he does not deserve that. Canby is a good man."

Martha almost recoiled under the violence of his words. His voice had phased from his usual smooth arrogance to a harsh growl.

"But I am wasting my breath, am I not," he concluded, "on the likes of you."

Martha knew a moment of self-loathing. She had tried to convince herself that what she was doing would hurt no one. Lord Canby wanted a granddaughter, and she was prepared to fill the bill. The old man would never know of her deception. However, she was possessed of a sudden, wholly unwelcome desire that the earl might think better of her. The scorn in his dark gaze pierced the wall she had so carefully built around her conscience.

"My lord," she said, forming the words with difficulty, "I promise you, I will cause the Marquess of Canby no pain. I will be the child of his heart and the joy of his final years."

The earl appeared to remain unmoved. Instead, he spoke in a minatory tone. "Do consider, dear lady. As I told you, I have set investigations in motion, and the people I hired are most thorough in their methods. I have not the slightest doubt there are one or more loose threads in your, er, interesting past that you have overlooked. Believe me, I shall discover them. And when I do, your charade will be at an end, and you will spend a very long time in a very unpleasant prison cell."

Martha clenched her fingers in her lap, but she replied smoothly. "You may investigate until your eyes bubble, my lord. You will turn up nothing beyond what I have told you."

The earl made no response for several moments,

merely gazing at her as though he contemplated a particularly repellent bug in his salad. At last, he spoke calmly.

"Very well, Mrs. Finch. I shall only say that I believe you will regret this night's work. And now, if you are finished, I believe we must be on our way."

## 6

Shortly after the carriage pulled away from the Grand Hotel, it passed Hyde Park, where preparations for a fireworks display were under way. It was growing dark by the time Martha and the earl made their way into what was for Martha the terra incognita of Mayfair, and flambeaux had been lit in the doorways of the elegant town houses. To Martha, they created a veritable fairyland.

*Even if they turn me out into the street after tonight,* Martha thought fiercely, her hands clenched in her lap, *I'll have this moment to remember. Me, Martha Sounder, riding in a fine coach with a fine gentleman, on my way to visit with a marquess in a bloody magnificent house in Grosvenor Square.*

She almost breathed the name aloud. She had never expected in all her life—at least, until a few months ago—that she might become a part of this exalted world.

Might. She addressed herself firmly. That was the operative word here, and she'd better not forget it. If the marquess could not be ensnared tonight, her cause was lost. On the other hand, if she could win him over, the Earl of Branford could frown and growl until his eyes bubbled, to no avail.

She shot a sidelong glance at the earl. The light from the flambeaux, slanting across the harsh planes of his face, lent them a sinister expression, but it could be seen under closer scrutiny that he wore his now-familiar air of boredom. He had apparently sunk into a fit of abstraction, for during the short journey, he spoke not a word.

At last, the carriage swung into the square, a vast empty expanse bordered by an imposing array of elegant homes. At one of these, the carriage halted, and almost before the vehicle drew to a full stop, the front door was flung open to disgorge a liveried footman who scurried to let down the carriage steps and to assist the passengers in disembarking. Another personage, standing in the open doorway, bowed as Lord Branford alit from the carriage.

"My lord," he murmured in response to the earl's casual greeting, adding a respectful "madam," to Martha before admitting them to the house.

Martha gazed about her as they entered a vast entrance hall. A glittering chandelier hung over a floor of marble marquetry that surged like a lake around her feet. It spread to lap at various doors leading into barely visible chambers before washing up against a staircase that curved gracefully upward.

"His lordship is expecting you, my lord," the butler, Hobbs, informed Lord Branford, who nodded. "He is waiting in his study."

Lord Branford turned, his face impassive. "Are you ready, Mrs. Finch?"

For an instant, Martha was seized by a desire to turn and flee from the house into the darkness outside. She pictured in horrifying detail what might ensue were she to pursue her present course. The marquess would instantly see into her soul. He would point an accusing finger and his stentorian "Out of my house this instant!" would be emblazoned in the air. The words would flay her and follow her into the night stinging like a thousand vengeful insects.

She stood for a moment, perfectly still. She breathed deeply and told herself not to be absurd. She had come too far and her hope of success was too great to be overwhelmed by her vaporish fears.

"Yes, of course, my lord," she replied calmly.

Hobbs escorted the little group upstairs. As they moved through the house, Bran glanced at Martha Finch. With his curious attunement to her mood, he could almost feel the tension that radiated from her. What was going through her mind? A careful last-minute rehearsal of her story? Was she exulting in the soon-to-be fulfillment of her schemes? Or—again he shifted uncomfortably—an eager anticipation to greet the family she had never known?

Martha darted a glance into the earl's saturnine face before lowering her gaze in a pretty assumption of modesty. Somehow, though he had made it perfectly plain that he did not believe a word of the tale she had spun for him, she was grateful that he walked beside her into the lion's den. She knew she must be mistaken, but she felt almost as though he provided a degree of support for her.

Hobbs stopped at one of the doors, which was immediately flung open. A tall gentleman stood in the aperture.

"Bran!" he exclaimed. "At last!" He flung the door wide. "Well, do not just stand there. Come in. Come in!"

The man glanced sharply at Martha as Branford ushered her into the room and she returned his gaze with equal interest. He carried his height well despite his years, with a slim elegance that bespoke his status and wealth. A mane of silver hair swept back from a broad forehead and aquiline features. He did not look the sort of man to be easily gulled, but according to Seth Pinfold, he was inclined to reach out to anyone claiming to be Felicity Marshall.

"Lord Canby." The earl's voice cut crispy into her reflections. "Allow me to present Mrs. Martha Finch."

Lord Canby took her hand in his. He stared searchingly at her, as though willing himself to see a remnant of the six-year-old face he had so loved. It seemed to Martha as though his piercing gaze could see into her

very heart and she trembled at the thought of the lie
that hid there, waiting to slither out into the open like
an obscene reptile, destroying all that it touched.

Abruptly, he folded her into a warm embrace.
"Welcome, my dear child." He nodded an abstracted
greeting to Branford and gestured him to a chair. He
guided Martha to a settee near the window and sat
beside her.

For a long moment, he said nothing, and the room's
silence roared in her ears. She struggled to remain still
and unmoved by his unrelenting surveillance, making
herself return his gaze with a degree of composure.

Watching her from his chair at the far end of the
room, Bran was forced to admit that so far she was
carrying her charade off to perfection. If she really
were Felicity Marshall, her behavior would have been
no different.

Look at her now, bending that serene, enigmatic
smile on the old man as he questioned her. From the
eagerness of his expression, he was already halfway to
believing every lie she spooned into him. Yes, from
the way she was managing her strategy so far, the
attractive widow was going to prove harder than her
predecessors to dislodge from the marquess's willing,
nay eager, suspension of disbelief.

Martha Finch, he reflected, had proved unexpected
from the moment he had met her. What was it that
was so appealing about the widow? To be sure, she
could not be considered an Accredited Beauty. She
was too thin, but she carried her angular body with
flair and grace. Her features were delicate, but pur-
poseful, and her eyes . . . Ah, her eyes. A man could
lose himself in their velvet depths.

But that man would not, of course, be he. Despite
his family's efforts, he had assiduously avoided parson's mousetrap. He had no aversion to the institution,
but, as he had told his importunate relatives on many
occasions, he had simply been unable to find the right
mate. Not that he lived like a hermit. He had enjoyed

the favors of many women, from bored ladies of the *ton* to a wide assortment of delectable ladybirds. He was, fortunately, immune to the charms of Mrs. Finch's sort of female. Well, perhaps not immune, but he knew when a spot of dalliance might be in order and when it was devoutly to be avoided. Not that Mrs. Finch had so far given any indication that she viewed him as more than a bothersome impediment to the scheme she was putting so neatly into play.

She had not fooled him, of course, with her wide chocolate gaze, or her melting declaration that she wished only to discover her true heritage. He forced his attention to the continuing conversation.

"Yes, my lord," she was saying, "I have visited London before, but infrequently—on buying trips with Matthew, so I am looking forward to seeing some of the sights while I am here."

Could it be, he wondered, that Martha Finch was telling the whole truth? That she really did believe she might be Felicity? Good God, he continued, his thoughts unwillingly plunging forward. What if she really was Felicity Marshall? He sat, stunned at this possibility, which he had not so much as considered until this moment. And why should he? It was inconceivable that if Canby's granddaughter had somehow survived the accident that killed her parents, she would not have come forward before now. At six, she had known her own name and where she lived. She could have told—but, of course, Martha claimed to have lost all memory of her life before the shipwreck. The truth, or a well-conceived ploy?

Bran shook himself. Of course, it was a ploy. The memory loss was just too coincidental, as was her story of her rise in the Murchison household due to the death of a ladies' maid.

He sat back to watch, with an unwilling appreciation, her next move.

"And were they kind to you—these fisherfolk?" asked Lord Canby.

The old man still held Martha's hand in a painful grip, but it was not this that caused a cold thread of discomfort to snake through her. It was the man himself who made her uneasy, so pitifully eager was he to hear about every facet of her life since she'd been found on the beach at Tenaby.

She had known from the start that she was perpetrating a fraud. However, she had rationalized her actions until she almost believed that if she was not precisely justified in her actions, she was acting sensibly. She knew that Lady Felicity Marshall was dead. But Martha was as certain as she was of sun and wind and rain that the child she had known only as Mary would not begrudge Martha her chance at security, at a life of ease and comfort such as she had never known. And, most importantly, the family she had always longed for.

*Mary, all my life I called you "little sister." I was mistaken, but I was not wrong about the bond between us. Was I? Mary, be with me in this.*

The marquess pulled the silver locket from his pocket and opened it. He gazed at the small, painted faces.

"You do not recall ever seeing this lady and gentleman?" he asked gently.

"No," whispered Martha, swallowing the pain in her throat.

The marquess sighed. "They are Felicity's mother and father—my son and his wife."

"Yes, so I have been told."

The marquess was visibly disappointed.

"I am so very sorry, my lord," Martha said. "I believe you were told that I have no memory of that time. I can only tell you about how I have lived since."

The old gentleman sighed. Rising, he carefully placed the locket about Martha's neck before returning to his chair. "I know, my child. I was hoping that you might carry some memory of the time when you were my darling girl." His gaze was bright with longing.

From his corner, Lord Branford spoke. "Sir, I think Mrs. Finch has taken up enough of your time this evening. Perhaps, when our investigation is further along, she can return, but until—"

The marquess sighed. "I suppose you are right, Bran." He pulled an ornate watch from his pocket. "It is getting rather late."

He turned to Martha and said slowly, "I still believe you may very well be Felicity, my dear, but Bran is right. We must have more facts. In the meantime, I would see more of you. I hope you will come to see me again soon—perhaps for dinner."

Martha swallowed to contain the disappointment that rose in her throat. "Yes, of course, my lord. Perhaps—oh!"

She stared at the marquess's pocket watch, glittering in the candlelight. The marquess, following her gaze, asked eagerly, "Do you recognize this?"

A wave of dizziness swept over her. "No—but your fob! I've seen it before—but smaller. It is etched with the portrait of a lady, is it not? Wearing an odd hat."

"This is astonishing!" exclaimed the marquess. He handed Martha the watch so that she could examine the fob suspended from the golden chain. "Not a lady—precisely—but the goddess Athena in her helmet. I used to let Felicity play with the watch, and she was so much taken by the fob that I had one made for her in miniature. She wore it constantly."

"Yes!" The room seemed to reel about Martha. Once again, the image of the small, pale face flashed before her. A tiny girl, dressed in expensive clothing— and— *Mary! What am I to do? I cannot tell them*—

"I had forgotten," she continued brokenly, "but—it was pinned to the shawl in which I was wrapped—I suppose it must have been lost some time shortly after my rescue, for I do not remember seeing it later."

Lord Canby turned to Lord Branford, his face

wreathed in a smile that seemed to light the room.
"Bran! Do you know what this means?"

Bran, gazing down at Martha, felt as though the
world had exploded beneath his feet. My God! Was
it possible? This woman, whom he had castigated as
an impostor, was, in truth, Felicity Marshall? His first
instinct had been to refute Martha's claimed recognition of the watch fob. A moment later, he realized
with stunning force that even the cleverest of frauds
could not have known about the little keepsake, or
recognized it just now.

Bran lifted a hand to Martha.

"Felicity," he choked.

7

For some moments, Martha could do nothing but
stare into Branford's face as a black vortex of confusion formed in her mind. She had spoken inadver-
tently, and for an instant, wondered at the wisdom of
this unplanned utterance. But the recognition of the
fob had struck her like a thunderclap and she had
blurted out the memory without thinking. What did it
all mean? It was simply more proof, she supposed,
that Mary, the child whose past she had usurped, was,
in reality, Felicity Marshall, for the embroidered shawl
and the attached fob had enfolded Mary, not her.

She was brought up short in her wild speculation
by a single word, uttered by Branford.

"Felicity!"

She stared up at him in profound shock. He believed her! Whatever upheaval the sudden memory
of the little fob had caused in her, she had at least
accomplished this. She had won! She had completed
her deception—not just of the marquess, but of the
Earl of Branford. The realization produced a repetition of that curious emptiness she had experienced

before. She wrenched her gaze from Branford. For God's sake, this was her moment of triumph. She must pull herself together.

She turned her face to Lord Canby and allowed her lashes to flutter over her cheeks. "Please, my lord," she whispered. "I—I don't know what to say. I did not expect to remember— Oh, this has all been too much! May I please be excused? May I please return to the hotel?"

"Of course, my dearest child. But you must not call me 'my lord.' I am your grandpapa. And you are my dearest Felicity." The marquess was almost sobbing. "You are returned to me after all these years. Of course, you may retire, but not to the hotel. You must stay here now. This is your home, and—"

"No!" The word was out before she could recall it. No, she must not stay here. Without examining her reasons, she knew only that she must leave Canby House. She must retreat to the neutral haven of the Grand Hotel, at least for tonight. Tomorrow, perhaps, she would be ready to make a triumphal entry into the home of Felicity Marshall.

To her surprise, Branford spoke just then, his voice cutting coolly into her heated reflections.

"No," he echoed, "it is not surprising that Felicity needs some time to herself at this moment."

"What nonsense," began the marquess. "This young woman is, without a doubt, my granddaughter. I wish to—"

"Please, my—Grandpapa," said Martha, her voice now clear and composed. "Lord Branford is right. I cannot tell you how it warms my heart to know that you believe in me and that you want me here in your home. But, he is right. I need some time to reflect. There will be plenty of time to begin our new life together."

The marquess made an impatient sound, but, after a long moment, stepped back.

"Very well, Felicity, but you will return tomorrow.

First thing. For there is much I would discuss with you. Of course you will want to do some shopping with Mrs. Coppersmith. If you are to go out and about in society, we must deck you out accordingly."

The marquess issued further instructions, almost babbling in his excitement, but at last, he embraced her once more and saw her from the house in Lord Branford's company.

In the carriage, Martha was intensely aware of the earl's intense scrutiny.

"It appears you have proved your case, Mrs. Finch. Or—no, I must call you Felicity now, must I not?"

"Because of a single, vague memory?" murmured Martha warily.

"Oh, no. Er, well, yes, but such a memory. Only the real Lady Felicity would recognize that fob."

Martha glanced up sharply, for his tone held a warmth she had never heard from him. His gaze, too, had lost its glint of speculative assessment, and he now looked at her, it seemed to Martha, with a certain— tenderness? Despite herself, a lovely warmth spread through her.

The streets were still thronged with revelers, and the carriage's progress was slow, but at last it swung into the hotel drive.

On their entrance to the hotel, Lord Branford steered Martha toward the desk, again occupied by Mr. Simmons. Good heavens, did the man never sleep?

Upon receiving the room key from Mr. Simmons, Lord Branford, to Martha's surprise, turned toward the stairs. Was he planning to launch another interrogation, despite his averred belief in her story? No, she couldn't bear it. She desperately needed some peace and quiet in which to mull over this abrupt change in her situation.

"It is very kind of you to have escorted me home, my lord," she said imperiously, reaching for the key, "but I believe I can find my way back to my chamber on my own."

The earl did not relinquish the key. Instead, he smiled benevolently—an expression that sat most peculiarly on his stony features.

"But, my dear, it is the duty of a gentleman to escort a lady staying in an establishment such as this to her chamber. He is obliged to open the door for her and inspect the premises for, er, marauders or burglars, or any other evildoers."

Bending a gaze of extreme skepticism on her escort, Martha shrugged and accepted the arm he offered for the journey upstairs.

Upon entering their chamber, she looked around the sitting room. To her dismay, Mrs. Coppersmith had apparently retired for the night. There was no sign of Peters, and only a single candle had been left lighted. Martha turned to Lord Branford with a nervous smile.

"Well, the room seems relatively marauder-less, does it not?" she said hastily. "I do thank you for accompanying me, my lord." She had remained close to the open door, and now she offered the earl her hand. "I would offer you some refreshment, but I hope you will excuse me. I find I am quite exhausted from the, er, events of the evening. It looks as though tomorrow will be a busy day."

The earl did not take the hint. Instead, he moved farther into the room.

"Indeed. Tomorrow morning, I should imagine you will find your grandfather knee-deep in preparations for your presentation to the rest of the family—and to the *ton* at large."

Martha fought the sickness that rose in her throat like bile. Dear God, why could she not produce a little exultance in this situation? She had won! Why did she feel like vomiting?

She sank into the nearest chair, a settee, without

taking her eyes from him. "My lord," she grated, "do you believe I am Felicity Marshall?"

Branford sat next to her, and Martha realized suddenly that she had made a poor choice of seating, for the couch was small and the earl was very large—and he was very close to her. His eyes glittered in the candlelight, but his expression was serious.

"I suppose I owe you an apology, Felicity, for until this evening I was convinced that you were merely the latest in a long string of unscrupulous fortune hunters. I must admit that I found myself wishing to believe you, for you seemed as different from that breed as cheese from chalk. My skepticism was too long ingrained, however. I hope you will forgive me for that. At any rate, tonight you put all doubts to rest, and I am delighted to welcome you home, Felicity."

Martha drew a long, shuddering breath. She could barely force herself to look at him. "You believe that my recognition of the fob was genuine?"

Bran chuckled. It was a lovely sound, she thought, so at odds with his formidable appearance that she was startled. "It took only a moment to realize that you could not have recognized a keepsake that vanished with Felicity's disappearance." His voice fell. "I must tell you, when I recovered from my initial shock, I was inordinately pleased at this revelation."

"P-pleased?"

"As I have told you, Stewart Marshall was almost a brother to me. Felicity—you—were the sister I never had. You were too young to participate in our activities—not that we would under any circumstances have allowed a mere girl to join in our games—but you have always been a presence—an enchanting presence—in my boyhood memories."

It seemed to Martha that the air about them had grown dangerously thick, and she was intensely aware of the silence of the room and the candlelight that enclosed them in an intimate pool. Hastily, she rose.

"I can only say, my lord, that—"

The earl came to his feet as well. "Please, you must call me Branford now. My particular friends, of which I hope I may number you, call me Bran. And now," he continued, "I shall leave you—although I hope you will spare me some time tomorrow after your morning with Lord Canby and your shopping expedition. I should like to show you about London a little."

Lord, please let him go—now. She didn't think she could stand another moment of his overtures of friendship. "That would be very nice, my—Bran." She nearly choked on the word.

Martha accompanied him to the door, where he turned to face her once more.

"I look forward to becoming reacquainted with you, Felicity."

He grasped her lightly by the shoulders and bent to kiss her cheek. His lips were cool against her skin and she stared slightly. She started to draw back, gratified despite herself at this brotherly gesture. But he did not release her. The next moment, his hands were on her back, gentle but insistent, pressing her against him. His mouth brushed her cheek once more, then traced the curve of her jaw in feathered points of flame until he covered her mouth with his. He cupped the back of her head, and it seemed to her that for a few instants he drew her very essence into him. Without volition, she opened beneath him, and her hands crept upward to move into the surprisingly soft, dusky hair that waved at the back of his neck.

The next instant, he pulled back from her so abruptly that her knees almost gave way beneath her. He said nothing, but stared for a moment into her eyes, his expression as wide and appalled as she knew her own to be. He released her swiftly and, still wordless, strode to the door. Then he was gone.

8

The next morning, Martha perused a copy of *La Belle Assemblée* as she waited for Lord Branford in her sitting room. She had just breakfasted with Mrs. Coppersmith, enduring her burblings of happy congratulations and plans for a shopping expedition. Now, she found herself in an oddly unsettled mood, and was having difficulty forcing her attention to the periodical. The events of last night still whirled in her mind like starlings flying before a storm. By this time next week, the return of Lady Felicity Marshall to the munificent bosom of her grandfather would have been thoroughly bruited about the *ton*. Properly gowned and shod and coiffed, she would be ensconced in Canby House, meeting family, receiving callers, and accepting invitations to balls and routs and afternoon tea.

And she was unable to take pleasure in any of it.

She had not known her conscience would prove so troublesome. She thought she'd reasoned out her scheme to her satisfaction. Was what she was doing so wrong? No, of course not. No one would be hurt, after all. On the contrary, one old man would be made extremely happy, and she, herself, could look forward to a life of ease and security. She had earned this, had she not, after the deprivation she had suffered for so long?

Then why could she not banish the guilt that tarnished her satisfaction? Why could she take no pleasure in the future that stretched so glowingly before her? The memory of Lord Canby's embrace flooded through her. His eyes had shone with unshed tears of gratitude. Dear God, no matter how she tried to rationalize the fact, she had deceived a perfectly nice man for her own personal gain. She was preparing to assume a position to which she had no right.

Abruptly, she squared her shoulders. Well, by God, her conscience was just going to have to get used to it. She almost laughed aloud. Yes, she would just have to suffer through three full meals a day, and beautiful clothes, and an endless round of pleasure. Oh, indeed, she thought she could manage that.

But, what was she going to do about the Earl of Branford? She had lain awake most of the night thinking about the embrace they had shared. Dear Lord, she had known the man for less than a day! The kiss on the cheek had been, perhaps under the circumstances, acceptable. It was undeniably pleasant. The kiss that followed had been shattering. Perhaps she should not have been surprised at her unexpected response to the touch of his hands and to the feel of his mouth on hers, for she had been strongly attracted to the earl on their first meeting. What she found astonishing and more than somewhat dismaying was a renewal of that sense of belonging. It was as though she had been searching all her life for the haven she sensed in the strength of his arms and the hunger of his kiss. Something deep within her told her with a bewildering certainty that she and this man belonged with each other and that their coming together at this moment had been ordained.

Which was absolute balderdash. Bran had said that he and Felicity had known each other as children, but she was not Felicity Marshall.

She shook herself. She would not think about this anymore, particularly since—

A brisk knock sounded at the door and Martha leaped to her feet, her heart pounding absurdly. She swung the door open to face Bran, superbly attired, as always, in gentleman's dress appropriate for escorting a young lady on an afternoon jaunt around the town.

She searched his face, but found nothing there that spoke of an embrace shared in a candlelit chamber. He stepped inside the sitting room and removed his hat.

"Good morning, Felicity. I see you are ready," he said courteously. "Shall we go?"

"Of course," murmured Martha, feeling as though she had just put her foot on a step that wasn't there. She hadn't expected him to fall at her feet after the scene last night, but she'd expected a little more than "I see you are ready."

Good Lord, what was the matter with him? thought Bran, watching Felicity take up her darned gloves and her reticule. He'd felt as though he'd given up a piece of his soul to this woman last night. And all he could come up with now was a wretched commonplace. He observed that she moved with her usual queenly composure, displaying no trace of the passion she had shown last night.

He hadn't had a farthing's worth of sleep, thinking about that passion. God knew, he hadn't intended to kiss her at all. At least, no more than that friendly little peck on the cheek. But he had no sooner felt the smooth warmth of her skin under his lips—no sooner than breathed in the scent of her—than he had—well, he had completely lost his senses. He'd kissed a lot of women, but he'd never felt this sense of union, as though he and this woman had been created for each other.

And she had responded! She had opened herself to him as though she were experiencing that same connection. Lord, it had been all he could do to draw away from her, for had the embrace continued, he, the vaunted champion of Lord Canby's interests, might have tumbled the old man's granddaughter on the floor. There must not be a repetition of the episode, Bran told himself.

In silence, he ushered Martha from the room, but once in the carriage, he drew a deep breath.

"It appears I owe you an apology, Lady Felicity."

He watched in bemusement the delicate lift of her eyebrows.

"Apology, my lord?"

"About last night. I took advantage of you. I—I behaved abominably."

A becoming flush spread over her cheeks. "I would dispute your use of the phrase 'took advantage of,' Bran. What happened was—unexpected, but I would be telling an untruth if I were to say I didn't enjoy it."

"You did?" Bran's pulse leaped like that of a four-year-old on Christmas morning. "That is extremely flattering, of course, but you are a lady, and—and my behavior was—"

"Please." She smiled enchantingly. "You are forgetting my plebeian background. Where I come from, a kiss between a man and a woman who find themselves attracted to each other is a wholly natural progression of events."

"Yes, but—"

"However, you have no doubt concluded that perhaps you were a little precipitate and that it must not happen again. In this, I heartily concur."

"You do?" replied Bran, feeling like a flustered schoolboy.

"Yes. I think we may chalk up the whole episode to an excess of sensibility due to the momentous events that occurred last night, and a certain intimacy in the scene. Do you not agree?"

"Er."

"Thus, I think it would be best simply to forget the whole thing," finished Felicity briskly. Since this was the sentiment Bran had hoped to produce during the course of his aborted apology, he should have experienced a measurable degree of satisfaction. What he felt, oddly, was a certain flatness of spirit.

Once at Canby House, Bran deposited Martha with a respectful Hobbs, leaving her with a promise to return to the Grand Hotel later in the afternoon for their excursion. Lord Canby received her with child-like enthusiasm and the morning was spent in reminiscences and the further revelation of details from Martha's expurgated past.

Mrs. Coppersmith arrived at the town house in time for a lavish luncheon served in an elegantly appointed dining room that overlooked the square. After the meal, when the marquess would have hustled her back to his study for more conversation, Mrs. Coppersmith insisted that the shopping trip must now take precedence over any other activity. Shortly thereafter, Martha found herself seated in the showroom of Madame Fourgette, London's premier modiste. Madame herself, upon hearing the identity of the very plain young woman awaiting service, condescended to wait upon mademoiselle in person, displaying a gratifying eagerness to be of service. A bewildering whirl of garments was produced, and for some hours, Martha floated in a sea of silks, satins, muslins, and cambrics. Ball gowns, morning gowns, and walking dresses were produced for her approval, as well as ensembles suitable for every occasion from the opera to a stroll in the park.

"I finally had to cry quits," said Martha with a laugh some hours later as she and Bran made their way once more from the hotel, this time in Bran's phaeton, with a diminutive tiger perched precariously in the back. "Not content with getting me up like a circus pony, Mrs. Coppersmith—or no, I forgot, she wishes me to call her Carolyn—dragged me bodily to every milliner, shoemaker, and haberdasher in the West End."

From the gratifying order placed by Mrs. Coppersmith, Madame Fourgette had been able to provide a few gowns to be taken from the shop immediately. In one of these, Martha had presented herself to the earl. Her walking dress, of jonquil sarcenet, was trimmed with a triple flounce, with a set-on of narrow ribbon in a dark green. An Oldenburg bonnet, embellished with a single, small green feather, was placed at a jaunty angle on an equally smart arrangement of glossy curls, courtesy of the ubiquitous Peters.

Martha savored the appreciation in Bran's gaze as he surveyed her. "To paraphrase the poet, my dear, you walk in sunshine—and I find you quite dazzling, if you will forgive me for saying so."

"I shall not only forgive you, but I encourage you to continue in the same vein—as I am vastly pleased with my new finery. Where are we going?" she asked.

"To one of my favorite places in the world. And yours, too, if I remember correctly."

Martha raised a quizzical brow, but said nothing until the phaeton pulled up in Berkeley Square, into a crowd of vehicles parked under the trees lining the square.

"Gunter's Pastry Shop," Bran announced. "Would you rather order something to eat out here in the shade, or would you like to go inside?"

"Oh, inside, please."

Bran handed the reins to the little tiger, with instructions to walk the horses, before guiding Martha through the crowd. Once inside, a serving maid led them to a table.

"Do you come here often?" asked Martha casually.

"Yes, although not as often as when I was a child. I used to come with Stewart and his grandfather—and you—if I happened to be in Town at the same time as the Benningtons, which was seldom. In fact, I must tell you that it was here that you informed me for the first time that you intended to marry me when we both grew up."

Martha's breath caught. "Marry you?"

"Indeed, you were most emphatic. Apparently you had acquired the notion that a young girl's first duty in life is to seek an eligible *parti*. As Stewart's friend, you felt my name headed the list, so why waste time searching further? I was given a direct order not to so much as think of marrying anyone else."

Martha laughed unsteadily. "What a hoyden I must have been! Well, my lord, you may consider yourself relieved of that obligation."

"Obligation? My dear, I considered I had won a prize of considerable value—and felt my future was now secure."

Despite the absurdity of Bran's words, Martha felt herself blushing. "Did you come to Town often?" she asked hastily.

"No, most of my youth was spent at my home. I was always rather at loose ends," he added, "when your family left to come to Town."

"Did you have no one else to play with?"

"Not in the immediate vicinity. And I had no brothers and sisters."

"Your parents did not enjoy coming to Town?"

Bran was quiet for several moments before he answered. "Oh, yes. In fact, they were here most of the time. They thought it better if I stayed behind. You see," he added somewhat painfully, "my father was very active in politics, and my mother relished her role as a political hostess. A small boy would have been very much in the way."

In the silence that followed, Bran cursed himself. How in God's name had he come to blurt out what he had never discussed with anyone? It was not the sort of thing he would have talked about even with Stewart. He looked at Felicity, who was staring at him. "I'm sorry," he said, the words sticking in his throat like burrs. "I don't know how I came to speak so."

"Perhaps because you have discovered an old friend," Martha said softly, before turning the conversation to more general matters. When they rose to leave, Martha reflected that she had never spent such a magical hour.

She knew she was being absurd, but she also knew that, come what may, she would always cherish the memory of this sunny, perfect afternoon.

9

Martha spent most of the next three days at Canby House in the marquess's company. On these occasions, she was accompanied by Carolyn Coppersmith. Bran was usually present as well. In the afternoons, when both Carolyn and Lord Canby retired for a nap, Martha and Bran spent long, warm hours coming to know each other. It was, she mused dazedly, as though she had been only half alive through all her previous years, until she had found him. Though he said nothing, she sensed that he enjoyed her company, as well. Certainly, he shared his feelings and thoughts with her in a manner she felt was unusual for him. She knew she had no right to his affection, but she could not help but revel in it. In his presence, she managed to damp the feelings of guilt that were becoming harder and harder to ignore.

One afternoon, the two sat before the massive piano in the music room. Though it reminded her forcibly of her days with the Murchisons, she was glad of an opportunity to reacquaint herself with an instrument that had lightened her meager existence with precious moments of joy.

Bran, she discovered, enjoyed playing the piano as well. He could not be called a virtuoso, but he obviously loved music.

"I must tell Lord Canby to provide a music master for you," he said. "When you learn to read music a whole new world will open for you. In the meantime . . ."

With his own hand, he produced a series of notes, then guided Martha to a repetition. Within a few minutes, she had learned to play several measures in a continuation of the portion she had taught herself.

"Oh, Bran!" she cried softly. "This is wonderful."

Perhaps, she thought with sudden pain, in her fraudulent new life as Lady Felicity, she would find fulfillment in learning to play this magnificent instrument. She turned again to Bran. "I cannot find words—"

As she gazed at him, Martha became immediately conscious, as she had before, that the seat she shared with Bran was very small, and that his closeness, as it had done on that other occasion, was producing an alarming effect on her.

She wrenched her gaze from him to concentrate on the hand he still held against the keys. At the same moment, Bran started and coughed self-consciously.

She rose abruptly. "I must go. Grandpapa will be—"

To her discomfiture, she discovered that Bran still held one of her hands in his, but when she tried to disengage it, he came to his feet as well, still retaining it in a warm grasp.

"We will continue your lessons at another time, I hope," he murmured.

"Yes," she replied somewhat breathlessly. "I should like that."

And still, he did not release her hand, but gazed into her eyes for an endless moment.

"Felicity," he whispered at last, "why do I feel that you have returned, not to your grandfather, but to me? I did not realize how I have missed you. But now—"

He drew in a sharp breath and, with a single, almost angry movement, pulled her into his arms.

His kiss this time did not begin as a brotherly salute. He took her mouth with an urgency that snatched her breath and destroyed her reason. She leaned into his embrace, pressing herself against him as though she might absorb him into her very soul. She wondered for a distracted instant how a single kiss could be so satisfying while plunging her into a maelstrom of wanting. His hands, moving along her back, created a sensation of liquid fire, traversing the length of her body. She seemed to become a mindless puddle of sensation, all the while reveling in the knowledge that this man wanted her with a ferocity that matched her own.

He pulled away from her for an instant, and gazed at her with a hungry intensity that she knew was mirrored in her own eyes. "Felicity," he groaned. "I have known you—as an adult—for less than a week—but I realize now that I have been waiting for you since the day they came with the news that you would not be back. And I never knew it. I've been searching all this time—without knowing for what or for whom I was searching."

*Yes!* she thought wildly as his lips met hers once more, hot and demanding, seeking and tender. She, too, had been searching—for love—for acceptance and belonging—for Branford. Dear God . . . ! She almost crumpled at the terrifying knowledge that swept over her so suddenly.

This time it was she who pulled back, feeling as she did so that she was tearing part of her away.

"I must go!" she gasped, hardly able to get the words out. She could not say more, but ran from the room, leaving Bran staring after her, white-faced.

For some moments, he stared blankly ahead of him. He could not believe what had just happened. He had resolved to treat Felicity with the courtesy and friendship that was due not only her position, but which had been a gift from his heart when they were children. He had not expected that his heart would rush to a recognition of a love he had not even known existed. All it seemed to take, however, to destroy his reasoned intentions were a few moments in close proximity to her.

For a moment, during the searing kisses they had just exchanged, he had thought that Felicity was experiencing the same revelation. She had clung to him with a passion that had almost destroyed what little control remained to him. The sweetness of her lips, the soft, slender curves that moved against him with an innocent, age-old wisdom, had created a maelstrom of wanting within him—not just to possess that lovely, slim body, but to become one with her in spirit, as well.

He walked slowly from the room and, in the morning room, he found Martha, seated in conversation with the marquess and Carolyn Coppersmith. Her gaze lifted to him as he entered the room, but he could find nothing there beyond a shuttered blankness that enshrouded him in a bottomless depression.

Martha's breath caught. Lord, Bran looked as though someone had struck him a blow. It had been painful beyond words to leave him without telling him of her feelings—but she had no right. Dear God, she had no right to love this man. What did he feel for her? Was she reading too much into the passion they had shared? She looked away from the earl as he chose a chair next to the marquess. As the afternoon died, he cast sporadic glances toward her, but she was careful to allow nothing of the chaos churning within her to show outwardly.

Lord Canby had arranged for a small dinner party that evening. Martha had already been introduced to some of the family members, and tonight she was scheduled to meet several more. She was unable to look forward to the festive little occasion with anything but unmitigated dismay, but at least, when the guests arrived, she was kept busy. She smiled and smiled until she thought her face would crack, but she was able to keep away from Bran.

She was conscious of his presence throughout the evening, however. He always seemed to be at the periphery of her vision, and she was aware that his glance strayed to her often through the endless round of introductions and her brittle acknowledgments of cousins, aunts, and uncles.

When the dinner party finally ended, Martha relaxed momentarily on the ride to the hotel from Canby House, grateful for Mrs. Coppersmith's presence in the carriage. When at last they entered the little sitting room, she moved immediately toward her bedchamber, pleading exhaustion from the day's events.

Bran bowed over Martha's hand with a cool farewell.

"I would like to see you tomorrow morning, if that is acceptable," he said before releasing her hand.

She nodded wordlessly.

"Privately," he added in a very odd tone of voice.

Martha's gaze, which she had directed assiduously downward, now flew to meet his. She dared not read what was written in his eyes. She nodded again, and with a word to Mrs. Coppersmith, he turned. The next moment, he was gone.

Outside the corridor, Bran leaned against the door. Good God, he was trembling like a girl. He had made his assignation with Martha unthinkingly. He did not know what he was going to say to her, he had only known that he must see her. He wanted to conclude the scene that had begun in the music room. He grinned to himself. Not that kind of a conclusion, though had she remained in his arms another moment, such might have been the case. No, he reflected, as he moved down the corridor and out of the hotel. He wanted . . . Dammit, he didn't know what he wanted. On his deepest level of consciousness he yearned to gain a commitment from her—a promise that now that she had returned she would never leave again. Never leave *him* again. He listened to himself in some amazement. This sounded very much like a marriage proposal, and surely he could not be contemplating such a step on such a brief acquaintance.

But that was the most astonishing part of this strange reunion, wasn't it? The sense that he had known this woman for a very long time. He had scarcely acknowledged the existence of Felicity when she had been his friend's tiresome little sister. Now, it appeared that she had held a place in his heart for all the years of her absence.

Bran had by now traversed the short distance between the Grand Hotel and Canby House. As he alighted from the carriage, another vehicle drew up just behind him. From it stepped a cloaked figure who called softly to him.

"My lord? Lord Branford? It is I, Jonathan Beddoes."

Beddoes! The man leading the investigation into the reappearance of Felicity Marshall.

"Ah, yes, Beddoes. I sent a message to you regarding the matter of Martha Finch. It must have missed you. I am happy to inform you your services are no longer required, sir. Mrs. Finch—that is Lady Felicity—was able to offer irrefutable proof of her identity. Thus—"

"Proof?" The other man stood very still for a moment. "I am certainly pleased to hear that, my lord, but I think perhaps you would still like to hear my findings."

Bran stood irresolute for a moment before nodding. "Very well. Come into the house. Lord Canby will have retired by now, and we can talk privately."

Once in the library, over a gratefully accepted brandy, Mr. Beddoes began to speak.

"Once I arrived in Tenaby, my lord, I found some difficulty in finding anyone who so much as remembered Josiah and Margaret Sounder. However, eventually I was able to turn up one or two remarkable facts. It seems that . . ."

Beddoes continued with a narrative that soon captured Bran's full attention.

In her bedchamber at the Grand Hotel, Martha stared sightlessly at the canopy above her. Dear Lord, she must deal with the knowledge that she was in love with Bran. She had felt a strong, almost preordained attraction to him from their first meeting, but the realization that had struck her so stunningly while she sat with him at the piano must now be faced.

Did Bran love her? The thought was a trembling deep inside her. He had not told her in so many words, but she had been aware of a certain transference—as though he had given up part of his very es-

sence to her—that must surely be an indication of
something warmer than mere friendship.

If this was the case—if Bran had fallen as deeply
into love as she had with him—and in a matter of a
few days—this was a disaster in the making. When she
had begun her charade, her plans had not included
the Earl of Branford, let alone the spark that had
ignited between them. Not that marriage with him was
impossible. The Marquess of Canby would no doubt
look with extreme benevolence on a union between
his beloved granddaughter and a man who was as dear
to him as a son. She imagined the earl's family would
feel the same. No, the problem was that try as she
might to smother her conscience, she could not enter
into a lifelong contract with a man she had shamelessly duped. She nearly gasped at the pain that shot
through her at this thought.

Then there was the marquess. She thought she had
won the struggle with her conscience in that matter,
but she knew now with appalling clarity that it was no
good. She could talk till her eyes bubbled about grant-
ing an old man his heartfelt wish, and soothing his
declining years and all the rest, but the ugly fact remained. She was swindling him.

She simply could not go through with it.

Martha sat up in bed. She must abandon her shame-
ful pretense. She could not, she decided further, face
either Bran or the marquess. She knew she was being
a coward, but she would leave the hotel at the earliest
opportunity—this very night, in fact, so that when
Bran came to speak to her she would be gone. She
would leave a note—but she would be gone.

The words echoed in her mind like the tolling of a
great bell announcing the death of a loved one. Tears,
as hot and hurtful as live coals, lodged in her throat
before welling forth to rain searingly down her cheeks.
She dashed them away and, throwing back her covers,
slid purposefully from her bed. It was too late in the
evening to think of leaving by coach—even if she had

enough money to buy a ticket to York, which she assuredly did not.

There might be another option, however. Glancing at the clock, she saw that it was still early by London social standards—not even midnight. Mr. Simmons might still be at his desk. Hastily donning the bettermost of her shabby muslins, she slipped from the suite and hurried downstairs.

## 10

An hour later, Martha had retired once more, this time in accommodations far less luxurious than those to which she had regrettably become accustomed. The bed was narrow and none too comfortable and it, with a small dressing table, comprised almost the entire furnishings of the little room tucked in a corridor near the hotel kitchen.

It had taken her some time to convince Mr. Simmons to accede to her wishes, but he was a perspicacious, kindly gentleman and he had already guessed a good deal of her story. After moving her meager belongings, she'd composed a note, which now reposed on a table in the sitting room of her erstwhile quarters. She had scribbled her painful message in stony despair, unable to fully comprehend the fact that she would never see Bran again. As she outlined the extent of her fraud, she knew full well he would certainly not seek her out. She would be fortunate, indeed, if he did not set the Bow Street Runners after her.

Sleep in her new situation did not come easily, but at last, she fell into an uneasy doze.

In Canby House, at least one of its occupants was experiencing an equally difficult time in gaining his night's rest. Bran did not so much attempt to seek his bed until dawn had begun to lighten the window frames. The interview with Mr. Beddoes had nearly destroyed him. His first reaction to the agent's revelations had been disbelief, then at last an agonized acceptance. Dear God, how could he have been so taken in? He was not sure how she had accomplished her trickery, but she had worked her will with admirable cleverness.

He had almost given his heart to the vixen—almost offered her a proposal of marriage! With her pansy brown eyes and her appealing air of vulnerability combined with what had seemed to him a compelling honesty, she had scooped him into her deception with the ease of a cat sinking its claws into a particularly succulent mouse.

His first instinct had been to hasten to the Grand Hotel, there to yank Martha Finch from her triumphant repose. Then he would pack her aboard the first coach to York. Or no, what he should do is report her to the authorities and let England's dubious system of justice take its course.

He soon perceived the impossibility of either of these options. Mrs. Coppersmith would no doubt be completely overcome if he created a disturbance in the hotel in the middle of the night. A different sort of disturbance, a scandal of the worst sort, would erupt if he was to turn her over to the tender mercies of the law.

Thus, Bran contained himself for the remainder of the night. Very early the next morning, after calling his valet for a shave and a change of clothes, he set out for the hotel.

"What do you mean, gone?" was his astonished response to Mrs. Coppersmith's tearful greeting.

"Peters came to me not a half hour past," the older woman sobbed, "to tell me that Felicity's bed had not been slept in and the poor girl was not to be found."

"She is not Felicity," snarled Bran, leaping upon what seemed the only salient point in Mrs. Coppersmith's tale.

"What?" came the blank reply. "What do you mean? She—"

"Never mind." Bran put a hand to his head. "What is this about a note?"

"Yes!" Mrs. Coppersmith snatched up a screw of paper from a nearby table. "See, it has your name on it. I did not read it, of course."

Bran stared blindly at the little piece of paper. He contemplated his name, scrawled on the outside. Strange that he did not recognize the handwriting, when every facet of her had become so familiar to him. But then, he reflected bitterly, he really hadn't known her at all, had he?

*Dear Bran,* she had written, and he was seized by a momentary rage at the use of the name he'd offered her in his deluded affection.

> *I am sorry. I can no longer continue the false-hood I began so many months ago. I am not Felicity Marshall. I can tell you only that I know that she perished in the shipwreck. She is truly lost to you. I can only apologize deeply for the pain my deception will cause Lord Canby—and perhaps, you as well. I am leaving London and I shall not return.*
> *Martha Finch*

"Does she really think," were Bran's first words, "that she will escape so easily—with a simple, 'I am sorry'? By God, she shall not!"

He tossed the note to Mrs. Coppersmith, turned on his heel, and ran from the room.

Once in the lobby, Bran hurried to the desk. Here he was doomed to disappointment, for Simmons was absent from his post. He was about to turn away, when the sound of voices drifted to him from the little office behind the desk.

"But, ma'am," said one of them, immediately recognizable as Simmons, "there has not been time to con-

tact the Grand Vista in Harrogate. I am sure there
will be no problem, for Mr. Williston is looking for
help there—and you would be eminently suited for
the position of assistant housekeeper—but it would be
wise to—"

"I've no doubt you're right, sir," a woman answered, in obvious distress.

Bran halted, his eyes wide. Spinning about, he hur-
tled around the reception desk and into the office.

"However," Martha Finch continued, "I do not
wish to stay—"

She looked up, startled, at Bran's abrupt entrance.
She whitened, and her attempt to rise was thwarted
by his heavy hand on her shoulder.

"Of course, you do not wish to stay," snarled Bran.
"I do regret thwarting whatever plan you have concocted to escape your just punishment, Mrs. Finch, but
you will come with me—to Canby House, for now."

All but jerking Martha to her feet, he turned to Mr.
Simmons. "And as for you—sir, I shall have something to say to you later."

Mr. Simmons, pale but composed, stood and placed
himself between Martha and Bran. Bran stepped forward belligerently, but at Martha's gasp, he swung instead to face her.

"Madam," he said icily, "you will do me the goodness to come with me. Now."

Gazing into Martha's stricken gaze, Bran became
aware of an appalling urge to pull her into his arms.
To comfort her—to tell her that none of it mattered.
Good God, what was the matter with him? He had
the adventuress in his grasp, and by the Lord Harry
she was going to pay. Grasping her arm, he pulled her
toward the door.

"My lord," Mr. Simmons said, stepping forward
once again. "It appears the lady does not wish to accompany you."

Bran did not deign to answer, merely putting up an
arm preparatory to pushing Simmons out of the way.

To his surprise, the manager resisted—and in a surprisingly forceful manner.

"I am very sorry, my lord, but I cannot allow you to bully a defenseless female," he said resolutely.

"Bully!" Bran returned explosively. "Look here, my good man, you are no doubt unaware of the crime this 'defenseless female' has perpetrated. In any case, it is none of your concern. You will remove yourself from my path, or I'll—"

"Please," Martha whispered. "Lord Branford, please let me explain to you first. I will do whatever you wish after that."

"Explain!" Bran could hardly get the word out past the lump of anguish that had settled in his throat. At the agony he perceived in her eyes, something within him collapsed. "Very well. If the suite I engaged for you is still empty, we will talk there."

Martha merely nodded and turned to follow Bran from the room, but not before Mr. Simmons stepped forward once again.

"Are you sure you wish to do this, Mrs. Finch?"

Martha nodded almost imperceptibly.

"Very well, ma'am, but should you need assistance, you have only to reach for the bell pull—or to cry out," he added meaningfully. When Martha still said nothing, Mr. Simmons produced a room key and gave it to her.

Upstairs, when Martha handed Bran the key, she glanced up at him quickly and in her gaze Bran read a shared memory. With a harsh growl he flung open the door and ushered her roughly inside.

"How convenient for you," he rasped, "to have found such a stalwart supporter. What did you promise the unfortunate wretch for his cooperation?"

Martha stiffened, and turned even more starkly white.

"Nothing, my lord. I went to him last night to tell him I wished to leave London with all possible speed, but that I had no money. I asked if he could place me in a position in the hotel until I could save up coach fare." Her mouth twisted. "I am a very good scullery maid. Mr. Simmons seemed to know something of my predicament—that is, he had heard gossip about my reason for coming here and sensed that something had gone awry." Martha dropped her gaze. "In any event, he allowed me to stay the night in the servants' quarters, and told me he thought he could place me in another of the hotels in this chain as an assistant to the housekeeper. He said, it would—"

Bran interrupted her with a chopping gesture. "Yes, well never mind all that. Let us speak of your fraud. I must tell you that I already know the basics of your little scheme. You see, my agent came to see me last night, and he told me that after questioning almost everyone who has lived in Tenaby for the last twenty-five years, he at last was informed that—"

Martha slumped, interrupting him in a voice that was like dry grasses rustling in a searing wind. "He told you that there were two children found on the beach that morning."

Into the silence that followed her admission, Bran's voice intruded harshly. "The other child lived only a few days. I assume it was she—"

"Yes." Bran had to strain to hear her. "The Sounders found two small girls, whom they named Mary and Martha. Mary wore a fine silk dress. I was naked. The silver locket was grasped tightly in Mary's hand and it was she who was wrapped in the woolen shawl embroidered with her initials."

"Then who are you?" snapped Bran.

"I don't know," replied Martha simply. "Though I cannot recall anything that had happened in my life before opening my eyes to find Josiah Sounder's face peering into mine, I remember twisting about to find Mary crying weakly beside me. I sensed that she was important to me. When Josiah brought me to Margaret, I watched with her as Mary grew weaker. I was terrified at finding myself in this unfamiliar environment, in the care of strangers, and I formed the belief that Mary was my sister. She became my only connection to a life I could not remember, and I grieved frantically when she died only six days later. I dreamed about her at night—I created fantasies in which we played together as sisters in the loving family we had lost."

"But," interposed Bran incredulously, "Felicity had no sister. What would another small girl-child have been doing on the Benningtons' yacht?"

"I have no idea," Martha replied again. "In any event, though I was happy during the years I spent with the Sounders, with their deaths, I belonged to no one. A yearning grew in me to discover my identity. It's hard to explain how badly I longed for a family— my real family. People who loved me and would take me to their breasts."

"Mmph. And when you discovered that the Marquess of Canby was looking for his granddaughter, you put two and two together to come up with a vision of a tidy fortune for yourself."

Martha expelled a sigh so full of despair that Bran almost lifted a hand to her.

"Yes," she replied softly. "More or less. About six months ago I overheard a conversation that led to my contacting a barrister, Mr. Pinfold. I learned very quickly that he is not too nice in his methods."

"Just the sort you were looking for," interposed Bran dryly.

Martha flushed awkwardly, but continued as though he had not spoken. "I was honest with him, and he apprehended immediately what I intended. He had no objection to the fact that my claim was apparently false. Indeed, he seemed delighted to assist me. The rest you know."

"And the life you described to me? Your struggle as scullery maid? And the Murchisons?"

Martha flushed again. "Everything was as I told you. I did learn to speak properly there, and to behave in a genteel manner.'' She rose from the chair into which she had sunk. ''I believe that it is all I have to say, my lord, except that I profoundly regret my actions. I wish I had never embarked on this ruinous deception.''

Bran's fingers clenched. ''May I ask what brought about your remarkable change of heart? A *crise de conscience*?''

''As a matter of fact, yes. I wanted desperately for the marquess to be my grandfather, and for all the uncles and cousins I have met to be truly mine. And, yes, I did relish the thought of never again worrying where my next meal would come from. But, in the end, I couldn't do it. The—affection I had developed for Lord Canby''—Martha lifted her head, and the misery in her gaze almost engulfed him. She paused for a moment before adding—''and you—loomed like a spectre at a children's party. I did not expect to have such a difficulty, but I did—and it became insurmountable.''

She moved to the door. ''I beg you, my lord, do not force me to face Lord Canby. What good could come of such a confrontation? I know the anguish I have caused him—but would my admission to him make him feel any better? Or perhaps you have decided to prosecute me for fraud. If so, I shall not dispute your charge.''

Again her voice had become almost inaudible, as though each word she spoke took an unbearable effort.

''No,'' Bran answered quietly, thrusting down the pain that churned within him. ''I have already determined that the less scandal arising from your despicable action the better. And yes, I suppose you are right about the possible effect of a confrontation with Lord Canby. In short,'' he finished, biting off each of the words so that they seemed to splinter against his tongue, ''though it would give me a great deal of pleasure to have you whipped at the cart's tail, I shall simply bid you good-bye and good riddance."

He moved to open the door for Martha's departure, but halted suddenly and wheeled on her. "I suppose you intended, as part of your inflated plan, to snabble yourself a juicy *parti*." He cursed himself for his weakness in speaking, but he could not stop himself from pouring out the hurt and humiliation that consumed him. "Do you know how close you came to achieving your dream of a golden future? My God, I believed you! I believed you were the playmate of my youth returned to me. A veritable soul mate!" He uttered a ragged laugh. "I was about to propose marriage to you. You could have been a countess." His laugh was a mirthless bark as he opened the door. "In any event, dear lady, you need not concern yourself about how to earn your bread in the future. I shouldn't return to your failing bookshop if I were you. Oh, yes, my agent discovered the true state of affairs there. No, you must pursue a career on the stage. I predict a stellar future for you there."

At this, a cry of such anguish broke from Martha that he turned to look at her.

"Bran—" she choked. "Please be Bran for me just this one last time. There was no pretense in—what was between us. Please believe that knowing I must leave you and that I will never see you again will be more punishment for me than even you could dream of." Her voice dropped to the merest whisper. "Goodbye, my love."

She spun away and ran from the room, leaving Bran to stare after her, white-faced. A moment later, galvanized into action, he bolted from the room after her, but she was gone. He moved forward as though to follow, but an instant later, halted, his shoulders slumped and his hands hanging loose at his side. Very slowly, he retraced his steps to the suite. Closing the door, he pocketed the key and made his way mindlessly down to the lobby.

## 11

Bran did not return to Canby House. He could not face the old gentleman yet with news that would devastate him. Instead, he drove aimlessly through the streets of the city. Eventually, he directed his phaeton toward White's, where he ensconced himself in the farthest corner of the smallest of the lounges. His expression was such that none of his acquaintances so much as approached him in his isolation.

All during the rest of an interminable afternoon, his thoughts circled in an endless, corrosive spiral. In addition to asking himself again and yet again how he could have been so taken in, he contemplated the unbelievable perfidy of Martha Finch. He remembered her warmth, the pleasure she seemed to take in his company, her seemingly genuine joy in being reunited with her "grandfather." Above all, he could not rid his mind of the memory of her response to his embrace. God, he would have wagered his life that the sweet heat of her kisses was genuine.

But it was not. Every thrust of her body, every gesture of giving, even her soft murmurings, had been false as a two-pound note. And he had believed. Oh, how he had believed. He might almost laugh, he reflected bitterly, if he were not occupied in watching his life shatter around him.

It was very late in the day when he came to the bitter conclusion that he should rejoice in the discovery of dishonesty before he had made a complete fool of himself. He had almost committed his life and his heart to the witch. Lord, if she hadn't already revealed herself, he might very well have believed any denials she might have made of Beddoes's report.

If— Wait a minute! *Hadn't revealed herself?* When she had written her note, she had no idea that Beddoes was at that moment telling his employer of the two little castaways. Dear God, she'd had no reason

to destroy the plans that had culminated so successfully. Unless—

He sat immobile for a few more moments, frozen
in thought. Then, with a cry, he fairly leaped from his
chair and stumbled from White's, nearly knocking
over a waiter as he did so.

On leaving Bran, Martha had fled to the little room
she had been assigned adjacent to the kitchen. She
flung herself on the narrow bed. Dear heaven, her
worst nightmare had been realized with the appearance of Bran in Mr. Simmons's office. His reaction
had been as she'd anticipated. She would never forget
his look of contempt, and she imagined she could hear
her heart cracking into great, bleeding shards.

Now, at last, she found a measure of release in tears.
All her hurt and grief poured down her cheeks until,
at last, when she could cry no more, she simply rolled
over on her sodden pillow and stared at the ceiling.

At least, she would not have to face Lord Canby.
In addition, she supposed she should be grateful for
the position Mr. Simmons had offered her in Harrogate. She need not return to York and the further
humiliation of turning over the bookshop to Matthew's greedy relatives.

Far into the afternoon, she contemplated her future,
an activity that brought nothing but the most profound
depression. She might look forward to a lifetime of
honest work at a reasonable wage, but she knew the
hurt would never go away. She would live the rest of
her life in an aching void, for she would live it without
Bran. How she was to—?

She sat up, suddenly, her bleak musings interrupted
by— What was that smell? Surely—yes! It was smoke!
She jumped from the bed and ran from the room,
turning first toward the dining room. She encountered
several servants scurrying between the kitchen and
dining room. She could detect nothing amiss in the
dining room. Retracing her steps, she slipped into one

of the other rooms along the corridor between the dining room and the kitchen. Here the odor of smoke was clearly detectable, but the servants in the corridor appeared to notice nothing. She fled to the kitchen, where she encountered a scene of unmitigated bedlam.

The cavernous chamber was insufferably hot, but she could see no flame apart from the cooking stoves, nor could she smell anything beyond normal cooking odors. Servants of every status scurried to and fro in a seemingly patternless rush. Some wielded utensils, some carried containers of food. The chaos centered about a large man with a prominent nose who stood in the center of the melee, bellowing in what sounded like French.

Martha approached the man, tugging on his sleeve for attention. "Pardon me, m'sieur, but I believe there is a problem."

Driving along Oxford Street toward the Grand Hotel, Bran found the thoroughfare unexpectedly congested, and was forced from his abstraction by the sound of bells and the clatter of fire trucks racing past him. He smelled the smoke for several minutes before he realized it emanated from the hotel. Then, as he drew nearer, he was appalled to see flames leaping against the evening sky.

It was some moments before he could force his way into the environs of the hotel, and at last simply leaped from his curricle, leaving it unattended in the crush of traffic. Running up to the hotel entrance, he spotted Simmons, assisting a portly matron with a hastily stuffed portmanteau. A distraught young woman pushed past him calling for someone named Hettie.

"I don't know, my lord. I have not seen her," Simmons responded breathlessly to Bran's frantic questions. "The fire apparently started near the kitchen. Mrs. Finch is lodged nearby, but surely she must have—"

But Bran was gone. He was denied entry through the hotel's front door by the throng of arriving firemen, and ran to the back of the building. He searched frantically for several minutes, colliding with a great number of people, none of whom was the one person in the world he sought so desperately. He turned to make his way back to the front of the hotel, but— Wait! Was that—? His eyes strained toward a figure just emerging from a rear entrance, leading a very young serving maid to safety. Her face was blackened almost beyond recognition, and her shabby gown was stained and tattered, but—yes! It was she!

"Martha!" he cried.

At the sound of his voice, Martha whirled, and with an inarticulate cry she ran toward him, her arms outflung.

He gathered her into a crushing embrace, pressing his mouth against her hair.

"Oh, God, Martha. I could not find you! I—thought I'd lost you." He drew back to look at her. "Are you all right?"

"Yes," she choked. "I tried to tell that odious man that the place was on fire, but he wouldn't listen. No one would listen," she went on, the words tumbling from her. "Until it was too late. Oh, Bran, I am so glad—"

She halted abruptly, gazing up at him, wide-eyed. "But—what—?" She lifted her gaze to him in a dawning, unbelieving wonder.

"Come," said Bran brusquely. "Let us get out of this."

Taking her hand, he led her into one of the many garden paths surrounding the hotel . . . Soon they had left the bells and shouts behind, and reaching a shady little bower, he guided her to a small bench nestled there.

"Dear Lord, Martha," he breathed again. "I've been such a fool. For a moment I thought—"

Bran could say no more, but pulled Martha into a

rough embrace. His mouth covered hers in a kiss of such urgent tenderness that Martha felt her heart swell in an unbelieving joy.

The next moment Martha thought her heart must have stopped, for she could not breathe—could not even think. This apprehension corrected itself almost immediately as she absorbed the wonder of Bran's embrace. Only a few moments ago, she had been plunged into a nightmare, of which the hotel inferno was only the culmination of an eternity of unremitting horror, beginning with this morning's confrontation with Bran.

Now, he had returned. He had been frightened for her! He was kissing her, just as though . . .

"Bran?" she whispered again.

"Dear God, Martha, I have been so very stupid. I almost let you get away from me, and I love you so very much. Can you forgive me for behaving like such a lout?"

A surge of joy, almost painful in its intensity, welled within her. Was she hearing aright?

"Bran—my dearest love. I can't tell you what your words mean to me, but I don't understand. I did a dreadful thing. You had every right to turn away from me. How can you love me? I am not deserving of anyone's love."

He shook her gently. "Martha, listen to me. Yes, what you did was terrible, but sometimes very good people can do very bad things. You are—although I will admit to a certain bias—a wonderful person. You tried very hard to do a bad thing—and your reasons were compelling—but in the end you couldn't do it. I am just sorry I did not realize that aspect of your actions until a few moments ago."

With an incoherent cry, Martha fairly flung herself once more into Bran's arms and for the next several moments, nothing could be heard in the little bower save a few muted endearments and the distant commotion still in progress at the hotel.

At last, Bran rose and assisted Martha to her feet.

"I think we'd better go now, my love," Bran said. "It is getting late, and we must find some lodging for you for the night."

"Indeed," replied Martha unsteadily. "I'd forgotten for a moment that I no longer have a roof over my head. Do you think another hotel—?"

"I think first we must repair to Canby House."

He had spoken gently, but once again Martha felt her heart lurch within her breast. "No!" she exclaimed. "Oh, Bran—I cannot face him. What must he think of me?"

"We will face him together, love, for if we are to be married—"

"Married!" squeaked Martha. "What are you thinking, Bran? I cannot possibly marry you!"

Bran's brows snapped together. "I beg your pardon?"

"You must marry one of your own kind. You must wed a lady—so she can bear you noble children. I am fit only for—"

Bran clamped his fingers over Martha's lips. "If you plan to finish the sentence as I suspect," he growled, "I shall be forced to inflict some serious corporal punishment."

He followed through on his threat by kissing her once more, firmly, thoroughly, and with breathtaking competence.

"You are a lady in every meaningful sense of the word. If you will have me, I mean to marry you with all the pomp and ceremony available. But, I think you will agree, we must see Lord Canby, and we must do it now."

Martha breathed an unwilling sigh of agreement. Lord Canby would, in all probability, never wish to see her again, but gazing into Bran's eyes, she was strengthened by the love she saw there, mirroring her own.

"Yes," she whispered. "We must go to Lord Canby."

At the town house, they encountered a scene every bit as chaotic as they had envisioned. It took some moments for Hobbs to answer the door, and they had no more entered the house than the marquess burst into the hall as though catapulted.

"Bran!" Lord Canby cried. "Carolyn has been here. She showed me the note!" His face darkened on observing Martha. "You! You have the gall to show your face here." His features crumpled suddenly. "My God, you—you thieving vixen, how could you do such a thing? Who are you? How could you have concocted such a convincing tale? Where did you get the locket?" He thrust his hand forward. "Give it to me this instant."

"Sir." Bran did not lift his voice, but his simple gesture had the desired effect of calming the old man. Bran drew Martha forward. "May we talk this out quietly—and reasonably?"

For a moment, the marquess stood still, radiating anger and hurt. At last, he said grudgingly, "Very well. Hobbs, have something sent to the morning room." Turning, he stumped from the hall, not waiting to see if the others followed.

Some minutes later, the little group sat before a comfortable fire, tea things arranged on a low table before them.

"Now, then," Lord Canby began, casting a glare at Martha, "I should have thought you on your way back to York by now. Unless you have some idea of cozening me further, which, let me assure you, will not fadge."

"No, my lord," murmured Martha through dry lips. "I merely wish to explain—and to ask your forgiveness."

"My for—!" The marquess fell into silence, as though overwhelmed at her audacity.

"Please," said Bran once more, "we thought it nec-

essary to make you aware of the circumstances. Hear
me out, sir. I promise, you will think differently when
you do."

The old gentleman said nothing, but flung up a hand
in scowling acquiescence.

The tale did not take so very long in the telling,
and when Bran was through, the marquess leaned forward, still frowning at Martha.

"I am so very sorry, my lord," she choked. "I know
what I did was horribly wrong. Please believe me
when I say that finding a family had become desperately important to me—although I must confess that
becoming the heiress of a wealthy peer held an unde-
niable attraction." She sighed. "You asked me before
who I am. I am sorry, I cannot tell you. I know not
where I came from or what my name might be."

At this, the old man rose to pace before the fire for
a few moments. He turned to face Martha once more.

"I know who you are," he said heavily. "Your name
is Serena Worth and you are my son's other daughter."

## 12

"What!" gasped Bran, echoed by Martha.

"But, I never knew of another daughter!" exclaimed Bran.

The marquess sat down again, and when he next
spoke, his voice was hushed.

"When my son—Bennington—married Jennifer, he
was already involved with a young woman. She was a
governess whom Ben had met on a visit to a friend
somewhere up north. Though he loved Jennifer, he
could not bring himself to cut the connection with his
mistress. Her name was Joanna. Joanna Worth. Even
after Jennifer conceived Stewart, Ben kept Joanna
under his protection. When Jennifer became pregnant
with Felicity, however, he vowed to break with Jo-

anna. When he went to her, she told him that she, too, was with child.

"I don't know what happened then, but somehow Jennifer discovered Joanna's existence. She went to confront her rival, and to her own astonishment as well as Ben's, she liked the young woman on sight. She felt deeply for the plight of her husband's mistress, and insisted Joanna be brought into their home. Ben, needless to say, was absolutely flummoxed. One hears about these bizarre arrangements all too often in society these days, but one does not expect such a situation to develop in one's own family. Nonetheless, Joanna was installed in Bennington House."

"I don't understand," Bran interposed in astonishment. "I was as close to your family as I was to my own—much closer, in fact. Yet, I never knew of any of this."

"Yes." The marquess coughed. "Well, that was my doing. When Ben came to me to tell me what was happening, I was outraged. When he refused to concede to my demand that the Worth woman be set up in her own establishment, I insisted that, at least, Joanna be hired as Jennifer's companion and that Joanna's child be passed off as the offspring of her and a soldier killed in battle somewhere. After a great deal of fractious discussion, he and Jennifer agreed.

"The infant, a girl named Serena, was born a few days after Jennifer gave birth to Felicity. I saw little of Serena, since, though Joanna and Jennifer became fast friends, the infant and Joanna remained in Ben's home here in London, where they kept to themselves. I was disturbed to learn that Felicity and Serena had become fast friends and played together constantly—almost as sisters. As far as I know, Ben remained faithful to Jennifer through their remaining years together. Joanna and her daughter never came to Canby Park, which is why you would not have seen her there, and, of course, Joanna and Serena never set foot in Canby House. Because of my aversion to the association, care was taken that neither Joanna nor Serena would appear in my presence, although, of course, I occasionally caught a glimpse of one or the other of them by accident. Stewart knew of Serena's existence, but was told only that the little girl was the child of his mother's companion.

"Oddly enough, there was a strong resemblance between Joanna and Jennifer. Both were tall and fair and slim. The two little girls were similar in appearance as well, with golden curls and brown eyes."

The marquess sighed heavily. "I was not told that Ben and Jennifer intended to take Joanna and Serena along on their yachting holiday, though I suppose, given the relationship, I should not be surprised."

A profound silence settled on the group then, until Bran spoke at last.

"You know," he said thoughtfully, "we have assumed here that Martha is Serena, but what if she is Felicity, after all?"

"What?" Martha and Lord Canby turned to him in surprise.

"Well, just consider. Serena's clothing would have been just as fine as Felicity's. The locket, found in Mary's hand, might well have been snatched from Martha's neck in the rough and tumble of their brief sojourn in the boat. The shawl may have been snatched up at random and thrown about the handiest child before dropping them both into the boat. And then," he concluded almost as an afterthought, "Martha is left-handed—as was Felicity. That seems to me a great coincidence."

He halted, gazing at the other two.

"Yes," said the marquess after another extended silence. "It is possible, isn't it?" he said wonderingly— almost pleadingly. He turned again to the young woman beside him. "My dear—"

Martha spoke at last, in a voice filled with pain and bewilderment. "Then, I still cannot be sure who I am. I have no wish now to claim what is not mine, but—"

Her voice caught on a sob. "I thought for a moment I had recovered my identity. I thought I was Serena Worth—not as exalted a name as that of Felicity Marshall, to be sure, but it was my place in the world. Mine alone." She glanced around. "I suppose I am talking nonsense," she concluded with a watery smile.

The marquess reached for Martha's hand and said brokenly, "My son had two daughters, one of whom I never acknowledged. I do not know which of you has been returned to me, but now I tell you, it makes no difference. You are my granddaughter, and if you will forgive an old man for his foolish intransigence so long ago, I would like very much to welcome you home—again."

He stood, opened his arms, and with a joyful cry, Martha ran into them.

Bran joined them to add his own expressions of satisfaction, and it was some minutes before the rejoicing abated and the tears were dried.

"So, what the devil are we to call you, my dear?" the marquess asked, smiling. "Besides, Granddaughter, of course."

After a moment, Martha opened her mouth to speak. Since the moment of her recognition of Lord Canby's fob, other memories had begun to surface—recollections, for example, of a magnificent house with sparkling chandeliers—and there was a tall, laughing man she called "Papadearest." Interspersed with these were faint images of another man—perhaps a younger version of the marquess?—upon whose knee she climbed for loving embraces. The time was approaching, she felt, when her identity would be produced from her own mind. Until then . . . She hesitated.

With a glance at his betrothed, Bran interposed. "I rather think the Countess of Branford has a nice ring. We can work out the informal address later. Do you not agree?"

After several moments of stunned silence, the marquess uttered a pleased shout. "Do you mean it, boy? My dear? You would not bamboozle an old man once again!"

"Never again, Grandpapa," whispered Martha—or Serena—or possibly Felicity.

"I can only tell you this," Bran declared with great aplomb. "I devoutly hope your next descendant will be a boy—and he will bear the name Stewart Marshall Storm, Viscount Weatherby, heir to the Earl of Branford."

"What a terrible mouthful to inflict on a helpless infant," chuckled his beloved.

It was not long before the marquess, quite worn with the events of the day, retired for the night, leaving it up to his friend the earl to deal with whatever protests might further issue on the subject of forthcoming progeny.

All of which were vanquished most successfully, and in a wonderfully effective manner, by the designated father of said progeny.

# The Management Requests
## by Barbara Metzger

*Proper supervision.*

Captain Arthur Hunter was limping badly. He would always and forever be limping badly, but he wouldn't be Captain Hunter for long. No, as soon as the War Office accepted his resignation, Arthur would be Viscount Huntingdon, an honor he wished for almost as much as he wished for that cannon blast at Ciudad de Santos. Deuce take it, he'd managed to survive Bonaparte; his brother Henry might have tried to survive that curricle race to Brighton. Arthur never wanted to succeed his brother, and he never wanted to be stumbling through Mayfair leaning on a cane, and he sure as the devil never wanted to be playing diplomatic dogsbody to foreign dignitaries. Unfortunately, he spoke German, in several dialects. And he'd been of some assistance at the peace talks. And the prince regent wanted his officers marched through the streets like conquering heroes for the victory fetes.

Victory, hell. The country should be in mourning for all the good men lost. Yes, the Peninsular War was finally over, but at such a cost no one should be celebrating. Try telling that to those fools at the War Office, though. All they were concerned with was the next parade. So what if the poor infantry soldiers were being dumped back on the streets with no jobs, no pensions, no way to support their families? They had their new medals and ribbons, didn't they? Bah!

Arthur would have traded every gewgaw and grosgrain for the chance to go home to the country, to learn to manage the family's properties, to be out of the deuced public eye. Instead he was suffering through another barrage, this time of bombast instead of cannonballs. Devil take it, if he'd wanted to be a sauntering park soldier he'd have joined the Horse Guards. If he'd wanted to be a swaggering swell with a smooth tongue he'd have joined the diplomatic corps.

And if he'd wanted to stay at the family residence in Cavendish Square, he wouldn't be limping halfway across Town. He'd learn to ride again, he swore, but not in view of the *ton,* so Arthur supposed he'd have to purchase himself a curricle. His brother's, by all reports, was reduced to kindling. Meanwhile, the streets were so congested Captain Hunter had left the hackney to walk. Even at his slow rate, he'd get to Huntingdon House sooner. And the sooner he'd paid his respects to Henry's widow, the sooner he could remove his dress uniform, rest his aching leg, and resort to a bottle of wine.

Seven years older than Arthur's eight and twenty, Sylvia, Lady Huntingdon, still treated him like a sticky-faced schoolboy. A series of miscarriages had ruined her looks; knowing that she had not protected the succession from second-son soldiers ruined her temperament. Still, she was nearly all the family Arthur had left except for some old aunts and distant cousins, so he made sure to call on her first, before she heard through the rumor mills that he was back in London. He handed his shako to Henry's butler Udall and quickly combed his fingers through his blond curls as he followed the poker-backed servant down the hall.

"At last!" Sylvia did not waste her breath on pleasantries. "I thought you'd never get here. Henry has been gone for over a year now. The least you could have done was sell out your foolish commission."

In the middle of a war? Arthur merely bowed over her plump hand, declaring that she looked well. She looked like a stuffed sausage, with a frizz of hennaed curls on top.

"Well? How could I look well with all the worries on my shoulders, the thousands of details I am constantly bothered with?"

Since the captain knew he had an excellent man of affairs in charge of the estate, one who communicated with him on a weekly basis, he could not imagine what had Sylvia in a swivet. He did stop wondering, however, why Henry undertook a reckless race to Brighton in the first place. "Yes, well, I am home now, so you may refer any difficulties to me. You have enough funds? The house is in order?"

She waved his questions aside with a lace-edged handkerchief. Her other hand held a lemon tart. "Of course it's in order. For the time being. Who knows what will happen next though, with a vagabond for viscount."

"Ma'am, I was with Wellington, not a band of Gypsies. Henry agreed I should go. He even bought my commission." Arthur looked around for a decanter, but saw nothing but a pot of tea, to his regrets. Udall was playing least in sight, wise fellow that he was. At least the lemon tarts were good.

"Faugh. Henry thought he'd live forever, too. Most likely the same as you do, with no thoughts to the future, to those dependent upon you. What would happen to me, I ask you, if you'd died of that wound?"

"You'd have a handsome settlement and the dower house at your disposal. No one can take those from you, no matter what far-off cousin is viscount."

"Gammon. They are all strangers, not real family. But now that you are here, you will do your duty, I am sure."

Arthur thought about that Austrian princess he was supposed to squire about Town for the Foreign Office and shrugged.

"Yes, and while you are looking around at the current crop of misses, you can be our escort, now that we are out of mourning and there are so many fetes and balls."

Arthur choked on his lemon tart and took a nasty gulp of too-hot tea. Looking around? Escort? We? He could feel a prickle at the back of his neck, the same kind of prickle that used to tell him there was danger ahead, enemies waiting in ambush. "I'm afraid I have duties still. I did write to you concerning this last assignment, didn't I?"

Sylvia swept his excuses aside like so many crumbs on her ample chest. "Nonsense. You know what is owed your family. An heir, for one."

"Surely it is early days for that. I have no intention of—"

And Sylvia had no intention of letting this wealthy, titled gentleman slip through her hands. "Yes, and I am hoping you will consider my sister Elizabeth. A lovely girl, well bred, of course, with a handsome portion."

Arthur recalled Elizabeth Ferguson from Henry's wedding. She'd been skinny, spotty, and shy then. He saw no reason to believe she'd improved with age. "Is Miss Ferguson with you in London, then?"

"Of course. Where else should she be, with all the festivities going on? We'll be much more comfortable now, with a gentleman's escort."

"I'm afraid that won't be possible, ma'am. As I explained, I am to be squire to Princess Henrika Hafkesprinke. In fact, I must find my lodgings shortly, in case she and her entourage arrive early."

"Lodgings? You'll stay here, of course."

Where he could find Miss Ferguson in any number of compromising situations, like his bed? Arthur congratulated himself on bespeaking rooms at the princess's hotel. He'd not wanted to discompose his sister-in-law, nor make her feel in any way de trop. Now he did not feel as though parson's mousetrap was closing on his good leg. He stood, with the aid of his lion's-head cane. "I really must be off."

"I won't hear of it. What am I to tell people when they ask why you are not biding in your own home? They'll think we've had a falling out. That I did not make you welcome. Or that you do not wish to know your own family. Or—"

Captain Hunter had been making his way out of the drawing room, with Sylvia trailing crumbs and complaints behind. As he reached the hall he pointed his walking stick at the stairs to the bedrooms, the steep marble stairs that climbed endlessly, it seemed. "You may merely tell anyone rude enough to inquire that I was unable to negotiate the steps."

"After you walked here?" Sylvia screeched.

"Quite right. Udall, find me a hackney."

More stairs, confound it. The blasted hotel had enough steps to lead straight to the top of Mt. Olympus, it seemed to Captain Hunter. Half-naked gods and goddesses looked down from every niche and on every painted, carved, or woven surface, to watch the poor mortals struggle upward. Arthur's suite was on the third floor, of course. His batman, Browne, clicked his tongue.

"It's a rum go, Cap'n. You'll be settin' that leg of yours back a month, less'n you intend to spend all the time in your room, eatin' there, too."

Worse, it would set the cat among the pigeons if he took accommodations more inhospitable to his leg than Huntingdon House. His sister-in-law would have an apoplexy, at the least.

"You would of done better, I'm thinkin', to bunk down in the library at Cavendish Square, less'n, a' course, you was plannin' on entertainin' that princess in your bedchamber."

Which was exactly what Captain Hunter was not planning on doing. He was not going to become her royal highness's lover, despite the knowing looks at the War Office and the grins at the Horse Guards barracks. Escort duty was one thing, tupping her Teutonic majesty was quite another. Besides, he'd already done so, in Paris, in his cups, which was most likely why he'd been chosen for this assignment. It was the German schnapps, Arthur recalled with a shudder, swearing never again, not even for the sake of world peace. Princess Henrika was nearly his height, nearly his weight, and nearly insatiable. His leg had required more surgery after that night, and infection had set in. Arthur was barely recovered now, and doubted he'd live through another amorous encounter with the heroically proportioned Hafkesprinke scion.

The captain ignored his servant's overly familiar comments. He and Browne had been through too much together to take offense, especially as the old sergeant only spoke the truth. "I'll see what I can do. Don't carry our bags up yet."

So Arthur limped back across the leagues-long lobby to the reservations desk. The clerk, who gave his name as Kipling, seemed ready to weep that he was not able to accommodate the captain, especially when Arthur reached for his purse. The Grand Hotel might be recently opened, but it was already gaining a reputation for its elegant appointments, for its kitchens, and for being so pleasantly located near the parks. In other words, the hotel had no vacancies. With so many visitors in Town for the victory celebrations, every facility of note was full, including this newest. Kipling puffed out his thin chest at the success of his establishment.

Arthur asked to see the manager. "Oh, Mr. Simmons is much too busy, Captain. And truly, there is nothing he could do."

Another guest approached the desk, simpering that his shaving water had arrived cold that morning, and how the deuce was a gentleman supposed to shave with cold water, he wanted to know. Many were the times on the Peninsula when Arthur shaved with tepid water, or no water at all, and he would have told the loutish lordling to grow a beard. That way, no one would notice that he had no chin. The desk clerk, of course, was trying to explain how they were still slightly short-staffed and what help they did have was somewhat inexperienced. The Tulip was not appeased and poor Kipling was near tears agin. Arthur stepped around the desk, managing to nick the fop's high-polished shoes with his cane, and knocked on the door marked MANAGER in gold letters.

Mr. Simmons was seated at a paper-strewn desk in a well-appointed office. He stood, straightening his waistcoat, when the captain came in. Arthur did not waste either of their times with preliminaries, he simply stated: "I am Captain Hunter, here to translate for the Ziftsweig delegation, and help plan Princess Henrika Hafkesprinke's reception for Lord Wellington. She was thinking of holding it at your hotel, by the way. Oh, I suppose I should be using my title now. That's Viscount Huntingdon, don't you know." He paused a moment for Simmons to absorb all the pertinent details, and calculate how much business the Grand Hotel could win or lose on the officer's say-so. "I need a room on the ground floor."

"I am dreadfully sorry, sir, ah, my lord. There simply are no available rooms, not on any floor, and none of the guests is due to leave soon."

Arthur was staring past Simmons to the tidy bedchamber and small sitting room tucked behind the office. "What about your quarters? If you don't have another residence, perhaps you could ask some of the staff to double up for a short while, freeing a room for you. I realize that's a great imposition, and a slight to your dignity, but I am willing to beg."

Instead of getting down on his knees, from which he was liable never to recover, Arthur removed his purse from his coat and started counting out pound notes. "Of course, this is in addition to the suite already reserved in my name. I might try the stairs occasionally, or dine there with her highness, so you need not worry about having to let those rooms out again."

"But . . . but my apartment?" Simmons had just recently returned from his sister's house, where he'd been recuperating from the gout. He did not wish to return there.

"You could use the desk here, of course. I'll be out most days, showing the princess the sights, you see." Arthur kept stacking the pound notes.

Simmons licked his lips. This would be his money, not the hotel's, wouldn't it? And Mortimer's room belowstairs was still vacant. Or perhaps he could convince the housekeeper to take pity on him and share her bed. "I'll do it."

"I thought you might. My man will help you move your things. He'll look after me so your staff won't have to, and he'll sleep on a pallet bed in the sitting room. You see how easy it is to keep your guests happy? Now if you would only provide some hot water . . ."

Happy? Arthur was nearly ecstatic. He'd escaped his sister-in-law, and could hide from the hot-blooded Henrika. Best of all, he wouldn't have to drag himself up those blasted stairs in public view. Compared to his tent in Portugal or the officers' quarters in Spain or the hospital in France, this cozy suite was heaven. A hot bath, a good meal served by his own fireside, a cigar, and a bottle of cognac—now that was Arthur Hunter's idea of a homecoming celebration. He fell asleep reading the paper Simmons had on his nightstand, a notice, it seemed, that the man was composing for the hotel guests: *The management requests* . . .

Children should be on leashes? No, that was pets.

## 2.

### *No loud noises in the public areas.*

Captain Hunter felt like singing, by George. It was
a new day, and he was that much closer to a new life.
He'd awakened early, with barely a headache from
the cognac, and well rested for once. He put on his
old civilian clothes, even though they were undoubtedly out-of-date, a bit threadbare, and tended to droop
where he'd lost so much weight after the wound and
the fever that followed it. Arthur's old coat was comfortable, however, and better suited to London in July
than his uniform. Gads, what an absurd idea, he
thought, holding the victory celebrations in the City,
in the summer. They should all be in the countryside
enjoying what the war was fought to preserve. Some
nodcock must have decided the Londoners deserved
a reward for living in the heat, dirt, and congestion;
most likely the same nodcock who decided to build a
Chinese pavilion in Brighton while his army went
hungry.

The day was not stifling yet. Better still, Arthur did
not have to face either his sister-in-law, Princess Henrika, or Boney, for at least a few hours. And only a
handful of the other hotel guests were stirring to see
him make his slow way to the dining room. He took
a table close to the door and proceeded to sample
nearly every dish on the hotel's menu: kippers and
omelettes and beefsteak and kidney pie, flaky rolls
and thick jam, all washed down with rich, dark coffee.
He sent his compliments to the kitchen, but the waiter
only told him to wait for dinner, if he thought breakfast was something fine. Their Monsieur DuPré had
been fussing with the menu since dawn.

Lud, Captain Hunter thought, his clothes would be
snug in no time at all. He intended to pay a call on
his tailor today, and his bank, the solicitor, and the

War Office. A visit to Tattersall's to see about a carriage was also on his agenda. If he had a curricle, at least he could ride in the nearby park or out to Richmond. A phaeton might be faster and showier, but the captain knew he'd need a ladder to climb aboard. No, a curricle would do fine, a red one with black wheels, or a black one with red wheels, with no crests on the door either way, Arthur decided over a bowl of fresh strawberries and cream. Then he pushed himself away from the table and hobbled back to his room to fetch his hat, whistling lightheartedly. He did whistle softly, as befitted the lush, hushed lobby.

But the Grand Hotel was not reposing in stately silence, even without Arthur's cheerful tune. Some kind of contretemps was occurring at the reservations desk, the desk Arthur had to step behind to reach his, or Simmons's, rooms. The complainant this morning was a female, so the captain could not very well poke her with his cane, although he'd like to, in return for having his delightful morning destroyed.

He could not see much of the woman from the back, although she appeared fashionably dressed, with only a few brown curls escaping a straw bonnet. She was of medium height, but of mighty voice as she demanded a room. Her companion was an older, more sturdy-looking female garbed in black who stood to the side guarding their trunks and trappings, wringing her hands and murmuring, "Oh, dear, oh, dear. Oh, my stars and scriptures."

She'd need more than a prayer to find a decent room in London this fortnight of celebrations, Arthur thought as he neared the desk.

The other woman, obviously the one in charge and in a pique, echoed his thoughts. "There has to be a room. Every other respectable hotel is booked," she shouted. "And we drove through the night to get here early."

A different, younger clerk was on duty this morning, and he was anxiously tugging on his shirt collar as he apologized once more: "I am that sorry, miss, truly I am, but every available room's been bespoke. The Princess of Ziftsweig is due to arrive today or tomorrow with her entourage, don't you know."

"I didn't know, but now I see your underhanded intent. You want more money than mentioned in your advertisement. A bribe, in other words."

"Oh, no, Miss Thurstfield. I couldn't find you an empty room for a monkey."

The female clutched her tapestry carpetbag. "I don't want a room for a monkey; I want a room for me and my companion, Mrs. Storke. And I want it now, or I shall complain to the manager, the owners of this establishment, every newspaper in Town, and . . . and the mayor of London. And they'll all listen, I'll have you know, because my father is Baron Thurstfield of Interlaken, near Windemere." She stamped her foot, in case the poor harried clerk did not recognize her ill humor.

Lord save him from pampered, petulant females, Arthur prayed as he tried to edge past the self-important harridan, especially green girls fresh from the country. By Zeus, if he'd wanted to encounter sharp-tongued, demanding ladies at breakfast, he could have stayed at Huntingdon House.

The young clerk gave him a beseeching look as he sidled by the desk, then seemed to shrink when he realized Captain Hunter was not his relief, come to rescue him.

"Where's Kipling?" Arthur asked.

"The dastard—pardon, miss—decamped this morning when some old bat—pardon, miss—hit him with her reticule because her chocolate arrived cold at her bedside. I'm George, the footman. Leastways I was until I got promoted an hour ago."

Judging from the lad's expression, Arthur did not think George considered his promotion much of a step up. Miss Thurstfield did not think much of an erstwhile baggage handler overruling her wishes. She tapped her foot again. George cringed. Arthur had seen such looks on new recruits facing their first battle. He wished he could help. "Where's Simmons?"

"Where he is every morning, telling that blasted frog—pardon, miss—in the kitchen that he's a better chef than Prinny's man. Else DuPré cries in the batter, ruining his pastries. Either that or Simmons is off sweet-talking the housekeeper hoping she'll—pardon, miss."

Arthur shrugged, not at the inner workings of the hotel, but that poor George would just have to deal with the difficult damsel on his own. Before he entered his room, the captain turned and glanced at George's tormentor.

Miss Thurstfield was the most beautiful woman he'd ever seen. No, she was not classically beautiful in the blond-haired, blue-eyed ideal, but she was appealing in a way that made ensuring the Huntingdon succession of paramount importance. Soft and smooth and feminine and absolutely adorable, she had brown ringlets framing a heart-shaped face, with a small, straight nose and a tiny smattering of freckles on golden cheeks. And she had lips just meant for kissing and a body meant for loving. Suddenly the July heat was welcome, for it kept Miss Thurstfield from donning her spencer, so Arthur could see the rounded rise of her breasts above the neckline of her gown.

He was not in love, of course. The captain did not believe in love at first sight, especially not with some bucolic beauty who was full of her own self-worth. He turned back to his door, the one marked MANAGER, and felt a touch on his arm.

"Sir?"

He looked down at the graceful gloved hand that sent a shiver right to his toes. Then he looked up, into her eyes. And what eyes they were, fawn brown, with green and gold flecks and black rims. They were honest eyes, trusting eyes, eyes that could mend a soldier's weary soul. Or send him back into battle, to make her world right.

"Perhaps you can help, my good man?"

He was not her good man, Arthur considered, not good at all, not when he was having lewd and lascivious thoughts about the young woman's luscious figure. "I am afraid there's nothing anyone can do for you, miss, without a reservation."

"But I do have a reservation. That's what I've been trying to tell this dunderhead." She put her carpetbag on the floor and untied the strings of her reticule to find a folded sheet. "See, I have confirmation for this date forward."

She had a reservation and wasn't just trying to bully poor George? No wonder the little dear was indignant. Why, Arthur would be tearing the walls down to find himself in London with no place to lay his head. Of course, he had Huntingdon House, the army barracks, any number of friends and acquaintances he could ask for a bunk, but he was not a well-bred young lady whose reputation had to be preserved at all costs. He could not begin to imagine what possessed her father to let such a beauty traipse off alone except for a dithery companion, but here she was, causing a righteous ruckus. None of the other top-drawer hotels would even accept an unescorted, single female, if there were rooms available, which there were not.

He looked at the clerk, who nodded. "But the ambassador said the princess needed the extra rooms. And it wasn't like there was a deposit or anything. The mort—pardon, miss, the young lady's name ain't even mentioned in the reservations box."

"Then it was erased. I was assured my accommodations would be available today, and I trust you gentlemen to make them available now, so poor Nancy can lie down." She raised her chin. "Is that understood, George, and you, sir?" She turned inquiring eyes on the captain, whose tongue seemed to have lost touch with his brain.

"Arthur," was all he could say. He could have said "Captain Hunter." Hell, he should have said "Viscount Huntingdon," since she seemed to think a title was a useful thing for tossing around. But "Arthur" was what he wanted to hear from those rosy lips. Of course he wanted to hear it lying down, with her beneath him, those shining curls fanned across his pillow. A baron's daughter, of course, was not for dalliance, however.

"Mr. Arthur?"

He tried to recall his wayward thoughts. A bed, that was it. She needed a bed and it could not be his. That is, it could not be the bed he was currently occupying. "I do happen to have a suite of rooms that might be available."

George coughed and rolled his eyes, but Miss Thurstfield gave Arthur such a smile that the clerk could have choked to death without Captain Hunter noticing. Why, that smile was enough to make Arthur forget that he was a crippled old soldier with a world of responsibilities on his shoulders. "They are on the third floor, however."

"But the only empty rooms there are yours," George protested.

"Exactly. Mine to hold for emergencies. This counts as an emergency, don't you agree, George?" He nodded encouragingly until George bowed his own head.

"If you say so, Captain."

Miss Thurstfield was too excited to notice the by-play. "Oh, the stairs won't matter. We have five stories in Interlaken, and neither I nor Mrs. Storke has the least difficulty. But these reserved rooms are not exorbitantly priced, are they?" She started to untie her reticule again.

"Oh, no. In fact, they are already paid for." Twice. And Arthur would likely have to bribe both George and Simmons their price again to forget that the suite was held in his name. Miss Thurstfield of Interlaken near Windermere could not be staying in a gentleman's apartments. "That is, we don't charge for them. Can't, since your misplaced reservation was the hotel's fault in the first place."

"Why, that is quite generous. I am sure the hotel will continue to be a great success if you strive to keep your customers so content. You can be sure I will recommend your establishment to all my friends when they travel to the City."

"And I am sure the management will appreciate your kind words." He turned the guest book for her to sign. "George, why don't you find someone to carry Miss, ah, Hope Thurstfield's bags up." He pulled the key out of his pocket and placed it in her palm, forcing himself not to hold her hand, or squeeze it, or bring it to his lips. Damn, but he was acting like the veriest mooncalf. He was not in love, by Jove, Arthur told himself; he'd just been living the soldier's life too long.

She gifted him with another heart-stopping smile— Lud, she had a dimple—and bent to pick up the satchel, which barked.

"You'll have to keep your satchel on a leash, you know. Hotel policy." Arthur was teasing, trying to work himself into confessing that he really was not part of the management staff. He had no excuse for letting her believe he was the concierge except that he'd been ensorcelled by a pair of brown eyes, which was, of course, no reason to continue her misconception. Besides, plain Mr. Arthur was no eligible *parti* for a peer's daughter. Captain Hunter was passable; Lord Huntingdon was a premier catch.

Before he could speak up, however, Miss Thurstfield graciously bobbed her head and said, "You'll be sure to make note of my room number, won't you, for when my intended arrives?"

Her intended? Miss Thurstfield was betrothed? Arthur's feet hit the ground, with his heart plummeting after. That French cannonball hadn't hit him half so hard. He nodded and turned to enter his room, the

one marked MANAGER. It might as well have said:
ABANDON HOPE, ALL YE WHO ENTER.

●          3.

*That all valuables be secured. The Hotel is not
responsible for theft or loss.*

Why should he bother with new clothes? The best
tailoring in all of England could not hide Arthur's
limp. What need had he for a curricle? So the fashionable world could gawk when he clambered down? No,
what he needed was some solitude and a bottle. Or a
ladybird, and a bottle. If he paid enough, perhaps a
Covent Garden convenient would not cringe at the
sight of his mangled limb. For sure no proper young
lady would look at him with admiration, affection, or
*amour*. Not that he couldn't find any number of mod-
ish misses willing to marry him; a title and wealth
could sweeten any bitter pill. Was it too much to want
a wife who wanted *him*, though, not his money or
social standing?

Thinking of money reminded Arthur that he needed
to visit his bank, no matter what other errands he put
off for another day. Putting up at this hotel was putting a hole in his pocket.

"Oh, my, what a lovely suite of rooms!"

Mrs. Storke was fluttering between the sitting room
and the two bedrooms, inspecting the water closet and
the wardrobes while the hotel's maids unpacked their
trunks. Hope's little terrier, Trumpet, was so excited
to be out of his traveling bag that he managed to get
in everyone's way. Hope was equally as pleased to be
so well situated. The rooms were the most luxurious
she had ever stayed in, including her chamber at
Thurstfield. Ever amenity she could think of was pro-

vided by the hotel, from the bowl of fruit to a selection of books and newspapers. And her window looked out over a tree-filled park, so she would not feel so homesick for the country. "You see, Nancy, coming to London was not such a bad idea after all."

"Oh, but what would we have done without that nice Mr. Arthur? I shudder to think what could have happened to us without his help."

"He was everything accommodating," Hope agreed as she placed the wrinkle-free papers on the floor in a corner for the little dog's use. She only hoped the poor servant whose duty it was to iron the newspapers did not hear of their current use.

"And devilishly handsome, didn't you think?"

She hadn't thought of much else since the hotel manager had come to their rescue. Why, every maidservant on the staff must be smitten with his blond hair and blue eyes, his broad shoulders and cleft chin. Even his hands were attractive, she'd noticed when he handed her the key, strong and capable, yet graceful in a manly way.

"Too bad about his limp," Mrs. Storke was saying around a bite of apple from the fruit bowl.

"He limps?" Hope found a silver bowl filled with sugared walnuts, so she nibbled on one. Trumpet had located a plate of biscuits, so he whined till Hope fed him. Nancy just shook her head and left to direct the maids in unpacking their gowns and bonnets.

Hope could not seem to get the handsome hotelier out of her mind. She knew he found her comely, too, for she'd seen that look in a man's eyes often enough in her nineteen years to recognize masculine admiration. What foolishness, though. As if her papa would let a mere Mr. Arthur court his daughter. He swore not to settle for anything less than a baronet. In truth, Hope could not envision herself living behind a reservations desk as Mrs. Arthur. But he was certainly well spoken and refined. She supposed he must be educated to hold such an important position, managing this enormous establishment.

Heavens, she told herself, it was more important than ever to locate Sir Malcolm, if her eye and imagination were wandering to upper servants and tradesmen. Papa would have her married to their gouty neighbor, Lord Ormsby, in a flash, if he suspected such a possibility. He'd given her this one last chance to enjoy herself at the victory celebrations and to find her errant intended.

Contrary to her papa's oft-stated belief, the intentions were not solely on Hope's part. Sir Malcolm Fredenham had spoken to her of his respect and affection, and they had sealed their understanding with a kiss. Before he could make a public announcement, however, Sir Malcolm had to inform his aunt and uncle in London, the relatives who were going to remember him fondly in their wills. And he wished to purchase a ring, he'd said, no trumpery bauble like those found in the hinterlands. Only the best would do for his bride-to-be, only a London jeweler's craftsmanship and artistry.

A month after he'd left, Hope had received a letter, the only letter she was to get, stating that Sir Malcom's uncle was ailing, begging his nephew to stay on. That was four months ago. The man must be either recovered by now or dead. As for her ring, that London jeweler had enough time to mine a deuced diamond, much less set it in a ring. Five months was long enough for a man to be away from the woman he loved, and too long for her father's patience. By the end of December, Lord Thurstfield had decreed, she'd be married and out of his house by the new year or he'd give her hand and handsome dowry to his good friend, Lord Ormsby. Ormsby was forty if he was a day, and covered in snuff and orange hair. Worse, he owned a vicious cur he entered in dogfights. No, Hope could not marry such a man. Trumpet would be a crumpet for the beast.

Hope believed her father's threats were occasioned by the recent arrival of a dashing young widow in the neighborhood. The widow's virtues, or lack thereof, were not suitable topics of conversation for innocents such as Miss Thurstfield but were the talk of the shire, nevertheless. The baron would never entertain the notion of inviting Mrs. Longstreet to his daughter's drawing room; entertaining her in his own cold, lonely bed was another matter entirely, an inviting matter that Thurstfield would dearly like to address before some other enterprising gentleman extended the widow his protection.

Hence Hope's journey to London, with her papa's blessings, but without her papa. His own duties and dislike of doing the pretty kept him in the country, he claimed, Mrs. Longstreet's name hanging between them. Of course, Lord Thurstfield believed his precious girl was traveling with her godmother, Lady Mildred Maythorpe. Lady Mildred knew everyone in Town, and was received everywhere. She fully intended to introduce Hope to every unmarried gentleman of her acquaintance. She did not intend to break her ankle tripping over her own cat.

Hope saw no reason to mention Lady Mildred's mishap to her father, since the news would only upset him. She left for London anyway, accompanied only by her companion and friend, not caring that she wouldn't receive invitations to Carlton House or the other grand social events. She only wanted to find her fiancé. Unfortunately, he'd never mentioned his uncle's name or address, nor any other friends. Surely someone in the vast city could give her his direction.

If she could not locate Sir Malcolm, however, Hope would not be precisely heartbroken, although she had found the baronet's countenance, company, and compliments everything pleasing. The decision to accept his hand had less to do with her heart and more to do with her head, and her father, telling Hope that she was nearing her twentieth birthday, and she'd already turned down every gentleman in the north of England, by her father's reckoning. She wanted to be married, to have a home of her own, and babies. She did not want those babies to be little Lord Ormsbys, covered in snuff and ugly orange hair, patrons of blood sports. So she had to find Sir Malcolm Fredenham, or find some way to meet other eligible *partis* before her funds and her father's patience wore out.

The new wardrobe Nancy was helping the maids unpack was a start. Au courant and elegantly copied straight from the latest fashion journals under Lady Mildred's supervision, the gowns were a showcase for Miss Hope Thurstfield's wealth and beauty and lady-like bearing.

Mrs. Storke dropped a pair of matching slippers and rushed to Hope's side near the window. "Oh, my lands and larks! You'll never believe what one of the girls just told me, my dear. There have been robberies, right here in the hotel! Valuables have been stolen right out of guests' rooms."

Hope scooped up her dog, ready to stuff Trumpet back in his satchel.

"Not that kind of valuable," Nancy chided. "Jewels and watches and cash!"

Hope glanced at the carved wood jewel box sitting in plain sight on the dressing table in her new bedroom. She planned on selling the contents if she could not find Sir Malcolm, to finance a fall Season in Town. Surely one of her mother's old friends would be willing to sponsor her, if Lady Mildred did not recover in time. With the jewels, Hope could take time to select a husband of her own, someone she could respect, if not love. With the jewels, she would not come empty-handed to her marriage even if her father disowned her or denied her dowry if he did not like her choice. She could not, under any conditions, afford to lose those jewels.

"The hotel must have a safe," she declared, stuffing her rings and necklaces and brooches into an empty embroidered reticule. She left out the pearls she intended to wear for dinner and a simple gold locket for the next day, before going to seek out that nice Mr. Arthur. No, Nancy did not need to run up and down all those stairs with her. What could happen in the halls of this magnificent establishment?

Captain Hunter called "Enter" when he heard the light tap on his door. Supposing his visitor to be Simmons, needing to use his desk, or his batman Browne returned from his errands at the haberdashers, Arthur did not bother putting down the bottle he was currently emptying. Still holding the bottle, he jumped to his feet when he saw Miss Thurstfield at the door instead. He winced, that she should see him like this, and from the pain the sudden movement caused his leg. "Yes, miss? What can I do for you?" he asked more brusquely than he intended.

Hope was staring at the bottle, rather than the tousled blond waves of his hair or the sleepy look to his blue eyes. "You're drinking, on duty?"

"My leg was hurting me." Now it hurt worse, thanks to this beautiful, bespoken female.

"But such a thing could cost you your job." No one she knew would keep on a servitor who imbibed, especially not in a position of such authority.

"No chance of my being dismissed, I assure you." He did put the bottle down and straighten his waistcoat.

She was still uncertain. "Your employers must be very understanding."

"What, to hire a cripple?" he bristled.

"No, to permit drinking on the job."

"I am not in my cups, dash it, so you can remove that scowl and the sermon. Ah, your pardon for speaking familiarly, miss." Damn, now he was sounding like that addlepate George. "You wished to see me about something? If you had rung, one of the staff could have taken care of your problem, I am sure."

"Since one of the staff is possibly the culprit, that would not have been wise."

Culprit? What, did one of the footmen ogle her? It was Miss Thurstfield's own fault for being so deuced pretty. Arthur found himself staring, if not precisely ogling. One of those brown curls was caressing her cheek, nearly touching her mouth. He almost reached out to brush it aside. "I am afraid you'll have to be a bit more explicit, Miss Thurstfield."

"The robberies, Mr. Arthur. I have come about the robberies." At his continued blank look, she went on: "There is no need to pretend, sir, to protect the hotel's reputation. All of the maids know things have gone missing recently."

"They have? That is, we have an investigation going on at this very minute. I am certain you have nothing to fear."

She plunked the embroidered reticule on Simmons's desk. "I am not so certain. I very much fear for the safety of my jewelry and wish it locked in the hotel's safe."

"The safe?"

"Surely the hotel has a safe for the day's receipts and the patrons' valuables. Even posting houses sometimes offer such a precaution."

Surely the hotel did boast a safe, but deuce take it if Arthur knew where it was or how to get into it. Now was the time to confess his imposture, but hell, she had a fiancé; he could have some fun. "Sorry, but only the night manager has the combination."

"That's ridiculous. What if I want to wear a ring in the morning?"

He shrugged. "It's a new hotel, you know. All of the difficulties have not been worked out."

"I see what it is. They have not trusted you with the information." She eyed the bottle he'd placed on the desk.

He might not be a hotel manager, but he was no sot either, by George. "The head manager trusts me implicitly. Why, he lets me sleep in his room. It's just that I have not been here long enough to learn all the ins and outs of the hotel. Luckily I did know about the special reserved suite. I trust the rooms met with your satisfaction?"

Reminded of what she owed this man, who was like no other employee she had ever encountered, Hope smiled. "Everything is perfect, thank you, especially the view."

And the view from Arthur's eyes was perfect, too. That smile was worth all the faradiddles he was telling, even if his soul were sentenced to purgatory. "I'll take charge of your treasures, then, and hand them over to Simmons myself. And I promise to watch him put them in the safe. If you come to me whenever you wish to remove a bit of jewelry, I'll make sure Simmons is available."

"Excellent, Mr. Arthur. Now here is a list of the pieces. Do you want to go over it, to familiarize yourself with the contents? You will be responsible for them, after all."

He had absolutely no desire to view her hoard of gems, of course, especially not when they might have come from the bastard she was betrothed to. On the other hand, he didn't want her to leave, so he nodded and swept his hand across the desk, clearing it of Simmons's notes and papers.

Hope poured the expensive jewelry out of the pouch, and ticked each item off her list as she showed it to Mr. Arthur, who was standing quite close to her in order to see better. She could smell his lemon and spice cologne and see the fine gold hairs on the backs of his hands. "My, it is growing warm today, isn't it?"

"Hmm," he agreed, inches away from nibbling on a dainty earlobe. He hadn't seen one necklace or ring, only her silken cheeks and long brown lashes.

"That's the lot, then," Hope said with a sigh, stuffing her fortune and her future back into the reticule. She handed the drawstring pouch and the list over to Mr. Arthur. "I suppose I should have a receipt, you know."

"A receipt?" His mind was benumbed by her—and by the half-empty brandy bottle.

"Yes, something back from you."

"You want something in return?"

"Yes."

So he gave her a kiss.

### 4.

*No spitting, fisticuffs, or rowdy behavior.*

*Whap!*

Arthur deserved the slap, of course, had been expecting it, in fact, but who would have thought this delicate flower of femininity had a roundhouse swing? He staggered back, but his bad leg gave way and he collapsed onto his back. Fine, he thought as he waited for the room to stop spinning, now he was a clumsy jackass as well as a lecher. What in the world possessed him to kiss Miss Thurstfield? Only a world of desire that grew every time he saw the woman. But he was no libertine, and she was no doxy to be mauled about. She was a lady, and an affianced one at that. Her blasted betrothed had every right to call him out. Thunderation, if she were not already engaged to be wed, he'd owe her an honorable offer. All he could offer now was his sincerest apologies, although he did not regret the kiss for an instant. "I am ashamed, Miss Thurstfield," he told her, still prone, looking up into her concerned eyes. "Perhaps I did have too much to drink after all. For my leg, don't you know," he hastened to add. "I swear such a thing will never occur again, gentleman's honor."

But he wasn't a gentleman, Hope thought. He was a jumped-up clerk, taking liberties not even Sir Malcolm had dared. The nerve of the scoundrel! The magic of his lips on hers! Why, she hadn't even struggled when he kissed her, hadn't so much as taken a step backward. In fact, Hope very much feared she'd put her own arm around the cad's neck. She knew for sure that she'd stared at him, dumbfounded or moonstruck, for ages before recalling that her virtue had just been assaulted. That's when she finally got around to slapping him. Angry at herself for not resisting the handsome rogue, she had swung with all her might, toppling poor Mr. Arthur. Good grief, she'd struck a crippled person! "I am so sorry, Mr. Arthur. I didn't know my own strength. Here, let me help you up."

"No, I can manage, thank you." He wasn't in his dotage yet, by Jupiter. "If you could just hand me my cane, I would be grateful."

Hope found a walking stick leaning against the desk and put it in his hand, then turned her back so she would not witness Mr. Arthur struggle to his feet. Bad enough she had to see the red imprint of her hand on his cheek when he finally stood and scrawled his initials on her jewelry inventory list. "There, now you have a receipt. If you think you can trust me, that is."

Hope was not sure. There was definitely something peculiar about Mr. Arthur, and the expensive, ornately carved lion's-head cane was merely one more discordant note. On the other hand, he obviously had a position of trust at the hotel, so her jewels ought to be safe, if her person was not. At least she was certain he was not the thief, for Mr. Arthur could never manage to sneak into the guests' chambers, even if he could climb the flights of stairs. "I would rather see my belongings placed in the safe myself, naturally, but I suppose I can trust you to see them there."

Trust him? The general had trusted him to carry battle plans for the entire Peninsular Campaign, by Zeus. And this milk-and-water country miss deigned to put her trinkets in his keeping? Arthur supposed he deserved that, too. He'd told Miss Thurstfield one rapper after another, masquerading as a caper merchant, and then pressed his unwelcome attentions upon her. In the back of his mind was the niggling notion that perhaps she had enjoyed those attentions, just a tad. Now was the time to confess his deceit, but how could he ever excuse such perfidy? She would despise him for sure, if she did not already, and that he could not bear.

Moving toward the door as if to say the disastrous interview was over, the captain nodded to acknowledge her tepid endorsement. "Your jewels will be safe, never fear. Now you are free to enjoy your visit in London without worry."

"Thank you. I'm sure I shall. Good day, Mr. Arthur."

"Good day, Miss Thurstfield," he said as he bowed her out of the room. "It was a very nice kiss."

Certain that her cheeks were flaming, Hope hurried across the lobby toward the stairs. Very nice, indeed!

"Did that charming Mr. Arthur take your jewelry away, then?" Nancy asked when Hope arrived, out of breath and out of countenance, back in their rooms.

Nancy would not think so highly of the villain if she knew what else he'd taken, but Hope just nodded, then suggested they go for a stroll in the nearby park. She understood that the Polite World went on the promenade in the late afternoons, so perhaps Sir Malcolm was among them. Or they could go shopping at the Bond Street stores Lady Mildred had recommended, and possibly catch a glimpse of him heading toward his club. Barring such a fortuitous meeting, Hope planned to ask whatever hackney drivers they employed if one of them knew Sir Malcolm's direction. In her admittedly small experience, jarveys knew everyone's coming and going.

No one knew of Sir Malcolm Fredenham's. One driver thought he'd picked up a toff by that name, but he'd only driven the swell from the theater to the

Coconut Tree, or vice versa. Or mayhaps it was the Daffy Club, and a nob named Windenham.

In her naivete, Hope did not think that any of the shopkeepers could help her, for she was patronizing milliners and modistes. Not a male was in sight, although one young seamstress did giggle about the gentlemen getting the bills. Husbands, Miss Thurstfield trusted, and Sir Malcolm was certainly not among their number.

They did not encounter him in the park either. Truthfully, Hope was wishing to come upon an acquaintance of her parents that she might recognize from their visits to the Lake District. Any member of the *ton* would know the baronet, and where to find him. But the park was thin of company. Either the Polite World had gone to their country estates, forgoing the victory celebrations, or they were in another area of the vast park, for Hope saw no one she could call upon. Nancy was upset with the men they did encounter, leering coxcombs who tried to scrape up an introduction to her little lamb, and she fended them off with her frowns. Trumpet was the only one who enjoyed the outing, barking at the squirrels and the ducks and the children and the flower-sellers crying their wares. Trumpet barked a lot. Developing a headache, Hope was glad enough to heed Nancy's advice to return to the hotel for a rest before dinner. Who knew? Perhaps she would recognize someone in the dining room.

The only one she recognized was Mr. Arthur, seated alone at a table right by the door. He was more fashionably turned out this evening, with a pristine white neckcloth tied in a complicated fold, and his wavy blond hair was smoothed back. Hope could feel her cheeks growing warm in memory of their last encounter as he stood when they passed his table. She nodded and kept walking after the waiter who was leading them to their table.

"Goodness," Nancy whispered, "what a progressive

establishment. The upper staff even gets to eat with the guests. Unless Mr. Arthur is assigned here to inspect the quality of the food and the service."

"Do you know," Hope told her once they were seated at a goodly distance from the disturbing manager, "I think Mr. Arthur must be something more than a member of the hotel's personnel."

"Well, he looks a treat, Hope dear, and he does seem genteel, but what else could he be, when he's working out of the manager's office and handling the hotel's business, like assigning our rooms and safekeeping your jewelry? I hope you're not getting any romantic notions, miss, for it won't do. My hounds and heaven, no. Your father would have palpitations."

"Oh, hush, Nancy. I am not imagining Mr. Arthur as any hero from a novel, nor do I have designs on his person. I just think he is more than he appears. That is, he appears more than he says he is. His manner of speech, even his dress this evening, and the . . . the air of confidence about him, give the lie to his position. I think he must be related to one of the owners, if he is not an actual partner in the hotel. Look at all the gentlemen stopping by his table to shake his hand." And all their ladies were simpering, she couldn't help but notice. "He has manners, too, for look at the fool trying to rise from his seat every time. No, don't turn to look. People might notice us staring."

"If you'd eat your dinner instead of watching Mr. Arthur, my dear, your interest might not be so obvious."

"I am not interested in the man, except in a scientific sort of way, of course, to solve the riddle of his identity."

Mrs. Storke shook her head. "Gammon. If I were twenty years younger I'd be dropping my handkerchief near that handsome fellow's table, too. But whether he be an owner or an employee here, it still won't fadge. In trade is as good as in service to your father, you know."

"Goodness, Nancy, I am not considering Mr. Arthur in light of a suitor, I tell you. I merely find him curious, like . . . like a duck out of water. That's it."

"And that's why you are looking daggers at the lady whose hand he just kissed? Eat your soup, Hope. It's delicious."

The rest of the meal was also, and extensive.

"My stars and salvation, if I ate like this every night, I'd be as fat as a flawn." Since Nancy was already well padded, a few more of Monsieur DuPré's specialities should have her bursting at the seams.

Hope ate more than her usual amount, too, trying the marvelously exotic dishes from the kitchen of a master chef. One was tastier than the other, so she kept eating. According to the waiter, Monsieur DuPré was second only to the great Careme, and quickly closing in on the Regent's chef's reputation.

Deservedly so, Hope and Nancy agreed.

After such a hearty meal, Miss Thurstfield and her companion decided to stroll through the hotel's lobby, admiring the statuary and artwork tucked into every niche. They encountered the pleasant young woman who had the suite next to theirs and introduced themselves. Lady Leverett invited them to attend one of the open-air concerts that evening with her and her husband. Hope was uncertain, having been endlessly warned against trusting strangers in the metropolis, but there was Lady Leverett's husband, smiling and patting Mr. Arthur on the back. Majordomos were notoriously excellent judges of character and class, Hope told herself, and hotel managers would be, too, so she accepted the invitation, happy to have a lady friend. Catching Hope's glance, the lady laughed. "Oh, everyone is delighted to have Arthur back."

Back? But the hotel had been open only a brief time. Hope could not ask further questions, in the flurry of fetching hats and shawls, and later she felt that prying into Mr. Arthur's personal life would have been rude. And reinforcement to Nancy's notion that she was top over tails for the handsome hotelier. She did ask after Sir Malcolm though, but Lord and Lady Leverett were visiting the City for the first time since their marriage four years ago and were not au courant with the latest *on dits* and arrivals. They promised to make inquiries for her, when they got around to paying duty calls or stopping by the gentlemen's clubs. Judging from the searing looks that passed between the pair, neither event would take place anytime soon. Lady Leverett did offer to speak to an old schoolmate about getting Hope an invitation to that lady's upcoming rout. "Everyone of note who is in London will be there, so you are bound to find your Sir Malcolm, if you can see him through the crush."

But the rout was nearly a fortnight away. Hope got up early the following morning, determined to continue her search. Over her chocolate and buttered toast, she considered her options. In Bath she could have consulted the master of ceremonies. In Interlaken the local news sheet told of every visitor, from Wordsworth to the wagon-maker's uncle. A person could get lost in London. And what if Sir Malcolm's relations were situated out of the City proper, or he was not partaking of the social events? How did one go about hiring a Bow Street Runner, anyway? Mr. Arthur would know.

She spotted him leaning on his cane outside the dining parlor, talking to the head waiter, and asked for a moment of his time.

Deuce take it, Arthur thought. Making his slow way out of the dining room, he'd seen her descend the stairs. He'd collared the maître d' about meals for the princess, who was already a day late, rather than have Miss Thurstfield watch him wend his ragged way back to the manager's apartment. Now she wanted to chat. She was wearing sprigged muslin today, he noticed, with tiny rosebuds embroidered at the neckline and

hem. She looked as fresh and as sweet as a spring garden, dash it, a garden someone else was destined to
pick. "Why don't we sit here, Miss Thurstfield?" Arthur
gestured toward a conveniently close-by grouping of
chairs and sofas, rather than make the journey to Simmons's rooms—or trust himself alone there with her.
After seeing her seated, though, he decided to remain
standing. The farther away from her, the more likely
he was to behave like a gentleman. "Now, how may
I be of assistance this morning, ma'am? Did you wish
a piece of jewelry out of the safe?" For a price, Simmons had given Captain Hunter the combination to
his personal lockbox, behind a muddy watercolor in
the manager's sitting room. "You could have sent one
of the maids with a note, you know. I would have
seen the item delivered instantly."

"Oh, no, I have no plans to wear anything fancy this
day." Now that she was facing the man, Hope was not
so sure how to proceed. He was looking caring and
competent and complete to a shade in fawn pantaloons.
How was she to admit that her almost-fiancé had scarp-
ered off before the banns were read? Or that she hoped
to use her jewels to entice another—almost any other—
gentleman into making her an offer? He'd think she was
desperate, at her last prayers, chasing after Sir Malcolm
or an eligible *parti*. He might even think she was considering a not-so-eligible match! But she needed his help.
Hope brushed one of Trumpet's hairs off her skirt and
blurted out, "I am looking for a man."

5.

*That gentlemen refrain from wearing boots and
spurs to bed.*

In the army, the cardinal rule of survival was Never
Volunteer. Now, however, at Miss Thurstfield's decla-

ration, Captain Hunter almost stepped front and center, shouting, "Me! Me! Me!" Even though the duty might kill him, he'd die a happy man. The small soldier was already standing at attention.

She couldn't mean him, of course. Arthur could not keep from grinning, though, as he asked, "Any man in particular?"

Oh, why had she thought he'd help? Hope was mortified that this . . . this counter-jumper found humor in her situation. She stood to leave. "I am sorry I took your time, Mr. Arthur, with my silly problem. I know you are a busy man."

He touched her sleeve for the briefest of seconds. "Don't go, Miss Thurstfield. I am never too busy to assist you. That is, it's hotel policy, don't you know, to be of service for the guests. Now, what kind of man are you seeking? A driver? A footman? A coiffeur, perhaps? Although I must say it would be a shame to cut your lovely curls."

Hope was more convinced than ever that Mr. Arthur was not what he seemed. No hotel hireling would flirt with one of the lady guests. He was flirting, wasn't he? Drat the man for sending her wits begging again. She studied the intricate pattern of the carpet for a moment, striving for composure. "I am looking for a particular gentleman, Sir Malcolm Fredenham, from Lancaster. Are you perhaps familiar with him?"

"I cannot say that I have ever heard of the fellow, but I have been out of the country till recently."

"Managing another hotel?"

"Managing." To survive, more like. "But I can make inquiries with the doormen at the gentlemen's clubs and such for you. If he is in London, he should not be too hard to locate."

"That's what I was hoping, but I could not call at those premises myself, of course. And I did not wish to hire an investigator, for that would make Sir Malcolm appear some kind of felon."

"Is he?"

"Heavens, no. He is a most respectable gentleman, a baronet, in fact. He simply forgot to give me his direction in Town."

"Sir Malcolm mightn't be the fiancé who was to call, might he?"

"Oh, we are not officially affianced. We have an understanding, you see."

Arthur did not see, not at all. How could any gudgeon let this goddess slip through his fingers? Any man fortunate enough to win her hand would be a fool not to put a gold band on it instantly. But that was assuming Sir Malcolm loved Miss Thurstfield, a notion that was easy to understand, but hard to swallow. Not that Arthur was in love with the chit himself, of course. He might wish to toss her over his shoulder and carry her away to his hunting box for a year to see if they would suit, but he was not such a nodcock as to fall in love with a woman after two days. He never had before, at any rate. For that matter, he'd never fallen in love, not even once, so he supposed he was no expert on the tender affliction. But if the Fredenham fellow did love her, Arthur reasoned, how did he "forget" to leave an address? That would be like forgetting one's name, like cutting off one's nose while shaving, like pretending to be an innkeeper. It sounded to the captain as if this benighted baronet was playing fast and loose with Miss Thurstfield's affections.

If he found him he'd treat the dirty dish to some home-brewed, for trifling with a lady. Then again, if Arthur found the jackanapes, Miss Thurstfield would likely make the betrothal official. Or get married by special license right here in London. But if Sir Malcolm stayed missing, Miss Thurstfield would stay single. Hope sprang eternal. No, Hope sprang to her feet again.

"I am certain his letter must have gone amiss, is all. But I so wanted to share the glorious celebrations with him here in Town. Thank you in advance for making those inquiries. I knew I could count on you, and your discretion."

"At your service, ma'am. Rest assured, I shall give your investigation the attention it deserves. Have you plans in the meantime?"

"I thought I might see a bit of the City, do some more shopping perhaps. I understand there is to be a military parade this afternoon to welcome some foreign dignitaries."

Oh, Lud, and he was supposed to be there, too. Not to march, of course, but to escort the Ziftsweig delegation, if they ever showed, in full regalia. "I am certain it will be quite a spectacle. But I cannot feel comfortable allowing two women to wander about the streets by themselves. Permit me to assign an escort to you." He held up a hand before she could protest. "And you need not fret about the expense. The man is already on the payroll, with nothing to do." Browne had been complaining just this morning that unless Captain Hunter visited his tailor and his bootmaker soon, he may as well pension his batman off. The sergeant would be just the ticket to keep Miss Thurstfield safe, and away from the reviewing stand. And Mrs. Storke seemed just the cozy armful Brownie liked best.

Hope left him then, but not without a smile of appreciation. She'd been right to consult the masterful manager, for now she felt confident again, buoyed by his care and consideration for her well-being. And his return smile.

Arthur watched her go, admiring the graceful sway of her hips and the softly rounded posterior outlined by the thin muslin gown. Then he realized his mouth was open so he snapped it shut before he'd be caught drooling like a dog after a juicy bone. Zeus, he had too much to do to stand around like a mooncalf. He needed a new wardrobe, and a new curricle so he might invite her for a ride in the park or take her sight-seeing himself. Now he had to add not finding

Sir Malcolm, which meant a call on his sister-in-law. Sylvia was one of the biggest gossips in Town; she'd know just where he shouldn't look for the feckless fiancé. Dash it, Arthur asked himself, what had he been about, wallowing in self-pity when there was so much to accomplish if he was to have a chance with Miss Thurstfield?

She was not engaged, only nearly so. As the saying went, there was many a slip twixt cup and lip, and Arthur meant to be standing by to catch the spill. He did not know how he was going to explain away his pretense, but he'd worry about being Viscount Huntingdon when he looked the part. For now, he was intrigued with the notion of courting a lovely young lady without fear of his wealth and title appealing to her more than himself. Meantime, the first thing he had to do was find the man who'd saved his life, now that he deemed that life worth living. Arthur hurried back to his rooms to collect his hat and inform Browne of his new duties, forgetting all about his limp or that others might be watching. Miss Thurstfield did not seem to mind; why should he?

"What do you mean, you cannot help me? I did not climb up those blasted stairs just to give my regards to the War Office, by Jupiter."

Arthur's happy mood had not lasted long. First he'd called at Lieutenant Thomas Durbin's family's home, only to find the knocker off the door. A surly footman at the service entrance had been no help, even after accepting Captain Hunter's coin. Then Arthur had gone to Whitehall, only to find that most of his acquaintances were off getting ready for the victory march. A smooth-cheeked soldier was left on duty, to his—and Arthur's—regret.

"Do you know who I am, Private?" Arthur shouted in his best battlefield tones.

"Yes, sir, Captain Hunter, sir. My lord." Everyone knew one of the most decorated officers of the last campaign. The private still could not get him Lieutenant Thomas Durbin's current address. "It's classified, sir."

"Cut line, Private. Since when is a junior officer's direction a matter of national security?"

"Since the lieutenant is being held for court-martial, sir. Orders are he's to have no visitors."

"What? What charges were brought against him? Dash it, man, I would know. The lieutenant saved my life."

"The, ah, charges include dereliction of duty, disobeying orders, disrespect for his superior, and desertion."

"Since his commanding officer was that fool Falcott, I am not surprised that disrespect for his superior is included, but the rest is hogwash. The lieutenant was one of the bravest, most valiant officers on the Peninsula, dash it. He ought to be leading today's celebration. And if you do not tell me his whereabouts, Private, you'll find yourself sweeping the streets after that same parade."

The lieutenant was in the guardhouse, and it took Arthur three hours to get him out. The hardest part was finding the officers to sign his release, once Captain Hunter had told his story: It was General Falcott who'd engaged the French while peace was being negotiated. Without support from the rest of the British troops, Falcott's infantry was cut down by the French. Sent by Wellington to find where the devil Falcott's brigade was and why the deuce they were not in camp, Captain Hunter had found the remnants of the unit. Lieutenant Durbin had rallied his handful of men to make a stand, despite knowing how hopeless their situation. Arthur fought by the lieutenant's side until the French withdrew, thinking reinforcements were arriving, and he could lead the intrepid troop back to the British lines.

On the way, though, they'd encountered yet another French gun emplacement, and Arthur was injured. He

would have bled to death right in the dust if not for
the tourniquet Durbin had tied. Then the lieutenant
and his men had stood over Captain Hunter, de-
fending him, losing more brave soldiers, until help arrived. No, Arthur would not let the lieutenant be
court-martialed for Falcott's feeblemindedness in
wanting to win one more battle, from his position of
safety.

But Falcott was a friend of the prince's, Arthur was
told. They could not make the general look bad. Since
Arthur was running out of time to return to the hotel,
change into his dress uniform, and get to the blasted
parade grounds, he very succinctly told everyone he
saw precisely how bad General Falcott was going to
look in the newspapers, the broadsides, and the print-
shop windows, when Arthur got done telling the true
story. And they could not stop him, by Harry, because
he was resigning. Besides, Falcott might be a friend
of Prinny's, but Captain Arthur Hunter was named
after Wellesley, his father's friend, not after Pen-
dragon, a mere folk hero.

The lieutenant was freed into Arthur's custody
pending an inquiry. A private, closed door inquiry, the
War Office officials begged. Arthur saluted without
comment and went to retrieve the lieutenant.

Durbin was almost choking to hold back tears of
joy and relief. He kept shaking Arthur's hand, until
the captain felt a lump in his own throat. Thomas was
pale and weak, for the guards had barely fed him, it
seemed, and never let him out of his cell for exercise
or fresh air. His clothes were filthy and his sandy hair
was matted. He could hardly walk to the hired carriage, so Arthur had to help support the younger man,
ignoring his own aching leg.

"Why didn't you send for me, blast it? You know
I would have told those fools what really happened."

"But you were lying near death in some peasant's
hut. The fever, my messenger said. No one else knew
what had occurred, and the army did not want too

many questions asked. They needed a scapegoat for all those brave boys who died that day, after peace was declared."

They both were silent a minute, remembering. Then the captain swore again. "Dammit, couldn't your uncle have vouched for you? Lord Avery holds great power in Parliament, so his word should have seen you exonerated."

Thomas shrugged his too-thin shoulders. "But Falcott is my uncle's bosom bow, which is why he bought me a commission in the fool's unit. Uncle Avery washed his hands of me the instant the army brought charges. He wouldn't listen to criticism of his old friend, and wouldn't have a coward in the family, he said."

"So much for family feeling. I suppose he left Town to avoid the gossip. The house is all shut up."

"That wouldn't matter. He disowned me, told me never to enter his doorway again."

"The bastard. Have you other family in London?"

The lieutenant shrugged again and then took a fit of coughing. Arthur rapped on the carriage roof and directed the driver to stop at the corner, where a stand had been set up for the celebrations, selling lemonade and oranges along with pennants and ribbons and whistles. Arthur was not sure how many more times he could clamber into and out of the coach before he fell straight on his face, but he fetched a jug of lemonade and a meat pie from another vendor.

When Thomas could speak again he told his rescuer that no, he had no other relations, and no friends, either. He'd learned that in prison, when none of his comrades answered his messages, until he'd run out of funds to send any more.

"So what will you do? Where shall I have the driver take you? I can't imagine you'd wish to go back to the barracks."

"About as much as they want me there." Thomas bit into the meat pie, not caring that the juice was

running down his chin. "I'll have to get my traps eventually, but no, I would rather sleep in the streets than
go there."

Arthur was not about to let Lieutenant Durbin
sleep in the gutter. He owed the lad for his life, and
for not asking about him sooner. But he couldn't take
him back to the hotel. There were no rooms to let,
and no space in Simmons's little bedchamber to put a
pallet. Besides, the young officer needed tending, and
Arthur would be too busy with his duties to Princess
Henrika to see to his welfare. Miss Thurstfield's suite
had plenty of room for an extra bed, and Arthur just
knew she and her companion would be competent and
caring, but it would never do, of course. Matters of
propriety would force this poor hero into some ramshackle riverfront rooming house until Arthur could
make other arrangements. There simply was not time
this afternoon, for Lord Wellington would have his
head for washing if he missed the ceremonies. This
was not the time to offend the general, not when Arthur needed his signature on Lieutenant Durbin's
release.

Then Captain Hunter recalled the perfect place to
take his young charge, a place overrun with idle servants, positively teeming with the gentler sex, and
abounding with amenities. Arthur ought to know, for
he paid the bills at Huntingdon House.

### 6.

### *That all bills be paid on time.*

"You said you needed an escort, Sylvia. Since I was
busy, I have furnished you with one."

"You always did have a deplorable sense of levity,
Arthur. I would have thought that now you had risen
to Henry's title you would have assumed a modicum
of his dignity."

"No, did you? But I am not teasing, you know. You lectured me at great length, if I recall, about my duties to the family. Providing you with a resident gentleman seemed to be a close second to providing an heir. I believe your words were that you had not had a good night's sleep since Henry's passing, worrying over the safety of the household with no man to protect you. Well, Lieutenant Durbin is the bravest man I know, so you should rest easy tonight."

"He is a coward! A deserter!"

"Rumors. All false. The lieutenant will soon be awarded a medal for his gallantry under fire." Even if Arthur had to give him one of his own.

As usual, Sylvia did not listen to any view but the one she held. "How dare you bring such a despicable creature into my home."

Arthur politely refrained from mentioning precisely who owned Huntingdon House, brushing at a speck of dust on his sleeve, instead.

Sylvia understood his unspoken message and changed tack, nearly grinding her teeth: "What I meant by a gentleman was a proper escort for my sister, as you well know. She'll be cut dead if she is seen on your lieutenant's arm."

"Nonsense. He will be accepted, nay, honored if you show your approval. I thought you had enough credit with the dowagers to sway public opinion, among the *ton* at any rate. I'll take care of the military."

Sylvia helped herself to another bonbon. She did not know whether to be flattered that her brother-in-law thought she held such power, or to be offended that he placed her with the dowager set. "I am not in my dotage, you know. But I do have considerable influence in the beau monde. I suppose such a thing as bringing him back into favor is not beyond my capabilities."

"The lad's uncle is an earl, remember, so it's not as if he's a mere nobody."

"But he is in such bad odor."

"He'll wash up nicely," Arthur said, choosing to misinterpret her latest complaint. Then he added, "He saved my life, Sylvia. Without him, Cousin Nigel would be viscount, and you would be living in the dower house in Suffolk, most likely with Aunt Aubergine."

Sylvia quickly popped another sweet in her mouth to replace the bad taste of such a dire fate. "I suppose we do owe him some kind of assistance. But to take him around with us?"

"I intend to see he is added to the guest lists for the ambassadors' balls and such, so you won't have to beg your friends for extra invitations. Of course you'd be welcome to accompany him, if you've a notion to meet the Ziftsweig delegation. And Miss Ferguson would be included, of course."

He was holding out a carrot, she knew, dangling the chance to hobnob with royalty. She could hardly do better for her sister, but Sylvia was never satisfied with one bonbon, or one carrot. "Do you know, I think it might be just the thing if we held a ball to reintroduce your lieutenant here. Of course there would not be time to organize a grand entertainment, but if you get your Austrian friends to come, the *ton* will flock after them." Who knew, perhaps Wellington would come. Or Prinny. She'd never held a proper come-out for her sister Elizabeth, what with mourning and waiting for Arthur to come home to pay the bills. Now seemed a golden opportunity. "That would truly show the Polite World that we welcome Lieutenant Durbin in our home."

"Oh, a ball would be much too much effort for a lady of your tender sensibilities. I'd never ask such a thing of you."

"Gammon." Sylvia jumped off the couch and rang the bell pull for her butler to bring pen and paper, her social calendar, and a fresh pot of tea, with those special seed cakes of Cook's. "Elizabeth can help pen the invitations. I wonder how soon we can have new gowns made up? And the ballroom chandelier will have to be taken down for washing. I never liked those crocodile-legged chairs in the Blue Parlor. I don't suppose . . . ?"

He waved his hand. "Send me the reckoning." He knew she'd never had intentions of doing otherwise, anyway. "We're all agreed, then, to make Lieutenant Durbin welcome at Huntingdon House?"

The question—the entire expensive discussion, in fact—was academic, as the lieutenant was already ensconced in the best bedchamber, being catered to by half the staff under the direction of Miss Elizabeth Ferguson. Sylvia had decided to have a spasm when Arthur introduced his houseguest, but the viscountess's sister had taken one look at the weary, woebegone soldier and began issuing orders for hot water, nourishing foods, a footman to assist him up the stairs, another to fetch him Henry's robe from the attic. Miss Ferguson had a backbone, it seemed. Arthur approved. In fact, he considered a match between the pair an unlooked-for stroke of serendipity. Elizabeth had a comfortable fortune; the lieutenant had none. Oh, Arthur intended to see that Durbin's uncle reinstated Thomas, but the lieutenant would have no army career to fall back on. A wealthy wife ought to suit him to a cow's thumb, if Elizabeth's coddling did not do the trick.

An excellent day's work, Arthur congratulated himself, taking leave of his sister-in-law with adequate time to get to the reviewing stand. "Oh, by the way, Sylvia, do you know of a Sir Malcolm Fredenham?"

"Fredenham? That dirty dish will never be on the guest list for any ball of mine, I can assure you. He came calling on my sister during the Season. I sent him to the rightabout you may be sure."

"What, is he a rakehell then?"

"No more than any other gentleman, from what I heard. But his pockets are sorely to let. Gambling, don't you know. He's hanging out for a wealthy bride, they say. Been turned down by more than one heiress's father. What, does he owe you money?"

"No, I've never met the man."

"I'm surprised. I'd heard he'd gone to Paris for the peace talks with the rest of his fast set. I assumed you'd encountered Fredenham there."

"I was a tad too busy for much socializing, even before my leg became reinfected. But do you know his direction?"

"He had rooms at the Albany, I am quite sure, but he gave them up when he went abroad. And didn't pay his rent there, either, I'd wager. I think I heard he left Paris with some foreigners, most likely hoping to make a match with a female who hadn't heard of his debts. If he returns now that all the celebrations and all the marriageable misses have moved here, you cannot want me to invite such a mushroom, Arthur, can you?"

"Assuredly not. We wouldn't want such scurvy scum sniffing around Elizabeth, would we?"

Devil take it, Arthur thought on his way back to the hotel, how was he going to tell Miss Thurstfield that her intended was in debt? Sir Malcolm, it seemed, was so badly dipped that Hope's dowry would not be enough to tow him out of River Tick. Either that or the baronet knew Hope's father would find out he was below hatches when they discussed settlements. The baron would have gone after him with a horsewhip. That's what Arthur intended to do, if the muckworm dared show his face in London. In fact, Arthur was looking forward to such an encounter. Telling a woman that her lover was a fortune hunter, however, was not a chore Arthur was anticipating with any degree of pleasure.

He donned his dress uniform as fast as possible without Browne's help, breathing a sigh of relief that he could put the other task off for a few hours. Standing firm in the line of fire was one thing; shattering a woman's heart was quite another. With any luck, he thought, she would discover her almost-afianced's treachery on her own. One of the other hotel guests might have heard of the dastard and informed her of his unprincipled intentions. Or his name might have been mentioned in the gossip columns along with his latest deep-pocketed prey. Or else he might just show up at the hotel and betray himself. Hah! If Arthur was that lucky, he wouldn't be limping.

Browne was an excellent escort, Hope and Nancy agreed. He made sure that they saw all the sights, that no one accosted them, that their packages were gathered for delivery to the hotel. He took them to Hatchard's for books and to Gunter's for ices. He waited patiently with the hired carriage outside the shops.

He was not, however, forthcoming. When Hope asked why he was not in the hotel's uniform, Browne muttered that he was employed directly by the cap'n.

"The captain?" Hope asked.

"That's St. George's up ahead, miss. Where the swells get hitched."

Later, when she asked if he had been with Mr. Arthur for long, Browne had wiped his damp forehead. "Too long, by thunder, if he's getting up to these queer starts."

"Queer?"

"Queen's Park is to t'other side of Town, but we could drive by there."

Browne also failed at getting them close to the reviewing stand for the parade. The roads were too congested, he said, and they'd left it for too late. But he had the driver park their coach in a shady spot, where they could get down to watch the marchers and listen to the military bands. Noticing that he stood at attention and saluted when the colors were carried past, Hope asked if he'd been in the army.

"Aye, and proud of it, miss."

"Was Mr. Arthur there with you?"

"Do you hear the bagpipes? Scots Grays must be marching next. The Ladies, they were called, on account of their kilts."

Hope thought about Mr. Arthur's air of command—and his injured leg—and decided that he must have been in the military. How fortunate that he and Browne had found employment, unlike so many other returning veterans.

They were too far away to hear the speeches, and Nancy was disappointed they could not catch a glimpse of the Austrian princess everyone was talking about. She was supposed to be a grandiose beauty and fabulously wealthy. Rumor had it that Princess Henrika Hafkesprinke was being considered as a match for one of the royal dukes, to provide an heir to the throne.

"But she is staying at our hotel, Nancy, so I'm sure you'll get to see her sooner or later. She might even take her meals in the dining room."

"And how the cap'n thinks to squeak through that is beyond me," Browne mumbled. "That is, the Twenty-third squeaked through old Boney's lines."

Hope dressed with special care for dinner that evening in her new jonquil silk. In case her highness put in an appearance, she told herself, certainly not to impress any mustered-out hotel manager.

He was sitting alone at his usual table nearest the entrance, making sure the dining room ran as efficiently as the rest of his hotel, Hope supposed. He, too, had taken extra pains with his toilette this evening, for his hair was still damp from his bath, and his neckcloth was tied as intricately as a dandy's. The midnight-blue superfine made his eyes seem bluer in the candlelight, and his coat fit him perfectly, stretching across his broad shoulders. He did not stand as they walked past. He did not smile and he did not invite them to sup with him, either, as Hope half expected. And half hoped. Dining with the staff could not be proper, of course, so she nodded and proceeded to her own table. The leek soup tasted like pond scum and the prawns in dill tasted like dust. The waiter anxiously asked if anything was wrong, and begged her to try the veal roulades, lest Monsieur DuPré feel unappreciated. So Hope moved the food around on her plate some more, feeling unappreciated. Nancy was eating enough for both of them, anyway, going into ecstasy over every dish.

Midway through the third course a hush fell over the dining room, and all eyes turned to the doorway. A woman was poised there, almost as if she were waiting for everyone in the room to stand and bow. Half of the diners did just that. One of the waiters bowed so low he spilled the contents of his tray. Princess Henrika had arrived.

Her highness was more beautiful than rumor had allowed, and taller. Majestically proportioned, she had hair so pale it was almost white, braided into a coronet that was woven through with diamonds and pearls, as if the princess needed more sparkle. Hope touched the yellow rosebuds Nancy had helped twine into her own plain brown locks, and sighed.

The princess had a magnificent bosom, too, though most of it was covered by more diamonds. The ruby pendant that hung in the vee between her breasts was just slightly smaller than one of Miss Thurstfield's—her breasts, not her jewels. Hope sighed again. Princess Henrika would never have to worry over a straying suitor, or winning a smile from a grim-faced concierge. She had everything.

As her large party moved toward the bank of tables reserved for them, her highness hung on the arm of her escort, laughing up at him, pinching his cheek, rubbing against his silk sleeve like a friendly cat.

"Scandalous," Nancy whispered. But Hope was not listening and she was not pondering the princess's morals. She was doing her best not to swoon right into

her haricots. The princess had everything, all right.
Including Sir Malcolm Fredenham.

# 7.

*That guests do not throw slops from the windows.*

She would *not* faint. She definitely would not cry,
at least not until later. Hope might throw the contents
of her wineglass— No, she was a lady, and a lady did
not cause public scenes. Visiting royalty appeared to
have its own standards, though, judging from the blatantly sexual display that had every eye in the room
focused on the Hafkesprinke heiress, and on Hope's
husband-to-be. Miss Thurstfield clenched her hands in
her lap, to make sure she did not shame her mother's
memory. Her fingernails were making indentations in
her palms.

"My saints and salvation, isn't that . . . ? Well, I
never!"

No, neither had Hope, and now she never would.

Nancy clucked her tongue. "I did not even know
Sir Malcolm spoke German."

"They likely converse in French." When they spoke
at all. The baronet was presently kissing the Brobding-
nagian beauty's nearly bare shoulder. Nancy gasped
again. So did Sir Malcolm when he raised his eyes, to
see his erstwhile intended staring at him across a platter of artichoke-stuffed pheasant. He stumbled, then
his face lost all color. He could not have looked more
guilty if he had canary feathers stuck in his teeth. He
whispered something in the princess's ear, almost having to stand on tiptoe to do it, Hope noted, and then
he left his party and headed toward Hope's table.

He was between her and the door; otherwise Hope
would have bolted. Instead, she was forced to paste a
smile on her lips for the benefit of all the curious

diners and waiters. Nancy mumbled something about snakes and sinners, and swallowed the rest of her wine. Hope swallowed the bitter taste in her mouth.

She did not raise her hands from her lap, so he could only bow at the waist, in exaggerated homage. "Hope, dearest, what a wonderful surprise to see you in London. I am amazed you got my letter so quickly, telling you I was back in the country."

"There was no letter, Malcolm."

"You must have set out from home before it had a chance to reach you. Silly puss, you could have missed me, for I was on my way north in a few days."

"How is your uncle?"

"My uncle? Oh, that uncle. He recovered so well that he decided to take a jaunt to the Continent. He needed me along, don't you know, to make the arrangements, and in case he had a relapse. I wrote you all about it."

"There was no letter."

"Dashed foreign mails. I, ah, do not see the good baron. Is your father not with you?" Looking around as if he feared an irate papa with a blunderbuss, Sir Malcolm seemed relieved when Hope explained that her father had stayed behind. "Then I will have to write to him, won't I?"

There would not *be* any letter. "That's not necessary, sir. I cannot imagine what you would have to correspond with Papa about."

"Ah, I can see I am in your black books, dearest, but I can explain everything. You see—"

Just then the princess called out from halfway across the vast room, "Malska, I vant to make the order."

Malska? Hope reached for her wineglass. She needed a drink, or two.

Like a dog being called to heel, Sir Malcolm edged away, but he latched on to her hand first and raised it to his lips. "We'll talk another time, my dear. How fortunate you are staying in the very same hotel. Right now I have commitments, you see. It would never do to offend the visiting crowns, would it? The whole peace treaty might fall apart."

As soon as his back was turned, Hope wiped her hand on her napkin. The she picked up her glass with trembling fingers but did not drink, merely staring into its depths, numb with the shock.

"My lands and liver! Did you hear him? He ought to be in Drury Lane. An oily customer as that one could play the villain in any number of farces."

"Hush, Nancy. People are staring. Are you nearly finished with your dinner? Would you mind leaving?"

Nancy stared longingly at the food still on her plate, but she dutifully started to gather up her shawl and reticule.

"No, you cannot leave," came a deep voice behind Hope. Strong fingers pried hers from the stem of the wineglass. "If you run away, he'll have won, and you'll know yourself as craven till the end of your days."

Mr. Arthur had come to her rescue once more. Hope looked up at him and attempted a smile. She was proud her voice only quavered slightly as she declared, "I am not a coward."

He squeezed her hand for a moment, then stepped back from the table, resting his weight on the lion's-head cane. "Of course you are not, Miss Thurstfield. That's why you shall stay and have the rest of DuPré's magnificent dinner, so no one can gossip about you and the princess's paramour."

His words removed any doubt she might have had, and any appetite. "No, I could not eat another bite."

"Of course you can. Otherwise monsieur will think his cooking is faulty. He'll throw a fit and resign, which will lose the hotel a great deal of business."

"And you would be out of a job."

"Something like that." His blue eyes twinkled at her, inviting her to laugh at his silliness.

Hope could not quite manage another smile, but she did pick up her fork.

"That's the ticket," he said, nodding, then lowered his

voice. "It has nothing to do with you, you know. Never think that. Fredenham needs money desperately."

"You knew?"

"I found out earlier this afternoon how deeply in debt he is. By the time I discovered that the dirty dish would be staying here, as part of the Hafkesprinke entourage, I had no chance to warn you." And he'd decided that if she saw the truth with her own brown velvet eyes, she'd believe it that much faster. Better a bullet to the heart than a knife in the back, he'd always believed. Besides, this way she could not blame the messenger. "From what I could gather, he was hanging out for an heiress all last Season, but his unsavory reputation followed him. Gambling debts, don't you know."

"No, I knew nothing, it seems. What a fool I was."

"Never! You just believed everyone was as good and honest as yourself."

Warmth flowed back into Hope's chilled fingers, down to her feet. "Do you look after every guest so kindly, Mr. Arthur?" He just smiled and gave her a roguish wink. Yes, she might live through her mortification. It was not as if her heart were broken or that she was a public laughingstock. Quite the contrary. She could see all the speculative gleams from the other dining-room patrons that she had caught the attention of two such dashing gentlemen. Yes, two gentlemen, for Mr. Arthur looked complete to a shade in his formal evening wear, despite his low standing.

In Interlaken, Hope might have been ridiculed. The neighbors would agree that she'd received her comeuppance for being so choosy about picking a husband. Here in London, though, only Nancy and this gentleman knew of her prior attachment. Nancy would never speak of it, and Mr. Arthur would never betray her.

"Artur." A piercing voice cut through the clatter and chatter of the busy dining parlor. "Artur, *liebchen*!" Ah, the unkindest cut of all. "Vere ist you, *liebchen*?"

Arthur raised his eyes to where the princess was
waving her napkin at him. He had to go. Henrika
would make a scene, else. She and the temperamental
French chef ought to make a match of it, he thought.
"Duty calls," he told the Thurstfield ladies, with
regret.

Trying to sound nonchalant and unfazed, Hope said,
"Of course," and forced herself to bring a forkful of
food to her mouth.

He bowed and headed toward the princess's table.
*Et tu, Brute?*

Arthur did not think of how he must appear, awkward as a three-legged turtle, tapping his way across
the room. He thought only of the hurt in his darling's
eyes. When he reached Henrika, she stood and threw
her arms around him, kissing first one cheek, then the
other. "Sit, sit, *liebchen*." Then she switched to German, begging him to join her, as these English lords
had no fire in them, not like her so-gallant Arthur.
She waved a scowling Sir Malcolm off to an empty
chair so Arthur might have the favored one, beside
her. As the baronet stood with his wineglass in hand
to switch seats, Arthur managed to stumble, unfortunately letting his cane swing up to knock Fredenham's
hand. The red wine spilled down the front of his white
inexpressibles. "*Ja, ja,* go change," the princess said,
dismissing Sir Malcolm. "Mine *engel* Artur keeps me
company."

Nancy and Hope took turns peeking at the luminar-
ies' table, which most of the waiters were tripping over
themselves to serve. "Now do you believe that Mr.
Arthur is not simply a glorified clerk?"

Nancy clucked her tongue. "He does seem to be on
familiar terms with royalty, doesn't he?"

"Familiar? If she was any more familiar she'd be
sitting on his lap. I'd wager they were lovers."

Nancy choked on a morsel of mushroom, but Hope
went on. "And I'd bet her influence got him his position at the hotel. Yes, and he's likely interested in her

money, just like Sir Malcolm." And just, Hope thought with a pang, like they had both shown herself flattering attention. "It stands to reason, for whatever circumstances forced Mr. Arthur into working for wages, he cannot wish to remain a hotel manager all his days."

"Never say he hopes to cozen her into marriage? He is devilishly handsome, but a workingman and a princess? That sounds like a child's fairy tale."

"No, I daresay even the audacious Mr. Arthur does not aim so high. I suppose he's merely trying to feather his nest at the princess's expense. Selling his favors like a . . . a light skirt."

"Never say so! Oh, my airs and archangels, he's a gentleman."

"My arse." Hope excused her language. "Your Mr. Arthur is a libertine. At least he is as tall as the Saxon siren. Come, Nancy, my stomach is quite turned by such licentious behavior. I daresay any lady would be offended."

Especially one who very much feared that *now* her heart was broken.

## 8.

### *That proper attire be worn at all times.*

Arthur could not call Sir Malcolm out, for a duel would only drag Miss Thurstfield's name through the mud. So he got rid of the muckworm by the simple expedient of taking the baronet's place as the royal fräulein's favorite. That was Captain Hunter's assignment, after all; putting paid to Fredenham's plans was his pleasure. Speaking of pleasure, the captain did not take Sir Malcolm's place in Henrika's bed, protesting that his leg could not manage the climb to her chamber, that he was not yet strong enough for the vigorous bedplay she favored. No one man was. Arthur thought, in fact, that he might just be saving the baronet's life.

Sir Malcolm was busy trying to save his skin. Once the duns saw that the baronet was out of favor with his wealthy patroness, they were after him like hounds on a fox. Fredenham attempted to reattach Miss Thurstfield's affections and her pocketbook—thin though it was compared to what he needed—but somehow she was never available. His messages requesting an interview never reached her suite, his notes begging for her forgiveness got misplaced at the manager's office, and the room number he was repeatedly given was repeatedly wrong. Unless he was ready to knock on every door in the hotel, Sir Malcolm was not going to visit his onetime meal ticket in her chambers. He could have waited in the lobby for her coming or going, but the bill collectors were gathering there. After a sennight of using the kitchen entry, and being threatened every time with the chef's butcher knife for disturbing Monsieur DuPré's creative efforts, Sir Malcolm was forced to flee London. He left without a wealthy, well-born bride. He did manage to get a ride in the carriage of a banker's widow from Harrogate, twice Hope's age, half as rich.

Arthur could not enjoy routing the enemy. For one thing he was too busy escorting the indefatigable Hafkesprinke contingent to every social event and tourist site. For another, he was having as hard a time seeing Miss Thurstfield as Sir Malcolm had. She had been taken up by Lord and Lady Leverett, who seemed intent on introducing Hope to every Tom, Dick, and half-pay officer in Town. They did not attend the same functions, and their paths seldom crossed in the hotel.

Not that seeing Hope would have availed him aught but the ague. The few times he did chance upon her, icicles dripped from her well-mannered greeting. At least she had not left Town. According to Browne, who had it from Mrs. Storke, a clod of a countryman was waiting to drag her to the altar there.

Just a week or so more, he calculated. The celebrations were winding down, the foreigners were returning to their countries, the *ton* to their estates. The day after his sister-in-law's ball he'd be free of the princess, free of the army. And free to court Miss Hope Thurstfield.

Hope decided to stay on in London, even though she was taking no pleasure in the sight-seeing or shopping or endless celebrations of Napoleon's abdication. If she'd seen one military parade, she'd seen twenty, it seemed, and fireworks were magical the first night. By the sixth night, they were just loud. But she stayed in Town, for her father's plans for her were even more dismal.

And she stayed on because she'd been invited to a grand ball at one of London's finest houses. Who knew, but the man of her dreams just might come waltz her off her feet. Hope doubted that would happen, for the man who was interrupting her sleep at night—and disturbing her days—did not dance. He limped through her fantasies. And sailed off with his behemoth barque of frailty.

Hope did some additional sight-seeing, visiting properties with a land agent, to see if she could afford a house of her own. She could not. Even if Hope could convince Papa to let her set up an independent establishment, though, Lady Leverett convinced her that she would be considered no better than she ought to be, a social outcast. Young women simply did not live alone. Hope had no desire to do so, either, but she had few choices. Her father would have apoplexy if she suggested finding a position, and she was not suited to be a governess or a companion anyway. Which left marriage.

If Hope was not to experience the love of a man, at least she wanted children to lavish her affection on.

Her little dog Trumpet was all well and good for cuddling and cooing, but she could not read him her favorite books, or braid his hair, or rock him in her arms. She'd be a good mother. Whether she'd be a good wife was less certain. The idea of begetting the infants of her imagination with any of the men she was meeting was sickening. Besides, her air-castle cherubs all had blond hair and blue eyes—and uneven gaits.

Hope studied the thick vellum invitation again. She did not know Viscountess Huntingdon. She did not even know the young lady who was to be among the evening's three honorees, or the lieutenant also mentioned in the fine copperplate. She did know the last name, and had no desire to spend the evening in company with the Austrian Amazon. Or her inamorato, Mr. Arthur.

According to Lady Leverett, however, the ball should be such a sad crush that she'd never spot anyone in the crowd. With so many of the Quality gone to their summer residences, Lady Huntingdon had invited everyone of note still in London to fill her rooms. Hope had to attend, the older woman insisted, for how else was she to meet eligible *partis*? Not loitering in hotel lobbies, for certain!

Hope decided to go, but not as anybody's country cousin. Or a heart-sore henwit. She cut her hair into short curls, despite Nancy's protests. Cropped hair was all the rage, Hope declared, and much cooler for the summer heat. She sent for her jewelry, all of it, and picked out a diamond and sapphire parure, then she found the most expensive couturier in London to create a gown to match the blue, with brilliants sewn across the silver lace overskirt. Miss Thurstfield even learned how to apply the hare's foot with a delicate hand so no one could detect the cosmetics, the darkened lashes, or the pinkened cheeks. She couldn't hope to compete with the Hafkesprinke heiress—a tallow candle might as well try to outshine the sun—but she knew she looked her best when the night of the ball finally came around.

So did Mr. Arthur. The enormous line waiting to greet their host and hostess almost came to a complete halt as Hope stood frozen on the steps leading to the Huntingdon House ballroom.

She had expected him to be there, of course, since Princess Henrika and her advisers and ladies in waiting and hangers-on were already enthroned on a raised dais near the orchestra. But Hope had not expected the hotel manager to be on the receiving line. Her mind went numb, along with her feet.

She had never expected him to be in uniform, either, no, not even if Lady Huntingdon had hired him for the night to manage her ball as efficiently as he and Mr. Simmons managed the Grand Hotel. But this was not the navy blue and white hotel livery she was used to, not by half. She thought for a moment he might somehow be that Lieutenant Thomas Durbin named on the invitation, but even at this distance there seemed too much gold on his coat, too many medals and ribbons and epaulets for a mere lieutenant. Nothing made sense. Hope tried to turn to leave, but the press of people was too great. She tried to find Lady Leverett and her husband, but they'd become separated in the crush. Nancy had said she'd find her own way to the chaperones' corner, when they gave their wraps. Hope was alone, and totally at sea. Drowning.

Then the bewigged butler called her name and people behind her shoved forward until she stumbled, practically at his feet. He took her hand and raised it to his lips. The delight that crossed his handsome face, the smile that was brighter than the enormous chandelier above them, would have gladdened Hope's heart, if that organ was not also numb. Her dear Mr. Arthur was a complete charlatan. An impostor, a deceiver. Whoever he was.

"How do you do, *Mr.* Arthur?"

"I can explain, Miss Thurstfield, I swear. Please save me the first dance."

"What, you are not injured, either?"

He raised his cane so she could see at least part of his act was real. "I meant we could talk then. Please?"

Before she could answer—a refusal, of course—the butler cleared his throat.

"Oh, yes, we need to move this confounded thing along. May I present you to my sister-in-law, Lady Huntingdon."

So he was related to the aristocracy. Her instincts, at least, had been correct. Perhaps he was Viscount Huntingdon's younger brother, an impecunious second son, taking up the hotel trade to support his expensive style of living. Hope was still trying to find some rationale, some excuse, she knew. She looked beyond him on the receiving line. "And your brother is . . . ?"

"Sadly departed, I am sorry to say." He addressed the rotund, ruby-draped female standing next to him: "Sylvia, here is the young lady I told you about."

Lady Huntingdon snorted, holding her lorgnette up to inspect Hope. "You mean the one you asked five times if she accepted my invite? How do you do, Miss Thurstfield? Arthur's been singing your praises. Call on me tomorrow." And she looked past Hope to the next person on line.

To the devil with protocol. Those overdressed, over-perfumed prigs on the steps could just wait their turn. "Arthur? Not Mr. Arthur?"

He flushed. "I am sorry, it just happened. I did not wish to embarrass either of us. It's actually Arthur Everitt Halliday Hunter, Captain, but there's more. I'm afraid I am—"

"His Grace, the Duke of Wellington," the butler intoned. The crowd on the stairs parted like the Red Sea, and Hope had to step aside before Lady Huntingdon trampled her on the way to take the general's hand. The last glimpse Hope had before she was swept into the ballroom was of the nation's hero sharing salutes, then slaps on the back, with her hotel manager.

Hope snatched a glass of champagne from the tray of a passing waiter. Then she grabbed another glass. If she'd dared, she would have seized the entire tray. It would not have been enough. By now, of course, she'd heard enough whispers and wisps of conversations to winkle out the enormity of her witlessness. What a fool he had made of her, this vaunted viscount. If she hid behind a potted palm and drank champagne, perhaps it would soon be time to leave. Or perhaps she'd pass out first. Either one was preferable to facing the two-faced fustian-flinger. Three-faced if she added his military career to that of clerk and peer of the realm.

He found her anyway, likely because the scores of footmen were in his employ, and they all remembered the sapphire gown, and the young miss concentrating on becoming castaway.

Arthur took the glass out of her hand, and the other one out of her other hand, and sipped from one before placing both in the palm tree's pot. "Come. No one should be on the balcony yet," was all he said, taking her firmly by the elbow and leading her to the opened French doors.

Of course no one would be outside yet; the dancing had not even started. And he, as host, should have been leading off the most elevated female in the room, Her Royal Highness Henrika Hafkesprinke. "The general has agreed to take my place since my leg will not permit," he said to Hope's raised brow. "And Lieutenant Durbin is leading out Miss Ferguson, so the other guests of honor are accounted for. Sylvia has decided not to dance, so she is presiding over the refreshments table. Come."

The cool breeze felt good on Hope's cheeks. Lights twinkled magically below from paper lanterns strung among the trees in the garden. The music was inviting.

And she wished she were home in her bed. Even if her father's friend Lord Ormsby was in it, too. Anything had to be better than listening to more lies, more silver-tongued schemes for her downfall. Hope gave Lord Huntingdon her back.

"Very well," he said. "Don't look at me. I cannot blame you. Just listen, please. That will be enough. First, you must believe that I never set out to deceive you. I simply did not want to be Viscount Huntingdon. That was my brother, who was raised up for the position since birth. I did not want to be Captain Hunter either, endlessly congratulated for surviving one endless bloodbath after another. Can you understand that I just wanted to hear my own name on the lips of a sweet girl? I did not want to think about my title, my battle record, or my bank account. I wanted someone to look at me, Arthur, with fondness, with respect. Was that such a terrible crime? Dash it, Miss Thurstfield, I would get down on my knees and beg your forgiveness, but I'd never get up, you know."

Hope turned to make sure he did not try anything so goosish. "I . . . I think I understand. I was pursued by Sir Malcolm for what I could bring, not for who I was. But what of Princess Henrika?"

"What of her? I knew her in Paris, so the government decided I was the best man for playing escort and keeping her from causing a scandal. She'll be leaving tomorrow, thank goodness, likely with a Prussian count in tow. She means nothing to me, I swear."

"But the hotel? What were you doing, pretending to be manager?"

"I wasn't. I simply borrowed Mr. Simmons's rooms to avoid climbing the stairs. You have my rooms."

"Oh, no! If word gets out, I'll be ruined. Staying in a gentleman's chambers, or permitting a man to pay my keep! You know how people will talk."

"Then I am quite prepared to do the honorable thing."

"Which is?"

"Offer my hand and my name, of course."

"Heavens, that is not at all necessary."

"It is to me. You already hold my heart, you know. In fact, I may as well make you a proper offer now. I was going to wait, to court you the right way, as myself. But I am so afraid you'll disappear back north, or find some handsome buck who can dance and who will never tease you, that I dare not delay."

"But we hardly know each other," she protested halfheartedly, for truth be told, he held the other half of her heart and soul, too.

"Then we shall have a lifetime to become better acquainted. Let us not waste a moment of it." With that he took her in his arms and kissed her, until she felt she was floating, on clouds. And he thought he could not dance!

9.

*No smoking in bed, no open, unattended flames.*

"Hush, my dearest," he said, placing a finger over her lips. "You don't have to give me an answer tonight. Just say that you will think about making me the happiest of men."

It was a good thing he did not expect an answer, for Hope couldn't have told him her name, not if her life depended on it. Her head felt like a hundred sparrows had landed inside, all flapping about and chirping. Which was more amazing, that her hotel manager was a hero viscount, or that he loved her? And if he'd lied so often and so easily in the past, could she believe him now? And if this was what one kiss could do to her, how would she survive being married to such a man? And, and, and, endlessly.

Then his sister was there. "What are you about, Arthur, sneaking off with a young lady in front of everyone? Do you want to destroy the gel's reputation? You are Huntingdon now, no ramshackle soldier, and it is time you acted in keeping with your dignities."

"I am trying, Sylvia. Lud knows I am trying to assure the succession as you keep insisting I do."

"Not on my balcony!" she shrieked.

It was his balcony, but she was right. This was neither the time nor the place for fervent declarations and fevered embraces. After gently brushing a disordered curl off Hope's cheek, he led her back into the ballroom, but he stayed by her side for most of the evening, introducing her to all of his friends as they paraded past to beg an introduction and a dance. The way he hovered at her shoulder or glowered at her would-be partners declared his intentions. When Lord Huntingdon led Miss Thurstfield into the supper room, no one doubted that an engagement was imminent, except for Hope. She was still pondering the conundrum of how Arthur could have deluded her by pretending to be someone else, if he loved her. Of course, the someone else was fond of her, too. She was getting a headache from all the questions, from all the champagne, and from all the gentlemen who wanted to meet her, now that she was suddenly in fashion. Still, she smiled at her dance partners, made polite conversation with the ladies, and even discussed the plight of returning veterans with the Duke of Wellington.

Arthur saw how weary she was growing, and how many men tried to lead her out to the balcony. 'Twas a toss-up whether she'd collapse from exhaustion first, or he'd challenge one of his former friends to pistols at dawn. The princess and her party had left, and so had the general. "You could leave now, my dear, if you wish."

She nodded gratefully, looking around for Lady Leverett for the first time all night. "Your friends left some time ago while you were dancing with that fop in the puce waistcoat. I promised to see you home. Well chaperoned by your Mrs. Storke, of course."

"But it is your party."

"No, it is my sister-in-law's, and has been a marvelous success. The lieutenant's uncle deigned to appear and has reinstated Durbin as his heir, and Miss Ferguson's father was closeted with him half the night discussing marriage settlements. And the princess was duly honored, and honored to go off to the next affair—literally and figuratively—with one of the czar's cousins. So my responsibilities have all been met, except seeing you safely back to the hotel."

Mrs. Storke was not much of a chaperone, snoring softly in her corner of the coach. She didn't see Arthur pull Hope closer to his side so she could rest her head on his shoulder, and he could rub his cheek against her soft brown curls. They did not talk, but the silence was comfortable, companionable. Things were not settled between them, they both knew, but this magical night was not to be shattered by any more hard questions.

It was shattered by the fire gongs, instead.

They could smell the smoke from blocks away, and hear the alarm bells ringing. The roads became congested with those trying to flee the fire, those arriving to help fight it, and those coming to gawk at it. Hope and Arthur stared out of the carriage windows, trying to discern the fire's location. "Dear Lord, it's the hotel!"

Indeed, the Grand Hotel was burning. Smoke poured out of the upper stories, although they could not see any flames, even when they rushed from the coach to make their way on foot, swerving around firemen and water wagons and lines of men in hotel uniforms and formal dress passing buckets. Arthur's man Browne was on one of the lines, but he left to report to his master. The fire had started in the kitchens, he told them, and traveled up the walls to the dining room, then to the guest rooms on the floors above. The manager's apartment was not afire, not yet, and Browne had managed to toss some of the captain's belongings out the window before the smoke grew too thick and everyone was ordered to evacuate the premises. The firemen were battling to keep the blaze contained at the right wing of the building, and looked to be winning that battle. A few of the guests were overcome with smoke, and a few of the maids were in hysterics. Miss Thurstfield's friends, the Leveretts, had returned in time to be rousted out, but they were safe at a friend's house, with whichever other of the guests they could gather into carriages to take to safety.

"Good thing they paid the fire insurance," Browne noted before he left to rejoin the fire brigade. Arthur said he'd find him as soon as he sent the ladies back to Huntingdon House.

Nancy was wringing her hands. "Oh, my stars and psalms! To think that we could have been in there, asleep in our beds!"

Hope was staring at the building. "But my dog is. I have to go find poor Trumpet."

Arthur grabbed her arm before she could take another step. "You cannot go in there, Hope. You heard Brownie. They have ordered everyone out. And the smoke would be too thick to breathe. Besides, your dog most likely ran out when he heard all the commotion. We'll find him around the back or down the block."

She was struggling to release her arm from his grip. "No, he only hides under the bed when he is frightened, from thunder or fireworks. He'd never leave on his own."

"Damnation! Very well, I will go, if you swear to stay here."

"No, Trumpet is my pet, my responsibility. The danger has to be mine."

He kissed her briefly on the forehead. "Don't you

realize yet, sweetheart, that I couldn't live without you?"

"You can't go in there, Cap'n," Browne protested when Arthur told him to pour a bucket of water over his head and on Hope's shawl, so he could cover his mouth. "Not after a cursed dog!"

"It's Hope's dog." That was enough for him. It had to be enough for Browne.

"But what about your leg?"

"It will do. You go to the women and make sure they stay put."

The climb was a nightmare, especially after he'd been standing all night behind Hope's chair. Arthur told himself he'd walk through hell for her happiness, and this looked like it, all smoky and stifling hot, and dark as the inside of a loan shark's heart. He had to hang on to the banister just to find the stairs. Going down was going to be worse, so he grabbed a coil of rope the firemen had left on the second landing and tossed it over his shoulder.

When he reached the third floor, Arthur could see flames down the corridor, hear the shouts of men with hoses and buckets and axes. Thankfully the fire was in the opposite direction of Miss Thurstfield's suite, his suite, that he was finally getting to use. He strained to see the numbers on the doors, then fumbled for the key in his pocket when he found the right one. She'd pressed it into his hand with a quick, "Be careful, my love." Her love dropped the blasted key and had to search for it with his hands along the carpet.

At last he was inside, headed for the bedchamber to the right, where he collided with the large bed. Now was not the time to think of his Hope in that big bed. The deuced dog had better be underneath, or he was leaving without him, before they both perished. "Come on, Trumpet, come to me. I'll get you out."

The dog did not believe him. Cursing, Arthur had to take the time to light a candle on the nightstand, muttering about the absurdity of lighting a taper in the middle of a conflagration. Then he had to get down on his hands and knees, with the candle. He'd strangle the little mutt himself, for this. There was Trumpet, cowering beneath the center of the bed, trembling so hard Arthur wondered that the little creature's bones did not break.

"Come on, Trumpet, come over here. I know you are frightened, but I didn't die from wounds in Portugal, and I didn't die from fevers in France. I am certainly not about to die in a hotel in London. Especially not now. Come on, I swear not to hang you with the rope. Blast you, come. Hope is outside. Where there is Hope, there is life."

Trumpet panted, but did not budge. Arthur reached back for his cane, and poked it under the bed, trying to send the shaggy little dog scurrying. "Come on, unless it's Gideon's Trumpet you want to be." The terrier just backed farther away.

"Of all the miserable mongrels in the world, I have to rescue one so dumb it doesn't recognize a friend?" Then Arthur recalled what else he'd encountered on the nightstand: a plate of sugar biscuits. He pulled himself up to his feet on the satin bedspread, and grabbed a handful of the biscuits before sinking down again. "Here, you dunderhead of a dog, have a treat, before you are toast."

The dog sniffed at his outstretched hand and inched closer. Arthur reached with his cane and snagged it in the dog's collar. He dragged the animal out and wrapped him in Hope's shawl, because he couldn't trust the terrorized terrier not to run back under the bed at first chance. But he could not hold to the stair rail, his cane, and the dog all at once. He shrugged out of his uniform jacket, thinking to make a sling with the sleeves, but he could hear the firemen getting closer, which meant the fire was also. So he stuffed the little dog down inside his shirt, held there by the waistband of his beeches. And felt a rush of warm liquid against his belly. "Bloody hell! Is that the thanks I get?"

Outside the room the thick black smoke was creeping along the hall carpet, toward the stairs. The lower floors might be engulfed by now, leaving him trapped. Arthur was not about to chance it. He unlatched a window and crawled through to the ledge. He could see a column, some window molding, a decorative medallion, nothing he could climb down or tie his rope to. Swearing, he climbed back inside, using one hand to protect the dog. He swung his cane around until it encountered the bed again, and he tied a loop around one of the heavy wooden legs, praying his knot was tight enough, the wood was strong enough, and the rope was long enough. He tossed his cane out the window before lowering himself over the ledge. He could hear shouts from below, and see faces turned his way in lantern light. No ladders, though, dash it.

Arthur was not as strong as he used to be, he quickly realized. Hell, he was not as young as he used to be, either. He had to keep kicking off the side of the building to avoid crushing the dog, which sent agonizing pain through his bad leg, and his palms were burning from the rope, but he kept going, for an hour or two, it seemed, before he felt hands on his legs, guiding him down. The hands caught him when he let go, and lowered him to the ground. Arthur sat up and pulled his wet shirt out of his waistband, sending Trumpet tumbling out, yipping, to race to Hope. People cheered and Arthur collapsed back onto the grass and Hope scooped the dog up, sobbing into Trumpet's scruffy, sooty fur. Then she handed the dog to Mrs. Storke and, kneeling, threw herself onto Arthur's chest, weeping.

"You did that, for me?"

She didn't know the half of it, but would soon, resting her cheek against his doubly damp shirt. He could only stroke her hair while she cried. "Hush, my love, hush. Everything is all right."

"Yes!"

"I told you I would find your dog. See, you can trust me."

"Yes!"

"And you can forgive me for deceiving you?"

"Yes! Yes, and yes, you noddy. That's my answer to your question! I will marry you, tomorrow if you can obtain a special license. I don't even care what name you put in the registry. I just want to share that name, and your life, whoever you are. Vagabond or viscount, Arthur, I love you. I think I must always have. I know I always will."

With Hope for all his tomorrows, Arthur knew he had finally come home. He could be anything she wanted, live anywhere she chose. He'd spend his days trying to make her as happy as she was making him at this moment.

He just prayed Brownie had saved him a fresh shirt.

# Promises to Keep
## by Allison Lane

### 1

London was huge and full of people.

Maggie Adams stared at the crowds as her hired carriage rounded a corner. Even knowing that London was the largest city in the world had not prepared her for its immensity.

It had taken two hours to reach Mayfair from the docks, though they had crossed only a portion of the city. She had seen areas of unimagined squalor, streets so elegant that her breath caught, and more people than she could count. A market square had seemed to hold the entire population of Halifax, yet more women had bustled along the next street than had huddled outside the mine after last spring's disaster. Every corner they rounded revealed more—piemen vying for a workman's custom, maids scurrying about on errands or flirting with handsome young footmen, horses jamming the intersections, delivery boys, shoppers, crones, pickpockets . . .

Never had she felt so insignificant—or so helpless. She'd already been turned away from every hotel Captain Harding considered suitable for ladies. What if the Grand Hotel was also full?

"I still think we should go to Adams House," said Alice stoutly.

"No. I promised Father to heal the breach with his

family, but he warned me to remain cautious. Arriving on their doorstep without warning will put me at a disadvantage. I must learn more about the family before making demands." To begin with, she must find out whether her grandfather was still alive. It had been twenty-eight years since her father had left home.

An altercation outside the window distracted her attention. Half a dozen men cheered on two youths, who were pummeling each other as they rolled about on the ground. A matron glared, then berated a gentleman collecting wagers on the outcome.

"You know how your father would feel about patronizing a second-rate hotel," Alice said, returning to their ongoing argument.

"The clerk at the Clarendon swore that the Grand Hotel is an excellent house."

"The clerk at the Clarendon thought you a rustic colonial with little money and less consequence."

Alice was right—not that she'd had any choice. Hiding her circumstances was another promise she'd made to her father. If she failed to heal this breach, she wanted no further contact with her English family. The only way to assure that was to hide her home and give them no incentive to look for her.

Yet dressing shabbily had been a serious mistake today. She had not understood how rigid the English were about class—far more than anyone at home. So at this hotel, her demeanor must convince the clerk that she was aristocratic despite her provincial gown.

The carriage pulled to a stop.

"It's impressive enough," conceded Alice as the door opened. Columns punctuated the facade, which overlooked a broad street divided by a tree-studded garden.

"Let's hope they have room." Maggie accepted a footman's hand down, but did not utter her usual thanks. She must radiate power.

Ignoring the elegant lobby, she stiffened her spine and marched to the desk.

"Good day, Mr. Simmons." She prayed the name-plate was his. "Mr. Louillier at the Clarendon believes you have a suite available—all he could offer was a single room. I trust you can accommodate me."

She glared in the way that usually cowed her employees, giving him no chance to assess her gown. It worked.

"Of course, madam."

She nodded regally. "Margaret Adams, of Halifax." This lie had little to do with promises. She could hardly admit being an American. War had raged between England and the United States for two years.

She signed the register and paid a week in advance, then sent Alice to deal with their driver. Exhaustion swept over her in a debilitating wave. The journey had been grueling—jolting along corduroy roads, canoeing down rivers, leading pack animals through dense forest. Eventually she'd caught a fishing boat to Halifax, where she'd boarded a ship for England.

But now that she was finally here, the uncertainty she had been ignoring returned. How was she to approach her family?

Deep in thought, she headed for the stairs and promptly ran into a gentleman.

"Pardon me, madam," he said stiffly, grabbing her arm to keep her from falling.

Flames burned her cheeks. "It was entirely my fault, sir. Are you all right?" Odd sensations radiated from his hand. "I should have been paying attention—though it could have been worse. I might have sent you sprawling." She winced at her babbling, for the words were embarrassingly true. She had been beset by clumsiness since leaving for England. Only last week, she'd nearly knocked the first mate overboard.

"Am I supposed to be grateful?" he asked coolly.

"That wasn't what I meant!" New heat flushed her face. She shook her head in an effort to restore wits scattered by his touch. Where had her sangfroid gone? He was only a man.

But *what* a man! His clothes were more fashionable than evening wear in Pittsburgh. A striped waistcoat peeked from under a dark blue coat stretched across powerful shoulders. Gray pantaloons showed off muscular thighs and impeccably polished boots. His eyes were an odd shade of green—something between old moss and a pale stone she'd once found along the river. Only his hair countered his elegance, framing his face in a riot of dark curls. She suppressed a ridiculous urge to test its softness.

"The accent is American," he said after quizzing her from head to toe. "But from neither Philadelphia nor Boston."

"Canadian," she countered, meeting his gaze in a test of wills.

He blinked, his eyes lightening with laughter. "Intelligent."

"What is your point, Mr.—"

"Widmer. Marcus Widmer. Forgive me. Your nationality is your own business, though this demonstrates why I resigned from diplomatic service. My tongue sometimes runs on its own."

"Maggie Adams, from Halifax." She offered her hand as if meeting a business acquaintance, then chided herself as he gravely shook it. "What can you tell me of the Grand Hotel? I had expected to stay at the Pulteney or the Clarendon."

"You and half the aristocracy." He offered his arm to escort her upstairs. "All the better London hotels are crowded because of Napoleon's abdication. In June, we entertained a host of foreign dignitaries, including several heads of state. In July, innumerable dinners honored Wellington. Now London is holding the public festivities. They will conclude tomorrow, but you should be careful when you venture out. Excitement often leads to rowdiness, and this heat has done nothing to soothe tempers."

She nodded, though London was cooler than August at home.

"As to your question, I've lived at the Grand Hotel since it opened last month. The service remains what Americans call spotty, but the prices are reasonable and the food is outstanding. Would you dine with me this evening?"

"My companion and I will be delighted," she replied without thinking.

Maggie shut the door to her first-floor suite, leaving Mr. Widmer to continue upstairs. What had possessed her to accept an invitation from a man to whom she had not been introduced? Recklessness was alien to her nature, but something about him scattered her wits. She still felt uncomfortably warm.

Or was it merely exhaustion?

She frowned, turning the encounter over in her mind. She'd spotted a flash in his eyes that usually denoted avarice, though that was unlikely. His examination would have convinced him that she was beneath him socially and probably naïve. Thus the only thing he could covet was her body. This invitation was probably the first step in a seduction.

The idea hurt. "Take care, Maggie," she murmured aloud. No one had ever piqued her interest so quickly. He exuded a powerful masculinity, which made him dangerous. If she hoped to keep her wits sharp, she must rest before dinner.

But first, she had promises to keep. She found pen, ink, and pressed paper in the sitting room's writing desk. Moving aside an oil lamp held aloft by a Greek maiden, she addressed a brief letter to her grandfather. With luck, he would be in London for the festivities.

Alice arrived as she was sanding the page. "What a wonderful hotel," she exclaimed. "They even have a dumbwaiter to haul the heavier luggage upstairs. I must include one when I build."

"Don't introduce too much ostentation," Maggie warned. "The Grand Hotel would overwhelm Pittsburgh. Most of those passing through cannot afford luxury."

"I know. I intend to start small, but I've every intention of serving the affluent. Pittsburgh has grown large enough to need a quality hotel, and mine will be the best." She ran her fingers over a black lacquer cabinet decorated with chariots and swans. "Mr. Simmons was soothing an irate dowager just now. He has a knack for knowing exactly what to say. I wonder if he would share information on hotel management with a mere female."

Maggie sealed the note, listening to Alice's chatter with half an ear. She doubted that the stiff Mr. Simmons would help, though if anyone could convince him to do so, it would be Alice Sharpe. Her former governess was the most persistent woman she had ever known.

Marcus berated himself all the way to his third-floor room. What was it about Maggie Adams that had prompted him to act the fool? Quitting the government had nothing to do with any lack of diplomatic skill. He had been a valued member of delegations to several countries. Never had he revealed any fact without purpose. So why had his tongue run away with him today?

*Wrong question,* his conscience announced.

The problem had not begun today, he admitted. He had behaved recklessly since quitting his position two months ago—arguing with his family, taking up residence in a hotel, allowing a pleasant flirtation with the maid to grow into a lusty liaison . . .

What a stupid idea that had been. Betsy expected him to set her up as his mistress, so breaking off the affair would invite retaliation—not that he'd considered doing so until half an hour ago, but one look at Miss Adams had banished any desire for others.

Maggie Adams. American, despite her denials. She was magnificent—tall enough to reach his nose, blue eyes, dark hair. Her manner might be almost masculine, but it formed a piquant contrast to the most delectable body he'd seen in years—his mouth watered at the image of cradling her breasts, of caressing her hips, of—

"Down!" he ordered his unruly passions. They were another change since quitting diplomacy. During the years he'd slaved to earn his superiors' respect, he'd been too focused on business to bother with more than an occasional encounter. Now he could rarely go a day without needing a woman. Yet Miss Adams was unobtainable. He could neither seduce an innocent nor court a foreigner. Inviting her to dinner had been stupid, but the words had emerged without thought—another new trait, and one he would rather do without. Now he must spend an entire evening lusting after someone he could not have.

Pushing the problem aside, he reviewed his afternoon meeting with Trevithick.

He was fascinated by inventions, especially those newfangled machines his grandfather derided. Diplomacy had never stirred his senses like the thought of operating his own business. Unfortunately, his talents lay in organization and oversight, so he needed a creative partner.

His family was appalled. Gentlemen did not dabble in trade. Nor did they display vulgar interest in things mechanical. Never mind that as the younger son of a baron's younger son he had no hope of achieving the title. Never mind that his interests did not run to agriculture, the church, government service, or even the military. As a gentleman, he was expected to emulate his ancestors.

"No," he vowed, pacing the floor. A large legacy from his maternal grandmother and a smaller one from his Great-aunt Margaret allowed him to follow his dreams. Change was inevitable, despite the hidebound thinking of men like his grandfather. A new order was coming. He must be part of it.

He had encountered progress wherever he'd gone. In Italy, Volta was producing electricity by immersing metal plates in a chemical solution. In Russia, a tinker had raved about his French cousin, Appert, who could pack meat in metal cans that kept it fresh for months. In the United States, he had watched gins separate cotton from its seeds in a fraction of the time slaves needed to do the job.

All had spurred his enthusiasm, but he was proceeding cautiously. He had so many interests, it was difficult to decide which to pursue, and his inheritance was not large enough to recover from mistakes. He knew too many men who had lost fortunes by backing unworkable schemes—like that canal venture Rutherford had embraced last year. If he decided to build transportation systems, he would avoid canals. Trevithick's engine would one day prove faster.

Of course, Stephenson was also working on an engine, which rumor claimed was superior to Trevithick's. Which inventor had the most practical design? Was it realistic to think people would accept miles of unsightly rails? At least canals appeared natural.

Maybe he should consider steam-powered ships instead of land vehicles. They were closer to becoming economically viable. Or perhaps he should look at manufacturing instead of transportation.

It was a daily argument that always made his head spin.

Setting aside Trevithick's proposal, he pulled out others and reread their claims. But for once, his mind would not stay on business. It kept drifting to a certain blue-eyed American.

Maggie ignored the dining room's ostentatious decor and concentrated on Mr. Widmer. She still wasn't sure what to think of him. Why was he escorting her to dinner? Seduction didn't fit his demeanor this evening. His warmth did not exceed propriety. Nor was he showering her with false flattery, as did

those seeking her influence with her father. Could he
possibly wish to be friends?

Her heart turned over. It was an insidiously attractive idea, but one she must suppress. Even if it were
true—and no one had ever approved her outspoken
manner—friendship would lead to sorrow when she
returned home. And risking a deeper attachment was
stupid. She could never remain here, nor would he
consider leaving. One day in London confirmed that
the English considered themselves superior to everyone else.

"Have you ever seen such huge mirrors?" asked
Alice, nodding toward the oval mirrors that flanked
the dining room's entrance, each taller than a man. "I
wonder if the fabled mirrors at Versailles can compare."

"I suspect so." Maggie bit back a sigh. Alice was
constantly comparing her various heritages—she'd
been born to an Irish indentured servant and French
trapper, then married an English baron's younger son,
who had tutored her in reading, writing, and social
graces. But at least Alice felt connected to the past.
Why had they come to England if not to find something similar for herself?

"I've read descriptions of the Hall of Mirrors," said
Widmer. "If I had not resigned government service, I
would be in Paris now and able to see it for myself."

"So why resign? Did you not enjoy the work?"
asked Maggie.

"Rarely." He smiled. "But it taught me much. Your
accent, for example. It is not from Halifax. Nor does
it match our former colonies. Where is your home?"

"Inland." His curiosity hinted at a different explanation for this invitation. Perhaps he considered her a
spy.

He frowned.

She tried a partial truth. "I came to England to heal
the breach between my father and grandfather, but if
that proves impossible, I want no further contact with
the family."

A waiter interrupted to describe the evening's dinner choices. But when he departed, Widmer resumed his probing. "You sound so uncertain of success that I am surprised you are trying. Or are you driven by curiosity?"

"That is part of it, for I know very little about my ancestors," she admitted. "But what are you doing now that you no longer work for the government?"

This time he accepted her change of subject. "Creating unconscionable scandal." He grinned. "My family has not decided whether to disown me or lock me in Bedlam."

Alice gasped.

"He is teasing," Maggie assured her. "What have you done that is so shocking, Mr. Widmer?"

"I wish to establish my own business, but trade is not a proper pursuit for gentlemen."

The waiter served plates of soup.

"Delicious." Alice tasted and sighed with pleasure. "Give my compliments to the cook."

"Monsieur DuPré is a *chef*, madam," the waiter insisted.

"He is more than a chef," said Widmer, laughing. "He is a temperamental *artiste* with a penchant for confronting anyone who disparages his creations. Only yesterday he brandished a knife at Lieutenant Forrester when he dared request that the sole not be smothered in DuPré's tarragon lemon sauce."

"Then we must do justice to his food." Maggie sipped a spoonful of the best soup she'd ever eaten, then resumed the conversation to keep from gulping the rest. She had not eaten since breakfast aboard ship. "Why does your family condemn honest business?"

"Tradition. I should derive income only from those activities approved by centuries of Widmers—land, investments, or service to the church or crown. Never trade."

"Forgive me, but farmers sell their products, and

investing gives one a stake in the business. So what is the distinction?"

"Distance. A steward oversees the fields, which are worked by laborers and tenants. Investing is likewise an aloof activity."

"Ah. A gentleman keeps his hands clean, relying on the labor of others to pay for his life of idleness." She could not keep the bite out of her tone.

"I take it you were not raised to idleness."

"Hardly." She smiled. "And you are rebelling against it."

He nodded. "I must do more than finance other men's schemes. Even if I cannot create something myself, I want to oversee its production."

"What sort of business are you considering?" Despite her resolve to eat like a lady, she had already finished her soup.

"I am not sure. I've been meeting with inventors, hoping to narrow my interests, but so far everything is fascinating."

"Which means you've not yet found your niche. One of our—"

The waiter returned to lay out the next course. And just as well. Describing the industries near Pittsburgh would reveal her home. "Who have you approached?" she asked, renewing her resolve to be mannerly after tasting the sauce coating a delicate fish. When she spotted Alice's gleaming eyes, she could almost read her friend's mind: *How can I entice this chef to Pittsburgh?*

"You would not recognize the names," he said with a shrug.

"You might be surprised. Are you interested in products—a better carriage spring or mechanical harvester? Or do you want to improve the manufacturing process itself—adapting steam engines to practical use or reinventing products using interchangeable parts? Whitney has done wonders with muskets. Since every weapon is identical, spare parts can be kept at hand, making repairs simple."

He stared, as if she had started speaking in Greek. "What do you know of such things?"

"Women are allowed to think where I come from. And we frequently discuss ideas." At least, she did. Her father had trained her to take over his business. But that was a topic she must avoid. She gestured to her plate. "Delicious birds. What are they?"

"Grouse," he said shortly, ignoring her diversion. "My interests are varied. Now that I have time to meet inventors, I feel like a starving child thrust into a room filled with sweets. When I speak to Trevithick, I can see networks of rails moving goods and people across vast distances. When I talk to Cayley, I become enthralled by his gliders."

"Gilders?"

"Birdlike devices that soar from cliff tops."

"How far?"

"A few hundred feet."

"That doesn't sound very practical."

"Few things are in the beginning," put in Alice. "But imagine how it would feel to float through the air."

"Imagine how it would feel to land on one's head," countered Maggie. Widmer laughed, drawing her eyes to his sensuous lips. His green eyes raised images of sunbeams sifting through young leaves.

"There are other possibilities," he continued. "Two years ago a company began installing gaslights on London streets—they've been used in mills for some time. Koenig is designing steam-powered printing presses. Steamships are plying Scotland's Clyde River, and one will soon serve on the Thames."

"America has had steamships on the Hudson for years," said Maggie in challenge.

That began a competition that lasted nearly an hour as they feasted on the best food she had ever tasted. She described the safety equipment added to the coal mines near her home. He countered with Davy's latest experiments on the nature of matter. She demanded details of how gas lighting worked in factories. He asked about Whitney's muskets and the machines that made interchangeable parts possible.

Fate was taunting her, she decided, scraping the last of the venison from her plate. Widmer was the most attractive man she'd ever met, reminding her of her father—the same quick mind, the same odd assortment of knowledge, the same fascination with diverse topics. Why couldn't she find someone like him at home?

A disturbance jerked her attention toward the door just as a huge man burst into the room, brandishing a cleaver. Flour dusted his golden hair.

*"Imbecile!"* he roared. "Who has dared to insult my sauces?"

"The gentleman is gone, Monsieur DuPré," said Simmons, producing a soothing tone despite his undignified dash into the dining room.

"Enjoy the farce," murmured Widmer, keeping his face neutral, though his eyes were dancing with laughter. "He entertains us at least twice a week—often better than the actors at Drury Lane."

"Why?" she whispered.

"He is French." He shrugged. "And he is determined to win London's acclaim. It infuriates him when anyone praises Jaquiers—the chef at the Clarendon. He doesn't understand that no one would dare disparage Jaquiers's food after paying such exorbitant prices for it."

Simmons might have been invisible for all the effect he was having on the volatile Frenchman. DuPré ranted. He gesticulated. He called the wrath of heaven down upon anyone who dared suggest a better chef existed in the world.

Without warning, he lunged at Alice. "Why ignore you zees work of art?" he demanded, pointing to her plate, where two mushrooms carved to resemble flowers graced a slice of venison. "Ze sauce, she is smooth, and rich with wine. And ze meat!" He kissed his fingertips.

"Truly perfect," agreed Alice, fluttering her lashes. "It begs to be savored, bite by delicate bite, not inhaled in a gulp like a dog would a stolen chop."

His laugh filled the room. "Ah, *chérie,* how delightful. A woman who knows food is above rubies."

"Above diamonds and rubies," insisted Alice in French, sending him into new transports in that language.

His hands punctuated his words, as did his shoulders and hips, providing a vivid contrast to the stiff English gentlemen in the room and reminding Maggie of an Italian family who had recently moved to Pittsburgh. His deep voice drew every eye, as thick as honey and as smooth as one of his sauces.

Alice matched him claim for claim, gesture for gesture, flattering his artistry and vowing to puff his talent to the highest in the land. She even thanked fate that the Clarendon had been full, for otherwise she would have missed the most exquisite meal of her life.

Simmons slipped out, his face sagging in relief now that the cleaver rested harmlessly on the table.

Alice kept DuPré talking until he had revealed his recipe for the venison's sauce. The moment he left, she laughed. "I haven't had that much fun in years."

"I cannot believe he gave you a recipe," murmured their waiter, starting at Alice in awe. "DuPré *never* reveals his secrets."

Maggie laughed. Alice's eyes had gleamed at the word *never,* for she loved a challenge. Their stay at the Grand Hotel should prove quite interesting.

"Only because those asking don't know how to handle him." Alice cut a bite of venison. "He is just like my father, using emotional outbursts to cow those around him. But he revels in flattery and will do anything to elicit praise."

"Recipes?" asked Widmer curiously, returning his gaze to Maggie.

She nodded. "Alice plans to open a hotel."

"I like good food," Alice explained. "I could never entice DuPré home with us, but at least I can duplicate his dishes." She cocked her head. "What was it you said about prices when he first burst in?"

Widmer smiled. "The Clarendon charges three or four times as much for a meal as the Grand Hotel, though DuPré's food is better. But the price gives Jaquiers a cachet no one dares deny."

"I prefer to decide for myself what I like and dislike," said Maggie bluntly.

"As do I," said Widmer, catching her eye with a look that pooled heat in her stomach. Maybe he was a rake after all . . .

The rest of the meal passed quietly, though DuPré returned to serve them a magnificent dessert with his own hands. Alice had obviously enslaved him. But a flirtation promised to keep them well fed.

## 2

Maggie stared at the note—the same one she had sent to Adams House yesterday. Someone named Robert had crossed her lines, denying any connection to her father, John Adams. A postscript informed her that her grandfather was dead.

"How dare they disown Papa," she spat, crumpling the letter. Pacing the room, she muttered imprecations against her English family. She should never have promised to approach them. But who could deny a dying man his last wish?

The memory formed a lump in her throat.

A tunnel had collapsed at the mine, killing four men and burying her father. Rescuers had dug him out, but he was too badly injured to recover. For a week, she'd hovered at his bedside as his delirium gave way to a coma and his life slipped inexorably away. Then he'd unexpectedly awakened.

"I'm dying," he'd whispered, his fingers clasping hers.

"No." The denial was automatic, though she knew he was right. Already his skin seemed transparent.

"Don't argue, Maggie," he continued in a stronger voice. "I haven't time. I don't want to leave you alone."

"You won't. I have Alice and Harry and Mr. Franco and—"

"That's business." His grip tightened as he fought for breath. "A person needs more."

"I won't wed Jeremy," she swore, naming the latest fortune hunter to come calling.

"He is no good. But you need family, Maggie. You need to know where you came from. I want you to heal the breach with my father."

She stared, for the request made little sense. "What breach?"

"We parted in anger." He shook his head. "Catherine was promised to my brother."

"Why did Mother accept him when she loved you?"

"It was arranged when they were children." He met her eyes, his own full of pain. "That is society's way."

"Boston society?"

"London. Father is a viscount." He paused to catch his breath.

She could think of nothing to say. He'd never hinted at such a background, though she had often envied his ease with powerful businessmen. But this was no time to discuss the past. His face was gray with fatigue.

"Family is important," he continued before she could urge him to rest. "Learn about yours. Go to England." Another pause. "My only crime was eloping." His voice softened. "But I cannot regret it . . . William hated Catherine. He hates everyone, so be careful. He won't welcome you."

"Where are they?"

"Adams House . . . London. Or Fielding Court . . . Kent. George Adams."

"Rest, Father," she said, stroking his frail arm. His gasps for breath tore at her heart. "We can discuss this later."

"No time . . . look for . . . box of papers . . . desk . . . prove your birth . . ."

"Father—"

"Promise, Maggie."

"Father?"

"Promise . . . but don't trust . . . hide this . . . until you know." He gestured weakly at the room.

"I promise." Tears streamed down her cheeks.

"Love yo—" His hand went limp as he slipped back into the coma.

Five months later, she brushed away new tears. He had died that night. The doctor could not explain how he had awakened, but the fact that he'd roused himself long enough to extract her vow gave it added weight. So she had come to England.

The box had held a packet tied with string. She'd been too grief-stricken to examine the papers then, but with this stinging rejection in her hand, she could postpone the task no longer. George might be gone, but the rest of the family remained. Pulling the papers from her writing case, she spread them across the desk.

Her father's will.

A statement of baptism, describing her as the daughter of John and Catherine Adams of Halifax, signed by her parents and a pastor.

A letter dated April 1783, addressed to Andrew Adams at a hotel in Paris.

"Andrew?" she muttered, opening it. Penned by Andrew's father, it referred to Andrew's recent week at the French court. Four more letters followed, all addressed to Andrew in Paris and mentioning social events Andrew had attended.

"Who is Andrew?" she murmured, setting the last one aside.

The next document was marriage lines, written by the captain of the *Mariner Queen,* who had united, on the high seas, Andrew Jonathan Franklin Adams and Elizabeth Catherine Anne Widmer. An accompanying note explained that they were listed on the ship's roster as John and Catherine Smith, immigrants.

She laughed. She had meant to ask George about her mother's family, for her father hadn't mentioned them. Now there was no need. Unlike Adams, Widmer was an uncommon name. Marcus Widmer must be connected.

The packet also contained a statement of death from the doctor who had treated her mother's final illness, documents related to her father's estate, Uncle Peter's will, and other papers that had nothing to do with her English families. It had not been assembled for her use, then. Separating the marriage lines, baptism record, and letters, she returned the rest to her writing case.

No wonder she had felt attracted to Marcus. Somehow she had recognized a tie. Perhaps she'd heard the name as a child.

Half an hour later, she took a seat in the hotel lobby. Marcus was out but would return shortly—or so Simmons claimed. She wasn't so sure, for if he was meeting another inventor, he might easily lose track of time. But she was too impatient to rely on a note, which he could set aside if he was rushed.

After ordering coffee, she distracted herself by watching the comings and goings of other guests.

A pale blonde wearing the entire contents of a large jewelry case swept down the stairs, accompanied by three men speaking what sounded like German. When Simmons addressed her as "Your Highness," Maggie stared. She would never have guessed the buxom woman was royal. In fact, she bore a striking resemblance to the Bavarian barmaid at the Riverboat Tavern, who required no assistance to oust rowdy drunkards.

A man with the blackest skin she'd ever seen burst through the door and hurried up the stairs, knocking a descending brunette into the banister. Obviously neither slave nor servant; he was too confident. But what was such a man doing in London? And in so elegant a hotel?

He was followed by a mother and son returning from the royal menagerie. The boy pounced on a design woven into the carpet, emitting ferocious growls.

"I'm a lion!" he shouted as the street door again opened.

A lapdog wearing a diamond-studded collar rushed in, barking ferociously.

The lad screamed.

Maggie jumped up to help, but the dog halted inches from the boy's face, looking pleased with the reaction it had provoked.

"Lady Augusta Mountrail! Can't you control that animal?" the mother snapped.

"Prince Theodore would never hurt a soul," declared Lady Augusta, scooping him against her bosom so she could press her face against his neck. "Would you, my sweet Teddy?"

Maggie regained her seat and gulped coffee to steady her nerves.

"One day that beast will go too far."

"He is not as unruly as Julian." Lady Augusta scowled at the lad, who was already feigning a new attack on a footman. "That boy deliberately tripped me yesterday. Teddy has much better manners."

Both women had hopelessly spoiled their charges, decided Maggie as they moved upstairs, their voices drowned out by a couple arguing over an invitation to a ball.

Marcus finally returned, deep in thought. When he failed to respond to her cheerful greeting, she stepped in front of him.

He nearly ran her down. "Miss Adams! But where is Mrs. Sharpe?"

"Shopping. I must speak with you."

"I have an appointment in an hour."

"I will be brief." She moved closer to the fireplace, away from Simmons's ears. "I need information about my mother's family."

"Your mother?"

"Elizabeth Widmer. She and my father eloped twenty-eight years ago."

Shock exploded through his eyes, dulling their green to gray. A surge of betrayal followed. She was too surprised by his reaction to question why she could read his eyes so easily.

Marcus stared at Miss Adams, suspicion tingling along every nerve. And lust, damn his uncooperative body. If only he hadn't recognized the awareness in her eyes last night. Knowing that she felt the same tug of attraction had made it difficult to sleep.

But he must set all feelings aside. Ever since *Life in London* had printed an exaggerated story about the Adams family that included all the old scandals, both they and the Widmers had been beset by pretenders. They had already exposed two men and a woman claiming Andrew Adams as their sire. At least this one had chosen a novel approach.

"Why did you say nothing last night?" he asked.

She shrugged. "I knew her as Catherine Adams, wife of John Adams. She died fifteen years ago. I only examined Father's papers this morning after his family swore that John was not related. Their marriage lines name Andrew Jonathan Franklin Adams and Elizabeth Catherine Anne Widmer."

"He sent you to meet his family, yet told you nothing about them?"

"He was dying. He begged me to visit England, said his father was George Adams, viscount, and that the papers in his desk would prove my identity. There was no time for more."

Clever or truthful? It was too early to tell, and he wasn't about to lay his own cards on the table until he learned considerably more about Miss Maggie Adams, late of America. She had already told him one lie. "What do you know of the Widmer family?"

"Only what you mentioned last evening. I had no inkling I was connected until now—assuming that we are speaking of the same Widmers. I did not even know my parents were English until the day Father died. He claimed Mother had been promised to his brother, but chose to elope. I suppose that's why they moved to Halifax." She shrugged.

"Andrew fled after stealing a fortune in jewelry and banknotes to cover yet another gaming debt," he said flatly.

"You lie." Her fingers curled, and for a moment he thought she would strike him. "Father was a hard worker, who abhorred any waste of time or money. A more honorable man would be difficult to find."

"Hard worker?"

"In Halifax, he worked on the docks, loading and unloading cargo. I don't recall those days, but I remember his years as a trapper, and those he spent cutting timber. There were other jobs as well. He died of injuries suffered when a tunnel collapsed in the mine."

"When was that?"

"The seventeenth of March. I only wish he'd died outright, like the others. He lingered for several days."

He pressed her hand in sympathy, sending another wave of desire rampaging through his groin. Andrew was innocent of the theft, though it was too soon to admit it. Mentioning the charge had been a test to see how much she knew. They had exposed one impostor by convincing him that Andrew's heir must repay that stolen fortune. "You say they never spoke of England?"

"Why should they? Our life was nothing like this." She gestured at the ornate lobby, with its frieze-covered cornices, Greek statues, and gold-leaf adornment. "We looked forward, not back. Father claimed that clinging to the past made it difficult to plan for the future—you should understand, for you said much the same thing at dinner. I can only recall two references to their youths. When Father was teaching me to ride, he mentioned his own teacher, Frank. And Mother claimed that the portrait in her locket depicted her mother, for whom I'm named."

"Maggie."

"That's what she called me, but my full name is Margaret Anne Hartley Adams."

He hid his surprise. It was unlikely that she would have known Margaret's family name, unless she'd uncovered a copy of Debrett's *Peerage* in the American wilderness. But he must investigate before accepting her. "Your father wished to renew ties with his family?"

"No. He had no interest in returning. But he did not want me to be alone in the world, so he asked me to heal the breach with his father and learn about my ancestors."

*Unless he had heard . . .*

Marcus suppressed the thought. March was too early for news to have reached America. Yet an impostor would know that. Miss Adams had sailed only a month ago.

*But grief saddens her eyes every time she mentions her father . . .*

"What other papers did he leave you?"

"Proof of my birth and their deaths. A note from the captain who wed them that mentioned their name change. Several letters from his father, written while he was in Paris in 1783." She shrugged.

She was hiding something. Ice formed in his stomach, confirming how much he wanted her to be real. Maggie was nothing like the other impostors. They had radiated greed from the first contact. "May I see them?"

"Of course." Rising, she led him upstairs.

The documents seemed genuine. He had seen George's hand often enough to recognize it now. The marriage lines were scrawled on letterhead from the *Mariner Queen,* captained by Joseph Barnsley.

"You mentioned a locket?"

She pulled it from beneath her bodice.

His doubts fled. He had seen that locket a thousand times, in the family portrait commissioned to celebrate his grandfather's marriage. The group had included his great-grandparents, his newlywed grandparents, his Great-uncle Henry, Great-aunt Margaret, and Henry's firstborn. His grandmother had worn the family rubies, but Margaret had eschewed the family emeralds, insisting on the locket Henry had designed to enclose her betrothal miniature. This locket. Elizabeth had taken it with her when she'd eloped.

For the first time, he stared at the miniature itself. The face was identical to the one in the family portrait.

"It would appear that we are cousins, Maggie," he said, shaking his head.

"Cousins?"

"Second cousins, to be precise." He pointed to the miniature. "She married my grandfather's brother."

"Good heavens!" She laughed. "I've never met a real relative before. So tell me about my family."

He complied, offering humorous anecdotes of various Widmers, though he refused to divulge more until he could swear he had verified every fact. The family would demand absolute proof before accepting her. Only after she was fully acknowledged as a Widmer would he approach the Adams family on her behalf.

### 3

Maggie waited until the footman finished laying the table before she sat down. She'd not seen Marcus in three days, but he had given her much to ponder. Her mother's parents were both dead—Margaret barely a month ago. If only she hadn't delayed two months before starting this journey. Yet travel would have been even more difficult if she'd left before the weather cleared. It had been hard enough as it was.

Her mother had been the youngest of six children, so there were numerous relatives on the Widmer side. Marcus had asked her not to contact them until he could speak with his ailing grandfather, the current Lord Widmer. She assumed that was where he'd been.

But she'd made no such promise concerning the Adams family, who already knew of her claims. So she'd written to her Uncle William and to his heir, Robert, explaining about her father's name change and asking to meet his English family before she returned home.

Now she smiled. In addition to breakfast, the footman had brought replies from each of them.

But William's response triggered her temper.

*My brother forfeited his place in the family when he embraced a life of crime,* he'd written in a slashing hand. *Even if you are not an impostor, I would never acknowledge his whore's brat. Should you set foot on my property or solicit others to support your claims, I will see you arrested.*

She frowned.

*Life of crime . . .* Marcus claimed Andrew had stolen a fortune in jewelry and banknotes.

*My only crime was eloping . . .* She believed her father, but he'd known that he would be arrested for the theft. Thus someone must have arranged evidence against him.

The past no longer mattered. William's antagonism

proved he had not forgiven Catherine's defection. To remove the sting, he'd convinced himself that she was unchaste. So he would never heal the breach.

She blinked back tears. Though she had only promised to make peace with George, William's rejection hurt.

Sighing, she opened Robert's letter.

He apologized for his brusque response to her first note, then invited her to dine with him at the hotel. *Shortly before his death, Grandfather searched for Andrew so he could beg forgiveness. Life is too short to cling to grievances. Perhaps in time, my father will also set aside his pique and welcome you.* He concluded with three pages describing the original rift.

She frowned. Robert could be no older than she, yet he wrote as if he had known Andrew intimately. His depiction bore no resemblance to her father. This Andrew was a rakish dandy and gamester, who was always in debt. He'd created further scandal by publicly insulting a powerful arbiter of fashion while in his cups. After George confined him to the estate in an attempt to reform him, Andrew had turned to thievery to support his excesses, then stolen his brother's bride.

Maggie snorted. The claims were patently ridiculous. Why would George have sought forgiveness if they were true?

Rereading both letters raised other questions. William obviously believed the charges, for he considered his brother a criminal. Since George had sought forgiveness, he must have found evidence that seemed to exonerate Andrew. Both men reacted logically.

But Robert's behavior was strange. Like his father, he believed Andrew guilty of every crime short of murder. Yet he applauded his grandfather's decision to seek forgiveness for driving Andrew away. Even blood shouldn't be *that* thick. If one of her managers embraced such irrational logic, she would fire him.

Marcus had said little about Robert, his reticence

proving his skill as a diplomat and adding to her suspicions. Now that she thought about it, he had said little about any Adams, though he must know them well. The two family seats shared a boundary.

The only way to learn the truth was to accept this invitation. At least the dining room was public. And Robert would be easier to handle than most of the gentlemen who called on her. He knew nothing of her situation. Whatever his faults, he was no Patrick Riley.

Patrick had been her first serious suitor. His charm had captured her imagination, spawning dreams of an impossibly Utopian future. But when he'd failed to win her father's support for his suit, he'd tried to abduct her. She had learned a valuable lesson that day. Never again had she disregarded her father's advice or believed any man's compliments. In the ten years since, she had become adept at looking beyond the surface to the avarice that always lurked beneath.

As she was doing now. Robert's welcome did not ring true. Perhaps he was befriending her merely to annoy his father—in which case, he was harmless. But maybe he wanted something.

"My cousin Robert has invited us to dine with him this evening," she said when Alice joined her. "We will meet him in the lobby."

"Why?"

Maggie shrugged. "I don't trust him. Why would he heap flattery on the daughter of someone he considers so vile? Most people believe the adage about the sins of the fathers." She handed over his letter.

"But how would he know about Pittsburgh?"

"Perhaps Grandfather's agent traced Father." She frowned, tapping the other letter against the tabletop. "No. In that case, Uncle William would also know."

Alice examined both missives. "I see what you mean. Robert's flattery does not match his opinions— unless he admires Andrew's supposed excesses. We must be cautious."

"So I thought. And it would be best to wear our oldest gowns."

Memories of Patrick still prodded her mind, so she stopped ignoring them. Her intuition had served her well in the past. Now it was convinced that Robert was a fortune hunter.

They arrived downstairs a quarter hour early, taking seats in the first parlor. Robert found them barely five minutes later.

No one would suspect they were related, Maggie decided, taking in his appearance. He might share her father's dark coloring, but his physique was nothing alike. Nor was his taste. Satin pantaloons and a gaudy waistcoat encased his slight frame. A blatantly padded jacket with enormous buttons emphasized his narrow shoulders. The ribbon on his quizzing glass was so long that it was tangled in the forest of fobs at his waist, so he fumbled bringing the glass to his eye.

He had greeted an acquaintance outside the parlor with studied ennui, but the moment he identified her, his manner changed.

"My dear Maggie," he exclaimed, dropping his glass as he bent to clasp her hand to his breast. The glass bounced painfully on her knee. "Had I suspected such beauty, I would have rushed to your side days ago."

She bit back a scathing response. Her intuition had been right. Not only was he lying, but he was doing it poorly. Patrick had delivered his flummery with far more conviction. But at least this proved that her attraction to Marcus had nothing to do with being second cousins. Robert shared even closer blood, yet she already wished herself elsewhere.

"Mr. Adams," she replied coolly, retrieving her hand. "May I present my companion, Mrs. Sharpe."

"Charmed." He did not even glance at Alice as he reclaimed her hand, gripping it so tightly that only a struggle would free her. "Shall we dine?"

Annoyance flashed in his eyes when she stood, for

she was taller by at least an inch. And temper tensed his arm when she deliberately stumbled, nearly tripping him. But he suppressed it, flashing another false smile. "I would have recognized you anywhere," he claimed, heading for the dining room. "You've the look of your father."

"Nonse—" She strongly resembled her mother, but scrabbling claws interrupted her protest, drawing all eyes to the grand staircase. Teddy jerked the lead from Lady Augusta's hand and hurled himself at Robert, barking loudly.

"Ignore him," Maggie said quickly. "He won't bite."

Robert ignored her instead. His foot struck, tossing the dog against a chair several feet away. "Quiet, you stupid beast!"

Lady Augusta screamed.

"What did you do that for?" demanded Alice.

Robert ignored her.

Teddy backed toward his mistress, snarling.

"That animal should be shot for insulting a gentleman," snapped Robert as he strode toward Lady Augusta. For a moment Maggie thought he meant to strike the woman, but again he kicked at the dog.

This time Teddy was ready. He ducked the foot, sinking his teeth solidly into the other ankle.

Robert lost his balance and crashed to the floor.

"Serves him right," muttered Lady Augusta, scooping up Teddy. She stalked off, murmuring soothing sounds into the dog's ear.

Maggie let Simmons help Robert to his feet. The incident had been illuminating. Robert's eyes had revealed fury and arrogance, but no fear. Even if Teddy had been attacking, he was too small to inflict serious damage. Most people would have tried placating the animal, but Robert had treated him like an annoying insect.

Nor did he hold her in higher esteem. By the time they reached the dining room, he had added conde-

scension to his incessant compliments, ignoring every
attempt to correct his false assumptions. He considered her a brainless rustic, and Alice might have been
one of the lobby's statues for all the attention he
paid her.

"London will seem overwhelming after living in the
wilderness," he said, patting her hand, "though escaping America must be the answer to your prayers. I
cannot imagine being trapped in a country overrun
by savages."

Nor could she. It was too late to avoid dining with
him, but she could at least discourage further contact.
She had no wish to pursue this connection. Yet he
was too arrogant to believe she found him boring,
so her best approach would be to give him a disgust
of her.

"I would hardly call them savages," she protested
sweetly. "We lived with a tribe for a time, and I've
several Indian friends. They are quite charming and
more honorable than many settlers."

He gasped, fanning himself with his handkerchief.
"What was Uncle Andrew thinking to expose you to
such horror? The experience has clearly muddled
your brain."

"Really? You sound shockingly narrow-minded.
There are many ways to live."

Unfortunately, he interpreted her words as an attempt at humor. Making another condescending remark about untutored colonials, he welcomed the
soup, not noticing that they had placed no order.

She described her winter with the Indians, embel-
lishing because she had been only five at the time, so
remembered little of it. An early snow had caught
them in the wilderness the year her father had tried
his hand at trapping. Unfortunately, her tale had less
effect than she'd hoped. Either Robert was not listening or his motives for seeking her out were unusually strong. A half hour later, he was still dumping the
butter boat over her head.

When three waiters arrived to lay out a new course, the lady at the next table snorted. "Shocking service," she snapped loudly. "We arrived at the same time, but have yet to see the soup."

Robert glowered at the woman, then administered a direct cut. "The problem with public dining is that one must share the room with encroaching mushrooms," he proclaimed. "Money will never overcome such obvious lack of breeding. As heir to a viscountcy, I will always be served first."

"Such arrogance," said Maggie, referring to Robert, though he assumed she meant their neighbor. The wait staff answered to DuPré, whose temper was legendary. His infatuation with Alice resulted in better food and service every day.

But she said nothing as she sampled a lobster patty. Meeting Robert had been a mistake. He talked incessantly, but she could not believe anything he said, even about the family. He exaggerated other people's faults to make himself appear saintly and shamelessly puffed his own consequence. Yet he ignored even blatant rudeness in his effort to convince her that he was hopelessly smitten.

She finally gave up. She'd met too many determined suitors to mistake his purpose, though why he would seek her hand was beyond understanding. Perhaps he was under pressure to wed and thought an insignificant colonial would be easier to control.

Yet that seemed unlikely. Two hours of acquaintance should have proved that she was rude, argumentative, and unwilling to change—she'd insisted on using a fish fork for the beef even though he'd corrected her twice.

Their waiter presented Alice with a frothy confection of fruit-filled meringue topped with sugared violets. "All day Monsieur DuPré has exerted himself for you," he said, bowing over Alice's hand. "He calls it Henri's Delight."

"Thank you, Matthew," said Alice. "Give him our

compliments. This was his best meal yet. And the service was exceptional."

"He will be charmed," said Matthew, winking.

"He will puff himself up until those nearby cower for fear that he'll burst," she countered, making him laugh. "But this time he deserves the praise—yet I shan't utter a word until I have the recipes."

Maggie choked. Not at Alice, for these exchanges had become a nightly ritual—DuPré believed she had the ear of society's most powerful arbiters of fashion. But Robert looked like someone had just thumped him on the head. He had seemingly forgotten Alice's presence.

"I am appalled," snapped the lady at the next table. "There is no excuse for catering to that popinjay! I swear the service is worse now than when the hotel opened."

"Then why are we eating here?" her husband demanded, draining his glass. "Give me my club any day. Never did like fancy plaster and all those foreign statues. Waste of good blunt. I'd wager Sir Michael cut corners on the construction to pay for such fripperies."

"Do you think so?" she asked, peering suspiciously at the ornate ceiling as a waiter set a platter of squabs on her table.

"Sure of it. No need to cover sound building with gilt. Take my club—good solid walls with sensible paneling." He shoved a pigeon breast into his mouth.

"Hardly elegant, though," said his wife, nibbling her trout.

"The fellow who designed this place was the same one who did the Ipswich Gardens Hotel. Hiding deficiencies under plaster frills did not work then, and it won't work now." He gulped another chunk of squab.

"Kitchen fires are common."

"Faulty construction. The wall behind the ovens was too thin. If the chef had been slower, the whole building would have burned."

Robert snorted. "That fellow should keep his mouth shut about things he doesn't understand. I was staying with friends in Suffolk when that fire occurred. Despite the rumors, it cannot have been more than a grease fire or the place would have burned to the ground—like Billings Hall. A single spark ignited a fire that spread so fast the family barely escaped. Generations of records gone." He sighed. "The paneling dated to Elizabeth's reign."

After hundreds of years, even thick beams would have been dry as tinder, but arguing would serve no purpose. It was time to end the evening. Yet curiosity prompted one last question. "Why does Uncle William refuse to see me?"

"He will come around," he said, frowning when she moved her hand out of reach. "But you remind him of Andrew's insane jealousy."

"Jealousy?" What lies would he repeat now?

"Andrew despised being the younger son. He hated knowing that Father would have the title one day, so he lashed out whenever he could." He shrugged. "The final straw was forcing himself on Father's betrothed, then abducting her. Father never recovered."

"Instead, he twisted the facts. My mother never wanted William, but no one listened, so her only option was to flee."

"A lady never contradicts a gentleman," Robert said, finally giving in to the anger she'd seen whenever she'd tried to provoke him. It was the first true emotion he had shown since confronting Teddy.

"I prefer truth."

"Females are incapable of comprehending truth." He held up a hand to halt her words. "Do not prattle about things you don't understand. Your father would never have admitted his crimes to you."

"Nor would yours. Heed your own advice, Cousin. You weren't there, either."

Robert took a deep breath, then donned another false smile. "I must take you firmly in hand if you are to go on in society, Maggie. Your barbaric upbringing will have you ostracized in a trice. I warned you about contradicting a gentleman. It is never acceptable."

Marcus stared at Robert's back as he placed his dinner order. He should have warned Maggie to avoid her Adams relatives until he could introduce her, but he'd assumed that she would leave the matter in his hands.

*Idiot!* She was no helpless maiden. The fact that she had come to England by herself proved that she was a determined woman who rarely relied on others. He should have known that she would shove the Adams family's rejection back in their faces.

So now she was at the mercy of Robert's charm. He hoped she was experienced enough to see through him. Robert's debts must be larger than anyone knew. Why else would he court a woman so different from his usual tastes?

He absently drained his wineglass.

If only it had not taken so long to authenticate her papers. Robert was dangerous. More than one innocent had fallen victim to his charm.

But he relaxed the moment he caught Maggie's eye. Her face lit up, the contrast making it obvious that she was barely tolerating Robert's company. To make sure she understood her danger, he scowled at Robert, shaking his head in warning. She nodded agreement, her eyes sparkling with suppressed laughter.

Relieved, he winked. He could almost read her mind—which was rather disconcerting. He'd never felt so attuned to another person.

Robert noted her inattention and glanced over his shoulder. "Be careful of that one," he warned her, administering a direct cut as he turned back. "He can never introduce you properly to society. Look at that insipid jacket and that dull waistcoat. The man understands nothing about fashion."

"But I have no interest in fashion," Maggie said,

pulling on her gloves. Her eyes now held only irritation.

Robert laughed as if she were joking, though Marcus knew she spoke the truth. She would return home as soon as she had carried out her father's wishes—which meant he must act immediately. At least explaining the Widmers was straightforward. Discussing the Adams family was another problem entirely.

4

Maggie frowned. Alice had not yet returned from her morning visit to the kitchen, and breakfast was growing cold.

She had declined to accompany Alice today, though she had done so two days ago, creeping down the servants' stairs into the bowels of the building. The kitchens were cavernous rooms kept uncomfortably hot by numerous cooking fires and four huge ovens. The smell of baking bread had made her mouth water, reminding her that she'd not yet eaten.

Assistant chefs had scurried about in apparent disarray, though they actually worked in concert to prepare a vast array of food. DuPré was a master of organization.

"Ze trick is in ze wrist, *chérie*."

His voice had cut through her study of the tricks he used to keep the kitchen running efficiently. Startled, she'd realized that he was teaching Alice how he introduced lightness into his creams.

"Hold ze spoon like so." He'd stood behind Alice, his hands covering hers as he demonstrated how to beat air into the cream. Several of his minions had stared in amazement.

Maggie grinned at the memory. DuPré had continued the lesson for nearly an hour, flirting outrageously the entire time. His voice had resembled honeyed velvet as he led Alice through the motions, nuzzling her neck between words. They were undoubtedly sharing another lesson today, but Maggie would not join them again. She did not belong there, as one of the maids had made clear. The girl had been so shocked to find her belowstairs that Maggie had felt obliged to apologize. Clearly, her standing as a lady would be in jeopardy if she indulged her curiosity again. Service would suffer.

Now she picked up the two letters that had arrived with breakfast. Robert's arrogant scrawl adorned one. The other had been penned in a precise hand that revealed nothing of its owner's character, so it was probably from Marcus.

A glance at the signature verified her guess. *Forgive me for ignoring you these past days,* he'd written.

Recalling that astonishing moment of mind-sharing in the dining room last evening, she blushed. She had lain awake long into the night, torn between awe that he understood her so well and regret that she must leave soon. They would never meet again—a fact she must not forget. She returned her attention to the page.

*Margaret Widmer's solicitor wishes to see you. I will call for you at eleven, if that is convenient.*

She frowned. What might her grandmother's solicitor want? No one in England had known she existed until a few days ago. And why now?

There was only one way to find out, she admitted, reaching for a pen and stifling a burst of excitement over spending the afternoon with Marcus. This was business.

After sealing her response, she poured chocolate and opened Robert's missive. He began with an entire page of compliments that ignored her curt dismissal last evening. Nor did he mention her rude and uncouth behavior. His persistence raised all sorts of alarms.

"Why the long face, Maggie?" asked Alice, hurrying in to claim her chair at the table.

"Robert wants to tour London with me this afternoon."

"Why?"

"An interesting question. He reminds me of Patrick Riley, though I can't imagine why he wants me. Did you ever hear such fustian?"

Alice read the letter, then smiled. "Not recently."

Maggie accepted the pages back. "We will decline this invitation. Marcus wants me to meet Grandmother's solicitor."

"Perhaps she left your mother something."

"That is hardly likely after twenty-eight years of silence."

"Love endures." Alice poured coffee. "It has the power to move mountains and link hearts, even after twenty-eight years apart. Your grandmother loved your mother deeply."

"How would you know?"

"Shortly after I became your governess, John drank too much and cried his eyes out over losing Catherine. He mentioned their elopement and admitted that her mother had preferred his suit to William's. Catherine had always been her favorite—perhaps because she was the youngest."

"Why did they cut all ties to England, then?"

"That wasn't clear, though I think John feared William. And after Catherine died, he expected her mother to blame him."

"What?"

"He had dragged her off to an uncivilized land."

"Nonsense! She could have died anywhere."

"True, but beware of your uncle, Maggie. If John feared him, he cannot be a good man." She disappeared into her room.

Maggie had no further interest in her Adams relatives, but Alice's warning reverberated through her head as she ate breakfast. By the time she dusted the last crumb from her fingertips, she had revised her plans.

"I think we should leave London for a time," she announced when Alice returned. "William is not a problem, for he refuses to meet me, but Robert might become a pest. He seems the stubborn sort."

"Ask Marcus what to do," Alice advised as she left to go shopping. "He is clear-thinking and must know Robert's purpose."

Marcus rested his hand on Maggie's back, absorbing her heat as he escorted her into Frankel's office. Touching her eased the tension in his shoulders.

They were late because of Betsy—again he cursed his stupidity. Since he'd broken off their liaison, she had plagued him with endless petty revenges—rearranging books, shuffling papers, spilling ashes in the wardrobe. Yesterday, he'd nearly sliced his throat because she'd chipped his razor. The cut would chafe under his cravat for at least a week.

Today, the papers supporting Maggie's claim had been missing. He'd finally found them under his mattress, but it was the final straw. He must demand a different maid when he returned.

He forced his mind back to business. Margaret Widmer had hired her own solicitor after her husband's death. Her marriage settlement had left her in control of her dowry, which had irritated her husband no end. And her will had shocked the entire family. Soft-spoken, docile Margaret had been hiding secrets for years.

"This is Margaret Adams, daughter of Elizabeth Widmer Adams," he said in introduction, then produced fair copies of the *Merchant Queen*'s sailing roster and log, which mentioned the wedding and explained the discrepancy in names. He'd also found official reports written by Captain Barnsley on identical stationery to that used for the marriage lines. Since years of dust had covered these records, he could swear that no one had looked at them since they'd been stored.

"Is Elizabeth living?" asked Mr. Frankel.

"She died fifteen years ago." Maggie pulled the doctor's statement from the documents he'd asked her to bring.

"Well before Mrs. Widmer." He steepled his fingers under his chin. "Your visit is well timed, Miss Adams. Only a fortnight ago, I sent to Halifax for your direction. Mrs. Widmer left five thousand guineas and a small estate in Somerset to her daughter Elizabeth, naming you as residual beneficiary in the event Elizabeth predeceased her. It was her hope that you would use the legacy to assume your rightful place in London society."

Maggie frowned. "Is the bequest contingent on my doing so?"

Marcus jolted to attention. It was a reasonable question for anyone versed in the law, but why would a lady from the wilds of America think to ask?

"No. The bequest is final, but she left a letter of explanation." Frankel handed her a thick packet wrapped in velum. "You may read it in the next room. I will be available to answer questions in half an hour." He gestured toward a door behind him.

Marcus led her into a small sitting room. She had been surprising him ever since he'd called for her, starting with her cool greeting and lack of questions. At first he'd assumed it was pique—after ignoring her for days, he'd arrived late for this appointment—but that no longer seemed reasonable. She'd glared when he'd produced his proofs, almost as if he'd betrayed her by verifying her claims. Maybe he should have mentioned this legacy earlier instead of leaving the job to Frankel.

He seated her in a comfortable chair. "Shall I leave?"

"No. I suspect you can answer most of my questions."

He nodded, turning to stare out the window as she broke the seal. A quarter hour passed in silence broken only by rustling paper. He wondered what she was thinking. Would this change her plans? His groin grew heavy at the thought of having her permanently in England. He had been fighting the urge to let her hair down and run his fingers through it since helping her into his carriage.

"Poor woman," Maggie murmured at last. "Alice was right. She truly loved my mother."

"No one knew how deeply she mourned the separation until after her death." He took a chair facing her.

"She never spoke of it?"

"The family never discussed Elizabeth. Until Aunt Margaret's death, everything I knew about the situation came from the Adams boys."

"In that case, it cannot have been flattering," she said dryly.

"It was not." He shook his head. "Not until Margaret's will was read did I demand the truth from my grandfather, Richard."

"Which was?"

"Richard Widmer and George Adams were neighbors and close friends who wanted to unite their lines through marriage. But neither of them had sired a daughter, so Richard offered his niece Elizabeth as a suitable wife for William. Margaret objected—she preferred Andrew even at the age of twelve—but Richard ignored her, attributing her dislike to a recent prank that had broken Elizabeth's arm."

Maggie tapped the letter. "She writes that Mother's elopement removed the light from her life and begs her to return home, condemning America as uncivilized." She shook her head. "Why does everyone in England criticize a place they know nothing about?"

"You must admit that the country is largely unsettled, though I agree that Boston and Philadelphia differ from London only in size. Your capital, however, is another story."

"You sound as though you've been there."

"Three years ago."

"Then you will understand that I have little incentive to live in England. I love the excitement. America offers opportunities I could never find here. Life can be hard, but the rewards are worth it."

"Your mother died at thirty-one, and your father was killed in a mine disaster."

"Mother died of an inflammation of the lungs—an ailment that kills people of all classes in both our countries. And I doubt that English mines are any safer."

He shrugged, though a viscount's son would never have worked in an English mine.

"I cannot accept this bequest," she said, tapping the letter. "Grandmother may have attached no conditions, but she clearly expected compliance with her wishes."

"But the inheritance is yours. Having proved your identity, Frankel has no choice but to transfer the property."

"I understand the legalities, but that does not mean I must keep it. Overseeing the estate would be difficult."

"Hire an agent."

"I prefer to manage my own holdings," she said absently.

Marcus pursed his lips in a silent whistle. Obviously Andrew had done well in America. Maggie Adams was no rustic, as he should have known from the beginning. The way she had shaken his hand had not been the untutored response of an ignorant girl but the habit of someone accustomed to the world of business. And there were other clues—her reticence about her father, her familiarity with legal proceedings, her indifference to the opulence of the Grand Hotel . . . She'd also recognized Robert's toadeating as the fustian it was, hinting that she had encountered the same thing in the past. And she was—

"Who in the Widmer family has the greatest need?" she asked.

"What?" The question jerked him out of his contemplation.

Maggie wondered what held his thoughts. He was staring at her as if seeing her for the first time. But she would consider that later.

Clearly this legacy was behind Robert's sudden infatuation. Five thousand guineas could support him for years, even without the estate income. Thus giving away the inheritance would remove his interest. "You mentioned my cousins—I believe fourteen others are descended from Grandmother. Who has the most need of property?"

"Michael is always drowning in the River Tick, but he would game away anything he acquired," he said warily.

"Perhaps I should be clearer. Who is both needful and deserving of help? Surely there is someone. This bequest should go to one of Grandmother's descendants, but I've no patience with gamesters."

His eyes flashed in surprise. How had he succeeded as a diplomat when his thoughts showed so clearly?

"Needful and deserving," he repeated slowly. "Edwin Jenkins is a captain, currently in Paris with Wellington's occupation force. Since military pay never covers an officer's expenses, he is perpetually short of funds. Thomas Widmer is vicar to a poor parish in Yorkshire. His income barely supports his family."

"Is Edwin married?"

"Not yet, though he has an understanding with his neighbor's daughter. Now that the war is over, he will make a formal offer."

"And leave the military?"

"No. He loves it. His wife will join him wherever he is posted."

"What about Thomas? Is he dedicated to the church?"

Marcus frowned. "I have never heard him complain, but I suspect he took orders to avoid buying colors. He would not have lasted a week on a battlefield, yet the family had no other position for him."

"And unlike you, he hasn't the means to strike out on his own."

"Or the interest. Few gentlemen are willing to tarnish their reputations with trade."

She nodded. "Very well. Thomas can have the estate and half the money. The rest will go to Edwin."

"You should think about this for a few days."

"There is no need." She met his gaze, holding his eyes until she was sure he understood her situation. When he nodded, she continued. "Grandmother remembered a young girl trained to English society. She would not have recognized the woman that girl became. Mother loved challenge and would have laughed at the idea of returning to England. I am no different. Thus I have no moral claim to her money. Let it go to those who are content to live in her world."

"But—"

"You needn't concern yourself with this, Marcus. I cannot accept it under false pretenses."

"Very well. We will put Frankel to work." Rising, he helped her to her feet, catching her by the shoulders when she stumbled. Sparks sizzled up his arms. "Would you like to meet my grandfather? He has changed since your parents eloped, and he now knows that Elizabeth chose more wisely than he. I fear your Uncle William is a wastrel."

It was a perfect solution to avoiding Robert. She smiled. "I came to England to meet my family. When shall we leave?"

"Tomorrow morning. In the meantime, why don't I show you about London?"

## 5

Maggie was closing her trunk the next morning when someone rapped on the sitting room door. Expecting Marcus, she pulled it open.

"Are you ready?" asked Robert, stepping inside before she could block him.

"What are you doing here?"

"Taking you to the balloon ascension, as promised. You will have seen nothing like it in the wilderness." His eyes gleamed just as Patrick's had that last day, snapping her to attention.

"I declined your invitation," she reminded him. It had been waiting for her when she and Richard had returned from visiting St. Paul's Cathedral and Week's Mechanical Museum. Sidling closer to the writing table, she fingered her reticule. "As I explained, I have other plans."

His voice hardened. "I am family, which makes me more important than shopping, Maggie, so cease this teasing. We've barely an hour to reach the launch site."

"I have no interest in balloons."

"I warned you about arguing with gentlemen." He circled the table she'd set between them, stopping an arm's length away. "A lady's first duty is to her family. If you insist on shopping, so be it. But we cannot risk having you bring dishonor to our name, so I must accompany you on expeditions until you learn society's rules."

"Since your father disowned mine, we are not family. Thus you have no voice in where I go or how I conduct myself," she said firmly. "No one would think you responsible for my behavior. Now leave."

"No." His eyes blazed. "You are an Adams. Your actions reflect on our name, so we must take care of you until you assume your proper place in the world."

"What is that supposed to mean?"

He smiled. "Your days as an ape-leader are over, my dear. The family has found you a husband—me."

"Absurd."

His fists clenched. "The family honor is at stake, Maggie. We have endured scandal ever since Andrew defiled our name. Only our marriage will suppress it. You will enjoy it more if you accept the inevitable like the lady you pretend to be. We will remain at Fielding Court until you learn to—"

"What fustian!" She wanted to smash a chair over his foolish head. *Family honor* indeed! "I've never heard anything so ridiculous in my life." But she could see the determination in his eyes. He would not accept her refusal. Loosening the strings on her reticule, she slipped a hand inside.

"I knew you were too stupid to recognize your good fortune." He shook his head as he stepped forward to seize her arm. "I must confine you to the country until you learn your place."

"Don't touch me!" She slammed a knee into his groin, doubling him over. Jerking the pistol from her reticule, she backed out of reach.

"You will—regret—this." His voice squeaked between gasps for air, making the threat sound feeble.

"Hardly." Her hand remained steady. "This is farewell, Cousin. Father was wrong to believe that rapprochement was possible. Either leave, or I shoot."

He tensed to attack—anger was eroding his sense—but before he could spring, Alice returned from the kitchens.

"What is going on?" she demanded, taking in the scene. "I knew he would make a nuisance of himself."

"We are discovered," wailed Robert, shakily straightening. "You are compromised, my dear. Marriage is your only hope." He produced a special license.

Maggie laughed. "English girls must be foolish indeed if you thought this scheme would work, Cousin. Find another pigeon for your trap. I will never wed you."

Fury flushed his face. "Do you wish to be cut by society?"

"If you had listened to anything I've said, you would know how stupid that sounds. I have no interest in the opinions of fribbles and wastrels."

"But—"

"No one would question us discussing family business unchaperoned."

"Further proof that you know nothing of the world."

"Of your world, possibly. But that society has no authority outside of England, and its scandals matter only to itself. The rest of us have more important things to think about. Now leave."

He stared at the pistol, clearly contemplating his chances of wresting it away.

"Do not underestimate me," she warned. "No one survives in the wilderness without learning to handle weapons. Will you go quietly, or must we summon the staff?" Alice had her hand on the bell pull.

"You will rue this day," he spat, raking her with such loathing she nearly flinched. "No one insults me with impunity." He stalked away, slamming the door behind him.

"Conceited oaf! What happened?" asked Alice, sliding the bolt shut.

"I'm not sure." She set down the pistol and sank into a chair. "He invited me to a balloon ascension. When I refused, he began prattling of honor and claimed that the family's name is in jeopardy—which translates into my having to wed him. But if he needs Grandmother's legacy that badly, he won't give up."

"Heavens!"

"Exactly." She glanced at her pistol, grateful she always carried it when traveling. "Are you sure you won't accompany us to Wyndmer Park? Robert is clearly dangerous."

Alice shook her head. "Simmons has finally agreed to overlook my gender and instruct me in hotel management. And Henri is teaching me more techniques each day."

"So how is our stalwart chef?" she asked, smiling.

"More puffed up than ever. He is a man of great appetites and even greater conceit."

"Take care. He seeks more than flirtation."

She laughed. "He is already carrying on with at least two maids, so you needn't fret. He thinks I will approach the Clarendon's chef if he annoys me. They are fierce rivals. Henri swears he himself is more talented, despite the fact that Jaquiers, not he, was once chef to the French king." She brandished several scraps of paper.

"What did he give you this time?"

"Henri's Delight," she said, tapping the top one. "That exquisite dove pie we ate last night, the meringue *glaces* in raspberry sauce, a towering *croquembouche*—Simmons raves about it, though I haven't sampled it yet—and several sauces."

"Good luck," said Maggie as another rap echoed.

Marcus smiled when Maggie opened her door. Every time he saw her, his longing grew, making it harder to remember that she would soon be gone. "Are you ready?"

"In a moment." She handed a pistol to Alice. "You have more need of this than we do. Keep the door bolted and do not leave the hotel alone. Robert may abduct you, hoping to force my hand."

They exchanged speaking glances.

Marcus frowned, but he held his tongue until they were in his carriage. "What was that all about?"

She shrugged. "Robert covets Grandmother's legacy, so he has decided to wed me. My refusal did not improve his temper. When will Mr. Frankel finish the transfer papers?"

"They will be ready when we return." Someone needed to teach Robert a lesson, he decided, frowning. But first he must warn Maggie of her real danger.

Postponing this discussion had been a mistake. He only hoped she would not kill the messenger. She might claim she had come to England because of the vow to her father, but he knew better. Andrew's death had left her alone. She needed family to fill the void in her life, so discovering the truth about the Adams men would hurt. Could she accept the facts, especially those that showed her father in a less than saintly light?

*Coward!*

His heart was more involved than he'd thought if he was ducking the job merely to stay in her good graces, he admitted in shock. But he could think about that later. Drawing in a deep breath, he launched the explanation he should have made yesterday. "Margaret's legacy is not Robert's goal—though he would consider it a satisfying bonus."

"What now?"

Cloudy skies made it too dark to read her expression, so he clasped her hand. Touching her was the only way to gauge her reaction. "I thought Grandfather could do this better, but I will try to explain."

"Explain what?"

"About Andrew and William."

"Is this about the theft that drove Father from the country?"

"That was merely their last contretemps." He stroked her fingers, momentarily distracted by their trembling. "Even as boys, William and Andrew were usually at odds, arguing with an edge that made others uncomfortable. Their pranks sometimes turned dangerous. And both suffered numerous unexplained injuries."

"Robert claimed that Father was jealous of William's position as the heir, but I cannot believe it."

"I suspect it was the other way around, but Andrew was not blameless. He retaliated against his brother's malice. And though his reputation as a gamester was exaggerated, he did lose three thousand guineas shortly before William was to be married."

"He would never do such a thing!" swore Maggie hotly.

"Maggie—" He caught her other hand, kissing it lightly. "We all make mistakes. The smart ones learn from the experience. I am not criticizing your father."

"Then what are you doing?"

"I am explaining the truth he wanted you to find. Personally, I think that card game was odd—not that it matters now. George paid the debt, but he and William reminded Andrew of his shame every day."

She relaxed. "So he made a mistake that his family refused to forgive. I suppose they believed the other charges, too."

"Of course." Relief warmed him. He should have trusted her sooner. "I suspect William started most of the rumors, for there was little evidence beyond the usual young man's wildness. He hated Andrew for being everything he was not—charming, intelligent, honorable, even better-looking. The final straw was when he discovered that Andrew and Elizabeth were in love."

"Yet everyone continued pressing her to wed William."

"They had no choice." He met her gaze. "The betrothal had been arranged when they were children. Contracts had been signed. Neither party could cry off without the other's consent, though William might have agreed if she had wanted anyone but Andrew."

"So Mother eloped."

He nodded. "When Margaret died, we discovered that your parents had written twice. The first letter confirmed that they had wed and swore that Andrew was innocent of theft. The second announced your birth. That was the last she heard."

"I should have realized she'd written. How else would Frankel have known about me?" She shook her head. "I don't know why there were only two letters,

unless Father feared retribution. Or maybe it was too
difficult—they moved to the frontier shortly after I
was born." She sighed. "You've tiptoed around the
subject long enough, Marcus. Was William responsible
for that theft?"

"All the evidence pointed to Andrew—supposedly
he had incurred another gaming debt. He swore he
was innocent, but George summoned a magistrate. By
the time the man arrived, Andrew and Elizabeth
were gone."

"That explains why they sailed under false names.
With his own father against him, he was helpless."
Her voice was shaking.

"George should have known better, but he only discovered the truth a year ago," he said wearily.

"How?"

"His valet spotted William leaving a forgotten secret passage. When George explored it, he found the
missing jewelry in a niche behind Andrew's old room.
He consulted Richard, but they could think of no way
to prove William was the thief. William could claim
that he'd just discovered the passage himself and that
Andrew had fled before he could recover the jewelry."

"Why keep it in the house?"

"He probably planned to find it when he came into
the title."

"Monstrous."

"I heartily dislike your uncle."

She nodded agreement. "Did George confront
him?"

"No. I think he was afraid to. William would dare
anything to protect his interests. If George and Richard had told the rest of us, things might have been
different, but they left the jewelry where it was."

"Robert claimed that George tried to find Father,"
she said suddenly. "I thought it was another of his
lies."

"George tried, but the task proved impossible. Andrew could have gone anywhere. It wasn't until Mar-

garet suggested Elizabeth was in Halifax—the subject arose in another context—that he sent an agent there. Unfortunately, he died a week later. When William learned about the agent, he recalled the man."

"Poor Grandfather. I wish we had known. Father would never have come back, but he would have been pleased that George knew the truth."

"That is not the end of the story, Maggie." He pulled her closer so he could see her eyes. "George's investigation turned up other crimes that continue to this day—or so we think; there is not enough evidence to put before the Lords. William is cunning, as is Robert. Both lie and steal and cheat, arranging that others will pay for their misdeeds. Fielding Court was entailed to William, but George willed everything else to Andrew."

"When did he die?"

"February—more than a month before your father."

She sighed in disgust. "No wonder Robert has been prattling about protecting the family."

"His allowance is much smaller than it used to be, which has not improved his temper."

"I will return it, of course."

He traced her wrist with is thumb. "Don't do anything rash, Maggie. We are talking about two estates and more than fifty thousand guineas. You need to think carefully before disposing of such wealth."

"We have already held this discussion," she reminded him. "I want nothing from them."

"But this comes from George, who did everything he could to keep it away from William and Robert."

She gazed out the window. Rain pattered against the roof. Marcus's fingers burned where they stroked her skin. If only she could throw herself against that hard chest and feel his arms close around her. Confronting her family's past left her feeling weak in ways the most complex business problem never did.

But she couldn't. Imposing on him for comfort

would cross a line that would ultimately hurt both of them.

"I will accept that much," she said finally. "He did recognize Father's innocence in the end, and Father's last wish was to heal that breach. Is there a residual beneficiary?"

"A third cousin, or possibly fourth." He shrugged. "I've never met the man. I suspect George chose him because the connection was too remote for the money to find its way back to William."

Maggie let the subject drop. She would talk to Richard Widmer before making any final decisions. But now she needed to place some distance between herself and Marcus. His leg brushed hers, weakening her resolve. She should have known that sharing a carriage would fuel her attraction.

But it must stop. They belonged to different worlds and would never meet again once she returned home.

Though the carriage was narrow, shifting put a small space between them. He withdrew his hand, turning his attention to the countryside. Stifling an unexpected burst of disappointment, she followed suit.

The heath they were crossing was very different from home. Even the wildest areas seemed tame. In sunlight, they would look downright inviting. Yet the scenery could not hold her attention. Thank heaven no one knew about her real inheritance. There was too much wealth connected to her name already. She would dispose of this latest legacy as soon as possible. Then she must leave if she hoped to reach home before winter. She should never have left.

6

Ten days later, Maggie returned to the Grand Hotel, more relaxed than she had been since her father's death. For the first time in her life, she felt connected to the past—not that she would remain in England; society was too formal and inflexible, and she had too many responsibilities at home.

She had been reminding herself of those responsibilities since admitting her danger in the carriage. It had been the only way she could keep Marcus firmly in the role of a friend.

He was the most fascinating man she had ever met—witty, intelligent, impeccably correct when necessary, yet carefree the rest of the time. Not only did he accept all her interests, but he honored the bounds she had set and even helped maintain them. Knowing they must soon part, he had not touched her again, though desire often heated his eyes.

He'd made sure that she enjoyed her visit, riding with her most mornings, escorting her to call on neighbors, and placating his grandfather. Richard had often been shocked by her outspoken ways, so Marcus's diplomatic skills had been in frequent demand.

But he rarely used them on his own behalf. She had heard shouting from the library more than once. Richard Widmer would never condone Marcus's plans—which confirmed her inability to fit into English society. Richard's cautious welcome would fade if he knew she ran a business.

She rapped on Alice's door, then hugged her friend when she answered. "You look wonderful!"

"As do you. The visit went well, I take it." Alice appeared more vibrant than ever. Flirting with DuPré agreed with her.

"Very well. Uncle Richard is a nice man, despite being quite pompous at times. I shocked him more than once, but we reached a reasonable accommodation. I wish you had joined me."

"I accomplished more by staying here. That silly chef has parted with dozens of recipes."

"Silly?"

Alice laughed. "You would not believe the contretemps yesterday. Two of the maids discovered that he was bedding both of them—I am amazed they didn't know long ago; it was obvious to everyone else."

"He must have bedazzled them."

"Probably. Henri is a powerful force."

"What happened?"

Alice's eyes twinkled with laughter. "When Fanny slipped downstairs to steal a moment with Henri, she found him kissing Pamela in the pantry."

"Henri should be more discreet. I suppose they turned on him."

"On each other." Alice shook her head. "Each accused the other of stealing her beau. Words led to blows. They'd reached the hair-pulling stage when the milkmaid burst in, furious because Henri was carrying on with a kitchen maid at the Clarendon. *That's* when they turned on him."

"Four liaisons?" Maggie choked. "How does he manage?"

"Four that I know of, though I suspect that last is merely a way to keep an eye on the Clarendon's chef."

"Words fail me."

"They did not fail the maids—or Henri, for that matter; they probably heard his protests in the attics. When Fanny shoved the milkmaid into a rack of pastries, the real fight started. The milkmaid—I think her name is Sally—retaliated. Pamela grabbed a syllabub and hurled it at Henri."

"Oh, no!"

She nodded. "I thought he'd been in a temper before, but you wouldn't believe the pandemonium that unleashed—arm waving, foot stomping, spitting, scratching. Food flew in all directions. Most of the kitchen staff joined in. It took Simmons and the footmen an hour to break it up. They are probably still cleaning the kitchen."

"You sound as if you were there."

"I was." She laughed until she had to sit down. "I never thought I could do anything so childish, but when the food started flying, I had to join in. It was incredible fun."

"Alice!"

"I know. Shocking behavior. And quite inappropriate. You would think I grew up in the wilds of North America." They laughed. "Matthew whisked me away before Simmons spotted me. He would never think me a suitable hotel manager if he knew I had peppered Sally with a dozen eggs and whacked Fanny with a loaf of bread."

Maggie shook her head. "Be careful, Alice. DuPré will be looking for new conquests now that his current liaisons are over."

"He only flirts with me because I keep turning him down—he likes a challenge," said Alice dryly, wiping her eyes. "Besides, you underestimate his charm. Matthew claims the tension belowstairs is thicker than old aspic, but each girl expects him to rebuff the others and remain with her."

Maggie stared. "Incredible. But watch yourself. What happens when he discovers that you've no intention of puffing his talent to London society? You know how wicked his temper can be."

"We will be gone in another fortnight—or have plans changed?"

"I'm not sure." Maggie's humor faded until her mood matched London's sooty air. "Grandfather Adams left a fortune to Father. I don't want it, but Marcus doesn't know the more remote Adams cousins well enough to advise me. Nor does Richard."

"What tale is this?"

"You were right about William." She explained why George had disinherited his heir. "Last week he denounced me as an impostor to Richard's face, then refused an invitation to the Earl of Candleigh's picnic because I would attend. And yesterday a groom discovered that the girth on my saddle had unaccountably frayed. I am convinced William is responsible."

"What about Robert?"

"He is capable of trying, though he has not returned home in months as far as anyone knows. He and his father haven't spoken since George's will was read. But he must be growing desperate—rumor claims he is beholden to several moneylenders. I agree with Grandfather's decision to disinherit them, but it will take time to decide who should receive the legacy."

"Take care to keep your plans secret, Maggie. Honor will fly out the window once people learn you are giving away money."

"I will say nothing. In the meantime, let's see what the kitchen can produce when the chef is beset by jealous women."

Maggie returned to the hotel late the following afternoon, seething with frustration.

George's solicitor was away, visiting a client. She could hardly discuss her business with a clerk, so she had to wait until he returned—not a situation she was accustomed to. Her own lawyer would run down women and children if it meant serving her faster.

*How arrogant,* chided her conscience.

She grinned, finally able to relax—which was good. She must hurry if she meant to bathe before dinner. As would Alice, who had stopped in the lobby to speak with Simmons. They had lost track of time while trying on bonnets.

She had entered her suite and was headed for the bell pull when a shadow moved in the corner. Her stomach clenched. "What are you doing here?"

Robert turned to face her. "You've had time to come to your senses. I can postpone the wedding no longer." His eyes belied his otherwise pleasant expression.

"There is no wedding."

"Arguing is useless." He fingered the Greek maiden atop the writing desk. "Either we wed or I kill you."

"Killing me would serve no purpose," she said, more calmly than she felt. Her pistol was in her bedchamber, but if she could keep him talking until Alice arrived, they could deal with him.

"I would prefer marriage," he agreed. "I need your inheritance to pay off my debts. But killing you would reinstate my prospects. Father would collect your estate as next of kin."

"No, he wouldn't. I have a will." The moment the words left her mouth, she cursed. She should have sworn that she'd already disposed of everything. Even if he knew Mr. Knowles was out of town, she could have claimed Frankel as her solicitor. Now it was too late.

"Bitch!" Fury flared in his eyes. "But that decides the matter. Marriage will negate any wills and make me independent of Father."

"I will not wed you."

He ignored her interruption. "I know a vicar who won't care if the bride is unwilling. Actually, he would sign the license whether you were present or not."

His sudden smile sent chills down her spine. She sidled toward the hallway, seeking another way to distract him. "No court would uphold such a marriage."

"But who would question it? A gentleman's word always outweighs a female's." His voice firmed. "You have no friends here. Several gossips saw us dining together, so marriage would surprise no one. Charles will do anything for a bit of the ready—his tithes hardly keep food on the table, let alone the opium he loves. I can forge your signature and use your companion as one witness," he added as his fingers closed around the base of the Greek maiden. "If I split the money with Father, he will sign as the other witness and swear you proposed the match yourself to rectify Grandfather's injustice."

He'd decided to kill her and forge the license, she realized in shock. He must not know that she'd spent ten days with the Widmers, any of whom would contest his claims. As would her American agent.

But her protest died unuttered. Alice was no good

as a witness unless she were also dead. He had clearly abandoned reason and would dare anything to claim the fortune as his own. Mentioning Marcus would endanger his life as well. She could not do it.

Robert lifted the statue and sprang.

The latch on the door jammed. Tipping the table into his path, she raced toward her bedchamber. Only her pistol could save her now.

He shoved the table aside and bounded after her, ignoring the vase she bounced off his shoulder.

As she jerked open the chest holding her pistol, the lamp crashed down on her head.


Marcus concentrated on a treatise on steam engines, pushing all other thoughts aside. At least he tried to. Maggie kept intruding.

Since returning from Wyndmer, he had avoided her, stifling his desire to see her, to touch her, to make love to her.

She had made it clear that she wanted only friendship, and he could understand her reasoning. Nothing would keep her in England. Thus he'd invented excuses that allowed him to hover over her without admitting that he cared—she was family and needed help to negotiate society's treacherous waters; she was a friend, who shared his interests and never ridiculed his aspirations; if he didn't watch her, she would fall prey to an unscrupulous wastrel like Robert . . .

He had needed the excuses to hide his growing infatuation. They kept him from thinking abut her inevitable departure. As did focusing on other topics—like steam engines and gas production and the mistakes he'd made in the past.

At least one mistake was well and truly past. When he had returned to the Grand Hotel, his possessions had remained exactly where he'd left them. Betsy had not slipped in to wreak havoc in his absence. She must have finally forgiven him.

"Fire!"

Someone beat on the door, jerking his mind from his work.

"Fire!"

Footsteps pounded along the hallway, accompanied by screams.

"My God!" He stared at the door. Smoke was seeping underneath. The air reverberated with terrified voices, clanging bells, and the distinctive popping of flames devouring green wood.

"Maggie!" he choked, fear baring the truth he had been ignoring for days. She was like no one else—warm, independent, caring, intelligent. He could not imagine life without her.

"Later," he muttered, grabbing his coat.

Another fist pounded on his door. He jerked it open to see Betsy running toward the servants' stairs. She blew him a kiss as she opened the disguised door.

Smoke filled the hallway. Clamping a handkerchief over his mouth, he raced for the nearest staircase. It was free of flames, but Maggie's rooms were in the other wing. Had she escaped?

By the time he descended two floors, he could barely see. The acrid odor of burning paint stung his nose and left him light-headed. Flames flickered hellishly behind billowing smoke.

Feeling his way past the grand staircase, he pounded on her door.

"Maggie!"

It was locked, but faint moans came from inside.

The fire was thirty feet away, lapping at the next suite. Fighting off dizziness, he threw himself at Maggie's door. And again. The third time it burst open, dumping him on the floor.

Blinking the sweat from his eyes, he choked. In here, the flames were only ten feet away, dancing in her bedchamber. He stared stupidly for a long minute before realizing they had eaten through the dining room ceiling. The fire must have started in the kitchen, two floors below.

"Maggie!"

"Help."

Her voice was so weak he was amazed it had penetrated the closed door, but at least it came from Alice's room. Maggie was dragging Alice toward the sitting room. Blood streaked both their faces.

"What happened?" he demanded, heaving the unconscious Alice over his shoulder. The flames were crossing the threshold between Maggie's bedroom and the sitting room. They seemed to be spreading at lightning speed, while his feet felt mired in mud. A year might have passed since he'd broken down the door, though it could only have been minutes.

"Robert is trying to kill us." When she stumbled, he grabbed her waist with his free hand.

"Can you walk?"

She nodded, then darted away. "My writing case!"

"There's no time to collect belongings!"

"I can't leave her recipes." She was already back and pushing the broken door aside. The flames in the hall were closer. Others raced up the grand staircase.

"Hug the wall," he gasped. "The east stairs are still free."

Her lips moved, but the fire's noise drowned her response.

Again time seemed suspended, though they were stumbling eastward at a near run. The smoke was thicker than ever, suffocating him despite the handkerchief. Alice weighed more with every step. Maggie tried to help him, but by the time they reached the stairs, he was so dizzy, he could hardly stand.

Smoke rolled up in a solid wave. They could never remain conscious long enough to reach the bottom. Remembering Betsy's dash along the hallway, he gestured toward the last niche in the wall. "Servants' stairs."

Thank God she was not prone to hysteria. She found the disguised handle and pulled. The air inside was nearly clear.

She coughed. "Can you manage Alice alone?"

The spiral was too narrow for two abreast, so he nodded. But Maggie must have known how weak he was. When he nearly fell from the last step, she caught him. Together, they shifted Alice to his other shoulder, then cracked open the door.

On this floor, the entire west wing was ablaze, and flames had spread to the lobby. But the door to the nearest parlor was ajar. Stumbling across the hall, he collapsed against the window frame.

"Hand Alice down!" Maggie shouted, pulling him out of a stupor. She'd opened the casement and jumped the four feet to the ground.

He complied. The last thing he remembered was Maggie tugging on his wrist.

Maggie tried to ease Marcus's fall, but she was too weak. They went down together in a sprawl of arms and legs. But at least he was out of the building. For a moment, she'd feared he would collapse inside. Even if she'd pulled herself back in, she could never have lifted him to the window.

"What happened?" demanded a man, materializing from the gloom. Night had descended. She must have been unconscious for at least two hours.

"Too much smoke," she gasped. "Help me pull them clear." Alice's face looked gray in the flickering light. Marcus didn't look much better.

"You're cut," the man said, touching her head.

"I fell." A crash sent flames roaring through the dining room windows. The ceiling must have come down. "We have to move," she said firmly. "Can you help?"

He summoned others, who carried Marcus and Alice to the park dividing Queen's Garden Road. The relative coolness made it easier to breathe. Cradling Marcus's head in her lap, she looked around.

The street teemed with people, garishly lit by the blazing west wing. Some sat in stunned silence, staring at the flames, but most were milling about, screaming, sobbing, or shouting orders.

A rope of sheets tumbled from a second-floor window above the dining room. A dark figure emerged, oblivious to the flames already threatening the fabric. But even as a scream welled in Maggie's throat, men tugged the sheet away from the window. A fireman directed a stream of water onto the flames, allowing the man to scramble safely down. The crowd cheered.

A shrill whistle cut through the noise. Before she could figure out who had signaled, a shout drew all eyes to a man wearing the soot-stained uniform of a kitchen servant.

"DuPré done it, I tell yuh. After that fight, 'e vowed 'e'd prove 'e were the best chef on earth. 'E's been in there two whole nights and two whole days, a-bakin' away. I told 'im this mornin' that wall was too 'ot. But 'e turned 'is nose up, just like you'd 'spect from a mad Frenchie."

"Nonsense," said Mr. Simmons calmly, pushing through the crowd toward the speaker. "The kitchen was designed for twice the ovens that are currently installed. They could burn around the clock for weeks without endangering anything."

"The wall was 'ot," the servant insisted stoutly. "Ol' DuPré were stokin' them ovens night an' day, yellin' fer more an' more coal. I tol' 'im the wall was burnin', but 'e don' care. Too busy boffin' the maids to listen to honest workers."

"The wall could not have smoldered all day," insisted Simmons. "Now cease this prattle at once."

"Prattle?" shouted someone.

Growls were already sweeping the crowd.

"What sort of hotel installs a madman in the kitchen?" demanded another. "He nearly stabbed my wife last week. And how do you explain that fight?"

"The flames are in my room," sobbed a girl. "All my new gowns are ruined!"

"Who's going to pay for my lost trunks?"

"And my missing jewelry?"

"Maybe it's the Frenchie what's been robbing us."

"He could have started the fire to cover his crimes."

*Robbing?* Maggie shivered, pulling Marcus closer. The crowd was becoming a mob. Two men held Simmons. The servant was inciting even more anger. Gratified to have an attentive audience, he regaled them with every complaint he'd ever heard against DuPré. Most of his claims were embellished, but his listeners didn't care. They wanted someone to blame for their losses.

She was wondering how to protect Marcus and Alice from a riot when the arrival of a clanging fire wagon distracted everyone's attention. Simmons jerked free and hustled the servant away. Tempers eased as new firemen jumped down to assault the blaze.

She relaxed, aware of her pounding head for the first time since Marcus had burst into her room.

Bells, horses, and a crying child formed a counterpoint to the crackle, hiss, and roar of the inferno, beating against her temples in unrelenting cacophony. Exploding windows showered spectators with glass. Firemen worked feverishly to pump water on the blaze. Others rushed inside to attack walls and floors with axes, hoping to contain its spread.

Smoke burned her throat. Heat baked the side facing the hotel. Plants withered before her eyes.

Alice groaned. Her color had improved and she was breathing easier, but Marcus remained inert.

"Marcus!" she cried, running her fingers across his face and through his hair. When he failed to respond, she slapped his cheeks and chafed his hands. How could she live with herself if he had sacrificed his life to save hers?

"Maggie?"

*Thank God.* "We're safe." She smoothed his hair one last time, then helped him sit up against the tree.

He coughed deeply, then took in the scene. "The crowd looks dangerous."

"One of the servants was blaming DuPré, which unleashed tempers."

"Why DuPré?"

"The servant swears the ovens overheated and set the wall on fire, but it had to be Robert."

"So you said. But if he wanted to kill you, why leave you alive?"

"He wanted it to look like an accident. He knows a vicar who will sign his special license without a formal ceremony—apparently the man is an opium-eater. Marriage would negate my will, so he could claim everything."

Marcus muttered something creatively vile.

"I agree. He smashed a lamp over my head, then waited for Alice. That was several hours ago—plenty of time to stage an accident that would shift suspicion to someone else. You said he was adept at such chicanery."

A shout rang out. "There he goes! The mad Frenchie! Make him pay." Half the crowd raced away.

"DuPré?" asked Marcus.

"Yes." She peered after the retreating mob. "I hope he escapes."

"He should. For all his size, he's quick." Marcus struggled to his feet. "I must tell the firemen about Robert so they can search for evidence. Will she be all right?" He nodded toward Alice.

"She is coming around."

"Wait for me here." Kissing her lightly on the forehead, he strode away.

7

Maggie sipped a cup of tea, relaxing for the first time since last night's fire. Marcus had commandeered a cart and brought them to Richard's town house.

Alice had wakened fully by the time they'd arrived,

but the doctor demanded that she stay in bed for a week to allow her concussion to heal. Maggie was under similar orders, but she'd come down to the drawing room anyway. Now she let her eyes take in the decor.

Unlike her sitting room at home, which was decorated in blues and creamy whites, this one had deep red walls and draperies. Red also figured strongly in the chair covers and carpet, complementing the dark woods of the ancient furniture. Under other circumstances, she might have found the intensity overwhelming, but today it was comforting. Even the room's clutter seemed almost cozy.

Footsteps on the stairs announced Marcus's return. She had lain awake well into the night, trying to accept the truths yesterday's terror had revealed. She should have known where befriending Marcus must lead. Yet what could she have done differently? She'd been doomed since running him down in the lobby.

"Any news?" she asked when he reached the drawing room.

"You are supposed to be in bed," he reminded her.

"I am not one of your fragile English maidens."

"True." He poured wine, then leaned against the mantel as he examined her. Apparently her appearance satisfied him, for he relaxed.

"The firemen confined the damage to three floors of the west wing, so my room was spared. My belongings reek of smoke, but are otherwise undamaged. Your suite was destroyed."

She shuddered, but they were lucky to be alive. When set beside that, the loss of a few possessions was nothing. And in truth, she had saved everything important. Alice's recipes and her father's papers had been in her writing case. The locket still hung from her neck.

"I spoke to the magistrate. He needs your statement but will wait until you are recovered. Robert is under arrest."

"They found enough evidence?"

"More than enough. He was seen in the basement just before the fire started."

"I'm not surprised. He went more than a little mad."

"Perhaps, though that would not matter under normal circumstances. Few people would believe a servant's word against that of a viscount's heir." He shrugged. "But this case won't come down to a gentleman's word. The fire clearly began in the basement hallway, climbing the wall to the dining room. The kitchen was untouched until the dining room floor collapsed into it. Thus the fire cannot have started inside the kitchen wall."

"I suppose he tried to emulate the rumors about the Ipswich Gardens."

"They weren't rumors." He joined her on the couch. "That fire really did begin in an overheated wall. What rotten luck that Formsby was nattering on about it the night Robert dined with you."

She refilled his glass, pleased that her hand remained steady. "It was actually good luck. Without Formsby's hints, Robert might have killed me outright. He took a chance, though. How could he be sure the fire would reach my suite before someone put it out?"

"A bucket of turpentine spread in the hallway. The pot boy saw him carrying it, but DuPré distracted his attention before he could mention it."

"So they arrested Robert."

Marcus nodded, but his eyes were troubled. Setting his glass on a table, he clasped her hand. "Not just for arson, or even for the attack on you. A maid died."

"Oh, no!"

"She had returned to the attic for her things—including a hoard of stolen jewelry—and was overcome by smoke."

"Just as you were." Her voice trembled.

"It's over, Maggie." He stroked her fingers as he'd

done in the carriage. "But I will never forget the moment I realized you were still in your room."

"It can't have been worse than when you nearly collapsed in that parlor," she admitted in a moment of weakness, then cursed herself. She had not meant to reveal her feelings. Nothing could come of them.

"I love you, Maggie." His eyes bored into hers.

"That certainly complicates matters," she complained, though her heart was trying to batter its way out of her chest.

"It doesn't need to."

She sighed. "I can't stay here, Marcus. I have too many responsibilities at home."

"I know. But I can come with you—if you'll have me."

She stared. Was he serious? "But women always follow their husbands."

"Because men are usually tied to estates. But I have no estate. I can live anywhere."

"You don't understand what you are offering, Marcus. I live in Pittsburgh. We are growing steadily, but you would hardly consider us a city, and we are remote even from the rest of the United States. Life is very, very different from what you know."

"It might be more remote than Washington, but I doubt it is odder than Russia."

"Don't make light of this." She blinked back tears at fate's cruelty. His offer was too good to be true. "You have so many ties here."

"Family, yes. But they will never approve of how I wish to live. Nor will my friends. Leaving will keep me from embarrassing them. And I don't enjoy the *ton* any more than you do. So will you marry me?"

She closed her eyes, a lifetime of wariness holding her back. She wanted to believe him, yet he could not imagine what life would be like. England was so small and so tame when compared to America.

"I do care, Marcus," she finally admitted, "but you don't comprehend what you're offering. It took me three months to reach London. Granted, I could have done it faster if I hadn't been covering my tracks, but not by much. If you go back with me, you'll never see your grandfather again—you know his health is failing; it will be years before you could return. And you would be leaving behind everything you've known."

"Trust me, Maggie. I've served in places just as different. If I am with you, I can live anywhere." He gripped her shoulders. "Yes, I will miss my family, but if I'd stayed in government service, I would have been posted to some foreign place anyway. The only family I need is you."

His words warmed her, but there was one last question. "Father trained me to take over his business. I won't give that up."

"You don't have to. I've dreams of my own, love, and the means to pursue them."

"Are you sure? I've been confronting fortune hunters since I was sixteen. You are the first man who ever looked at me and saw Maggie Adams instead of money. No one else can tolerate me for long."

"Just what did your father leave you?" he asked, then kissed her forehead. "American men must be very strange. I cannot imagine anyone not wanting you."

"Thank you." She squeezed his hand, then gasped when he pulled her against his side. She melted into him, knowing this was where she belonged. "As to my inheritance, it started with Uncle Peter's glassworks— I always called him 'Uncle,' though in reality, he was Father's partner and the creative genius behind the company. He made some of the most exquisite glass I've ever seen, but mostly he produced sturdy ware that settlers could afford. Pittsburgh is where they board the flatboats that take them down the river."

"I am not following."

"The easiest way to move west is to follow the Ohio River, which begins where two smaller rivers join at Pittsburgh. Many people bring little with them. Some buy goods before hiring flatboats. Others wait until they are settled—we ship glassware to a dozen river towns."

"So you inherited part of a glass factory."

"Actually, I own the whole thing. Uncle Peter died in a factory fire ten years ago, leaving everything to Father." She sighed. "By then, Father had started other businesses."

"Which are—"

"He bought fifty thousand acres of land."

Marcus choked.

"America is huge—much larger than England. The bulk of our land is unsuited for crops, but it holds coal and iron."

"He owned the mine where he died?"

She nodded. "He'd just completed plans for building an iron works. It should be running by the time I return. And we supply much of the timber for the local boat builders."

"Pittsburgh sounds like the ideal place to start my own company." Visions of steamboats and locomotives flitted through his head.

"You are serious."

"I love you, Maggie. I can't live without you. Discovering that your home fits my own aspirations is merely a bonus. Do I get an answer now?"

"Yes. The thought of leaving you behind has bothered me more than I wanted to admit. I love you, Marcus."

He pulled her closer, kissing her as he had wanted to do since she'd run him down in the lobby. Passion exploded, newer than the world to which he'd committed himself, hotter than the fire they'd escaped last night. He needed all of his control to keep from taking her immediately. By the time he lifted his head, he was shaking.

Maggie was more than willing to continue. She had not expected his lips to ignite so much heat. It spread and sizzled until even her toes tingled. When he pulled away, she moaned.

"Later, love," he promised. "I won't dishonor you by anticipating our vows, though if we don't restore a little propriety, I may change my mind."

She stroked his cheek. "Can we be married here, or would it be easier to wed at sea like my parents?"

"Here. We owe the family that much. I will get a special license tomorrow. Alice should recover soon, so we can wed in a week or so." He smiled. "Are you financing her hotel, by the way?"

"No. She's been my governess and companion since Mother died. Father left her more than enough to follow her dream."

"I wish I'd known him." He kissed her again, then resolutely put her aside. "I can't think when I'm holding you, but we must make plans. William is already swearing that Robert is innocent. He remains powerful enough to have his heir released on the promise of sending him abroad. Neither of them will forgive you. You will take the place of your father in their minds."

"So we must hide our destination." She sighed.

"We can go to France, then take a French ship to America using false names."

"Good. I really do not want to retrace my steps so late in the year." She frowned, contemplating her uncle's displeasure. "William will also hate anyone to whom I give money, so turning Father's legacy over to another Adams could bring disaster."

"I doubt he will actually harm anyone. That would be too difficult to hide."

"Perhaps not, but he *will* put pressure on them. I would rather not have that on my conscience. The estates can go to the residual beneficiary and one other remote cousin—you must help me decide which. But I will put the rest into a trust."

"For what?"

"To help scientists and inventors."

His eyes glowed. "An excellent decision. We can arrange it when Knowles returns."

"Perhaps I should establish a similar trust at home," she began, but he distracted her with another kiss.

"We will have plenty of time to discuss it, love. I would rather concentrate on us." He pulled her into his lap, running a hand down her thigh. "I love you, Maggie."

"And I, you." Her arms tightened around his neck. "May you never regret leaving England."

"I won't." This kiss was even better. His good intentions slipped away unnoticed as passion again exploded between them. She was his. Forever.

Some promises were impossible to keep . . .

**SIGNET**